Also by Joan Brady

The Unmaking of a Dancer

Theory of War

Death Comes for Peter Pan

The Émigré

BLEEDOUT

A Novel

Joan Brady

A TOUCHSTONE BOOK
Published by Simon & Schuster
New York   London   Toronto   Sydney

TOUCHSTONE
Rockefeller Center
1230 Avenue of the Americas
New York, NY 10020

For information regarding special discounts for bulk purchases,
please contact Simon & Schuster Special Sales at
1-800-456-6798 or business@simonandschuster.com

Designed by Melissa Isriprashad

Manufactured in the United States of America

10   9   8   7   6   5   4   3   2   1

Library of Congress Cataloging-in-Publication Data
Brady, Joan.
  Bleedout : a novel / Joan Brady.
    p.   cm.
  "A Touchstone book."
  1. Lawyers—Crimes against—Fiction.   I. Title.
  PS3552.R2432B57   2004
813'.54—dc22   2004055374

ISBN 0-7432-7008-8

For Alexander and Flora

Author's Note

If we get right to the heart of things, the South Hams District Council is responsible for the existence of this book. Their relentless pursuit of me through the courts took on an almost messianic quality and focused my attention as never before on issues of justice and injustice. Without the expertise of Nigel Butt, litigator, and Dr. Walter King, inventor, they would have had me dead in the water long ere now. Or maybe in Holloway.

I have named the fictional South Hams State Prison in their honor.

1

BUT WHY DID HE KILL THEM?

Try as I might, I cannot find an answer that satisfies me. Stephanie assures me that I would understand if I could see him, but I've been blind for a quarter of a century. I cannot make out as much as a man's outline in full sun. And yet even on the first day I met him, he gave off a sense of threat as soon as he entered the room. He was only a boy then, a couple of months short of sixteen, and already a multiple murderer who would have been on death row if not for his age. That could hardly be it, though. I was used to murderers. I knew the rattle-clank of chains and leg irons.

The more I think about it, the more I think it must have been the way he breathed; I swear I could hear his fury at the very oxygen that gave him life as he took it into his lungs and let it go. The Chernobyl meltdown had dominated the radio for almost a week, and I remember thinking, "Rage is the nuclear core that powers the boy."

All this intensity failed to tell me why he killed them. It still does.

Twenty years of living with the question, and now I find myself in the absurd situation of a man about to be murdered—without the hope of my answer first.

◄○►

A truck approached along Route 97 out of Springfield, Illinois, going toward Petersburg. A slanting, bleak, early-morning sun shone, but there was no warmth in it. This part of America is fiercely cold in winter. The truck slowed as it passed through the gates of Oakland Cemetery and hit the buckled road that is never repaired until spring, then continued over a small rise ringed round with naked winter branches. Papaws grow here, larch and beech too, and the south fork of the Sangamon River is almost close enough to see.

This is one of the most famous burial places in the country. It's the site of Edgar Lee Masters's *Spoon River Anthology* and the grave of Ann Rutledge, beloved of Abraham Lincoln, "wedded to him," as Masters's poem on her gravestone reads, "not through union, but through separation." Edgar Lee himself is buried here. So are his wives, his parents, his grandparents, his nephews and their wives. So are dozens of characters from his poems, Mitch Miller, Lucinda Matlock, Bowling and Nancy Green.

Hannah Armstrong is buried here too. She stitched Abe Lincoln's shirts and foxed his pants; she's the one who told him on the day he was elected, "They'll kill ye, Abe." Not far from her lies Chester Gould, who created Dick Tracy. And not far from him, there's Johnny Stompanato, gangster, stabbed to death with a kitchen knife by Hollywood goddess Lana Turner's daughter and buried with full military honors under the personal direction of that mobster of mobsters, Mickey Cohen.

Despite such colorful dead and despite one of the prettiest woodlands for miles around, a vast, bulbous water tower is what sets the tone. It's blue and white, and looms over the countryside atop a single spindly stilt, garish, ungainly, intrusive. The graves look shoddy, even Ann Rutledge's and Johnny Stompanato's. They reek of cheap and cheesy haste, death stashed away as fast as possible: a glance at a shiny catalogue and a quick talk with an oily somebody who promises to handle all the unpleasantness. A few relatives do come to pay a pious postfuneral visit with plastic flowers. But by the time winter gets its teeth in, even these meager offerings have faded under a coat of grime and dirt.

Beyond the main set of graves, the paved road ends.

The truck slowed to a creep here; a sign on its baby blue side read P. M. Wurtzel and Son in elegant copperplate lettering. It jounced along a rutted dirt path past a cluster of trees and into a secluded area, a tiny Eden where there was only one grave, different from the others, a delicate, hand-carved stone rather like the ones found in English country churchyards. The dogwood that overhangs it blooms every spring. The truck stopped. Six men bundled out and stamped their feet against the cold.

The ground was solid ice some five to six inches beneath the surface that morning. In olden days, winter corpses piled up in the woodshed until spring and the thaw; these state-of-the-art workmen set up a propane heater—a model specially designed for the purpose—and began defrosting. They powered up a generator for the pneumatic drill, reamed out holes for stakes, erected poles and strung ropes to build a frame. What emerged was a sturdy tent, and how unexpected it looked in the cold landscape, this touch of summer gaiety escaped from the state fair. It was summertime inside too. Portable heaters warmed the air; brilliant green AstroTurf covered the floor except where the ground defroster stood. Chairs stood in orderly rows, a lectern in front of them.

Only then did the crew remove the ground defroster and begin to dig. But when they finished, the hole was only two feet square and three feet deep, just big enough to take in an elderly aunt's cat or maybe her Pekingese. More AstroTurf went down into the gap; they patted it into place as cooks might pat dough into an irregularly shaped pie pan and then began to gather up their tools in preparation for the boss's arrival.

This was an important funeral. The press would attend, and the crew sensed excitement in the air.

My name is Hugh Freyl. I am a corporate lawyer, and I went blind in O'Hare Airport only half an hour before the last flight to Springfield.

At the time, I was deep into the hydra-headed litigation spawned by the merger of Michigan Genetic and Westman-Boyle. There was $800 million at stake, and the route to this pot of gold was littered with class-action suits, accusations of covert premiums, secret share deals, illusory poison pills. No corporate lawyer can resist a case like this, and I had just about mastered enough of the detail for a plan of action to emerge.

I cannot imagine why I should have felt abruptly restless. Nor can I imagine why I left the safety of American Airlines' business lounge or why I wandered out into the concourse or why I sat down there in among the bustle of people. But the last thing I saw was Terminal Two's high-vaulted ceiling. I looked up at it, then rested my head in my hands and closed my eyes. When I opened them again . . .

Not a thing. Nothing. A blank screen.

My beautiful Rose had migraines; she had described the blind spots that preceded them—and always went away. I told myself to be calm, to wait it out. I told myself this too would pass. But even as I mouthed the words, I bolted off my chair, stumbled, half fell, reached out, caught hold of somebody, started to babble.

"Please help me. I do not know what's—"

The somebody shook me off.

I stuck my arms out in front of me—there were people everywhere, I could hear them—and yet somehow, magically, there was only empty space around me, eye of the storm, pin-the-tail-on-the-donkey at a children's party. I lunged out and managed to snag a passerby.

"You've got to help—"

"Let go." It was a man. I had him by the coat, and he yanked at it.

"Find me a doctor." I could hear pleading in my voice. "Please help me to—"

"Let go of me!"

"I need a—"

"Just let go, huh?"

"I cannot see. I know there's a medical station by the—"

"Sure, sure. Wait here, huh?"

And he was gone. I waited. Nobody came.

I caught hold of a woman next. She escaped with a shriek. I caught another. She listened and disappeared. I got a man who found me a place to sit down before he disappeared too. I sat there for . . . I could not possibly say. It seemed hours. I did not dare get up. My legs felt gelatinous; I knew I would never find my way to another seat.

And then she came to me: "You okay, mister? You're looking kind of peaked."

It was a wavery voice, impossible in a young woman, but not weak or aged either; when she left me—ostensibly to find that elusive doctor—it did not cross my mind that she would come back any more than the others had. And yet five minutes later I had a whole medical team around me.

"Where's my Good Samaritan?" I said to them. "Please. I must thank her. I must speak to her."

"Don't you worry none," came that wavery voice. "This here's a doctor. He's gonna fix you up. You gonna be okay."

"I hardly know . . ." I had not wept since I was a boy; I was so grateful that tears poured down my cheeks. "How can I ever thank you?"

"No need for that, sir. Anybody'd have done the same."

◄○►

At ten-thirty, just as the workmen packed away the last of their tools, the media began to arrive at Oakland Cemetery. WICS-TV had come from Decatur, where there had been mysterious attacks on three McDonald's in a single week; the CNN crew had traveled overnight from Biloxi and a story on the run-ups to the Miss Winter Orange beauty contest. Video technicians wielded shoulder cameras, filming this grave and that vista; audio technicians tested microphones; interviewers jockeyed for position. Print and radio reporters arrived with notebooks, tape recorders, still cameras.

All were in place by the time the president of P. M. Wurtzel Funeral Home arrived. The son and heir of the original P. M. Wurtzel himself was fresh-faced, aggressively young, pink-cheeked, athletic if somewhat overweight, a Bible-belt product of vitamins and virtue. He bowed for the cameramen, who dutifully filmed him and the box he carried so decorously, a small, highly polished wooden thing decorated with a filigree design in polished brass.

At eleven, Springfield's matriarch, Becky Freyl, arrived in the family Lexus SUV and got out, helped by the substantial Lillian, her cook and companion. Microphones, interviewers, tape recorders rushed forward. Cameras rolled and clicked. At eighty-seven, Becky was tall and fine-featured, as intensely feminine as the southern belle she had always been, but she ruled this town with the sharp wit and the painfully sharp tongue that had whipped it into shape sixty years earlier when she arrived from the big city of Atlanta to marry into the Freyl family of Springfield.

Interviewers began talking even before they reached her.

"What about the investigation, Mrs. Freyl? What about David Marion?"

"Is Marion still in custody? Four days is a long time to hold somebody without a charge. Can you comment on that?"

"Do you think they've got the right man?"

"Do *you* think he killed your son?"

Becky did not flinch. She stared them down with an old-fashioned schoolmarm's cold disapproval, not the slightest attempt to cover her face or avert her eyes. No hint—beyond pursed lips—of the pain they were causing her. Composure this imperial is rare. These crews had never run into it before, and they fell silent in front of it, awkward, sheepish, uncertain.

"Would you kindly let me pass?" she said then. Her voice carried only a whisper of a southern accent.

The questions erupted again.

"You get them cameras out of here," Lillian said, taking over. "You know you ain't supposed to talk to her. You *know* that. What's the matter with you anyhow? Ain't you got no respect for nothing? You bother her with one more question, and that's the last one you ever ask in this town, you hear me?"

The flock retired in disarray, and Becky resumed her stately progress up the AstroTurf path toward the tent.

Once inside, she turned to P. M. Wurtzel's president. "And you are?"

He cleared his throat to emphasize his illustrious name. "*I* am D. Morrison—"

"Yes, yes. The undertaker," she interrupted.

He bowed. "*Bereavement consultant,* ma'am. At your service."

Becky frowned at the vulgarism, looked around her and noted the little box that P. M. Wurtzel's president had placed on the chair his crew had set beside the freshly dug opening in the ground. "What's that?"

"We have been privileged to place the deceased's mortal—"

"A jewelry case? You've put my son in a jewelry case?"

"Oh, no, no, no. No, no. This is the very finest in our top range for loved ones who have been cremated. You yourself chose—"

"What is he doing on a folding chair? Hugh hated chairs like that. They wobble. Take him off at once."

P. M. Wurtzel's president was flustered. He blushed. He shifted from one foot to the other. "I'm afraid the workmen broke the altar when they—"

"Do you always blame your shortcomings on other people, young man?"

"Oh, no, ma'am, I assure you—"

"Can you not at least cover it with some of that"—she gestured at the AstroTurf—"that hideous material?"

Over the next few minutes, cameras recorded snippets of other mourners as they arrived in cars as elegant as Becky's and climbed the AstroTurf path to the tent: lawyers, doctors, bankers and their wives, the cream of society, members of that most exclusive of clubs, the Springfield One Hundred—some of them with a full five generations of Illinois history behind them. But when Senator John Calder arrived, cameras surged forward.

"What about the future, Senator?"

"What do you think of the Governor's Mansion, Mrs. Calder?"

"What about Governor Szymankiewicz? When are you going to start getting him out of there?"

Everybody said John Calder was going to be the next governor of Illinois. The election was a year away, but Szymankiewicz didn't stand a chance next to Calder. *Everybody* knew that. How could it be otherwise? Nobody could pronounce that tongue-twister of a name. The press had gleefully dubbed the poor man "Sissy." Besides, John Calder was the one who had the Freyl fortune and the Freyl connections behind him. Even more important, he was Springfield's own son; he'd been born and educated with other local kids. He'd giggled over bowls of garlic-laden chili at the Dew Chili Parlor and got drunk at dances at the country club. He'd worshipped at the feet of Libby Jennings, high school sweetheart, and crashed his father's car into a motel out near White Oaks Mall. Then, to top it off, he'd come back from law school in Chicago to practice in the town just like Springfield's most famous lawyer, Abraham Lincoln. And like Lincoln, John Calder was one of those rare figures whom the camera loves. Practically every picture of him ran, no matter how mundane the setting. Which is to say that whatever John Calder did was news. Whatever his young wife did was news too; in this cold graveyard she clung to his arm and smiled adoringly up at him. She was elaborately coiffed, dressed in multiple layers of mourning, hatted and veiled. A reporter from the *Illinois Times* noted all this into a tape recorder. Sometimes Mrs. Calder made her own clothes; as soon as the press discovered one of them, women all over the state employed seamstresses to copy her.

The senator wore a somber overcoat and a stiff collar; nobody should look too comfortable at a funeral. "This is no time for speculation or politics," he said. "I am here to mourn my friend and to do what I can to support his family through this terrible hour. Hugh Freyl was a great American. His death is a blow to the country and to freedom itself."

It was an eminently quotable speech: short, to the point, emotional but not sloppy: it would make the opening slot on evening news programs throughout Illinois. The cameras followed the senator into the tent. His head was bowed. His pace was reluctant but brave. Perfect.

Inside, the Calders embraced Becky, who bore up under their tributes with rigid shoulders and a straight back, just as she had borne up under the attentions of lesser mortals. All the seats in the tent were full. The minister arrived last, tall, thin, decorous if a little pinched—the cold, perhaps. His ears and nose were a startling pink. He whispered to Becky, held her hand, whispered some more, went to the lectern, opened his prayer book and began.

" 'Man, that is born of woman, hath but a short time to live and is full of misery. He cometh up and is cut down like a—' "

And who should walk through the opening to the tent but David Marion himself.

2

I SPENT MY FIRST YEAR AS A BLIND MAN GOING FROM
doctor to doctor and test to test. One famous Chicago authority announced
that I had ocular larva migrans, an infection caused by roundworms in the
intestines of dogs and cats. Another insisted on a rare inherited condition
called Leber's optic neuropathy, while a colleague of his scoffed at nerve
involvement of any kind. Between them they ruled out all vascular ailments
and injury. The only thing the experts agreed on was that I had suffered
sudden bilateral painless visual loss. Their joint diagnosis boiled down to an
idiopathic condition, which turns out to be an elegant way of saying that
no one had any idea why I had gone blind in two seconds flat.

I ended the year as helpless as I had begun it.

Sudden disablement is a terrible shock to the system. When the able-
bodied call people like me brave, what they really have in mind is, "Thank
God I don't have to do anything about you." I hated them for it. I hated
them for being able to see when I could not. I hated them when they
helped me, and I hated them even more when they failed to help or
made no effort to do so. Furniture, knives and forks, toothbrushes con-
spired to hide from me, and I hated them too. Learning Braille seemed
like an admission of defeat. So did using a cane or any other tools the
blind rely on. I spent my days slumped in front of a television I could not
see, listening to the sound tracks of old movies.

The sad and humbling fact of the matter is that bitterness at this
level bores everybody, even the one who feels it. One afternoon, grudging
and complaining, I allowed Rose to coax me into some lessons in Braille.
To my surprise I turned out to be good at it, and I had forgotten how
much pleasure there is in mastering a new skill. Then one day—it was very
sudden—the thought that a guide dog might allow me to walk outside on

my own seemed exhilarating. So was the thought that I might find my way around inside the house with a cane.

I spent the next six months as a resident at the Lincoln Center for the Newly Blind about a hundred miles north of Springfield. I had to learn everything again like a child: how to overcome such obstacles as rain, snow, gutters, gravel; how to negotiate a doorway in a strange house and cross a four-lane highway; how to make a mental map of my route in-doors as well as outside; how to boil an egg and find a water glass on a table without knocking it over. I even learned some wrestling and judo to heighten my grasp of space relationships. Equally important were simple social techniques: how to attend a concert, a parade, a state fair; how to handle a menu in a restaurant and go dancing in a nightclub.

It was in pursuit of this last goal—an evening on the town—that I ran head-on into the hardest lesson the newly disabled have to learn and one that no school is equipped to teach even though all of them try very hard to prepare their pupils for it.

The evening began well—perhaps too well. There were twelve of us in a party that included our instructor, several partially sighted pupils from the Center and several of the wholly blind like me. Dinner was at Las Cruces, a catfish restaurant on the banks of the Illinois River. The food was good. So was the wine. The talk was animated, and I remember a sense of burgeoning confidence, almost elation, as the meal progressed. After dinner, we left in taxis for a night spot called Nemesis—a painfully apt name as it turned out—on the other side of the river.

A band from Carbondale was playing that night; the atmosphere was heady and noisy as we paid the cover charge at the door. Waiters pushed tables together for us. I had only just sat down when our instructor touched my shoulder.

"You'd better get up again, Hugh," she said. "We've got to leave."

"What's the matter? Is somebody sick?"

"They're throwing us out."

I knew from her voice that she was not joking, but the evening was so full of promise that I could not quite take it in. "Whatever for?" I said.

"The manager is right here beside you, and he is adamant."

I am basically a peaceable man, a firm believer in negotiation. But my reaction was the instant, visceral rebellion of a five-year-old when his favorite toy is snatched from his hands. "If he wants me out," I said, "he is going to have to drag me."

"Now you just look here, mister," came the manager's voice, a meaty baritone, full of swagger and demand. "It isn't safe here for you guys. It's crowded, and I sure as hell am not going to find myself sued when one of you gets hurt. You're going to be spilling drinks all over the place. You're going to be bumping into people and knocking over tables. Who's going to take you to the bathroom when you got to go? Tell me that, huh? My staff got too much on their hands to babysit you."

Ignorance and callousness are hard enough to bear, and I had already learned far more about them than I wanted to know. But this time there was loathing: black skins, yellow skins, Muslims, foreigners, women—and the disabled. Blind, Down's syndrome, deaf, legless, epileptic: what difference does it make? "We are no more likely to spill drinks than you are," I said, and I had to fight to keep my voice steady. I turned to the others. "Please sit down. We have every right to be here."

The manager withdrew without another word. We tried for a few minutes to recover the party mood, but it was a lost cause; we were all in agreement that the evening was over by the time we heard the wail of police cars—which none of us associated with ourselves. I was just getting up to find my coat when I felt a policeman's hand on my shoulder. "Sir, if you don't leave I'm going to have to arrest you," he said to me.

I sat down again at once. I crossed my arms. "Are you aware, Officer," I said, "that Illinois was the first state in the union to institute a White Cane Law? I believe the year was 1937."

He sighed. "Okay, guys, we got no choice."

They handcuffed my hands behind my back and jostled me into a squad car along with two others, both of whom had backed up my protest. It is not easy to describe a first taste of unadulterated humiliation. They say that doctors have no grasp of disease until they have been seriously sick themselves. Lawyer that I had been, I knew nothing of the burn of injustice. I had no idea what it did to people, and I was sunk so deep in it that I only half heard the charges against us: remaining on land after having been forbidden. I alone was singled out for aiding and abetting others to commit this violation of the City Code. A date for an arraignment was set, and we were released on our own recognizance.

I had a bad night, but by morning, I knew what to do. Before noon, I had composed my first legal letter since going blind. I addressed it to the city attorney, a Mr. Phillip Ross, and I laid out for him a clear case against the city and the police department for false arrest and for violation of the White Cane Law. I gave him two weeks to reply. I noted at the bottom of the letter that copies were going out to newspapers, both local and statewide. A media outcry followed. All charges were dropped, but by this time, not one of the twelve members of our ill-fated party was willing to let it rest. We formed a legal committee. We brought suit on behalf of the Center and ourselves. We won just over $500,000 in damages, and with it, the Lincoln Center built and equipped the first computer department in the country dedicated solely to the needs of the blind.

But what was most important to me personally was that I was back. I had reclaimed the tools that I had lost. I was in business again.

Somewhat to my own surprise I found that the cutthroat world of corporate law still intrigued me more than the civil rights that had nudged me back to my profession, and yet blindness had changed me subtly as well as obviously. I felt the need—almost a vocation—to help other people in some simple way, something comparable to what the Center had done for me. My friends and colleagues thought the idea was just sentimental. They enjoyed teasing me with proposals; I have forgotten which of them brought up the Illinois State Education in Prisons program—always in need of part-time teachers—although it was just another dinner-party joke. I remember the laughter, and yet I knew at once that I had found what I was looking for.

I do not doubt that criminals should be segregated from law-abiding citizens. But I despise the idea of degrading people just for the sake of it, whether the people are the disabled, the poor, the old or the convicts we put behind bars. Of all of us, prisoners have it worst; their humiliation is continual, ritual, extreme. Part of the reason it persists is that most inmates are ignorant; they do not have the tools that allowed a blind man like me to make a stand for his dignity. Most convicts must burn—as I did—with the injustices of the system under which they suffer. Education alone delivers the weapons to fight it.

I put my name forward.

◂◦▸

I had been teaching for nearly three years when young David Marion appeared on my list of pupils. I was not called in on his case because he expressed a desire to learn—he most emphatically did not—but because he was so young. As far back as 1917, Illinois state law required that children be educated to the age of sixteen and to the literacy standards of the sixth grade; this boy was only fifteen, and his record stated that he could not read at all.

"Good afternoon, Mr. Marion," I said to him. There was no reply, so I said to the guard, "Would you kindly remove his manacles? Nobody can learn if he's in chains."

The guard refused. I insisted.

"Now you may go," I said to the guard.

He refused. I insisted.

When David and I were alone, I turned to him. "You do not belong in this facility, Mr. Marion. I will arrange a transfer at once. But that's a . . . curious name to have . . . in here: Marion."

It was more than just "curious." The prison was Marion Federal Penitentiary at Marion, Illinois, south and a little east of Springfield, and it is a barbaric place, the most violent and repressive in the entire federal system, the true heir to Alcatraz. By the time of my first visit with David, it was already the repository of many of Alcatraz's former prisoners. Institutionalized racism, institutionalized religious intolerance, inedible food and inadequate portions, solitary confinement for ninety days for minor infringements, minimal medical treatment, mass reprisals at the slightest infraction, routine beatings, rape—gang rape, individual rape, private rape, public rape.

To bestow the name Marion on a child sounded like a curse to me—and so it turned out to have been when I learned a little more about the boy. It is hardly surprising that there was no reply to my comment.

"Mr. Marion?"

"I ain't going nowhere."

"This is a federal prison, and yours is not a federal offense."

"I want to stay where I am, you hear me?"

"I hear you."

"You won't do nothing, right?"

"There is not even a Young Offenders' wing in this institution."

"Ah, fuck it."

"You were convicted of murder in a state court, Mr. Marion. How did you come to be in a federal prison?" He did not answer. "You most certainly do not belong here, not under any circumstances. You are only fifteen years old. Do please understand that my only purpose in arranging a transfer is to make your life more bearable. I am certain that you will adjust readily to the change."

Again he did not answer. I sighed irritably. "I suggest you open your book. Perhaps we can discuss a transfer later."

"Jesus, you don't know nothing about nothing."

"The book, Mr. Marion."

But he was clearly too preoccupied with the transfer to respond. I found this reaction as puzzling as the extraordinary tension that the suggestion had aroused in him. He made me think of an animal just seconds after the trap has snapped shut over its leg or the prisoner at the bar who has just heard a death sentence delivered, and I wondered a little nervously if I had been hasty in asking the guard to remove his chains. Perhaps he had become sexually entangled with one of the inmates. Such things are very common in prisons, especially with boys as young as he, who are often mercilessly abused and exploited by older prisoners. The lives of these victims can be miserable beyond our imaginings; all manner of horrors can be held over their heads to keep them compliant—beating, mutilation, enforced prostitution, threats to friends and family on the outside, even death—easily frightening enough to provoke the kind of reaction I sensed in David Marion. As a lawyer, I knew I must get this vulnerable young person away from the penitentiary as quickly as possible, with his cooperation or without it.

The tense silence stretched between us until I was almost ready to call the guard, then abruptly he relaxed, as though he had managed to steel himself against the move or had resigned himself to whatever it entailed.

"You're screwing me over, you asshole," he said, "and you don't even know it."

"I cannot for the life of me see how a move to a less repressive facility could be other than an improvement."

He gave a snort of contempt. "So you're here to teach me reading and writing, huh?"

"Among other things."

"Like what?"

"Is that a serious question?"

"Christ, you're nothing but a goofy old blind guy."

I leaned forward in my chair. "I certainly cannot deny being blind," I said, "although I assure you I wish with all my heart that I could. But despite my limitations, I do see some things clearly. First, I can see that your self-control is not absolute. You would not be behind bars if it were. Secondly, I see that your intellect is adequate to the job I have been set to carry out on your behalf. Finally, I can see that you are not aware of how very ignorant you are. It is here that I can be most helpful to you, because I am sorry to inform you that the uneducated are the unempowered in our society and that neither your self-control nor your intellect will get you anywhere—behind bars or out in front of them—unless you have access to power. Blind though I am—'goofy' though I rather hope I am—power is precisely what I have to give you, and I will do my utmost to fulfill my task."

There was a pause. "Where the fuck did you get a hold of a spiel like that?"

And so the lessons began.

-◦-

There was no chair for David in the funeral tent. Of course there wasn't. He stood by the opening, holding the canvas flap against the wind; the minister fluffed himself and began a second time.

" 'Man, that is born of woman, hath but a short time to live, and is full of misery. He cometh up and is cut down . . .' "

Imagine somebody who had always kept his word in a world where nobody does. Imagine somebody who had actually delivered the power he'd promised in that elegant, early speech. Then this very same person proceeded to get his pupil out of prison to make use of it. For eighteen years, Hugh was visitor, teacher, adviser. And finally, liberator.

How could such a man be reduced to something that would fit into such a *little* box?

3

THE GRAVESIDE SERVICE FOR HUGH FREYL WAS MERCI-
fully short, and the funeral guests departed for a buffet lunch at his
mother's house some ten miles southeast in Springfield itself.

Springfield is the state capital of Illinois. Lincoln practiced law
here for nearly a quarter of a century; he ran for senator here both as
a Whig and as a Republican, and even though he lost both senatorial
bids, he initiated his campaign for president here. To this day, he
brings in hordes of tourists that keep the town's cash flow so healthy
that his birthday is celebrated as a major holiday for a patron saint.
Springfield grew into a big town on his back, 115,000 strong, and the
Freyls have been its leading family since long before he arrived in it.

Right at the beginning the Freyls bought large tracts of land
both in the middle of town and in the surrounding countryside;
there are streets named after various forefathers and a square dedicated to Becky Freyl's husband, dead of a heart attack over a decade
ago. The Rebecca Freyl Museum of Art houses the work of artists
from across the country, and the Rebecca Freyl Opera House was
nearly complete in a special plot just off the Capitol Complex. Becky
herself lived beneath a pure copper roof in a stately structure surrounded by a private park. The funeral guests took roundabout
routes to the house to allow for the few minutes of preparation that
would be necessary.

By the time Allen Madison, president of the Springfield Federal
Bank, pulled up in his Cadillac with his willowy and still-handsome
wife, there were already two dozen cars along the driveway. His
wife sighed irritably as he rang the bell beside the massive oak door.

"We're late," she said.

"If you hadn't bawled on that pancake you slap all over your face, we'd have been here first," said the banker. He was a dour, bitter man, very proud of his presidential name and his resemblance to the affable Ronald Reagan—which really was marked if he got drunk enough and the light fell on him from just the right angle. But he hadn't yet had his first drink of the day, and morning light is always harsh. He gave her a cold glance. "You didn't even like Hugh Freyl."

"How can you say such a thing? I adored him—especially looking at him. Pity I never got much closer than that."

Tall, long windows flanked the front door; the son of Becky's staunch protector and servant, Lillian, opened it for them. "Morning, Mr. Madison, Mrs. Madison," he said. "If you can just step this way, Mrs. Freyl will be right with you."

The couple were wholly familiar with the elegant Chinese slates in this foyer; they knew the graceful arch of the staircase that rose up to the bedrooms above. They'd been coming here for a quarter of a century, dinners, cocktail parties, Sunday lunch. But this morning there were so many people packed into the space that the quarried floor tiles were barely visible and the living room beyond was blocked from view. The banker's wife—her first name was Ruth—hadn't counted on a receiving line; it clogged the flow of new arrivals like a supermarket checkout at rush hour. Besides, her shoes were patent leather and a little tight. She let Lillian's son remove the coat from her expensive shoulders, and she turned distractedly to embrace her closest friend and bridge partner, the broker's wife.

"Where's Piet?" she asked.

These two women had known each other since they were children; they'd been the most popular girls in town all the way through school, but the broker's wife hadn't held on to her looks the way Ruth had. Not even plastic surgery could disguise a thin neck barely supporting a head that wobbled pompomlike on top of it.

"He got here early," the broker's wife said of Piet, her husband. "The bastard."

"Trouble?"

"Need you ask?"

"Oh, dear," said Ruth a little absently, craning her neck to see who else was corralled in the foyer. Hugh's four senior partners at

Herndon & Freyl clubbed together as they always did, wives on their arms—all except for Jimmy Zemanski. Hugh's doctor and his wife were there along with the biggest Angus breeder in the state and his wife. The owner of Wake & Field Engineering, who supplied toilet fixtures to motels throughout the Midwest, stood just behind a grouping that included two identical blond heads. Why do women of uncertain age insist on that shiny gold? It makes them look so haggard. Anyhow, those two bleaches meant that the mayor of Springfield was right on the point of entering the sanctum beyond with his twin daughters and probably their husbands, too.

The crowd in the foyer thinned more rapidly as Hugh's partners began their way through the receiving-line formalities. Ruth's friend, the broker's wife, shifted foot to foot. "Only six to go," she sighed.

Ruth turned to her with a delighted smile. "David Marion's already in that room, you know."

"No! He's here *too*? That beat-up Chevrolet is *his*?"

Ruth nodded. "I wouldn't be surprised if he got us a mention in the society pages of *The New York Times*."

The broker's wife laughed. "Not even the maid would drive a heap like that."

"Come, come. It's a classic. She probably couldn't keep it up."

At the entrance to the living room stood the senator and young Mrs. Calder, both of them at Becky's side. When the Madisons finally got that far, Ruth and the senator's wife kissed cheeks. The senator shook the banker's hand and held it in both of his (he was famous for this handshake).

"Sad business. Sad business," he said.

"A difficult time for us all," said the banker.

Then came Becky herself. Ruth would have kissed her too if that unyielding back had not indicated that the time for such things was past. Ruth stumbled a little—fearful that she might not be doing precisely the right thing—but managed to deliver the little speech she kept in reserve for the bereaved at funerals. Becky cocked her head to catch every word. The banker received the same rapt attention. Becky thanked them both graciously and said, "Please have Lillian give you something to eat and drink."

The Madisons moved on into a living room that was airy, rich-textured, as elegant as any featured in style magazines from New York and San Francisco. There was a Japanese subtlety to the arrangement of pictures on the walls and the artifacts on tables and shelves, even in the tapestry that Becky had designed herself: these things showed an éclat that everybody here had the money to indulge in if only they'd known how. How easy it was to see that she was born to the sophistication of Atlanta. No wonder she was still arbiter of the town's taste, bellwether of its manners, its style, its pursuits.

The large room was crowded. At one end stood a mahogany dining table laden with platters of rare sliced beef fillet and German potato salad, bread, china, silverware. There were bottles of Scotch, bourbon, martini mixings, a bucket of ice and frozen glasses. Lillian presided. Becky's liquor was always the best, and the guests collected drinks and drifted into little groups. Ruth Madison floated out of her husband's vicinity and toward Piet, husband of her best friend. They had recently come to a private arrangement that included Tuesday and Friday afternoons at the St. Nicholas Hotel; the affair was only a month old, and standing near each other in public brought with it a tantalizing, illicit charge.

"I've had such a hard year," she whispered into his ear; her large brown eyes sloped downward at the outer edge, giving her the vulnerable charm of a night animal in the forest.

"What is it?" he said, solicitous, worried, knowing from her voice that she wasn't talking about Hugh.

"Hems were up in January and down again by November. It's so much work."

His smile was a little uncertain. Her coquettish humor had enchanted him ever since he was a boy, but he didn't understand it any better now than he had then. He strained to think of something sophisticated to say. Nothing came to mind. Fortunately, the crowd eased around them just then. They caught sight of David Marion at the same moment—and both forgot their game entirely.

There he stood—this gate-crasher of graveside funerals and private funeral parties—right out in plain view. Or rather, there he leaned against a wall across from the mahogany table, glass in hand, a tall man, heavily muscled as long-term convicts tend to be, body relaxed into a belligerent indifference as though he had as much

right to be here as any of them, *more* right than they did. And yet
amid all the black finery he wore no tie, no jacket, crumpled jeans,
crumpled shirt open at the neck, sleeves rolled just short of his el-
bows. A moat of empty floor space surrounded him.

"How could he show up dressed like that?" Ruth said to the broker, who only shook his head. "I bet he's slept in those jeans for a
week. What do you suppose he thinks he's doing? Spitting in our
faces? He hasn't shaved in days either. Plainly he hasn't."

They watched in fascination as Becky made her way toward the
pariah in their midst. A hush fell over the entire company.

"Mr. Marion," Becky said. Usually her height gave her an edge;
she could look most men straight in the eye. To her annoyance, she
had to look up to this one.

"Mrs. Freyl," he replied. The voice had a gravelly resonance to
it, and the tone was both gentle and polite, which was surprising—
even a little alarming—because the tension in him was palpable.

"We did not expect you."

"No."

He nodded to her and turned toward the feast on the mahogany
table as though she'd suggested he lead the company in partaking of
the food; so far none of them had yet been able to distract their attention from the liquor long enough to consider eating. The guests
shrank back to let him pass. At the table, he picked up a plate; they
watched transfixed as he speared the first slices of beef from the
platter. Then he spooned up the first of the potato salad.

"We ain't got no beer, David," Lillian said, "and you're sure
enough going to need something to drink with what you're eating."

He cocked his head at a collection of bottles. "What's that?"

"This here? We got some red wine."

"It'll do."

Lillian filled a glass, handed it to him. "David, don't you pay
them folks no mind, you hear me?" Her eyes took in the roomful of
guests as she spoke. Then, hands on hips, she addressed them in
that strong voice of hers, "Ain't the rest of you going to eat any of
the food I done prepared in Mr. Hugh's honor?"

The guests hurried to line up like good boys and girls. Ruth
found herself separated somehow from the broker and next to his
wife again. As the two women picked up plates, they watched

Becky and the senator disappear off in what they assumed was the direction of a telephone.

"They can't be going to call the police, can they?" said the broker's wife.

"I'd guess at damage limitation of some kind."

"*I'd* guess the damage is done."

"There's something about a man that big, though, don't you think?" said Ruth, looking David up and down.

The broker's wife laughed. "Ruth Madison, you ought to be ashamed of yourself."

"Oh, I am. I am."

There was a panther in the zoo out at Lake Springfield that prowled back and forth across his cage the way David moved; its musculature shimmered with fury beneath its pelt. The zookeeper stuck bleeding meat on the end of a long pole to feed the beast— none of the other big cats required such extreme caution—and Ruth wouldn't have dared get any closer to David than that even though it was last summer's dreams of him, not the broker, that had led to her month of afternoon appointments at the St. Nicholas Hotel.

"Becky says he was born for the electric chair," said the broker's wife.

"Nonsense," said Ruth, who had an unexpectedly literal mind. "Illinois uses lethal injection. Or rather it doesn't do anything at all anymore." There'd been a moratorium on executions for several years, and it was likely to stay in force until John Calder got into the Governor's Mansion to revoke it.

"He killed Hugh," said the broker's wife. "I know it. You know it. So does everybody else."

Ruth bit her lip. "I went down to the *Illinois Times* yesterday and looked up the original report."

"Yeah?"

Ruth nodded. " 'Two men dead at Fowler & Son Garage.' "

" '*Two* men'? Oh, *that* report. How long ago was that anyhow? It must be twenty years if it's a day."

The story had plastered the front page, photographs of the dead men, another of the very young David—a school picture, probably—with tousled hair and cocky grin. He'd been at his foster father's garage out near White Oaks Mall with his foster father and foster brother. There hadn't been any witnesses to what happened; a customer had returned to pick up his car and found what looked at first like no more than a kid beaten to his knees in some kind of brawl. But a glance in the pit beneath his car was enough to send the customer reeling out of the garage screaming for the cops. Two of the brawlers were dead. They were *real* dead too, messy dead, sprawled in a stew of blood, brains and black engine oil.

When the police arrived, the lug wrench David had killed them with lay on the garage floor right out in plain view.

◄◦►

A panther can see the world from behind his bars even as the world can stare in at him, and for David, this rich and elegant room in Becky Freyl's house didn't have much of an edge on an oil pit with the stench of death in it. At least death was real. Everything on show here was pretend. These people reeked of greed and shallow, stagnant convention.

He watched them pick at their food. Some sat. Most stood, plates in one hand, setting glasses down on strategically positioned coasters so they could juggle knives and forks. Their concentration was split between him and the liquor while his attention was on them alone. He was an expert watcher. Prison trains a person in the art. It's not that there's little else to do in a cage; it's that prison is a jungle. It's a place for predator and prey, a place where panthers belong, where everybody is to be feared: guards, other inmates, *everybody*. All it takes is a single unanticipated gesture, and you're raped or mutilated or dead—or all of these. This lot? An endangered species. Not one of them would last twenty-four hours. Even so, their behavior was wholly familiar to him.

Sometime around the middle of his sentence, Hugh had given him a copy of a little-known work of Emile Zola's called *Death;* he read it with great curiosity because it showed him that people on the outside react to death just like people on the inside: the full gamut from deep grief, through sadness, passing regret, hypocrisy, simple pleasure, right on up to hard-headed calculation. Rebecca Freyl's guests added only sanctimonious references to the much-vaunted "closure." Most of them were well along in the familiar process of distancing themselves from the dead man, jockeying for position, trying to decide who would bear the mantle of successor at the Sangamo Club, the country club, the cocktail party, the dinner table, the legal world. This dividing up of the dead man's garments was the only reason David had forced himself to come here: to see if one of them snatched at the spoils too hungrily.

Most of them had avoided his gaze, but as he was getting ready to leave he caught Helen Freyl's eye across the room. She looked away at once, but he knew perfectly well that she'd been watching—just like the others—to see what he might do.

Helen was Hugh's daughter, pretty as well as bright, very much her father's heir—as serious a scholar as he was, educated at Choate Rosemary Hall, a Phi Beta Kappa graduate of Vassar, a doctorate in physics from Columbia. Her hair was dark where her father's had been light, but she had his startling-green eyes; she had his cheekbones too and the crisp family features. She even had something of his quirky rebellious streak, dressed in pale blue among the mourners in black. Part of what had made Hugh attractive was that he wasn't aware of it himself; she was the same. She was one of those soft women; in this, she was just like her mother. Her skin was so fair that David could see blue veins beat at her temples, and she bruised easily, a trait she despised.

She was standing with Jimmy Zemanski, the partner at Herndon & Freyl who had arrived alone. Jimmy had been fidgeting because her attention was not focused exclusively on him. It did not help—not at all—that she was as preoccupied with David as the rest of them. Helen was *Jimmy's*. He saw himself as Hugh's heir, the youngest of the four senior partners in Herndon & Freyl. He was tanned, square-jawed, smooth-skinned, cowlick in the hair. His handmade suit showed off an all-American's bulging muscle to perfection—halfback at UCLA. Well, near enough to perfect: there's time and chance and all that, and the guy was several years past forty. The ruddy cheeks probably had as much to do with liquor intake as with tanning bed—alcohol was the town's weakness—and the suit hid a roll of flab along with the sinew and bone.

But he was a man of substance like the rest of them, and it showed. Helen's exchange of glances with David, that quick lowering of her eyes: these were things he could not allow to go unremarked any more than he could allow a jailbird motherfucker to walk out of here unchallenged. Besides, there's security in numbers; there were nearly fifty people in the room. Jimmy gave Helen's distracted shoulder a proprietary pat, picked up his drink and took a few steps toward the arch to block David's path.

"How you doing, David?" he said in a courtroom voice that threw another hush over the room.

David nodded his head in token greeting. "I'm just on my way out." As he'd been with Becky, he was polite, even gentle.

"Come to pay your respects, have you?"

"Something like that."

Jimmy lifted his drink to salute the rumpled clothing. "My, my," he said. "Quite the fashion plate, aren't we? Is there some point you're trying to make?"

"Your plans didn't leave me enough time to change."

Jimmy gave a short laugh. "Not me, friend. A few days in the clink was an order from the dowager herself. Last thing she wanted was the likes of you fouling her nest today. She's mad as hell about it. So is the senator, I bet. In fact, I bet the entire police department is cowering behind doors until the storm dies down. By all rights that leaves some unfortunate desk-job cop stumbling all over himself with apologies. You're probably going to cost some poor bastard his job this very afternoon."

There was a pause. David made a move to step forward into the foyer, but Jimmy stayed where he was. The funeral guests held their breath. "Is there something I can do for you?" David said.

"You? Do something for me?" Jimmy lifted his drink as he had before. He eyed David up and down. "Nah. Not a thing."

David nodded his head, a token bow this time. Still Jimmy held his ground. "You don't really want to get in my way, Jimmy," David said then.

Jimmy moved out of his way at once.

◄o►

I never intended to teach anything beyond basic reading and math, and the only difficulty I expected—and for the most part encountered—was working out ways to mediate between my disability and my pupils' sight.

But the people who became my charges were astonishing to someone like me. Long-term prisoners are raw, stripped down, painfully direct. Their reaction to what I had to teach them often mirrored my own grudging and yet hopeful first approach to Braille, and I sensed in all of them the same bafflement I still feel myself.

But it did not take long for me to realize that any sense of community I might have felt with them was illusion. Prisoners are different from you and me. They're aristocrats in the world of pain. Most of them are born to it, and their life stories still shock me. Few had anything I recognize as a childhood. In an effort to understand them, I sought out books on sociology and childhood psychology, but such studies are written by highly paid, earnest college professors with degrees from Brown and NYU, dry academics from comfortable homes who know as little as I do, who could not possibly grasp what lies at the heart of lives like these. Their texts rely on statistics, bare-bones case histories and classifications reminiscent of consumer satisfaction sheets handed out by market researchers on street corners.

Despite David's youth, he had been convicted as an adult in an adult court; hence the murders he committed were a public matter. All prior records, while he was still officially a juvenile, were privileged. I did not see them until much later, when I became his lawyer as well as his teacher. My textbooks would have deposited what I have learned of his upbringing into a category entitled "Abuse and Neglect" and a subcategory entitled "Very Extreme Violence." The writer in one of my books set up a checklist: tick the box next to the words that apply. That things like these form part of any child's life is horrifying; that they happen so commonly as to figure in the dry form of a chart is enough to take the breath away. If a reader ticks seven out of nine of the boxes below, the subject fits the category. In David's case the reader would have to tick them all and still be a long way away from a sense of what had actually happened to him.

bite	break bones	infect with venereal disease
hit with a fist	burn or scald	threaten with, use knife
beat up	tie up with rope, wire	threaten with, use gun

Apparently David comes from nowhere. Until he was six or seven he had no birth certificate, no last name, no official existence. The fact that the birth was not registered leads me to assume that he was born without medical attention. No place of birth is indicated either, but the east side of Springfield is likely, since his grandmother had an apartment there, and he went to live with her almost at once. His mother disappeared without a trace.

He first came to the notice of Child Welfare Services when an unidentified neighbor made a furtive telephone call about a little boy who never went to school. The social worker assigned to the case found him playing in the gutter outside his grandmother's tenement. Her apartment was locked, and she was away for the day. The social worker's report states that the boy was badly bruised. He was also dirty, infected with lice and impetigo, malnourished and very, very hungry. He was not even registered at school.

Not long ago, I sought out that very same social worker and spoke to her myself. She had never forgotten him; there were very few children she disliked, but she had mistrusted this one on sight, even though she figured he wasn't much over six years old. She told me that she won his confidence by buying him a hamburger and a chocolate milk shake. "What's your name?" she asked as he wolfed down the food.

"David."

"David what?"

"David."

"Your last name, kid."

"Just David," he spat at her.

"Don't you talk nasty to me, or I'll take that milk shake away."

"David Marion."

When they finally tracked down the grandmother, she said, "He don't have no name. David, that's him. He's a bad, bad boy. He's always doing something bad. Some days I call him David Marion 'cause that's where he's going to end up: the pen at Marion. You just wait and see. His mother was bad too, nothing but a whore what didn't have no name neither, and his father never was at all. David nothing or David Marion. Take your pick."

◄◦►

David made his way across the vast, open space of the Freyls' foyer. A crystal chandelier hung above the Chinese slate floor, and the beveled panes of the tall windows on either side of the front door put glitter into the light from a weak winter sun. He found his coat, a leather jacket as inappropriate as his crumpled jeans. He was putting it on when Becky Freyl and John Calder emerged from the study.

"I'll join you in a minute," Becky said to the senator.

"You're sure you can handle this yourself?" the senator said.

"I am not a child." She turned to David. "Mr. Marion?" There was no warmth in her voice. "I have to talk to you."

"Sure you do."

"The others are waiting for you, John," she said to the senator, who still stood beside her indecisively.

"Listen, Becky, maybe I'd really better—"

"Please do as I ask." The senator gave David a worried glance, started toward the living room, hesitated, then went on. "In here," she said to David. She led him back to the study.

This was where Hugh worked, where he and David had talked so many times in the two years that had followed David's release from the South Hams maximum security prison northeast of Havana, Illinois, where the best catfish in the state can be caught. The study was a gentleman's club of a place, large, wood paneled, leather sofa, deep carpet, velvet drapes, a beautiful room by anybody's standards. It had always made David intensely uncomfortable. The world outside a prison was an alien place to a man who had spent his adult life in a seven-by-ten-foot cell—open toilet in the corner—when he hadn't been in solitary or chained to the floor in one of the punishment blocks. But the luxury on show here didn't bring to mind the sort of remote heaven most men dream of inhabiting; it had all the feel of a honeyed trap.

Hugh's specialized technology for the blind only heightened the sense of threat. It looked to David as though it belonged in a silent *Frankenstein* movie, where Hugh was the great doctor and David the monster. The acoustic hood had cost a fortune; it was a trash-can-like object designed to mute the Braille embosser's terrible racket, but it resembled a generator for the power that was to be injected into the corpse on the doctor's table. The even more expensive jumble of metal and wires in a transparent plastic case—the Braille display that let Hugh's fingers read the computer screen—could easily have been the capacitor that stored the power and delivered the huge jolt that got life going.

Becky sat in the captain's chair behind this barrier of equipment and the tangle of wires that connected its various elements. "How dare you come here today?" she said to David, who stood before her.

"You didn't make it any easier for me."

"I instructed the police to hold you in custody until the funeral was *over*. They failed to follow instructions." David said nothing. "You haven't been very helpful, have you? Friday evening until Tuesday morning at the police station—and not a single, solitary word out of you. The desk sergeant tells me you wouldn't even give them your name."

"Are you going to ask me to sit down?"

"You won't be here long enough." He turned to leave at once. "All right, all right. Have it your own way. Sit. If you *must*."

He took off his jacket, tossed it on the leather sofa and sat beside it, leaned back, stretched his arms out to either side of him along the sofa's substantial back. There's something about physical grace that makes insolence all the more insolent—it seems to come so naturally—and Becky was not pleased. "You are an embarrassment to my guests," she said.

"You could have stopped me at the door."

"That would only have compounded their embarrassment. Explain yourself," she said.

"How do you want me to go about that?"

"What I cannot figure out is *why* they let you go."

"They just could have remembered the law."

"I imagine silence was . . . prudent from your point of view, but it can hardly be said to be reassuring for my family, can it?"

"I'm sorry."

"My son is brutally murdered, and you're sorry? That's the best you can say for yourself? You're *sorry*?" Her misunderstanding was deliberate; it was just what David had expected of her, which she sensed and which infuriated her. "I'd have thought you'd be anxious to help all you can," she went on—very tart—"if for no other reason than to dispel the suspicion that inevitably surrounds you." She picked up a pencil, tapped it on the desk, set it down again. "Have you nothing to say for yourself?"

"What about?"

"Don't you *want* to explain yourself? If I were in your position, I would be very eager to do so." David said nothing. "Innocent people protest their innocence."

"They're stupid."

This is the truth. If a person is arrested for *anything,* the real professionals—whether they're criminals or lawyers—keep their mouths shut. Open your mouth to state anything, and a diligent interviewer can find something in it, no matter how innocent or trivial that something may be, to indict you.

Becky pursed her lips. "Just look at you,"she said to David. "How dare you arrive at Hugh's funeral unshaven? How dare you come to my house in this condition?"

"Get to the point."

The pale winter sun filtered through into this room as it did into the foyer, its slant so steep that it lit up dust particles floating in the air. There was an unseemly burst of laughter from the living room beyond, and Becky's lips pursed tighter. "I *told* Hugh that any attempt at rehabilitation would never work on a man like you," she said to David, "and that was long before I even knew what you'd done."

"People want what they want."

"However that may be, only five minutes ago, I finally learned *why* you went to prison."

For a moment David was taken aback. "Haven't you always known?"

"I do not lower myself to details of that nature."

"You're the only one here today who doesn't."

"My son's intellectual weakness was the idea of a noble savage." She eyed David with disdain. "I could never understand it myself. A savage is a savage. He thinks like a savage. He responds like a savage. No combination of taming, training and high-minded intention is going to alter that. But even people as brilliant as Hugh are reluctant to let go of their dreams."

Becky expected obedience from her subjects. She expected fear and a drop or two of blood in tribute. And yet David kept his gaze on her face as she spoke, not a flicker, not even a blink. That was *her* trick. Seeing it in this low person made the police chief's cowardly evasion of her outrage a few minutes ago even more intolerable. "To imagine I presided over a table," she went on, "where a man like you dined as a guest, not once but many times. I had no idea you'd committed such a terrible, disgusting . . . I'd never have permitted it. Never."

She shivered with distaste.

"And *still* you keep quiet," she said. "My son is murdered. His murderous protégé is taken into custody—and refuses to speak. I should think simple gratitude for what he did for you would soften your heart. But no. Not a word. Not even to me, his own mother, in the depths of her grief." She paused for David to apologize. When he did not, she went on irritably, "Did you kill my son or didn't you? This is the question. There is no other."

It was a question he had expected, but not so boldly or so soon. Next week perhaps, in the form of a royal summons to her lawyer's office. Or perhaps in the person of Hugh's lovely daughter. But Becky was claiming it for herself. She *needed* it, just as half a dozen guards equipped with truncheons and rib-spreaders need a prisoner to beat. He could not help a bemused admiration for her. She was as old as God; she faced him alone, which takes more guts than any guard he ever met—far more than Jimmy Zemanski had mustered just a few minutes ago backed by a roomful of supporters—and her timing was accurate enough to catch him off balance.

"There's nothing to tell you, Mrs. Freyl," he said.

"You do not deny that you killed my son?"

"As I say, I haven't got anything to—"

"Am I to conclude that you admit it?"

"You'll conclude whatever you want to conclude no matter what I say."

She studied him a moment, savoring the blow she was about to deliver. It was the one pleasure she was likely to get on this terrible day. "I know you are in some way responsible for Hugh's death," she said. "I have no proof, but I *know* it exists. The police will find it. Believe me, they will. The moment they do—the moment they find the slightest shred of evidence that places you within miles of the scene—I will hunt you down and destroy you. In the meantime, if you come anywhere near this house I will have you arrested. Do I make myself clear?"

David shut the door to the study behind him and headed for the front door across the foyer, zipping his jacket as he went. The wake was in full swing in the living room: clink of glasses, shush and murmur of voices, tensions easing under the torrent of liquor and the presence of John Calder, town luminary—as well as the absence of David.

He didn't notice Helen at first.

She stood at the far end of this elegant space, a patch of misty morning sky in her pale blue dress, but it wasn't sky he thought of when he caught sight of her. Hugh had had a favorite toy when he was a child; he'd kept it all his life until he gave it to David, who'd had no toys except the ones he stole. He'd never imagined things like this even existed: an antique brass kaleidoscope, jewellike patterns that shifted at the slightest tremor despite a shiny exterior as tough as they come: a glorious, ordered beauty that is no more than a trick of mirrors—and nothing inside but broken shards of glass.

Helen's brows were knit across a fleeting range of expressions that moved so quickly he couldn't quite catch them—grief? puzzlement? pain?—and yet there was a smile on her face too. She raised her glass to him.

"To my father's murderer," she said.

There was barely a split-second delay in the zipping of his jacket. But she caught it, and her smile deepened before it disappeared completely.

THE AREA OF SPRINGFIELD WHERE DAVID LIVED WAS A
dangerous place; it was the very same area where he'd lived with
his grandmother as a small boy, no part of the Freyls' town that
rocked itself to sleep on goose down and dreamed of summer hem-
lines and hostile corporate takeovers. It was a hellhole, a free-for-all.

You name the crime: it was daily currency here. Police did not
patrol the streets anymore. When they were called, they crept
around the long way hoping that by the time they finally arrived
there would no longer be a need for them. Burglaries, carjackings,
gang wars, beatings, stabbings, drive-by shootings, guns everywhere,
drugs hawked on every street corner like cotton candy at the circus.
The only legitimate businesses were liquor stores and loan sharks,
and they operated behind heavy-gauge metal-mesh enclosures,
wrapped up tighter than spider eggs in a cocoon. Everybody black
hated everybody white. Everybody white hated everybody black.
They hated their own color too, if not quite as much as they hated
each other. Boys roamed the streets in wolf packs, priding themselves on the ability to snuff out a life as quick as they could down a
bottle of liquor or smoke a joint. No wonder, either. Nobody in
town gave a shit what went on here. Even on a good day the streets
were upended-garbage-can filthy.

David parked the ancient Chevy he drove—a white two-door
Impala dating all the way back to 1967 when cars were big and
horsepower really mattered—and walked past battle-torn buildings.
His apartment was five flights up, past the sound of bouncing bed
springs and the grunts of whores and their johns. At first sight, the
desolation beyond his front door seemed of a piece with all of it.

Grime on the windows was so deep that the rooms were twilit even at noon. But as soon as the eyes became accustomed to the light, the room showed itself to be as ordered as a military barracks. The furnishings were spare and austere: single bed, two straight chairs, round table in the center of the room, minimal kitchen facilities. Pens, paper, envelopes lay in precise formation on a desk against one wall along with computer, printer, scanner.

David had lived here since his release from South Hams State Prison two years before, and back then it had seemed to him too wonderful a place even to covet in his dreams. The splendor of it had dazzled him, disoriented him. Sometimes he awoke with a start and didn't know where he was. He paced the floor, running his hands over surfaces just to reassure himself that all these miracles were actually there in the room with him. There were drapes across a window without bars. The bed had sheets and pillows. The mattress wasn't lumpy; it didn't lie threadbare on a concrete shelf. Not even the prison hospital block was so comfortable. Nor was there any stench from an open toilet in the corner. He could shut the door and be by himself; he could open it and go get himself a pack of cigarettes or a can of beer. He could walk eight paces in a straight line and still not reach the opposite wall. But most of all, it was *his*. He could do with it whatever he wanted to. No bed-wetting cellmates screaming with night horrors in bunks above him. No guards to trash the order he'd imposed just because they were bored and a few moments of bullying amused them.

Even so, anybody who'd never done time would have found it amazing to think that during the past two years, a man had showered, shaved, dressed in rooms that would pass in gentler eyes as no more than a slum—had somehow made himself respectable enough to arrive at the ornate Freyl mansion and eat a three-course meal on a damask tablecloth. There *were* ties to that world, though. Prints by the Dutch graphic artist Escher hung on the walls: a round tessellation of angels and devils disappearing off into a circular infinity and several of the studies of impossible buildings and illusion staircases. Even more telling were the two bookcases that ran floor to ceiling on either side of the desk. The lower shelves had already been packed into cardboard boxes—at this stage in a house move, it's hard to tell whether a person is moving out or moving in—but the top shelves were still full of books. Nobody else around here owned as much as the Bible. Nobody would have been caught dead reading it.

A man even bigger than David squatted over one of the boxes with a book open in his hands. He looked up and shook his head as David entered the apartment.

"Un-uh." He shook his head again. "You taking *all* this shit with you?" He tossed the book back in the box.

David took off his leather jacket. "Good to see you, Tony."

"You're a couple of days late."

"I had a few problems."

"So they tell me. I'm real sorry to hear about that."

David was surprised. He was touched, too, because Tony had never been sorry about anything in his life. Tony was a true American, named for the American way of life: Tonio Liberty Schama, a personal tribute to the Liberty Bell, as he always said, the symbol of freedom itself. He had all the country's guiltless self-interest; he was even his own personal melting pot. His eyes were blue; they were the first thing anybody noticed about him because there had plainly been an African ancestor or two somewhere along the line. Not that he looked black. Not that he looked white either or Asian or any identifiable ethnic group; traits of one seemed to appear on his face then slip aside abruptly to admit the traits of another. And yet in spite of this complexity, he presented the world—just as his country does—with a deceptively simple face that smiled a lot, kept its secrets buried deep and gloried in an oversize body built out of solid muscle.

He and David had grown up together until David went to prison. Or rather, they had seemed to. It was more half together, half apart; they'd fought their separate ways in and out of foster homes and juvenile detention centers that somehow managed to allow them to meet up again and again, tearing them apart each time only for their paths to cross yet once more. These meetings and re-meetings had come to have a fated feel for both of them, a dreamlike intensity that provided the only continuity that either had to rely on in their rootless lives: brothers in shit if not by birth. Tony was the one part of David's past that he could recall without hate or fury or pain or fear, and the bond had held all this time.

They'd started working together almost as soon as David got

out of prison. David had not remotely expected to find that it was as easy to make money when he put his mind to it as it had been before he went to prison, but he'd always had ideas. He'd always been the brains of the two of them, the leader. Carjacking, mugging, dealing when they were kids: it was usually David's inspiration and David's plan. It's true that Tony had chafed in his secondary role from the very beginning, even when they were both small boys, but with David around, the money and the kicks came rolling in an awful lot quicker. Nobody could deny it—and together they made a formidable pair.

"We got to rejig the Kingston job," Tony said. "I hate those big old buildings. Why can't they locate them closer to Springfield?"

"They came to you?" David flicked on a light.

"I didn't crawl around on my knees."

"Same day?"

Tony nodded. "Next Monday."

"Same cut?"

"Yeah. Long as we rejig it. She kick you out?"

David flicked the light off again. "They figure I killed him."

"Well, fuck me," Tony said with a laugh. "Big surprise."

David's criminal record didn't start out so different from the other convicts I taught: shoplifting at the age of seven, stealing car radios at eight, dealing at nine. At twelve, he was released illiterate—aggressively so, according to the reports on him—from a juvenile detention center.

But three years later, at only fifteen, he was tried as an adult in criminal court—the gravity of his crime put him beyond the reach of the juvenile system—convicted of two murders and sentenced to life without the possibility of parole. There are very few youngsters like this among the prison population. The evidence against him was not strong in legal terms, but the records given me—I was issued a modicum of background material on all my pupils—stated that he had signed a confession and that his bloody fingerprints were on the murder weapon. For some reason, the file included a short newspaper story on the case that dwelled on the gore and said little more than that the dead were his foster father and his foster brother, a boy a few years older than he. The harshness of the sentence doubtless reflected the brutality of the killings and the fact that there were two victims; David's history of delinquency could hardly have helped.

His record in prison was not commendable. In fact, I am sorry that his is one of the most violent in the hundred-year-long history of South Hams State Prison, where I had him transferred within a month of our first meeting because there was no place available in a juvenile facility. It is also true that he has an extensive psychiatric record, but such records are common in prisons like South Hams and Marion where convicts are chemically restrained. If officials inject a man with massive doses of Thorazine, it is prudent—to say the least—to diagnose him as schizophrenic first; such interventions come under periodic review by various state commissions.

All reports indicated that David's final foster family had been kind to him. The social worker's three-month evaluation revealed a devoted, close-knit group who managed to persuade him that there was another way. He did continue to truant from school, but he stayed off the streets and out of trouble. He worked in the garage his foster father ran out near White Oaks Mall; he showed a gift for car mechanics and indeed anything mechanical. He spent a great deal of time there, just as he did at home helping his foster mother.

And then one day he killed her husband and her son.

I researched the details more fully later on, when Stephanie and I were engaged in our campaign to free him; Stephanie was my personal assistant and, I am happy to say, my friend. Reports of David's offense did not make for easy reading. Forensic evaluation showed that he had beaten the two men to death with the lug wrench the police had found beside him and that he had gone on beating the bodies long after they were dead.

According to the record, he waived his Miranda rights as soon as he arrived at the police station. After that, his behavior reverted to normal; he refused to speak at all, not one word, not even his name, for more than an hour. The interviewer was a sergeant by the name of Norton Wellwood. He applied no pressure, offered the boy cigarettes, smoked with him and talked on in an easy monologue as though David were the son of a close friend.

"I was looking at the oil pan," David said at last. I would doubt that more than two or three adults in his entire life had spoken to him with the sergeant's patience.

"What about the other guys?" said the sergeant.

[No answer is reported in the transcript.]

"All three of you in that pit?"

[No answer reported.]

"That's a lot of guys for one oil pan, ain't it?"

[No answer reported.]

"What'd they want with it?"

"Got twenty-five bucks extra for sticking sommat like 'clean oil pan' on the work sheet."

"You expect me to believe that?"

[No answer reported.]

"You telling me all that manpower was just standing around checking an oil pan that didn't need nothing done to it?"

[No answer reported.]

"Two full-grown guys and one kid in that pit just staring at it?"

[No answer reported.]

"Ah, Christ almighty. How'd the fight start?"

[No answer reported.]

"Give me a break here, David."

I began to like this Sergeant Wellwood. Most policemen are quickly institutionalized, much as doctors and prison guards are; to find one not only capable of the patience and becoming genuinely puzzled by his subject: this was almost a miracle. When the boy did not reply this time, the sergeant reverted to his discursive approach.

"You know, I bet you're gonna be a big guy when you grow up. I bet you get a real spurt when you're sixteen or seventeen—something like that. My kid was only little when he was your age too, but he had them big feet, just like you. Now the bastard's taller than me and still growing. Makes me mad as hell. I mean, what are you, anyhow? Five six? Five seven?"

[No answer reported.]

"And there you are beating the shit out of two guys twice your size. You didn't plan nothing, did you? Huh, David? You wouldn't do a thing like that, would you?"

[No answer reported.]

"How the fuck you totaled them and not the other way around?"

[No answer reported.]

"So why not lay off them when they was out cold?"

[No answer reported.]

"Come on, kid. Talk to me. I can't help you if you don't talk to me.

There wasn't any fight going on anymore. It was over. Why the fuck you have to go on beating at them till you got nothing left but red mash for heads?"

Yet once again there is no record of an answer.

◄o►

The garage that David's foster father once ran out near White Oaks Mall had been bulldozed and cemented over, and yet his mind flirted with garage pits, oil pans and long-dead memories while he and Tony ate faded sandwiches at a booth in Cockran's.

Cockran's was open all day and all night. It had been an east side fixture forever, booths lining the walls, a row of tables down the center, bar with high stools, pool table upstairs. Not that it was particularly inviting. The plastic seats were torn. The aluminum fixtures were cheap. A television blared, and the heavy smell of beer mixed uneasily with the fog of cigarette smoke that hung over the customers. But it was a tough place, the toughest in town. No bar in Springfield had a reputation to match it; every streetwise kid dreamed of spending his evenings there. Nobody—*nobody*—went there for a first time unaccompanied by an old patron and walked away intact.

Except David. His appearance in search of Tony when he got out of prison two years ago had become a legend all its own.

A handful of suckers wandered in each year; they'd become an occasional entertainment that everybody looked forward to. Some guy, some stranger to Springfield or the east side, would open the door like Cockran's was an ordinary bar and just walk in; the whole place went on the alert. There's always a shiver of anticipation when somebody's about to get beat to a pulp. The regulars would let him get halfway to the bar so he had to make a choice between diving for the can off to the left or the door he'd just come in; watching him figure the odds was all part of the fun.

David was ten paces into the room when Fat George sauntered up to him and said, "Going somewhere?"

You can always tell a guy who's been inside. There's the prison walk first off. There's a roll to it. It lays out the territory, and David sure as hell had that. Then they're pumped; there's nothing much to do inside but pump iron. But there's the prison look too. The slightest hint of a stare—even a glance—is a challenge, a gauntlet thrown down. Life inside is hard enough; inmates avoid eye contact. Not this guy, though, which was weird. That look in the eyes didn't have anything to do with the size of him either; he was bigger than most, but the east side is full of big guys. So are prisons. And it wasn't the muscle you could see on him; there are lots of guys like that around too. But this one stared at you straight on without even blinking. In South Hams prison they used to say only cops and crazies looked like that.

Fat George took his time. A whole minute must have ticked by before David said, "You don't really want to get in my way."

No snarl. Just a statement of fact like a weather forecast and precisely the same thing he'd say to Jimmy Zemanski at the Freyl funeral party.

"Hey, boys," George said, "I think we got us a live one here."

"Perhaps we should discuss this over a drink," David said deferentially, stepping to one side as though to accompany George to the bar.

"What's there to talk about?" George said, but he turned anyway—the natural reaction—with a quick smile for the others.

The shift in position was all David needed; his first blow caught George with a bent elbow right between the eye and the ear. The movements that followed were so quick and so accurate—direct hits to the Adam's apple and the spleen—that George was down before he knew what was happening to him. He brought down a table and its chairs with him. Glasses smashed. Ashtrays and bottles flew. If you don't want a man to get up and take you from behind, you have to keep him down; the heel of a boot hard across the fingers is very effective. The next strike—too erratic for the others to predict and too fast for anybody to get in a word of warning—landed on the sternum of an overweight used-car salesman, the weak spot in the group. With him on the ground gasping for breath, David had maneuvered himself outside the circle even as the others were still scrambling to form it. Bodies make excellent shields; from behind these two, David caught hold of the arm that came at him next and levered it across his own hip. The crack of the bones as they broke was as loud as a gunshot, more than enough to shock the room into silence.

Only then did Tony spin around on his stool. A smack of his hand on the bar broke the spell. "Well, well, well, as I live and breathe," he said, "if it isn't David Marion in the flesh."

They'd met at Cockran's many times since then. The table where they sat with their sandwiches this night was piled with newspapers that had covered the murder of the eminent Hugh Freyl. Tony had gathered them up, knowing David would want to study them; for the last hour or so, they had been reading, comparing, sifting. *St. Louis Post-Dispatch, Chicago Tribune,* Springfield *State Journal-Register* and *Illinois Times:* front-page stories that ran to full-page spreads inside, rundowns of life, career, family, photographs with governors and corporate leaders, comments from two ex-presidents. Smaller stories appeared in *The New York Times, The Washington Post* and the *San Francisco Examiner.*

"A lotta words that don't add up to much," Tony said.

"Yes," said David.

"Don't even say if he was shot or stabbed or strangled. That's the part that gets me. How can they sit on it so tight? Usually there's a crowd of guys just lining up outside to give the papers whatever they want. What you going to do? You got to do something."

David lit a cigarette, inhaled deep, held the smoke in his lungs.

"Sounds to me like nobody found out nothing much," Tony went on. "A screwball maybe, but getting inside that building means even a screwball got to have *some* idea what he's doing. Somebody was thinking here. Somebody was planning something. Which means you just got to be suspect number one on anybody's list, right? Otherwise, it's nothing but a practical joke." He cocked his head; he'd always loved practical jokes. "Not a bad one at that, come to think about it."

David only nodded.

"Question is, what *can* you do? There's not anyone you can even talk to."

"I'll find him," David said, letting out the smoke at last.

"Maybe it's a her. Ever think of that?"

"In that case, I'll find *her.*"

5

PRISON TEACHES A MAN TO KEEP SECRETS EVEN FROM
the people closest to him—*especially* from the people closest to him.
David waited until Tony was ready to leave Cockran's; it was somewhere near enough to midnight when he headed alone toward the
area of downtown Springfield where legal offices and government
buildings cluster.

Herndon & Freyl had occupied the same address for eighty-five
years—the most prominent of the law firms, a name to conjure with
for all that time. The building was handsome, solid, old. It looked
impregnable. The block was enclosed by structures on all four sides
except for a parking lot behind a barbed-wire-topped wall. By day,
there was an entry phone, a guard in an anteroom and a receptionist behind the desk in the front lobby. All night long, an armed
guard remained on duty. There were chinks in this system, though,
even if they were visible only to the likes of David.

The chain-link fence blocking the parking lot entrance was a
playground climb for him. He was walking across the lot itself in
seconds. The whole area should have been tied into an alarm system of some kind years ago. Of course it should have been. A modest brick structure nestled in one corner of the lot where the
manager sheltered during the day: an obvious weak spot. What kind
of idiot figured he could secure it with a Kwikset deadbolt?

There's an age-old secret to lock picking: it's *easy*. Anybody can
do it. Thieves have been doing it since the history of locks began, and
locks began as soon as there was something worth stealing. Members
of the great medieval locksmiths' guilds swore oaths in blood to keep
the secret of simplicity because it gave them the power to exploit the

rich, who were too lazy to penetrate it themselves and so assumed thieves were too stupid to do so either. Today's locksmiths hide it just as deep and for exactly the same reasons; otherwise, they'd be out of business tomorrow.

David had learned to force his way through a Kwikset before he was ten years old. Apply a light torque while moving the pick back and forth across the pins; this is called "scrubbing" the lock. One by one the pins push up to the shear line. The drive pin catches in the hull—the part of the lock that doesn't rotate—the plug turns; the lock opens. David was inside the manager's shelter in less time than it had taken him to climb the gates.

The shelter exited into the well at the backs of the buildings, one of which housed Herndon & Freyl. As he saw it, this was just inviting trouble, especially when the crucial connecting door between shelter and well was locked with a Schlage. It's true that a few years back they advertised the Schlage as unpickable, but nothing stays unpickable for long. These days, $20 buys a dedicated Schlage Wafer Pick Set from any number of Web sites: "Quick and easy to use," one site reads. "Comes with complete instructions."

In five minutes—the fence and three locks behind him—David was opening the fire escape door that led straight into Herndon & Freyl. He had been here before at night, and more than once. The first time was within weeks of his release from South Hams prison. He wasn't at all sure why he'd broken in then—perhaps just to prove to himself that he hadn't lost his touch. That doesn't explain subsequent break-ins, of course, but because of them he knew the building better at night than in daylight, when he'd seen it only as most other clients of the firm saw it: front door, security desk, receptionist, elevators, secretaries, waiting rooms.

He shut the door to the fire escape behind him—gently, carefully—and listened for movement. Nothing. The beam of his flashlight revealed a vast open-plan space; flimsy white partitions—a foot off the floor and five feet high—cut the floor into its many cubicles. Aisles ran between rows of them like streets; there were no doors. During the day the whole area bustled. This was the Data Research Department of Herndon & Freyl, full of ambitious college graduates tracking down the detail that most legal firms leave to the overworked law students, paralegals and associates who occupied a higher floor of this building in keeping with their more elevated status. The amount of paper in a law firm is terrifying. Single cases can fill dozens of boxes, sometimes hundreds. The young people on Herndon & Freyl's second floor scoured the correspondence for dates that didn't match up, snippets of information that didn't mean what they were supposed to mean, data that in fact suggested the opposite of what was claimed for it, shifts in a story over months and, of course, simple old-fashioned lies.

At night, the deserted floor was a papier-mâché ghost town, a curiously soulless place, more like an overgrown maze for rats than a complex for people to work in. It reminded David of prison, and he felt at home in it despite himself. On his several night visits he hadn't been able to resist wandering from cubicle to cubicle, all of them identical on the outside, each personalized on the inside, pitifully so to his way of thinking; at South Hams, he'd always felt cut to the heart by the efforts prisoners made to impress themselves on the section of concrete and bars they had no choice but to inhabit, two to a cell when they were lucky, three or four when they weren't: the guy who decorated his wall with obscene pictures of his mother, the ancient man who almost crowded himself out of his bed with a cardboard model of the ship he'd served on in World War II, the kid who covered everything—including his shoes and underpants—with drawings of Bugs Bunny.

But it had not been just the fact of these prison relics that had intrigued David. It was their evanescence. They were mirages, all of them; they shimmered for a moment and were gone. Guards entered a prisoner's cell to search it on a daily basis anyhow, but they could enter it at any time and it was their absolute right to destroy what they found there—a right they often exercised. These cubicles at Herndon & Freyl were more sedate than most prison cells: photographs of boyfriend, girlfriend, mom and dad; mobiles of planets or fish or atomic particles; travel posters, cuddly toys, print-covered Kleenex boxes. And then of course computer equipment dominated them rather than concrete sleeping shelves and open toilets. But the magical thing to David was that not one of them was a mirage for the person who worked in it; it remained intact until the occupant *chose* to alter it.

He left by the service stairs and climbed past the third floor, which housed the back stacks of Herndon & Freyl's famous library, thousands upon thousands of volumes, the biggest of any law firm in Illinois. There were banks of computers here too as well as copiers, shredders, micrographic equipment, viewers, scanners. Next came the floor where law students, paralegals and assistants worked in quiet carrels that came down to a carpeted floor; they researched the technical side, case law, statutory law, Supreme Court decisions, rules of court, the vast outpouring of legalese that makes up the framework of a case. On the fifth floor, the junior members of the firm and their secretaries worked in offices that ran along either side of a narrow library. David was especially cautious here—junior members sometimes spent late hours over cases. The top floor, the sixth floor, was where Hugh had worked along with his senior partners.

The stairs brought David out near the room reserved for Hugh's personal assistant. He opened the door and shone his flashlight around: book-lined walls, filing cabinets, computer equipment. His inspection was deft and quick. He went through the connecting door into Hugh's office, the largest on this floor, the corner office with windows over the Capitol Complex. Office position is critical in any firm. Hugh was top man, principal partner; his was the top office, even though he could not see what was on view. The forensic team had finished here on Friday, the day the police had picked up David.

While Hugh was in residence, computer technology for the blind dominated everything just as it did his study at his mother's house: a full repeat of those fiercely expensive boxes of toys—acoustic hood with Braille embosser, Braille display in a transparent box, speech synthesizer, scanner, tangle of wires and connections. There was no sign of any of it now. Hugh's law degrees no longer hung on the wall. Several bookshelves had been cleared; piles of new volumes stood on the floor waiting for the secretarial staff to index them in their new location. An alien bank of bookcases stood by the wall beside one of the windows. Only the old desk still had pride of place. But then it would, wouldn't it? It had been Herndon's desk. Herndon's father had inherited it from his great-grandfather, who had been Lincoln's partner as well as his friend and his wildly inaccurate biographer; Hugh inherited the desk when the younger Herndon died. Every partner in the firm coveted its burled cherrywood sheen.

David glanced over it; he flicked open the topmost folder.

Herndon, Freyl & Zemanski
Attorneys at Law

Jimmy had wasted no time in laying his claim as heir apparent to the firm. Embossed stationery on linen paper. Very elegant. Hugh dead no more than a week, and he already had a couple of reams of it on hand. Well, what difference did it make? Herndon had been dead for a full ten years. As far as Jimmy was concerned, Freyl had been dead even longer than that.

David opened the door from Hugh's office to the library.

If clients had appointments with senior partners, a receptionist took them through here; offices branched off the library on the top floor just as they did on the floor below. But everything here was on a grander scale. The library's arched windows were double size, floor to ceiling like the bookcases; they gave a lovely light during the day. David shone his flashlight into the darkness. The single important detail revealed in all those newspapers was that Hugh died right here in this room.

David's examination this time was painstaking, detailed. He ran his fingertips over the surfaces and edges of the two long oak tables in the center of the area. He checked their undersurfaces as well as the surfaces of the bookcases, chairs, ornate radiator covers, windowsills, moldings on the walls. There had been no mention of a struggle in any of the newspaper stories, but the scars he found everywhere—some very deep, some superficial—made it clear that what went on was more than just a struggle, probably a lot more. The depth of the cuts indicated metal weapons, at least one of them angled at the working end, all of them swung in a frenzy. The sheer number and spread across the sixty-foot length of the room—walls, fixtures, furnishings—had to mean either a long-lasting attack or a number of attackers closing in from various angles. It was almost as though the room itself had been the target, as though a gang of teenagers had attacked it with garage tools and iron bars. There must have been blood everywhere, sprays, splatters, pools of it, just as there had been all those years ago at the garage out near White Oaks Mall.

He surveyed the book-lined walls. Some volumes dated back to a rare archive that included the first law books issued after Illinois became a state in 1818; the other titles ran a full range up to *Theories of Illinois Corporate Law* and *The Rule of Reason in Bankruptcy* published less than a month ago. Many were missing now, perhaps some of them too bloodstained to be salvageable. Many others showed efforts to clean covers, spines, exposed pages. Even so, there was a warmth in these heavy, heavy tomes on Illinois law. Floor to ceiling, one end of the library to the other: they had a special feel for David, a special smell—a special promise all their own.

◄o►

The day after I first met David in Marion Federal Penitentiary, where he clearly did not belong, I made a few telephone calls, pointing out to the warden that David had committed no federal crime and was not pending trial on a federal charge or being held as a material witness; therefore the warden lacked any jurisdiction over him. When I next saw David he was in South Hams State Prison.

I had hoped he would be relocated to a youth correctional facility or a young offenders' wing of a state penal institution, but the prison system is always full to bursting, and no appropriate place was available. South Hams was by no means ideal; it was a maximum security prison without any special provision for juveniles. It was also an old installation, dating back to the early part of the last century, and its equipment was as outdated as the stone buildings that housed its inmates. But it was a better place for him than Marion. The food was a definite improvement; so were the accommodations. Prisoners had more freedom to move about; rules were neither as rigid nor as harshly enforced, and there was a larger library than most prisons have as well as an emphasis on education as a route to rehabilitation. For this reason, my visits were easier to arrange, and it was certainly easier for me to get to him; the prison complex is only a few miles beyond Havana, a small town on the Illinois River, just about a quarter as far away as Marion.

An added bonus was that I could pick up the famous Havana catfish on the way home. There is a high pier there right on the river's edge where customers can buy straight from the fishermen themselves. Now that David is a free man, I almost never go there anymore.

But in those early days I came to dread his smoldering, unresponsive presence at what passed for reading lessons. I knew that he felt I had betrayed him on our very first encounter by arranging the transfer, although I cannot for the life of me understand why he should have taken the move so badly. I asked him once not long ago, but he would only give me that standard answer of his, "The past is a waste of time." He always says that whenever he does not want to explain or delve deeper, but this time there was sadness in his voice, or so it seemed to me, anyway—something of a weary resignation as though I could not possibly understand the meaning of the question, much less any answer he might make to it. Even so, I am quite sure that resentment of my interference in his prison accommodations lay behind his determination not to let me get close enough to him to teach him anything. He was so certain his obstinacy would make me give up that I became determined not to let him win. Within a few sessions, I knew that adult education readers were not going to work. Adventure stories, comic books, even *Playboy* magazine—banned from any prison cell at the time—fared no better. I made up flash cards with words in ink for him and in Braille for me.

That was when it became interesting. David began to learn Braille, and yet he seemed to remain steadfastly ignorant of written English.

So I said to him, "Mr. Marion, you are a very intelligent person. You pick up Braille even though nobody wants to teach it to you. This is, I am happy to tell you, the chink I have been looking for in your armor." I readily admit I was as pleased with myself as I sounded. "What your new-found grasp of Braille indicates to me," I went on, "is that you can also read written English, at least a little. In teaching the illiterate to read, the only serious hurdle is the basic principle of the technique. It is the Everest each pupil must conquer. Afterward? Well, afterward is much easier. What I am saying to you is that the ability to grasp any written language—not just a language made up of the letters you are familiar with—is prima facie evidence that the Everest has been conquered."

He said nothing.

"Now the question becomes, how do we play the game from here? Suppose we start at the end instead of the beginning. What do you think? Should we give it a try?" I pulled a heavy volume out of my brief-case. "This is the third edition of *The American System of Criminal Justice*, by the great jurist George F. Cole. I think you just might enjoy it."

No reaction.

"I have cleared the book with all the relevant authorities, Mr. Marion," I said. "From today forward, it will serve as your official reading primer."

A pause. "I hate people shitting me."

"I assure you, I'm telling you the truth."

Another pause. "What do you care?" The words were as defiant as ever, but this time there was a gentleness to his voice that I had never heard in it before and something of a hush about his person.

"I suggest we begin with the introduction," I said.

6

DAVID HAD BURIED THE EVENTS SURROUNDING HIS FOS-
ter father and foster brother as deeply as the rest of his past, but the
trouble with bodies is that sometimes they get exhumed. His arrest
as a suspect in Hugh's murder had had all the feel of replay to it: six
cops, two squad cars, handcuffs behind the back, couple of body
blows to show who's top dog, rough hustle into the police station.
Then came the desk sergeant. There's always a quirk like that, some
bizarre piece of irrationality to reinforce the sense of an old trap
closing in.

David had recognized the guy at once. He was related to the first
police officer who'd interrogated him all those years ago—maybe
even his son—the first cop he'd been stupid enough to talk to since
he was about six years old.

State-raised kids like David learn to keep their mouths shut
when they're barely out of the cradle. At first, it's more in the line
of superstition: if you talk to foster parents—or social workers or
cops or teachers or anybody like that—you're doomed. Kids have to
be maybe fourteen before the full extent of it dawns on them, before
they realize that it's not just fate, that it's far worse than that, that
the very law of the land does not apply to them, that it hardly ever
punishes anybody for hurting *them,* although it sometimes punishes
them for *getting* hurt. If they say anything—anything at all—somebody's going to have them for it. By this time, it hardly matters
whether what rules the mind is superstition or reason or faith.
Whatever it is, is there for good, and it never leaves, no matter what
happens. In David, the twin enemies of fate and state had main-
tained a united front despite Hugh and all the years of intellectual

gymnastics. Or perhaps it was *because* of the formal teaching that the hold was so tight. After all, didn't Hugh himself introduce David to Robespierre's famous words?

> *Bring me the truest patriot in France.*
> *Get him to write six lines on any subject,*
> *and I'll find something in them to hang him.*

How could anybody put it better? And it has to be said that David's belief in the collusion between state and fate ended up meaning that he agreed with Becky Freyl; he'd known for as long as he could remember that he'd been born to be executed. An equally undeniable truth was that Hugh's murder would fulfill this destiny all too quickly if he couldn't find a fall guy.

So David had to get a line on what the police knew about the murder. The newspapers had revealed almost nothing. His midnight visit to Herndon & Freyl had told him a few things, but mainly it had lengthened his list of unanswered questions. There was little point in a daytime visit; none of Hugh's friends and colleagues would speak to him, much less see him. But cops: they're another matter. They love to talk. They blabber about cases, especially high-profile cases like this one, just as doctors blabber about patients; and cops in the same family are practically joined at the hip. The guy's son or nephew or whatever would have a lot of details because everybody at the station would know them. If David could learn just a little of what was already on the record, he might have some idea what move to make next.

Trouble was, he could no longer quite remember the name. There had been several interrogators during that time whose names had welded themselves into his memory, but not this one; and his aversion to police stations meant calling there could only be a last resort. Eastwood? Milkwood? Wildwood? The only part he was sure of was "wood" and he was sure there'd been more to it than that.

An Internet search can find anybody anywhere, and home addresses of policemen are not protected by law. David formulated combination after combination—Woods, Woodward, Woodford, Woodgate—ran searches on each, phoned every listing in and around Springfield that even resembled such a name. At last he found an N. Wellwood in Pleasant Plains, a tiny town ten miles out of Springfield. A man answered and he knew the voice at once, even remembered the full name at once: Sergeant Norton Wellwood. He'd expected reluctance and found it, but an hour later the old policeman called him back and agreed to meet him on Saturday night, three days off.

Those three days were an eternity that only David's hard-learned prison patience allowed him to endure, and when Saturday finally came, he arrived half an hour early at the ersatz Mexican bar on the south side of Springfield that Wellwood had suggested. He found the man already in a booth with a largely finished margarita in front of him.

"Can you drink a pitcher of those things?" David said to him, easing himself into the bench on the other side of the table.

"I thought you'd never ask."

David signaled for the waitress to bring a pitcher of margaritas. "Thanks for coming," he said, turning to Norton. "I wasn't sure you would."

"Me neither." David took out a pack of cigarettes, offered it to Norton, who shook his head and watched David cup his hands over a match. "You had me worried, kid. Know that? You had me worried for years. I used to wake up in the middle of the night worrying about you."

"Oh?"

Norton shrugged and studied his empty glass. The remains of salt around its edge sparkled in the dim light. La Casita ("the realest Mex bar in town") shrouded its dinginess with red-shaded wall lamps and the bland jollity of cantina music: vilhuela, guittaron, trombone, flute.

"Your son followed in your footsteps," David said.

"Fucking bastard acts like he's my boss. Keeps on telling me how the world works. Jesus, I hate being retired."

"You were good at your job."

"Yeah? You think so?"

"I usually have the sense to shut up."

"Come off it, David. You gave me diddly-squat. I got to take a piss."

David watched Norton struggle out of the booth. Was it really possible that the burly cop—who was strong enough in himself to show concern for a boy—had turned into this soft and sagging old person? And the boy who had been at his mercy: what trace of him remained in this tall and powerfully built man?

"I'd a recognized you anywhere, know that?" Norton said, answering the unspoken question as he eased himself back into the booth. "Don't you never get tired of being mad all the time? Makes me tired just looking at you. Where'd you learn to talk so fancy, anyhow?"

David tilted his beer bottle in a toast. He'd picked up a Carta Blanca at the bar on his way over to the booth. "The Illinois State Education in Prisons program," he said.

"You're shitting me."

"No."

"You even sound kind of English."

"I had a teacher who was educated in England."

"Freyl?"

"His mother sent him to Harrow."

"That a college or something?"

"High school. He went to Oxford after that."

Norton chuckled. "You really are a ding-dong, know that? To think that little bum I questioned turned into . . ."

He shook his head and trailed off as the waitress appeared with a pitcher of frozen margaritas and several salt-rimmed glasses for him. She set a bottle of Tecate in front of David, who picked it up and stared at it absently.

"We run out of Carta Blanca," she said. "That okay?" David nodded. She wore a bright Mexican skirt and a low-cut full blouse, but she was one of those sturdy Illinois farm girls with freckles and strong teeth, a living, breathing incarnation of ketchup, Coca-Cola and yellow American mustard on a hot dog. "That'll be $15.25," she said.

"You can get that crap you're drinking in the Piggly Wiggly," Norton said to David. David nodded again, gave the girl a twenty and told her to keep the change.

"Police procedure seems to have changed in the last twenty years," he said to Norton, lighting a second cigarette from the butt of the first.

"They rotate them. Know that? Two years max, and they're

back on the street doing fuck-all. How the hell can you run a force like that? Nobody knows nothing about nothing."

"Sounds familiar."

"These goddamned kids down there, they got no nose for it no more. Okay, okay, it ain't their fault. They been told they can read it in a book. Kids is stupid. They believe what you tell them. Some things don't come out of books, David."

"I know."

Norton really did seem to think a cop was a truth seeker, who was not opinionated or prejudiced or prone to hasty judgment. He said it with such conviction that it sounded almost possible. He said he'd done his damnedest to live by the motto "I work for God." But what the fuck does it all add up to in the end? His wife was fooling around and his son was a shit. He loved his daughter, who had the prettiest blond curls you ever did see, but she lived in New Jersey with a stockbroker and never came back to the Midwest. He'd had a triple bypass two years ago, and now there was something funny going on in his legs. Every night he had to get up half a dozen times and threaten his prick with felonious assault to get as much as a dribble out of it; to prove the point, he took himself off to the can twice more during the next hour and a half.

David called over the waitress and ordered a bowl of tortilla chips and some guacamole. He had a delicate sense of timing, and he figured it was now or never.

"Tell me, Sergeant," he said. "Would *you* have pulled me in for the Freyl murder?"

"Jeest, nobody's called me that in a hell of a time. Sounds good, don't it? Sergeant Wellwood. How many days they hold you any-how?"

"Four."

"And you didn't say nothing to them in all that time?" Norton laughed. "You learned your lesson good, didn't you? I used to wish my kid . . ." He looked down at his empty glass, then poured the dregs of the pitcher of margaritas into it. He was slurring his words pretty badly. "I don't know. Maybe I'd a pulled you in if it was up to me. Maybe not. It sure looked like your work, didn't it? We ain't had a guy beat that bad since they scraped them guys of yours off that garage pit."

None of the papers had reported the method of Hugh's murder; those four days of questioning had skirted the issue with care, and nobody but David knew of his after-hours visit to Herndon & Freyl. An oil pit in a garage is very different from an elegant library in a law office. There's no denying it. And yet David suddenly remembered the clang the lug wrench made against the metal of the car above the pit. Once or twice—many years ago now—the thud it made on mashed bone had jolted him upright in the middle of the night. The state of the furnishings at Herndon & Freyl could easily have meant a similar savage contest. But there were so many scars and they covered so much of such a very large room. Which left him with a more urgent sense of the questions that had come to him during that illicit visit. Several attackers? An unclear purpose?

If only he could have been certain the sergeant was carrying a tape recorder or there was a bug in the booth. The police hadn't pressed charges against David for the Freyl murder because they didn't have anything on him. There could be no other reason; they'd have loved to pin this on him. The slightest trace of anything would have sufficed. Wellwood could so easily have told them about tonight's meeting: "Give him just enough to chew on," they would have said. "Let him think you're telling him what he wants to know. These guys are vain. Maybe he wants to know we recognize him from the way he goes about his killing even if we can't get him for it."

"You're telling me Hugh was badly hurt," David said to Norton.

"Yeah, you could say that." Norton watched David take a deep drag, hold it a little too long, let it out slowly. "You want something from me, don't you, kid?"

"Yes."

"Don't sound like you to butter up an old cop for nothing."

"I need to know what the police know."

"I don't know nothing about that."

"You know the condition of the body. That doesn't sound like nothing to me."

"So I know a little. So what? Why the fuck should I tell you? You going to tell me you didn't kill him?"

"Will it influence your opinion?"

"Just might."

The Tecate tasted exactly like the Carta Blanca that had preceded it. Not that David would have noticed the difference between one beer and another. "I never lied to you, did I?" he said.

"You never told me nothing."

"What's the difference?"

"There's other ways of looking at that, especially for an old choirboy like me who was looking to be a priest till he was eighteen."

"Christ wouldn't answer Pilate."

Norton laughed. "Boy, oh, boy, you really are something, aren't you? Not even a heartbeat to come up with a Mickey Mouse like that. You never told me you was innocent." He laughed again. " 'Course, Christ didn't neither. What do you want anyhow?"

"Information."

"That's what you got me out here for, huh?"

"Yes."

Norton sucked at the dregs of his margarita. "It's a fine point, my friend, but I ain't sure that getting an old cop liquored up so's he'll spill his guts is exactly ethical. I might have to ask my snot-nosed kid about that."

David stubbed out his cigarette, then took another from the pack and lit it. "You knew what I wanted all along, didn't you?" he said.

"Well, what the hell, I *sure* do like them margaritas."

"Could you manage another pitcher?"

"You bet I could." David signaled the waitress, and Norton settled himself back in the booth. "See, I figure to myself like this, maybe if I give David what he wants, *maybe* he'll . . . I always felt bad about you, kid, always wanted to do something to—Aw, what the fuck. I already said too much anyhow."

The cantina music pumped away in the background with a singer this time, a deep voice but a woman's, something about forgetting. The sound system was too muddy for David to get more of it than that.

"Was anything taken?" he said. "Papers, documents?"

"Hell of a mess: probably all kinds of crap missing. Looked like kids having a field day in daddy's desk. 'Course them lawyer guys always got secret enemies. They make too many undesirable contacts."

"Like me, you mean."

"From what I hear it did look kind of personal."

David stubbed out the cigarette he'd lit only a moment before, tapped yet another fresh one on the table, put it in his mouth but somehow could not bring himself to light it. "What about Athena?"

"What's that?"

"The guide dog."

"Oh, yeah. Funny name for a dog. Funny-looking dog too. How come he called her that?" David shrugged. "Not a sign of her any-where. Guess he didn't take her with him that night. Not a smart move."

"Might it have been kids? A gang?"

"One guy."

"Only one?"

"Only one."

"You're certain about that?"

"Some kind of analysis of footprint patterns or something. I don't understand nothing about that."

"What footprint patterns?"

"Like he was wearing them booties the forensics guys wear. Know what I mean?"

David considered the point. "Any idea how he got in?"

"During the day, they figure. Like a regular customer or some-thing. Must've hid somewhere. Wasn't no sign of nothing else."

"But not a robbery gone wrong." It was a statement, not a ques-tion.

"Look, kid, all I really know is Freyl fought back pretty good for a blind guy that couldn't see nothing of what's happening to him." Norton watched him a moment, then said, "I got to get to the can." He tried to pull himself to his feet and fell back into the booth. David was staring fixedly at the tabletop. Norton gathered his strength, managed to ease himself out of the booth, started toward the restroom, then turned back.

"Promise me something, David."

David looked up at the voice.

"Don't never get old, huh?" Norton said.

7

IN DAYTIME, A PRISON IS A JUNGLE. AT NIGHT IT IS A
zoo. The telltale noises change when dark closes in. Guards do regular
rounds then; they come and go as they please, heavy boots echoing down
metal corridors, huge collections of keys jangling, dogs straining at the
leash. There's nobody to watch over the helpless, much less intervene.

Rich and law-abiding people like me remain very innocent in such
matters. Rose and I used to ponder over drinks in the evening—log fire
burning, leg of lamb in the oven, wine open on the sideboard, warm bed
upstairs awaiting us—how we would manage such nights. The irony was
by no means lost on us either. We struggled for comparisons and thought
only of hotels that had not lived up to their reputation or an overnight
stay at a friend's house with the air-conditioning broken and the baby
awake at two in the morning. The worst we could come up with was an
all-night party at an Italian ski lodge and a clumsy chambermaid cleaning up after a drunk.

I asked David to write me an essay on the subject.

By this time, he had been an inmate of South Hams prison for a couple of years, during which I had visited him once a month. My designated
role in the lives of such as he was to achieve a sixth-grade level of literacy. There was no reason—and usually no wish on either side—to continue
contact after that. David was by far the brightest of the people I taught;
he should have been long past any such level by now. I even suspected
that he studied Cole on criminal justice when he was alone in his cell, but
I had no proof of it; at lessons, he read halting snatches from the book in
a voice swamped with boredom. But I have to admit that the more he re-
sisted, the more I was intrigued. Why defy me for so long? Did this young
man never give in?

And yet however hard I tried to win him over, I could not find another subject that provoked any hint of the excitement that book had kindled in him. I did not expect anything much from the essay either, although despite himself he had the rough beginnings of some style as a writer. I had given him a copy of Keats's "To Sleep" because Keats called sleep the "soft embalmer of the still midnight." It was a dare, a taunt, part of the game. I hoped it might stir up some response in him.

"Do you mean to tell me, Mr. Marion," I interrupted (he was reading his brief attempt out loud and in the same halting, bored tone), "that you can manage on no more than two or three hours?"

"So what?" His hackles were up at once.

"I'm filled with admiration. Sleep has always seemed a waste, and yet I cannot function properly unless I have slept a full eight hours. Is there a trick to it?"

I had never before asked him direct questions about himself, and I think this combined with the unexpected compliment took him off guard. "Most guys in this fucking hole grab at sleep like it was candy." I was delighted to hear feeling in that voice; but as soon as the words were out, he was wary again, doubtless sensing a trap—or maybe fearing some other betrayal—in this slight shift of the ground rules between us. "Can't get me no purchase on it. Don't know why."

David still couldn't manage more than two or three hours of sleep despite a wide selection of licit and illicit drugs. After he left Norton Wellwood, he knew he would not sleep at all, and he set out into the Springfield streets that angled off from his apartment in the slums of the east. He often ran at night. But this night was different. Tonight there was a fierce edge to his pace. He ran past bars he knew well and saw nothing, past pool halls and whorehouses, laughter, heavy rhythms of rap music, the occasional abrupt violence—fight, mugging, break-in—that punctuated the dark. None of these intruded on his brain any more than the long stretches of emptiness between them.

His route zigzagged gradually westward across the first set of train tracks and into the commercial center of town. Here he hit a concentrated patch of Lincoln nostalgia, a brittle and sugary distraction from the hard-driven deals in government, business and law that go on here: Lincoln Home, Lincoln Family Pew (under Tiffany glass), Lincoln Herndon Offices (a short sprint from Herndon & Freyl). He saw none of it.

Six blocks farther on, still zigzagging, he passed another tug at the heartstrings, a wedding-cake dome atop a handsome stone structure, lit up against the night. This is the Old State Capitol, the very place where Lincoln spoke his famous words, "a house divided against itself cannot stand"; it's a monument that does stand—and stands proud—just as Lincoln would have had it, but it stands alone and just about midway between the two sets of tracks that divide this profoundly divided town. David saw none of this either.

Across the second set of tracks came mile after mile of small front yards and clapboard houses that belonged to factory foremen and bank clerks, respectable people with dogs and mortgages. The night was moonless, starless, overcast. Dawn didn't break until he reached the tree-lined streets and stately, porticoed houses of the far west. The sun would rise soon despite the clouds, because the sun shone here every day, and this is because here stood the dwelling places of the chosen few who lived the American dream in all its splendor, the owners of the factories, the banks, the law offices, the machinery of government.

And yet this was where Hugh's own wife died, on the very boulevard where David awoke from his daze. It was a true boulevard out of a French city, a wide strip of trees, shrubs and grass dividing the street into two lanes so that its elegant houses looked out onto an urban parkland instead of each other. He had not planned to come here, did not want to be here, could not imagine what had brought him here.

The past is a waste of time: the dead are dead.

Even so, he stopped his run to glance around him at the very spot that changed the direction of his life as surely as it changed the substance of Hugh's.

◄o►

Rose was impetuous. She was a decisive, controlled, fast driver; but she was as impetuous in a car as she was everywhere else. It was one of her greatest charms. She and Helen and I started out together, a Christmas vacation Wednesday and a semicircular route designed to deliver me to a dental appointment and Helen to her riding lesson. The first part of the journey went as planned except that it took longer than it should have, and Rose's impetuosity was getting the better of her as it always did when she was late. She hated being late.

I was already in the dentist's chair when the accident happened.

When Helen was little, Rose had developed the habit of thrusting out her right arm whenever she stopped short to keep Helen in her seat. She didn't give it up even when seat belts came in, even though Helen was securely belted up, and Rose alone was the one in danger. She never fastened her own belt unless Helen or I scolded her; she was always in too much of a hurry. It became one of those family games of threat and defiance, Helen and I would describe horrific head wounds and Rose, irritably fastening her belt only to please us, would say, "Well, at least I won't have to listen to you two anymore."

And so she didn't. The police told me afterward that the car hit a patch of black ice and skidded into one of those cotton trees that drop fluff over the street in summertime. Helen wasn't badly hurt—a few cuts and abrasions—but the car was so mangled that it took more than an hour to cut the two of them out of it. By that time Rose was dead. Twisted metal from around the broken windshield had made a profound cut from under her chin on one side, up between the eye and ear on the other side and down again over to the back of her head; skin separated from skull in a modern version of an old-fashioned scalping. She would have bled to death even if this had been her only injury, but there was also extensive internal damage that drained her dry before the scalp wound had a chance.

Helen would never talk about the experience except to say that Rose had thrust out her arm as usual before they hit the tree. Poor Helen repeated the point over and over, as though it formed some impassable barrier in her mind: the familiar, final, protective gesture of her mother's life. I could not talk about the accident at all, and yet no single thought entered my head that did not end in the wreckage beneath that cotton tree. Nights blended into days and days into nights, the hours a wasteland, a total desolation, an absolute negative. I ate, drank, slept but I have no memory of meals or sleep. Even the simplest domestic duty so oppressed me that I could not perform it. I felt I had gone blind a second time—deaf, dumb, insensate too—and I hated everybody and everything, just as I had the first time around. Except that this time I hated Rose too. I hated her for not being there to stroke my brow and coax me back from the edge of the abyss to which her death had brought me.

My solution was hardly original, but it came highly recommended by the Hemlock Society: two grams of quinalbarbitone and a plastic bag over the head to complete the job. I redrafted my will. I put my affairs in order. Toward the end of what was supposed to be David's final lesson with me, I assured him that he would enjoy his work with my successor, whom I had chosen carefully and who was much closer to his own age. Perhaps with this person, I told him, he might be able to break through the barriers that I had been unable to help him through myself. The air around him went abruptly truculent. I got nothing further, not a single word. I turned to pack away my books.

Then he said, "You selfish prick. You're going to kill yourself, aren't you?"

"Mr. Marion, I did not remotely imply anything of the—"

"You think guys like me can't see what's goin' on? Well, I got news for you, asshole. We ain't that dumb. It's written all over your fuckin' face. You're gonna slit your throat and drop us in the shit where you found us. You forked us out. You're gonna toss us back. Right?"

I paused, then continued packing. "Your gutter language proves only that your thoughts are no more fully articulated on this subject than on many others," I said.

"Jesus, listen at you. You don't get it, do you? I told you we ain't that dumb. You come in here with your books and words and promises. All that shit about 'power.' What the fuck was wrong with me? I had me something I could control. Sure, it ain't nothing the likes of you would ever a wanted. But it was mine. You hear what I'm saying? It was *mine*. Why didn't you fuck off when I told you to? What right you got to come in here and tell me what I got ain't worth nothin'? that what *you* got is what I want? What's all that 'power' worth now, huh? You don't know from nothing about what's hard in a life, you motherfucker—not from nothing. How the fuck can you even guess what you done to the guys like me you're gonna leave with their dicks hanging out?"

"You are an ignorant and foul-mouthed young man, Mr. Marion."

"I trusted you!" he shouted. "I never trusted nobody in my life before. All this time I thought you was a bigger man than that. Jesus, what an asshole."

I was trembling as I left him. It was not until the middle of the night—I woke abruptly—that I suddenly realized he had never given so long a speech in all the time I had known him.

I flushed the quinalbarbitone away. The next morning I composed a letter to him, telling him I would be with him as usual for the following lesson. I addressed him for the very first time as "David" to let him know that he had guessed the truth and was alone responsible for my change of heart. We never spoke of the matter again, although he let me know he had understood me in the subtlest of ways. He never again swore in my presence. From that day on, his spoken grammar improved markedly. But most important, it became clear to me that at long last he was allowing himself to change direction, that for the first time in his life he was prepared to channel his explosive fury into something positive.

Perhaps he never knew that he also became my emotional mainstay and remained so for a considerable period. On the other hand, even before he satisfied his examiners that he had reached a sixth-grade level, he and I came to the tacit agreement that his education would continue. I knew—if he did not—that it was as much for my sake as for his. But his progress was astonishing, more than enough to sustain the interest of any teacher. I realized I had been right; he'd been holding back for as long as I had known him—and holding back a very great deal.

I introduced him to history and novels. He was puzzled by fiction—perhaps a certain literalness of approach dictated by a life as hard as his had been. History came much more easily to him. I am sorry to say that it is not a subject with which I can claim great familiarity, but I could see that in it he exercised what I think of as a lawyer's ability to collate material, analyze disparate sources and knit together credible pictures from fragments of information. Over the years that followed, we spent a great deal of time on philosophy and politics, where his opinions were passionate if, in my opinion, naïve. I even managed to teach him some of the French and Latin I had learned as a schoolboy in England, although I was even less qualified in languages than I was in history and I feared for his accent in both of them.

But I do not do him justice. It is a rare privilege to be given a gifted pupil, an almost unheard-of privilege for one involved in teaching prisoners, and I wanted only the best for him. I felt I was building something new and fresh, something untrammeled and beautiful in the midst of that squalid prison and despite his own squalid past. Urban savage into man of culture: this was my creation. Every night, I went to sleep considering where best to go next with him and woke in excitement at possibilities that seemed to clamor for precedence.

Only gradually did I realize that I still had a role to play in the lives of my daughter, my mother, an unexpected and surprising number of my other pupils. But I am most profoundly grateful to him because if he had not turned my logic on its head—where logic like that serves the living best—I would never have had the opportunity to meet Stephanie.

8

THE SCREEN ON DAVID'S CELL PHONE READ "STEPHANIE Willis."

"Yes?" David said.

"David? David Marion? What a wonderfully unexpected pleasure to get a message from *you*."

"I've been trying to get hold of you for days."

Stephanie had been Hugh's personal assistant during the time he had been working to get David out of prison; Hugh had talked about her a lot, and David had listened to the stories the way he listened to stories about Hugh's family, straining to understand a life as alien to him as anything out of a science fiction novel. Not that Hugh had spent all that much time, proportionately speaking, on himself and his life; but he used these stories to illustrate points that David could not have understood otherwise: why a child might cry when left alone in a train station or a woman feel put down in the company of bank presidents and senators because her father was only a druggist. These people—Hugh's circle—were characters from a magical world of comfort and innocence that locked away wild beasts like David and forgot them except as Sunday afternoon curios or evidence of their own moral superiority. Even though David had never met Stephanie, he figured her reception of him was likely to be as cold as anything Hugh's funeral party guests could dish out. Why should it be otherwise? Her failure to return his calls certainly hadn't surprised him, and yet the warmth in her voice now and the way she put the words: that was a surprise. He was on guard at once.

"How *are* you?" she said. "It's so extraordinary to actually hear your voice at last." But before he had a chance to change the subject, she rushed on, "Something's the matter, isn't it? Is it Hugh? Is he all right?"

"You haven't heard?"

"He couldn't be in trouble, could he?"

"He's dead."

There was no response.

"Ten days ago," David said.

"How?" She could barely get the word out.

"You don't want to know."

"No. Of course I don't." Then she added, "Tell me."

David sketched an outline of the reports in the newspapers along with some of what he'd learned from Norton Wellwood: a murder that had taken place in the library of Herndon & Freyl, a single attacker with a blunt instrument made out of metal, Hugh alone at the time without even his guide dog. He did not go into the extent of the damage or the condition of the body or the resemblance—in his mind if in no one else's—of the marks in the library to the working end of a lug wrench. Nor had he any intention of telling her he'd been picked up for the murder himself. If she'd missed Hugh's death in the papers, and nobody in Springfield had contacted her, she'd obviously missed any stories of David's days in jail as well. Any mention of that, and he knew she would jump to the conclusion that Becky had simply assumed—who was a more likely killer than David?—and he'd learn nothing.

She seemed to take in what he told her. At least she said nothing until he was finished.

"You still there?" he said when the pause grew to an uncomfortable length.

"I can't make the pieces fit in this tale of yours. It all keeps slipping sideways."

"I need information."

"Oh, David, what for?"

"You know what I mean."

"Do I? I guess . . . No, no. There isn't anything I could say that would mean anything now. I'm sure you know everything I do—more than I do. It's been well over two years now since I left Springfield. I haven't been within a thousand miles of it in all that time. When was the funeral?"

"Just under a week ago. Last Tuesday."

"Oh, God, David, what's the good of a world without Hugh Freyl in it?"

"Zemanski has himself installed already."

She gave a mirthless chuckle. "Dear Jimmy."

"So?"

"You plainly don't like him any better than I do."

"Hugh trusted him."

"Do you really think so?"

"Don't you?"

"Goddamnit," she burst out, "why do people work so hard and so fast to destroy what's best? Can't they even wait to come up for air? I hate that town. I really do. It was bad enough before—all that eye-scratching and coffee-klatch pretension—and now it decides to kill Hugh. Look, David, a lot goes on there that nobody knows about—or admits to knowing anyhow. I wish I didn't know about it. I've never run across so many desperate people fighting so hard for what isn't worth having. I suppose some of them are no more than sad and greedy, but a few of them are really bottom of the barrel. I bet Jimmy was painting his name on the door the minute he made sure Hugh was cold."

There was no sign today of the weak, winter sun. David sat at the round table in his east-side apartment, and it was as bleak, raw, gray inside as it was outside. The packing crates that lined the walls closed in on the room, and yet there was still no sense of disorder even though David had the newspaper articles spread out in front of him, searching through them yet again for some hint—something, anything—that he might have missed on earlier readings.

"Can you give me anything specific on Zemanski?" he said to Stephanie.

"What difference would it make?" There was desperation in her voice. Desolation too. "What difference does anything make?"

"There are things I need to know."

"Things?" The word was almost a sob.

"Information," he said irritably.

"Oh, Lord, I'm so sorry, David." She wrenched her focus toward his concerns with a determined if ragged exhale of breath. "Of course you have to find out what happened. This must be terrible for you. Hugh loved you like a son. He really did." There was no reply David could bring himself to make. Hugh's stories had not managed to bridge the deeper gulfs between David and the free world, and he had no idea how to deal with comments like hers, especially when they came at him so unexpectedly. Straightforward attack? Sure. No problem. But sympathy hurt him in unreachable places; there were no muscles he could contract against it, no pressures he could apply. He felt swamped, stripped, raw. "I don't mean to sound so unhelpful," she went on. "I guess I can't think straight at the moment. I can't really . . . Look, I can be on a flight to Chicago by—let's see—two o'clock this afternoon. Three at the latest. An hour at O'Hare. Another will get me to Springfield. There's a flight in at about ten, isn't there?"

"What do you want to come here for?"

"Oh, David, don't sound so angry. Please."

"I don't want you here. Just tell me about Zemanski."

"There isn't really anything I can tell you over the telephone."

"Then you're no use to me."

David clicked off the phone. It rang again at once. "David Marion, don't you *dare* hang up on me. Now, you listen here, I have three weeks' vacation stored up. I will be in Springfield this evening."

"What *for*?"

"Because it's what *I* want. I don't give a damn what you want."

"You expect me to believe that?"

"I don't care whether you believe it or not."

There was a pause. "You're not going to like what you see."

"I can manage. David?"

"What?"

"You take care of yourself, huh?"

"What's that supposed to mean?"

"Don't go getting yourself into any more trouble until I'm around."

He sighed, irritable again. "Okay. Okay. I'll pick you up at the airport."

◄◦►

Hugh had often said that despite Stephanie's warmth, she was as tough as they come. He had also told David that she was a descendant of tough people, of the Russians who sailed across the Bering Strait during the West Coast's fur rush that preceded its gold rush by more than a hundred years. These invaders—some came all the way from St. Petersburg and Moscow—eliminated the sea otter population along a thousand miles of shoreline and made huge fortunes in the process. Maybe they didn't do much intermarrying with the Kodiaks, who were fierce, and the Aleuts, who were friendly, but the Russians and the natives certainly got together. Stephanie was living proof of it.

Even though David had never met her before, he recognized her the moment she appeared at the door to disembark from the tiny sixteen-seater United Express airplane. Those warm red-browns in her skin were easy to trace, but the broad forehead and widespread black eyes could just as well have been Russian as Kodiak or Aleut. It was hard to tell how old she was. He figured thirty-five, maybe a year or two more or less; she had the kind of skin that doesn't age. It was even harder for him to decide if she was beautiful or handsome or neither of these things; faces as strong as hers aren't usual in women. But what dominated even across an airfield was an artless-ness and an unself-conscious curiosity that was Russian to the core.

David knew that Hugh had loved her; even from this distance he could easily see why, and he steeled himself against her. His experi-ence in such matters was sketchy at best; the last thing he needed was another complication in his life. He hadn't gone to prison a vir-gin—not by any means—but only weeks after finishing eighteen years of solid male company, he'd got himself embroiled. A young woman had visited him inside, and he'd begun a correspondence with her; he'd come to wait impatiently for her letters, his hands trembling as he opened them, his heart in his throat whenever he thought about her. Then he met her on the outside, and nobody could have been less well equipped than he to handle the explosive intensity of what happened. It had ended badly. Thereafter, he'd rel-egated women to a matter of negotiation not unlike the haggling that had gone on between him and a downtown used-furniture dealer over the round table in his apartment. But once or twice the relega-tion cost him in ways he couldn't understand, and he had no inten-tion of allowing Stephanie to turn into another such time.

"So where's this famous Chevy?" she said to him, hugging him spontaneously, then holding him out from her a little to scan his face. "You're even better looking than your pictures. Did you know that?"

"What pictures?"

"Strings of numbers across full-face and profile of the dangerous murderer. I've seen them all. It's your family album: I used to get the feeling I was watching you grow up when I looked through them."

"How'd you manage to get two bags onto that plane?" he said, reaching for them. The weight of them came as a shock. "What's in these things anyhow? Sand?"

She smiled. "I have some material here that just might interest you."

"Oh?"

"I'm afraid I irritated a whole lot of people toward the end of my time at Herndon and Freyl. I kept a lot of records too—dug up some that just might have a bearing on Hugh's death. Probably not, but it's worth a try anyhow. There was so much going on that I couldn't make sense of. Still can't. That's why I couldn't tell you anything useful over the phone—too much material and no routes into it that I could make sense of myself."

"You irritated people? You mean Jimmy?"

She sighed. "Why *do* I dislike that man so much?"

Springfield Capital Airport is out to the north of town. It's a small airport, desolate in the way small airports always seem to be; David and Stephanie walked past vending machines and semilit empty spaces to the parking lot out front and David's Chevrolet Impala. He'd been in the process of a paint job when Hugh died; the fiberglass fill was nearly finished, the rubbing-down had a long way to go, and the large body looked battered, a pitiful relic from a boisterous era of car making. She studied the Chevy from this angle and that as he loaded her bags into the trunk.

"Impressed?" he said, putting the key into the ignition.

"It's the most amazing piece of machinery I've ever seen. How old is it anyhow? twenty years? thirty? What could possibly persuade such a tired old engine to turn itself over?"

"How about faith?"

"I wouldn't have taken you for a man of faith."

"Whatever works."

"And to think Hugh wasn't sure you were a pragmatist. He was funny about people, don't you think? As shrewd as they come with the ones he didn't like and not anywhere near so good with the ones he did." She scanned David's face as she had before. "I bet you're a little like that yourself."

He turned the key in the ignition. The car purred to life at once, and he maneuvered it out of the parking lot. "Where do you want to go?"

"The Great Western isn't too bad. Or at least it didn't used to be. I hate flying. Why do the wings have to tremble like that?"

"Have you had anything to eat?"

She shook her head. "I don't know what's the matter with me tonight. I'm not usually this whacked by a plane journey. I really *need* to get to a bed. Are you free tomorrow? I'd love to take you to lunch at Norb Andy's. We could talk there. Hugh and I used to go there a lot."

"What time do you want me to pick you up?"

"You don't have to do that. After all, I forced myself on you, coming here. I'll rent a car. Meet you there about twelve-thirty?"

"I'm free all day." He nodded at her, a chauffeur's hat-tipping gesture. "At your service."

"Well, that's a change for the books. I thought you didn't want me to come here at all."

"I can bow to the inevitable as well as the next guy."

"I bet you can't."

"Try me."

"What about work? You must have a job or something."

"I'm tied up tonight, but that's it."

She looked out at the orange glow of the arc lights that lead away from the airport. The rain was just beginning; the forecast was sleet turning to snow in the small hours of the morning. It was going to be a bad night. "Norb Andy's is the only place I miss in this godforsaken town," she said sadly. "That and the Pair-a-Dice, I guess. But I'd like to see—" She broke off, then began again. "Would you mind awfully taking me to the cemetery first? I know it doesn't make much sense, but I'd kind of like to see where he is."

◄◦►

I have never mastered the trick of feeling faces. I only wish I had. I still wonder what Stephanie looks like. I suppose it should not matter to a blind man, but I would dearly love to know, although I knew I wanted her

near me the moment I heard her voice. It was warm and open, and somehow it seemed to have a smile at its center.

Not that her first words about me were particularly inspiring. What
she said was, "Please show Mr. Freyl to a chair, Janet."

I had been brought to emergency at Memorial Hospital with my wrist
broken in a minor accident of the sort that people like me are prone to.
She was deputed to make certain that I filled out my insurance claim
form before I left the premises; from the way voices moved in the air
around me—the blind develop a crude form of sonar—I could tell that the
room we sat in was one of those tiny spaces beneath staircases and beside broom closets.

We went through the usual routine: name, date of birth, address,
marital status, insurance company, type of coverage.

"Would you mind telling me your name?" I interrupted.

"Oh, I'm sorry. It's Stephanie Willis."

"Mrs. Willis?"

There was a pause. "Whatever you like."

"Not Mrs. Willis."

"Not really."

"Why have they put you in this horrid little room?"

She laughed, and the laugh was as promising as her voice. "Are you
English, Mr. Freyl? Only an Englishman would use a word like 'horrid.' "

I shook my head. "Only educated there, but I cannot seem to get the
sound of it out of my voice. Do they at least pay you well?"

"I'm afraid there are just too many people desperate for jobs like this.
It does pay the rent. Near enough anyway."

"Is there any pleasure at all for you in it?"

"Mr. Freyl, we really must fill out the rest—"

"Please tell me."

"Why would you want to know a thing like that?"

"I've always been interested in . . ." I paused for the simple reason
that I had no idea how to finish such a sentence. All that interested me
was this woman with a smile in her voice. "I guess I would just like to
know if you are happy here."

She laughed again and said, "Mr. Freyl, I have never been so bored in
my entire life. No, that's not altogether true. Yesterday was definitely
more boring than today—nobody asked me an unexpected question yesterday—and tomorrow is going to be like yesterday. So will the day after

and the day after that. On the other hand, I have a high boredom threshold. Sometimes I think I even enjoy being bored—although not very much. Now, if you can tell me the name of your insurance company, I'll—"

"I need a new personal assistant."

Within a month, she was installed in the office across the fire escape from me, and I was aware almost at once that my judgment about her had been correct. She is one of the few people I have known—my childhood playmate, the eminent Senator John Calder is another—who has an instinctive sensitivity about the blind. I do not believe she had ever known anybody in my condition before, and yet she knew without being told to identify herself when she entered a room so I knew who she was and to notify me when she was leaving the room so that I did not end up talking into thin air. She used words like "look," "see," "blind" as though I were perfectly normal, and she did so even as she cautioned me about stairs, curbs or obstacles in my path. She knew to look directly at me when we spoke so that I could follow her voice with my eyes and face, and she even seemed to take pleasure in the delicate social nicety of placing my hand on a doorknob or the arm of a chair so I could orient myself.

She was as intelligent as she was sensitive. Her gift for describing people and surroundings was so great that I sometimes had the sense I was seeing them myself. She was not afraid of hard work either. When I turned the records of my various pupils over to her, she put in evenings and weekends on top of our daily schedule to make certain she mastered all the important detail in them; she realized at once that David Marion was a special case for me; she spent hours with his file, and she came to me one afternoon in some puzzlement.

"It says here he signed a confession."

"Yes. Yes, I know."

"But the social worker says he was functionally illiterate."

"The confession is what mattered in those days. Whether it was signed or not was largely immaterial."

"You're kidding me." I shook my head. "That's dreadful. You could fit anybody up for anything."

"These days we are more aware of the potential for abuse."

She harrumphed in disapproval. "Anyhow, this one was signed. It says so right here."

"I do not think he was illiterate. He's one of those very bright people who pretend stupidity to get an edge on the rest of us."

"Well, I suppose . . . No, damnit all. That's not the point. Don't you see? It just doesn't add up. Everything I know about this guy comes from the snatches in this file and your stories about him, and signing a confession, whether he could read it or not: it just isn't the way he works. I'm sure it isn't. If they handed him a confession he wouldn't look at it. I bet he wouldn't let on that he knew it was in front of him. I bet he never even killed anybody."

I shook my head. "The only question is why."

"You can't be that certain."

"I've known him way too long to doubt it."

She thought a moment. "Damn. I want him innocent."

"I know."

"He was so young. Fifteen! Just a baby."

"Childish pranks can have disastrous consequences."

"A prank!"

"Use whatever word you like. It will not alter what happened."

"Couldn't he just have been in the wrong place at the wrong time? an easy arrest? and an easier conviction?"

"Highly unlikely."

She paused. "One bad act doesn't make him irredeemable."

"Of course it doesn't," I said. "Over the years I have known him, I have watched him develop into an entirely new person. The pity of his sentence is that it does not allow for change."

"And you don't swallow this confessing stuff. You couldn't. Which is to say the cops could have fitted him up for that part of it. Only a couple of months ago—it says so right here—'Infraction of Rule 3201' . . . What is that?" I shrugged. "Well, whatever it is, all he had to do was admit he'd done it. He spent ninety days in solitary instead."

"I think he likes solitary."

"You're a thoroughly irritating man, did you know that? It's the feel of the thing that's wrong. Some of the other foster families that took him in sound as nasty as they come. The last one"—she rifled through the paper—"doesn't seem like that at all. They seemed to be really trying. So why didn't he kill one or two of the others? the ones who deserved it? Why does somebody like him let the bad guys off and kill a family that treats him decently?"

"Precisely the question that bothers me," I said, "and you do have a point about confessing."

"I'd love to know what he has to say about it himself."

9

FOR NEARLY FIFTY MILES, ROUTE 55 HEADS SOUTH OUT of Springfield as straight as a plumb line, not a single bend or swerve. Then it begins a gentle westward swing toward the vast expanse of the Mississippi River and across to the big city of St. Louis. David drove. Tony hated being a passenger, and he was a restless traveler even when he was at the wheel. His temper took on something of a manic edge as the trip wore on; his ceaseless banter kept pace with his mood.

"How come you drive this old heap anyways?" he was saying, but David knew there was no need to answer. "You got plenty of cash to buy something nice. I mean, you're rolling and you don't got commitments like me. You could get, lemme see, how about one of them . . . Hey, I betcha I know. I bet it's because this junk heap got a carburetor and plugs and points and shit like that like you used to work on when you were a kid. Right? Hey, David, I'm talking to you serious now. You keep on about the past being a waste of time, well, if you ask me, you're *living* in the past. One of these days, you're going to have to bring yourself up to the present, see things the way they really are, learn about fuel injection and antilock brakes. That reminds me, did I ever tell you about . . ."

And he went on to a practical joke he'd played that had nothing whatever to do with cars, although it did have to do with the past. Perhaps that was it. Perhaps that was the connection. Tony had talked like this ever since he and David were children, swinging from one topic to another via an internal logic of his own that was unavailable to anybody else. He was laughing delightedly about the time he'd covered himself in ketchup and played dead when one of his foster families got back from the store, and then—bubbling over—he went on to the time he'd silently unzipped his fly at the checkout in a supermarket and pissed in an old lady's pocket, then waited until she reached into it for her money.

Prison had taught David to value silence above almost everything else, and tonight he craved it. He lit one cigarette after another, each from the stub of its predecessor, and did his best to block out what he could of Tony. He sifted again and again through the few meager items in his store of facts from Norton Wellwood: a single attacker, death drawn out, something personal. If the police didn't have an awful lot more than this after ten days of investigation, they were going to have a hard time pinning it on anybody— even David. They just had to be asking themselves who would bother to beat a blind man to death. It's messy, time-consuming; he couldn't believe they didn't have some better idea what had gone on. Stephanie's hint at Zemanski—and the records that weighted down those heavy suitcases she'd carried off the plane—became more tantalizing with every passing moment.

Tony rattled on regardless. "I keep thinking about that snazzy funeral, you know, the Freyl thing. It's like when my dog died. That little hole and all. Know what I mean? Not being big enough for the man? Did I ever tell you about my dog? Big old dog. It was the Labor Day weekend—up in the nineties and awful humid— and the vet had to freeze him for a couple of days so he wouldn't rot before we got him buried. I had me a friend out near Pawnee, and they had a place called Boot Hill where all his ex-dogs were buried. So Mutton was going down to join his friend Emily the beagle. I called them, and this guy—his name was Albert Pogomuller, poor motherfucker—he dug a hole for the grave. But it was for a dog curled up and my dog had died with its feet stuck out and that's how it froze. See what I mean? The hole was too little. See? Just like Freyl, huh?"

The weather had set in as hard as the forecast promised. In front of David, the beam of the Chevy's headlights scattered and billowed in sleet that turned gradually to fine, dry snow. Everything else was blackness. The winter fields that stretched out icy on either side of the highway could just as well have been ocean or the Rocky Mountains.

"Let's take a look at the plans," David said when the Mississippi was no more than twenty miles away.

The two of them had worked jobs like this one ever since David got out of prison, with him as the central figure—the strategist, the brains—just as he'd so often been when they were children to-gether. Tony unrolled a sheet of paper, an architect's plan, and lit it with a flashlight.

"We got some serious shit this time," he said. "Only the one exit, monitored day and night—two guys on both shifts. Double door entry system. This here"—he pointed to an icon on the plan—"means they got X-ray monitoring of their mail. Cute, huh?"

David kept his eyes on the road ahead. "How about the perime-ter fence?"

"They're certainly trying hard. Makes me think of the time—"

"Stick to the fence."

"Okay. Okay. Looks like they got movement sensors here . . . and here and . . . practically everywhere. Timer lock on the gate."

"On the *gate*?"

"SafetyGauge sold it to practically every sucker on the list."

"Fences are your territory."

"You damn betcha."

"So?"

Tony laughed. "The fucking thing shorts so bad in weather like this that you got to shut the supply off. It's got to be one of the stu-pidest products in the whole country. I can't figure how you sell it to anybody, kindergarten, dog pound, Salvation Army. How stupid do you have to get to buy something like that?"

There was silence in the car for a minute, then David said, "Surely not everyone remembers to turn off the fence when there's a storm."

"You blow this one and you got a whole day's work ahead of you. Makes maintenance mad as hell. They got to have figured that out by this time. It don't make sense otherwise. How long they had the system? two years? three? We just cross our fingers and cut right through."

"Some people never learn."

"Nah. Trust me. It's gonna work. There's the usual blind spots across the yard. All that's left is walking up to that CCTV of yours . . . Ah, come on. Don't shake your head like that. You didn't get access cards?"

"The computer circuit is closed," David said. "I couldn't hack into it. There wasn't any way I could slip us into the database inside."

"They got to match us up to pictures *inside*? What's the point working out the fence at all? Jesus, I just been wasting my time, huh? All this for . . . what? What are you figuring to do, huh? Fly through solid steel? *Now* what are you shaking your head about?"

David controlled the wheel with his left hand; with his right he reached out to the plan. "The ceiling over the entryway . . . here . . . it's suspended. All we need do is hug the wall to the left of the camera—they'd have put it about . . . here—and the ceiling shields us. It's just one of those design faults. We slip past the trap without ever involving the security check and activate the electronic strike . . . here."

"How come you know the camera's there?"

"Standard procedure."

Tony studied the large sheet of paper. He shifted it upside down to orient himself. "I don't see a suspended—"

"Take a look at the elevation."

Tony bent over the plan again. When he straightened, his laugh was again that childlike delight of the practical joker. "There's just got to be some kind of prize for guys as dumb as this. I'm going to set up one myself. Know what? I'll make us a fortune. Ain't one of them guys going to know *nobody's* come a-calling"—he rapped out a beat on the dashboard—"until they make their rounds tomorrow morning."

A few minutes later David parked the Chevy. The wind had intensified, and the snow was driving hard—visibility was very low. He and Tony put on heavy coats; they gathered their gear together. Then, heads down to do battle against the weather, they set out toward the illuminated area and the high perimeter fence that surrounded the U.S. Customs Bonded Warehouse at Coopersville, Illinois.

10

WHILE MY LIFE BEGAN TO KNIT TOGETHER AGAIN AFTER
Rose's death, my daughter Helen's shattered into smaller and smaller
pieces. She slipped from the top of her class at school to the bottom of it,
and there she stayed. But that was the least of it. I could hear her sob herself to sleep at night; sometimes she awakened screaming. In the morning,
she denied everything: no bad dream, no nightmare, no tears, even the
screaming had not happened. Nobody could force more out of her than
that, not one of the endless parade of psychologists, psychiatrists and
other counselors who tried. Medication helped her sleep but only if it was
heavy enough to turn her into a zombie during the day. As for the accident itself, she insisted she could not remember anything. If pressed, she
would come back with some question like, "Why do you hate me?"

There are times when my mother's harsh approach to life has its at-
tractions; everything becomes simpler when you squeeze what you cannot control into a neat category, trim off the edges and start again from
there. She had sent me to school in England because I had formed friendships that she felt were beneath me; no American institution would take
me far enough away from them. Besides, an English-educated son was
just what the snobbery of the day called for. She pressed me to do the
same with Helen.

"Helen needs to achieve a physical distance between herself and her
unhappy memories," she said. "She needs to be able to concentrate on
the affairs of young people." When I protested, the stance hardened to
the adamantine. "It is a mother she needs now, and you are no substitute
whatsoever for that, my dear. Neither of us is. Not for this task. I'm too
old, and you are a blind man preoccupied with his work and his other interests. Furthermore, you must be aware that she blames you for her

mother's death. First you failed her by going blind, then you let her mother die: hardly the Hercules an eleven-year-old girl dreams of in her father. As a woman, I can assure you that if she doesn't separate herself from these preoccupations, she will never see that they make no sense. You will lose her forever, and the guilt will destroy you both."

There was too much truth in what my mother said, however painful, for me to deny it. I managed to keep Helen inside the country. No more than that. She ended up on the East Coast at Choate Rosemary Hall. But I have to admit that despite the pain it caused me, it was the right thing to do. Almost at once, she found herself in a science class taught by one of those rare and wonderful teachers who can turn an academic subject into high romance. Helen began to blossom. She threw every ounce of her troubled thought into mathematics and physics, and she graduated summa cum laude. Nothing seemed able to stop her then. She sailed through Vassar and then Columbia in under six years.

My mother says she is even prettier now than Rose was, that she has Rose's slender elegance and the wonderful softness that makes you ache to touch her. Odd that she should have my eyes. It worries me a little, although I cannot imagine their color has anything to do with going blind; and they must be quite startling with her dark hair and very fair skin. Perhaps all this—it adds up to something as vulnerable as it is formidable—is why she acquired my mother's protective coating and painfully sharp tongue. But the sense of tragedy she carries with her is her very own. So is the intensity of her preoccupation with the strange world of modern physics, where everything depends on who is looking and nothing is what it seems. No other Freyl has developed enough grasp of the subject to pass a high school examination on it, much less submit a doctoral thesis titled "Collision Theory and the Absorption of Radiation in Matter."

How proud and happy Rose would have been—how proud and happy my mother and I are—to know that Columbia is going to publish Helen's thesis in the spring and that she has come home for at least a couple of years to teach at Southern Illinois University at Carbondale.

◅◦▻

While David and Tony were driving back to Springfield from the bonded warehouse, their night's work successfully completed, Helen stood naked in a bathroom that was a stainless-steel and ebony wonder. Even the toilet basin glimmered beneath an ebony seat. The expense on show was plainly terrifying; yet the light was lousy, and the mirror was only the front door to one of those nasty cabinet things over the washbasin. She opened it: a couple of after-shaves inside, hair cream in a dirty jar with a few hairs stuck in the cream, something in an octagonal bottle "for the masculine chest" (dye most probably). She picked up the tube that lay beside it. Face scrub? She read the label carefully. Ah, exfoliant. Then what does he need the electric razor for? She took it gingerly out of its box. How could he bear to put this thing to his face? And before break-fast at that? The stench of old flesh collected in it was enough to make the hardiest of women gag.

She replaced the razor, shut the cabinet door and concentrated on her own face. A quick survey showed her mascara to be intact. A small mercy, but definitely a plus of some kind.

The light in the bedroom was no better than it was in the bath-room, but at least it was intentionally bad: soft focus, ceiling mounted, the result of some *New York Times* article entitled, say, "For the Discerning Male." The furniture was functional, heavy, oversize, awkward; straight lines, leather and some coarse-knit ma-terial, colors muted to black. In a word, ugly. Just like the oaf in the vast bed on the other side of the room. Not that he was so bad awake, but asleep? with his mouth open? She tried not to look at him as she dressed and ended up staring at the fabled George Blanda's hand-signed football instead.

Which was not all that much of an improvement.

She had barely followed last night's drivel about . . . What was it about anyhow? Oilers and Titans? Do football teams really have names as dumb as that? He'd played on some team with this Blanda person, an end or a halfback or something. What could "halfback" pos-sibly mean? A single-cheeked ass? She hadn't said that of course. She'd just said, "Then what did you do?" in the fascinated-sounding way that she and her girlfriends had practiced at school, all those years ago among so many fits of giggles. She knew she did it perfectly too be-cause he'd got so interested he almost forgot to bed her. She'd had to steer him back to the idea herself. Well, what the hell. If she concen-trated on hating *him* for a few minutes, she knew she'd get a little re-lief from the other hatreds that pressed in on her so relentlessly.

Besides, what *else* was there to get out of all that sweating and groaning? It is the true mystery of the male of any species, human, ape, rhinoceros: slap of heavy flesh and a heavy odor, high as a kite on testosterone, jerking himself off into anybody or anything that stands still long enough (unless it's willing to coo over football). Then he says something along the lines of "How was it for you?" as though he's delivered himself of a dainty cup of tea on a butler's tray.

And yet she had wanted something from him. Comfort. Solace. Maybe what her father hadn't been able to give her: she wanted the dreams to stop. She kept thinking they would. She wanted things to be as they had been once, way back before the car crash when blood had stayed inside bodies where it belonged and that gray stuff . . . She'd known it was brains. Eleven years old, never even cut up a frog in a biology class, and she'd known she was looking at her mother's brains spilling out over an alpaca sweater all the way from Peru. The only person she had left was her father, and all he cared about was her dead mother. That was when Helen knew she wanted only to be dead herself.

No, no, don't think about that part of it. If she didn't think about it, she might not dream about it. Concentrate on that chunky statuette instead. Or was it a designer toy? maybe a sex aid? She picked it up. Look at the damn thing: as gross and ugly as everything else in this room. Suppose she raised it above the sleeper's head with both hands and brought it down with all her strength . . . Well, it's a healthier dream than the other one, isn't it? Besides, who wouldn't want to beat this guy's brains out?

"Oh, Jimmy," she said to him, "can't you shut your fucking mouth even when you're asleep?" But she said it under her breath because she was almost dressed, and if she woke him now it was going to be even longer before she could escape.

11

DAVID WOKE ABRUPTLY, BREATHING HARD AND COVERED in sweat despite the cold. It was before dawn; he'd gone to bed as soon as he'd got back—it couldn't have been more than an hour or so before—from the long drive to the bonded warehouse near the Mississippi River. He hated sleep. It wasn't just that he couldn't get enough of it. He hated the dreams it brought just as Helen did. His dreams repeated themselves like hers too, and this morning he'd awakened from the one he hated most: the dream about the Monaghans.

He'd gone to the Monaghans when he was just eleven, the same age as Helen when she lost her mother. David was already a veteran of the system by that time, a hardened, smart-ass street kid who believed in nothing and yet ached for a family, a mother and a father like the kids on TV with Action Man and Little League baseball and maybe a ride in the car on Sunday. But who the fuck would give anything like that to a kid like him even if they had it to give? After all, he knew the ropes. He'd been there. He'd seen it all, most of it anyhow. When they took him away from his grandmother, he'd gone to the Franks. They got their kicks by putting out cigarette butts on his arms and back. He still had the scars on him. The Petries came next. They fed him rotten meat. He was so hungry he ate it. When he threw up, old man Petrie used to pin his arms behind his back and force his head down into his own vomit—beat him shitless when he wouldn't lick it up off the floor. After that, there was a stay at a juvenile detention center where they locked boys into a tiny dark room for days at a time. Dirty milk carton of water and a piece of bread night and morning. No bathroom privileges, not even the toilet. Then there was . . .

But what difference did crap like that make? Every single kid in the center knew the score. They all saw their lives as wild dogs might, as an endless series of smash-and-grab raids on warmth and food from which they were beaten off with fists, sticks, cigarette butts, whatever was nearest. The only way to survive was to hate so hard nobody could reach you, and the only interest David had in this new set, the Monaghans, was in finding out just how they planned to exert their power over him—and mapping out some kind of escape route before they hurt him too much. That's what it was all about. Power. No wonder Hugh's first speech to him in prison about power made such an impact.

The caseworker wore little clicky heels when she took him to the house early one summer evening; her toes came through holes in the front. She'd painted her toenails pink—David had stared fixedly at them—not recently enough, though: the polish was chipped. There was a high privet hedge around the yard of the house she took him to, and that was scary because it meant these Monaghan guys didn't have to worry about neighbors. Sometimes neighbors could be relied on to help if things got real bad. Usually not, but sometimes. There was a flight of cement stairs down to the front door. The caseworker knocked, made David say, "Hello, Mrs. Monaghan. Hello, Mr. Monaghan" and kept her hand tight on his neck while she blabbered the usual social worker junk. Then she walked out the door alone, a happy lady, little clicky heels skittering up those steps as fast as she could go. David figured that social workers got some kind of a kickback for closing a file no matter how many times it had been closed and reopened before. He sat at the Monaghans' kitchen table and stared at them. Sometimes if he looked nasty enough, they'd send him away before they really got into the swing of it. It's less fun when the kid looks like he won't cry. The table was red. He'd never forgotten that first view of it: dark red linoleum with an aluminum edge.

"He is *very* dirty," Mrs. Monaghan said to Mr. Monaghan. She had creases all over her face: old. The old ones are the meanest. "Do you want to take a bath, David?" she said, turning to him. "We have a real pretty bathtub with old-fashioned taps—Bud found it in an old house a couple of blocks away—and we got some bubble bath in specially for you."

David had heard about drowners. They hold your head under

the water. He'd never had drowners before. They wait until you're nearly dead, then let you up to breathe a little so they can do it some more. "Don't want a bath," he said.

"Well, I can't say as I blame you much," Mr. Monaghan said. "I never was one for baths either. Specially at dinnertime. Food's more like it, I'd say."

"Ain't hungry," David said, although he was *starving* and the kitchen was full of cooking smells. The thing is, you can never tell what kind of traps they're laying for you, especially when they start out sounding nice.

"You mind if we go ahead?" Mr. Monaghan said—very politely—as though David was the school principal or something. David shook his head. Mrs. Monaghan set the table for two and busied herself with meat from the oven, potatoes, lima beans, plates, glasses of milk. "We know an awful lot about you, David," Mr. Monaghan went on. "It doesn't hardly seem fair, does it? You probably want to know a little something about us."

David shrugged. He couldn't have cared less.

"I build roofs for people—that's my business—and I'm sorry to say it's not going real well at the moment. Even so, Mrs. Monaghan here, she takes good care of me. She'll do the same for you if you'll let her. We got two kids of our own. They're all grown up now, and they live far away. You sure you won't have a little meat and potatoes?" David made no response. "Why don't you just set out a plate for him with a little bit on it?" he said to his wife. "Maybe he'll be tempted to join us." Mrs. Monaghan put a small portion in front of David, knife and fork beside it, folded paper napkin with daisies around the edge; then she sat and bowed her head. Mr. Monaghan bowed his head too. "For what we are about to receive, may the Lord make us truly grateful."

Old *and* religious. David hunkered down inside himself. This was going to be *really* bad.

The Monaghans ate and talked as though David wasn't there at all: some client or something that wouldn't pay up. So he figured, what the fuck, why not eat before they get to whatever turns them on? He ate the food in front of him. Mrs. Monaghan refilled his plate. He emptied it. She laughed. "I'm glad to see you're a good eater, David. I never did trust a man who didn't like his food. Now, Bud, he's always eaten up well, and you see what a fine man he is.

Though I have to admit to you that he was a wild boy when I first met him, not promising at all—except to me, of course. I fell in love with him the moment I laid eyes on him."

David had never eaten so much in his life.

Mr. Monaghan took him outside and they tossed a ball back and forth. That's the sort of stuff you always have to do on the first day or so. God only knows why, but it must have worn David out after all that food because he didn't remember going to bed. The next thing he knew he was waking up in the morning in a room by himself with a window and clean sheets and a pair of pajamas on him. That was when he realized he'd been bathed in his sleep. There were clean clothes to wear laid out on a chair. He dressed and went downstairs, drawn by the smell of breakfast. The Monaghans were at the red table again: orange juice, eggs, bacon, toast. Afterward, they took him shopping. They bought him jeans and shoes that were so new they still had labels on them. Then came a barber, then a hamburger and an ice-cream soda, then back to the house, a couple of hours of TV, dinner at the kitchen table, tossing the ball in the backyard, bed.

Sunday was much the same except that they spent the afternoon at the Lincoln village at Petersburg. He'd never been there before—it was supposed to be like when Abe Lincoln first came to Illinois—and he really liked the look of it. Everything was clean. Everything was simple. Of course, it was all fake. The good stuff is always fake.

All this happened in summertime—no school—and things went on the same way for a week while David got tenser and tenser, waiting for the blow to fall. Another week went by. He couldn't wind himself any tighter, but you're nuts to relax. That's when they get you. He didn't give an inch. He wasn't friendly. He spoke very little and when he did, he was surly. He ate, drank, slept—and waited. Meantime, he cased the neighborhood stores, gas station, café; this was one of the times when Tony was in a nearby family, and they went out thieving together like they always did. It was a good neighborhood for it too. Lots of people left doors unlocked during the day, and clerks in the stores nearby were just plain stupid. David stole from the Monaghans as well, whatever he could find: money, videos, food, a camera, a tape recorder.

They had to know it was him. They couldn't help knowing, and yet they stayed not just nice but more than nice. They fed him, entertained him, even fussed over him. So it was going to be sex. That's what he figured. He was a cute kid. Cute kids know they're going to get something shoved up their asses sooner or later. What the hell, most state-raised kids expect it, cute or ugly. He'd been lucky that way so far. He barricaded his door at night.

One day they took him out to White Oaks Mall, and David picked up a little metal car he liked the look of. He slipped it into his pocket.

At once Mr. Monaghan was bending over him. "You'd better put that back, David," he whispered.

"What you talking about?" David said, as nasty as he could.

Mr. Monaghan knelt down beside him. He took David's shoulders in his hands. "Look, David, we don't mind if you steal from us. They told us you would, and we expect it. The neighborhood stores, well, that's harder but we can handle it. I wasn't an awful lot better myself when I was your age. But that store detective over there . . . You didn't see him, did you? over there by the fire escape? Well, he saw you lift that car same as I did, and sure as shooting he's going to take you to court if you keep it in your pocket. You know what the court's going to do: it's going to be reform school this time, and there's not going to be a single thing we can do about it. Now, I don't know about you, but Mrs. Monaghan and I, we'd really hate to lose you. I mean that. We really would. You mean an awful lot to us."

It was the strangest, gentlest of revelations. They'd seen, encompassed, forgiven. David burst into tears, and a small, critical piece of his armor slipped. The Monaghans began adoption proceedings that very same day. That night David forgot to barricade his door.

But he sure as hell paid the price for that chink they'd forced in his armor. He'd been right in the essentials of the thing all along. It just came from an unexpected quarter. Another month and school began. He truanted. He'd always truanted. Social Services never bothered any of the other families because of it. This time they got huffy, refused the adoption on the grounds that the Monaghans could not control him and took him away to a group home. He kicked and screamed. They had to tie him to the bed and starve him to shut him up. If he'd hated the system before, there was no limit to what he felt now.

Even so, the Monaghans stood by him. They made sure they always knew where he was. They sent him Christmas presents, the first he'd ever had in his life. He ran away to them a couple of times from other homes. They visited him in juvenile detention centers when he got sent there and in prison after that, both Marion and South Hams; as soon as they realized he'd become a heavy smoker, they sent him cigarettes as well as the meager limit the prison allowed of chocolate, fruit, coffee, creamer, toiletries. They wrote him regularly. They were the first people he wanted to see when he got out, even before Tony.

That's when the dream began—the very night he'd seen them for the first time as a free man in eighteen years. It was always the same after that. He was back in the garage out near the White Oaks Mall. The mangled bodies of the Fowlers—foster father and foster brother—lay in the oil pit where he'd left them. The police had him on his knees facing away from the carnage, hands cuffed behind his back and somehow—the way things happen only in dreams—he managed to twist around just as they turned over the bodies to begin an examination.

And the faces of the people he'd murdered were the faces not of the Fowlers but of the Monaghans. They lay entwined in an eerie, comfortable embrace amid the blood and the black engine oil.

◄o►

At eleven o'clock, some seven hours after he awoke from his dream of the Monaghans, David pulled up in front of Stephanie's motel for the trip out to Petersburg and Oakland Cemetery. The cold had intensified further as it often does after a snowfall. Even so, she was waiting for him outside the reception area. Despite his own upset—the dream had thrown him badly—one glance at her was enough for him to see that she was feverish and chilled at the same time, a cold, the flu, something. Her face was flushed and pinched.

"Go back to bed," he said, rolling down the window and calling out to her.

"I've rented a car. It'll be here in half an hour. I don't want you to catch this."

"Hugh's not going anywhere."

"I know."

"You're going to make yourself really sick."

"I know it's ridiculous, David, but I just have to go."

"Get in."

She was retreating. "No, no, no. You'll catch cold too. I'll call you as soon as I'm better."

"Get in," he said again.

The messy town fringe that litters Route 97 going out of Springfield is several miles long. New and shiny gas stations stand cheek by jowl with battered and deserted ones; motels of twinkling neon and busy industrial plants are only an empty lot away from dilapidated motels and deserted industrial plants that look like bomb sites. But the harsh edges of yesterday were softened under last night's snowfall and the morning's heavy cloud cover. Plows had been out since dawn; even so, the Chevy's progress was slow over the icy, gritted surface.

When the water tower of Petersburg finally appeared, gourdlike atop its stalk, it looked hazy and artificial to David as though it were some giant Mexican music maker, a mariachi or whatever out of Norton Wellwood's La Casita—an object that made no more sense against the midwestern sky than Stephanie's insistence on visiting a graveyard with a cold coming on, and yet both were somehow reassuring. There was no wind. No branches moved in the trees along the road. Beside him, Stephanie seemed smaller, buried deep in her massive winter coat. He turned into the rough road that leads to Oakland Cemetery. The new snow was six, maybe eight inches deep, and he'd been figuring that they would have to slog all the way from the highway to Hugh's grave. He wasn't at all sure she could manage a hike like that. Maybe she had Kodiac blood in her veins, but this was no morning for the unhealthy—Kodiac or otherwise—to visit a grave.

But another Springfield worthy had died that week; the cemetery road had been cleared again in preparation for the funeral. David drove over a small rise. The pneumatic drills started up as though on cue. The noise increased steadily past the famous graves: Ann Rutledge, Emma Jerusha, Edgar Lee Masters and all. It reached a peak at the site of a partially erected tent, where a crew of men were hard at work. The cleared road ended here. David stopped the car; he and Stephanie got out and fought their way toward the Freyls' private hillock.

David disliked graveyards at the best of times, and it was way too cold to be wading through one this morning—as well as too noisy. The ground beneath the snow was as frozen as it had been on the day of Hugh's funeral, and it took a good fifteen minutes to reach the plot. Stephanie was out of breath; she leaned heavily on David's arm. What could she think she would find here? Why waste effort on bones and ashes? What's the point of a graveyard anyhow? To supply roots for a rootless existence? assuage the guilt of the living? proclaim their triumph over the dead?

David did not doubt her sincerity; he could feel her tremble as they stared at the ground, and he knew it was not only fever. And yet there was nothing to be seen here except Rose's pretty marker—no sign of Hugh at all. The gravestone would not go up until the ground thawed, and the depth of new snow was more than enough to hide all evidence of his recent arrival; no single undulation in the snow betrayed the position of the diminutive hole or the tent that had housed an entire funeral party. It was as though nothing had changed at all in the years since Rose died; only the tracks of a squirrel were fresh, a sidelong scramble from nowhere to nowhere.

Stephanie shivered. "I loved him," she said, staring down at the blanket of white.

"Yes."

"Oh, David, wasn't he *wonderful* to look at? I never could understand why he thought he was ugly. Did you? I mean, how could anybody with those green eyes of his be ugly? with crinkles all around them when he smiled? and dimples too? Maybe it was because the smile was crooked. Maybe he thought . . . I mean, sometimes when people look in the mirror and see a crooked smile, they think it's ugly even though everybody else knows it's charming, and then maybe he figured it could only have got worse as he got older or maybe he exaggerated the memory of it because he couldn't see it. The funny thing is, I could never figure out myself just why he was so appealing. It wasn't just the look of him either. I used to think and think and dissect and dissect . . . and still I never figured it out. I fell in love with him the moment he walked into my office at Memorial, and the most amazing part of it—even that very first day—was the quality . . . I could never quite bring myself to believe it existed, not in all the time I knew him, but whatever had been absolutely impossible before seemed possible as soon as he appeared. He was just plain so *alive*. And he believed in things. He thought he could change things, make them better. He really *believed*." David nodded. "How could somebody like that just cease to be?"

"He never understood why you left."

She glanced at David, frowned in puzzlement, then looked down at the squirrel tracks in the snow across Hugh's grave. "That's a strange thing to say."

"His feelings ran pretty deep."

She shook her head. "I thought they did too for quite a while, but I just . . . I just imagined it. I saw what I wanted to see even though it wasn't there."

The pneumatic drill stopped. There was a moment's dead silence, broken by the mournful, descending cry of a screech owl, unusual during the day but then this day was dark even for winter. David scanned the trees.

"Mrs. Freyl called you in for a talk," he said.

Stephanie nodded, pulled out a handkerchief, coughed into it.

"I see," said David.

And so he did. He'd been called in for his very first interview with Becky almost two years ago now, almost two years before Hugh's funeral party when she'd exiled him from the house. Only a few days away from a life sentence and solitary confinement at South Hams, and she'd offered him $50,000 to leave town, get away from her son and the family. At once. As soon as he could pack a bag. Without waiting for his response, she'd opened her checkbook and begun to write.

"That's not much to start cold in a strange place," David had said. "Not for someone with a prison record."

"You will destroy my son if you stay here. Is that what you want?"

" 'Destroy' him, huh?"

"That's what I said."

"Not too likely."

"I refuse to haggle."

"Whatever you say." He'd turned to leave the room.

"$100,000," she said. David had turned back but merely spread his hands. "That's my final offer. Well? Speak up, young man. Surely that's enough to satisfy your greed."

"It's tempting."

"You'll never hear an offer like it again." She wrote out the check, signed it with a flourish and handed it to him.

He'd scanned it—then returned it to her. "Mrs. Freyl, I hate being pushed around. If I take this to leave Springfield, I'll *have* to stay, and I'm not at all sure—"

"Now, you wait a minute—"

"—that I *want* to stay here. I don't like the town much. I never have. Keep your money for now. If I change my mind, I'll get back to you."

That was why, standing with Stephanie beside Hugh's grave, David had a good idea what she was going to tell him about her own interview with Becky before she said a word more. After all, Stephanie offered youth, enthusiasm, warmth, humor. How could the Freyls compete with riches like that? But Hugh was Becky's beloved only son, and she was not a woman to give up her possessions without a fight.

"She was doing her best to spare me," Stephanie began, "and she was very . . ." Stephanie shook her head as she had before. Grief is bad enough on its own. Add weakness and fever to it, and the words come tumbling out. "She said he was too embarrassed to speak to me himself. She said he was embarrassed by the pressures I put on him and that he couldn't respond . . . couldn't possibly return . . . She said I didn't have the background in law for my work to reach the standard he required, but he couldn't bring himself to fire me because I was . . . oh, God, this is so . . . because I was too dependent emotionally. It was true too. I knew it. Sometimes you can love somebody too much. I hadn't realized that before. It gets in the way of everything. I'd always thought . . . She said if things went on as they were, I'd destroy his friendships, his work, his standing in the community—his whole life—and make an awful fool of myself in the . . ." This time Stephanie trailed off into silence.

" 'Destroy' him? She used that word?"

"Even the remains of feeling he had for me: I'd destroy that too."

"She's afraid of you."

"Oh, come on, David. She's not afraid of anybody."

"You were the one I wasn't certain about. I couldn't tell enough from his stories."

"What stories?"

"Things you told him."

"He talked to you about me? Did he really?" But her pleasure was only fleeting, and she rushed on before he had a chance to answer. "Don't be kind to me, David. I can't bear it. I knew she didn't like me much. How could she? The Freyls were . . . They were the *Freyls*. My father was a pharmacist in a little town in Oregon. I never even graduated from college. Even so, it hadn't crossed my mind that I was embarrassing him. And now he's—"

She broke off, coughed again, shook her head again. David watched her a minute. Mrs. Monaghan had told him that a gypsy all the way from Hungary had stopped her in the street once and offered to tell her fortune for $25. The fortune hadn't come to much—it could have applied to anybody and the accent was so strong most of the words were garbled anyhow—but a bargain is a bargain. Mrs. Monaghan handed over the $25. The gypsy stared at her as though she was nuts. "You can forget all that junk," said the gypsy, dropping all trace of accent, "but I'll tell you this for free. You're too soft and too straight." David figured the same thing applied to Stephanie.

"The name of your father's drugstore was Katz," he said. "One of a northwest chain. He worked there for fifty-three years, and the townspeople paid off his mortgage for him when he retired. You'll think what you want to think, but Hugh could hardly *stop* talking about you. His mother is a great believer in the principle of divide and conquer."

"I don't know what that means."

"It's very effective."

"I only wish . . ."

"Wish what?"

" . . . that I could believe I hadn't imagined he felt about me as strongly as I felt about . . . Loving somebody too much makes you stupid, insensitive. I saw in him only what I felt myself, not what was there. It's called projection. I read all about it in a library book."

"You could have asked him."

She shook her head once more. "I knew I'd have to pay for being so happy. I knew it couldn't last: that's how I knew Mrs. Freyl was right. The idea that I was embarrassing him was . . . I couldn't bear it. It makes me cringe even now. All I had left was . . . I don't know, maybe a few shreds of pride. Not worth spitting at, but . . ."

Stephanie's distress was so great that she forgot what Hugh had told her about David—that he never smiled—and so she assumed that a smile was what gentled his features. "You and the guide dog threatened to upset the old woman's domestic arrangements," he said.

Stephanie laughed despite herself. "Athena and me?"

David nodded. "She does not take kindly to rebellion in the ranks."

◄o►

Some weeks after Stephanie expressed her doubts about David actually confessing to the crimes that put him away for life, she brought up the point again. I had not forgotten, but I was not at all sure how to inquire into the matter.

By this time, my lessons with him were in the form of a seminar for two. A high school diploma and an undergraduate degree (with a major in history) were behind him. There are a number of universities that allow for extension degree courses for prison inmates—it was the University of Chicago in his case—and he had graduated with honors, a pleasing result for me since it confirmed my own impressions of his ability. But a restlessness with academic constraints set in not long after he started work on a Ph.D., and while a doctorate was easily within his grasp, work on it developed into little more than a pretext for my continuing appearance at South Hams State Prison. We chose books and then discussed them. I often used details from my own life to clarify material that he did not have the experience to understand, and yet he never revealed more than the bare minimum about his life—past or present. This reticence made me reluctant to put questions to him.

"What you tell him about how you live has just got to seem like it comes out of some shining fairy tale," Stephanie said. "Maybe he figures a guy like you couldn't possibly be interested in a life like his, much less whether he'd signed the confession that got him where he is. Or maybe he just doesn't know how to talk about it. Or maybe he thinks you wouldn't believe him if he did."

"I might not."

"There. You see?"

"You really think I should ask?"

"What's there to lose?"

So on my next visit, I did.

"The past is a waste of time," David said.

"Why do you always say that when you do not want to answer a question? It could mean almost anything."

"Didn't you tell me once that if a lie gets told often enough, it turns into truth?"

"Are you telling me you did not confess?"

"No."

"Then you did."

"I can't see what difference it makes anymore. Besides, you're not my lawyer, are you?"

"That makes a difference?"

"Just forget it."

When I reported this back to Stephanie, she said, "I knew it! He never signed that confession. He never confessed at all."

"I do not think you can jump to that conclusion," I said. I often found David puzzling, and the conversation did seem odd. On the other hand, even though I tended to see him as something of my own creation—a man of intellect that I had helped mold out of an ignorant and violent social outcast—much as I felt I owed him personally, I knew that few convicts will admit guilt or fair process, especially to outsiders like me. And as I saw it, he had made his wishes plain. "He as much as told me to mind my own business," I added to Stephanie.

"I don't buy it," she said. "I read about this guy—he got a Pulitzer Prize for something—and he called Illinois the 'false confession capital of America.' "

I shook my head. "Wasn't he talking about Chicago? Confessing to two murders could hardly have slipped David's mind."

"Maybe if somebody else had asked him the question, maybe then he'd have fudged, but . . . It just doesn't work, Hugh. Not when it's you who's doing the asking. He always gives you some kind of answer."

"That is just what he did. He told me to 'forget it.' "

But she was not going to let me off that easily. "I don't see how come he feels he needs to evade you on this kind of thing. I mean, I can imagine why he doesn't want to tell you about his childhood and whatnot. You'd probably be horrified. But signing a confession? You're a lawyer. Stuff like that is your business. I bet he really thinks you couldn't care less whether he confessed or not. Maybe he wishes you were his lawyer. And maybe . . . Maybe your idea about its slipping his mind isn't all that wild. He isn't exactly what you'd call stable, is he? Or at least he wasn't in those days. Nobody with a couple of grisly murders behind him is your normal Joe in the street. People plead insanity all the time. Maybe it was true in his case."

"He did not enter such a plea."

"So maybe his lawyer was lousy."

I shook my head. "Public defenders are better at their jobs than most people think, and David's would have to have been almost wilfully bad to miss an opportunity like that if it presented itself."

"That doesn't prove anything about anything, except that David's case could have been an example of what most people figure is the rule. Besides, maybe he was in a fugue state or something. Isn't that what they call it? You do things and you don't remember anything about it? Even normal people black out whole periods in their lives."

I laughed. "You are putting more imagination into this than it merits."

"Maybe you aren't putting in enough," she said tartly. "This is your guy, and he doesn't have anybody to protect him but you. Can't we get a look at what they have? One way or another? At least some of it?"

There was such conviction in her voice that I could not resist. Besides, her dig at my imagination stung a little. I hated to think she might find me dull. So I paid a visit to the Old Records Division of the Springfield Police Department.

If David had been tried as a juvenile, we could not have seen his record. But he had been tried as an adult; the police paperwork on him was no more sacrosanct than any other criminal's. His arrest and sentencing took place way back in the stone age before computerization. In those days the police kept everything in cardboard boxes piled high on metal rack shelving; the process of putting them onto microfiche is slow, and nobody had yet got around to dealing with any records as old as David's. A discussion with a somewhat too motherly clerk, a short wait on a hard bench, and the clerk came back with a sheaf of papers. She let me heft it.

"Where's the binder?" I asked.

"Probably got lost years ago."

Records of homicides are usually kept in three-ring binders called mur-

der books that are sectioned off into autopsy protocol, witnesses' interviews, photographs and the like. She began feeding this unruly cache of
unbound pages into a copier that clanked and groaned while she explained
in far more detail than I wanted that the department's state-of-the-art
equipment had broken down only hours before and that this ancient machine was the only one the suppliers had on hand to fill the gap. She was
the kind who talks about everything to everybody. When we had exhausted
the subject of photocopiers, she turned her curiosity on me.

"What kind of dog is that?" she said. "I never seen one like that before."

"A cross between a Labrador and a poodle: a labradoodle."

She laughed. "Nah! You're having me on."

"As eager to please as Labradors and as allergy-free as poodles. They
were bred in Australia first."

"Yeah?"

"Most dogs make my mother sneeze."

"How old is he?"

"She," I said.

"Ah, isn't he cute? Kind a funny-looking—I got to say that—but real
cute, just like one of those great big stuffed dogs for kids. He must be
your very best friend in the whole world. I had a dog once. He died after
I'd had him only a year or so. Can't remember what it was. Distemper, I
think. That's a dog's disease, isn't it? What's his name? huh? Dogs like
that got names same as other dogs, don't they?"

"Athena."

"How come you call him that?" She made cooing sounds at Athena,
who did not respond. "He deaf or something?"

"She's on duty."

The clerk cooed again. Again Athena did not respond. "You know
what I think? I think all them dogs should be friendly. I mean, you got to
live with them, don't you? They're supposed to be your very best friend.
You shouldn't let them give you a bad-tempered dog. It's not right."

Back at my office, I handed the material over to Stephanie for sorting and an initial evaluation. "Why haven't they given you the whole
file?" she said when she had finished going over it. "Where's the famous
confession?"

"Is it not there?"

"It's plainly supposed to be here. The covering page says"—she shuffled the papers—" 'Disposition of Case: Subject (David Marion, juvenile) confessed that he did on Tuesday September 13 unlawfully kill Charles Gerald Fowler, mechanic, and Jackson Peter Fowler, juvenile. Subject signed a confession to that effect on Monday September 19 as appended to this document. Subject sentenced to life imprisonment without possibility of parole at Springfield Criminal . . .' and so forth. But there's no sign of a confession."

I sighed. "I am afraid records do get lost over the years, and the loss of the binder would only have made matters worse."

"How come you're not more interested in this?"

"It is just the way things are, Stephanie. We are probably lucky to have found as much as we did. Corrupted and missing files are major problems in dealing with old cases."

She shuffled the papers again. "Apparently they found bloody footprints and bloody garage tools—the first guy who interviewed David says so—but he only says they 'found' them. There aren't any pictures or test results or anything. Know what I think? I bet they never took any. There's supposed to be some stuff in an 'evidence locker,' David's lug wrench and the clothes he was wearing and a couple other things. So there's got to be something solid somewhere."

"I am afraid its contents would have been routinely destroyed after his conviction."

"You're kidding me."

I shook my head. "The case was final."

"Well, it doesn't leave us with much except for this bloody fingerprint that—"

"A fingerprint?"

"She shouldn't have given you the negative, should she?" Investigators use photographs to preserve manifest prints—ones clearly revealed to the eye—sometimes enhancing them with various reagents to sharpen contrast and improve visibility.

"You don't mean it," I said.

"Sure looks like a negative to me."

"Why is it such a pleasure when a police department makes a stupid blunder?" I said happily.

"Where are fingerprints supposed to be?" Stephanie asked.

"The evidence locker. It is an almost unheard-of breach of protocol for fingerprints to reach the murder book at all."

I spent the next several hours sifting through the file myself.

Modern computers have changed everything for people like me. Braille translators have been on the market since before I went blind; because of them, we could read anything entered on disk. The very first speech synthesizers were available then too, which meant that machines could read out loud to us. The technology was as expensive as it was cumbersome in those days, but prices have fallen as steadily and innovation has leaped ahead as quickly here as elsewhere in the field. We have astonishing freedom of access now. Hundreds of Internet sites are devoted to such abstruse aids for the blind as orienters that speak out the positioning of the mouse, sophisticated embossers that can print Braille on both sides of a page and display mechanisms that allow fingers to read a computer screen.

Which is to say that most of the information available to the rest of you is now directly accessible to people like me; there is even a whole world for us alone that you do not know exists. There are dozens of sites devoted to fascinating arguments over such matters as the white cane vs. guide dog debate. There's a lot of bitter humor too: "What is it with sighted people anyway? Why are they so obsessed with guide dogs' names and ages? This is a mystery to the blind. And why do the sighted tell so many tales of dead dogs they have owned? dead pets of any variety?" It may horrify the sighted to know there are even porn sites devoted to the blind and careful reviews of prostitutes who cater especially to us—as well as reviews of those who cater to the rest of you.

As for David's record, all I had to do was feed the material into my scanner. My virtual touch system means that I could even examine the fingerprint for myself, and I had to agree with Stephanie; the negative seemed in very poor condition. There were a number of oddities in the file itself that caught my attention, but David's interrogation at the hands of Sergeant Wellwood interested me most at the outset, partly because of the character of the sergeant himself and partly because his interview was the first interview after David's arrest—its date was given as September 13—and it was also the only interview to be found in the file.

Yet the record stated clearly that David had been questioned over the course of almost a full week: "Description of Interrogation: Subject (David Marion, juvenile) was interrogated for 35 hours over 7 days from Tuesday September 13 to Monday September 19."

12

THE APPROACH TO THE FREYL HOUSE WAS WINDING AND
forested. The road outside the property disappeared quickly from
David's rearview mirror. Snow had begun falling again as he left the
coughing and miserable Stephanie at her motel twenty minutes before; by now visibility was low. Only the Freyls could keep a road
like this clear under such circumstances. A bridge crossed a small
stream, and the house appeared, but it was no more welcoming this
time than it had been after Hugh's funeral a week ago. An ancient
oak hung as heavily over the pillared front porch as a Mafia enforcer; the colors were as dark and cold as the wind that flapped
David's coattails about his legs when he got out of the car.

He skirted an industrial carpet cleaner's truck that blocked the
entrance, climbed the wide steps to the veranda porch and rang the
doorbell. It was Lillian who answered. "Morning, David," she said,
pulling him into her arms. She was a big woman, not fat but solid,
strong, mother of five daughters and three sons, grandmother to a
dozen already with two more on the way. Her movements had the
certainty and authority of the matriarch she was. "You're a sight for
sore eyes," she said to him.

"That bad, huh?"

"You betcha." She brushed snow off his shoulders, hugged him
again, patted his back, let him go.

"Carpet cleaner?" he said, cocking his head toward the truck.

"She done put Athena down. Didn't want no more dog hairs in
the carpet. Says she can smell them. Says she always could."

"When?"

"This morning."

"I thought those crossbreeds were specially good for that kind of thing."

"I couldn't never smell nothing. Never found no dog hairs neither."

David took off his coat, shook the rest of the snow off it, threw it over the banister of the fine old staircase. "What does she want me for?"

"David, she don't tell me nothing. Just said you was coming this morning. She's waiting for you in Mr. Hugh's study."

"Only last week I wasn't allowed within a mile of this place."

"Week can be a long time sometimes." Lillian led David across the vast hallway and knocked on the study door. "He's here, ma'am."

The response was slow in coming and muffled when it arrived. Lillian opened the door to reveal Becky sitting behind Hugh's desk precisely as she had sat at her interview with David during the wake.

"You may go, Lillian," she said.

"Yes, ma'am."

"Shut the door behind you."

"Yes, ma'am."

Becky looked David up and down. "*Shaved* this time, I see," was her only comment. No greeting.

David inclined his head. "Mrs. Freyl."

"You'd better sit down."

A straight-backed chair faced the desk, and she indicated that he should take it. He moved it to one side and sat on the leather sofa as he had before.

"Your manners have not improved," Becky said.

"What's this about?"

"I spoke to Samuel Clark yesterday. I cannot imagine how so eminent a jurist can support the abolition of the death penalty, but no one can doubt his word. Certainly not I. He says you were in Washington, D.C., with him the night my son was killed."

"Yes."

"Is that all you have to say?"

"Yes."

The police had picked David up on Friday; his one telephone call had been to Samuel Clark only to find that Samuel couldn't be reached until after the weekend. David hadn't cared. All he had to do was wait; Hugh's funeral wasn't until Tuesday morning, and he'd had little doubt that Samuel would have him out in time for it. There was pleasure to be had in anticipating the Springfield Police Department's discomfiture; an outraged call from a U.S. Supreme Court judge couldn't help stirring up enough trouble to overwhelm a directive even from Becky Freyl—and then some.

Samuel represented the liberal edge of a conservative Court. He and Hugh had been friends for most of their lives, childhood playmates at Lake Michigan where both had had grandparents, fellow students at Yale Law School, best man at each other's weddings, godfather to each other's children. Samuel had practiced criminal law, served as state's attorney general and as a judge in the federal district court before he was appointed to the U.S. Supreme Court, but the work responsible for the great honor—in his mind as well as in most other people's—was a book that became known as *Clark on Prisons,* a meticulously researched, wide-ranging study of a penal system that was creating a more ruthless criminal class by generating hatred and rebellion in the strongest few while destroying hope and self-respect in all the rest. It had begun as a jurist's private diary of recidivism rather than a book. Only when he'd decided he just might have something did he discuss it with Hugh, and Hugh thought of David at once. There are so few inmates who have the insight or the capacity to put what really happens on paper; and Samuel needed the testimony of an insider, somebody articulate enough to reveal the human face as well as the human cost behind the statistics. The moment he saw David's photograph, the project took shape in his mind.

"Oh, my God," Samuel said, staring down at the mug shot, "look at the way he smolders."

David was luckier than most when it came to mail from the outside; there's nothing so prized in prison as letters. Even so, he received very few. He heard from Hugh only when there was a formal, tutorial reason to correspond, from Tony perhaps every couple of years if he was lucky; short, homey notes from the Monaghans arrived once a month as regular as clockwork. Samuel was witty, literate, discursive; he wrote frequently, and he was clearly straining to understand the life of extraordinary savagery and fear that the most ordinary of prisoners led in American prisons.

This is to say that the correspondence itself was a highly cherished diversion. But it became far more. Everything changed when Samuel injected his daughter Vivian into the equation. She was studying for a degree in anthropology at Washington University in St. Louis, which made her the ideal interviewer of a man who lived in the uncharted society of South Hams State Prison only 125 miles away; she came with a video recorder to interview David on her father's behalf. The day was graven into David's mind. They sat on opposite sides of a glass barrier, the microphone between them cutting off syllables and making voices tinny. He'd never seen anyone like her except in the movies, pretty, animated, bright, funny, dressed and groomed as only old money can do it, lush in the way only young women can be, that physical opulence, somehow both gentle and luxurious, that is nothing short of agony for a man who can only look. In that single interview, she turned David's stoical resignation to a life behind bars into an abrupt, driving passion to be free.

As for Samuel himself, his exchange with David made him famous; *Clark on Prisons* became an instant classic, and few doubted that it secured him a seat on the Court.

He'd told Becky that David was in Washington for a two-day visit to make an assessment of the security system in his home on the very night Hugh died. Samuel received more death threats than his share, and as he said to her, he had no intention of dying just because the right side of the law isn't as efficient at creating protection systems as the likes of David are at penetrating them. Samuel had quite enjoyed his conversation with Becky; he was at his most severe and judicial, a particularly pleasing role. He gave her the impression that something secret and important had gone on as well, something that as a private citizen she could not be privy to. She hadn't liked that. He'd also made it clear to her—although his approach was very circumspect—that he didn't approve of private citizens exerting pressure on local police departments to hold an uncharged man in custody beyond the legal time limit. Nor did he approve of Supreme Court justices having to exert pressure to get such a one released in time for the funeral of his friend and mentor.

That she hadn't liked at all.

"Why on *earth*," she said to David, "didn't you tell the police where you were at once?"

"No."

"Do you even know where to begin?"

"I have begun."

"How?"

"What kind of money are we talking?"

"Name your figure. Cash on delivery. Nothing if you fail."

David could not help his amusement at the haggling that had appeared so fast on the heels of her refusal to haggle just as it had the first time almost two years ago. "Suppose you pull out that check you wrote me for $100,000 a couple of years ago," he said. "We'll decide on the final settlement when the job is done."

"Nobody's worth $100,000." Her tone was at its iciest.

"Too bad."

"Certainly not *you*."

"Come now, Mrs. Freyl, it's the price you yourself put on me—and for the much less onerous duty of just leaving town."

She pursed her lips. "You said you had begun already."

"I spent an evening with someone who was able to give me some idea what the police know. I examined the library at Herndon and Freyl. I've drawn up some charts, tied some ideas together, done a little research. None of Hugh's circle will talk to me—except Stephanie Willis."

"*She* could not possibly be of any use to you—or to anyone else, I might add. As for Hugh's friends and colleagues, they will talk to *me*—and hence to you as my representative. You could hardly have examined Hugh's offices in full daylight. I presume you broke in at night." David made no response. "Just as I thought. Did you find anything?"

"The newspapers left out a lot."

"What?"

"You don't want to know."

"But you value it?"

"Yes."

"Well, it's a start—as you say. What guarantees do I have that you will do as you're told *this* time?"

"None."

She sighed furiously but took out a checkbook and began to write. "My name should open any doors you need to open. As far as

I am concerned, you may talk to whomever you like, however you like, utilizing whatever tactics you like. I will back you to the hilt as long as I can see logic in your procedure. My only concern is that you achieve a credible result." She tore off the check and held it out.

"Tell me something," he said, taking the check and scanning it. "What do you consider a 'credible result'? "

"As I say, I want this person tracked down."

"That's it?"

"What else could I want?"

"You tell me."

"I want him *found.*"

David tossed the check onto the desk. "I'm not a detective." He turned to leave again.

"Wait," she said, half stumbling in her anxiety to get out of her chair. "Of course that's not all."

"It isn't, huh?"

"Mr. Marion, I want the same thing you want."

"No, you don't."

"How could *you* know what *I* want?" The angry intensity in her voice surprised him into turning to face her. She couldn't meet his gaze at first. She looked out the window beyond him, then down at her desk, picked up the pencil she'd been tapping, stared at it, put it down. "I do not approve of Illinois's moratorium on the death penalty." He waited. "You are the only person I know who is—how can I put this?—not inclined to toady to the minutiae of the law."

He shook his head with the unexpected admiration he'd felt for her the week before when she'd thrown him out of her house. Here she was, frail to begin with and worn down with grief, yet she was tackling him on what she assumed was his home ground—not hers at all—and her timing was so precise she'd caught him off balance this time too.

"Let's make sure we understand each other," he said. "Are you really suggesting a hit?"

Her cheeks were a little flushed with the audacity of it. "I want you to deal with this person as justice in this state would deal with him if it hadn't been watered down by corrupt fools."

"You're sure of that?" he said softly.

"I would not have allowed you in my house for any other reason."

He studied her a moment, then nodded. "Hand over the check."

"Are you up to what I ask?"

"You'll just have to wait and see, won't you?"

◄◦►

By the time David left Becky snow was falling very heavily. Illinois usually has a single snowstorm each winter; a second right after the first is just plain bad luck, and this one seemed determined to show it was king of the field. The wind howled. Snow whipped the face hard enough to sting. As Lillian let David out of the house, he lowered his head against the onslaught. He didn't see—couldn't possibly have seen—the man heading toward the stairs to the Freyl house until they collided.

The man slipped, reached out to catch hold of David, missed. David caught him as he slipped again. A massive bunch of red freesias fell to the ground, an arterial spurt across the fresh white snow.

"I'm *so* sorry," the man said as David helped him to his feet.

David recognized the voice at once: Senator John Calder, no less than the great man of Springfield, the man everybody said was going to be the next governor of Illinois. He'd braved this terrible weather to express his sympathy in person to his old friend, the grieving dowager. There's an unexpectedly rocky time that comes when the formalities of death in the family are over, especially when the dead is a child. He brushed snow off his coat while David held him steady on his feet.

"I'm really very grateful to—" the senator began. But he stopped in alarm as soon as he saw who his rescuer was. He snatched himself away from the support. The last time he'd seen David was after Hugh's funeral, when Becky had sworn to have this dangerous criminal arrested if he came within a mile of her house again. She'd said nothing to indicate she'd changed her mind. Besides, nobody likes coming face-to-face with dangerous criminals.

"Good morning, Senator," David said.

"Why are *you*, um . . . ?" the senator began, but could get no further. Most unexpected. He was *never* lost for words, and yet not a single one of those professional niceties he mouthed every day without a second thought—to staff, public, press, anybody and every-body—was willing to come to his aid.

"She likes white ones better," David said, retrieving the flowers for him. Freesias were Becky's favorite.

"Does she?" The senator's voice had an absent sound to it, but worry skittered across the fear that was already on his face. He bent over to brush snow off his coat. "Clumsy of me . . . um . . . to fall like that." He took the flowers from David and struggled as before for some standard phrase that would get him out of this situation without further delay. "I loathe winter," he said at last.

David nodded—assent, agreement, courtesy, any or none of these—stepped aside, and the senator headed toward the house.

◄◊►

Nearly two decades and several shifts of location are quite enough to ac-count for the loss of all kinds of records, especially records as old as David's. Even so, Stephanie was adamant. If there was a confession, where was it? If there were further interviews with him, where were they?

"I bet the rest of his murder book is there somewhere," she said. "It's probably got mixed up with a bunch of other people's records at the bot-tom of the box. Don't you think it's worth trying once more? I mean, just ask the clerk to take a better look or something?"

So I went off again to the Springfield Police Department's Old Records Division. The clerk was apologetic and even more motherly than before, but after an hour's search she came back to me puzzled. "I can't find a trace of any of it now. See, I figured maybe—"

"The file is gone?"

"—some of the papers could a just slipped out of the folder and into the box over the years, but now . . . Yeah. Like you say. The whole thing's gone."

"Surely nobody has pulled it?"

"Nah. And I put it back right where I found it. I have a very orderly mind—makes my husband mad as hell—I always put everything back just exactly right. It's got to be here somewhere. Somebody must a moved it by accident or something. Don't you worry. I'll ask around. Leave it with me, okay?"

When there was no word in week or so, I went back—but the file was no longer available. "See, they been doing some kind of study of old cases," the clerk said. "Statistics or something. They been transferring boxes and boxes of them old files. I didn't figure they'd got to this stretch yet. Nothing else is missing—not that I can see anyway. I guess they must a found a cross-reference or something and forgotten to tell me about it." She cooed at Athena.

"What's his name?" she asked as she had asked before: precisely the same question in precisely the same tone. "How old is he?" she went on before I had a chance to say a word. "I had a dog that died. Don't know what it is about animals. They keep on dying just when you get real attached to them. You don't really want to be stuck with an unfriendly dog like that, do you? You don't have to have him, you know. Want me to write somebody for you?"

"It's the file I need. Who is doing this study? Any idea?"

"Some university or other."

I wrote the Springfield Police Department asking them to release David's murder book under the provisions of the Illinois Freedom of Information Act. When there was no response within the statutory seven working days, I wrote again asking if the lapse in time constituted a denial of my request. The reply came back that the file was "officially missing" but that a copy might be found in the district attorney's office or the public defender's.

But it turned out to be officially missing in both those places as well.

13

BY THE TIME DAVID REACHED THE STREET HE LIVED ON, snow had been falling heavily for at least two hours. Even the east side looked picture-pretty wrapped up in it, roofs piled high, front yards and sidewalks blanketed; even here, the wind was strong and snowflakes knew how to swirl and eddy with all the enchantment of a newly shaken glass paperweight. Two long ruts where the street should have been were the only evidence of traffic until David's ancient Chevy appeared. There was no sound, though—the storm's muffle was absolute—not even as the car crawled to a stop. David got out and made his way toward his apartment building.

Inside, up the five flights, and a blast of freezing air greeted him as he opened his door. These were not the rooms of yesterday. The books in the bookcase that once made so much difference—that once marked this apartment out from the neighborhood—were nowhere to be seen. The place was deep in what almost looked like snow from outside, that swirled and eddied just like that. But this stuff wasn't snow. It was paper, little squares of printed paper. Pages from David's beloved books. Torn out and shredded. *Thousands* of pages. The windows were open wide. It was icy cold. The only familiar items were the big round table in the center, the sealed packing crates ready for the move to come and Tony, who squatted amid the eerie disorder. He stood up as David entered and shook his head.

"Like what you done to the place," Tony said.

David gazed around him. If you can't show anger, show nothing. Nothing at all. Certainly not fear. "Leave me alone," he said.

Tony picked up a couple of scraps of book pages and glanced from one to the other. "This stuff was dumb enough before. Now what do you expect me to make of it?" He glanced from scrap to scrap again, then laughed. "I don't know. Now I come to think of it, I guess I can read it somewhat better like this. Why don't you give them ugly pictures of yours the same treatment?"

Education reroutes the pathways in the frontal lobes of the brain, and David had become a highly educated man. But nothing changes the ancient limbic part that nestles beneath those frontal lobes, and Tony knew precisely why David had destroyed his own books. He didn't know that a nightmare had triggered it, of course—the Monaghans beaten to death in the very garage pit where the Fowlers lay all those years ago—but Hugh's murder had ripped apart the fabric of David's life, and this chaos was a serious show of blood. Tony knew it. Nobody knew David the way Tony did. Nobody. They'd met when they were kids of about seven years old in a joyous raid on a garbage can, God knows what-all flying in every direction. Right at the bottom they'd found a little metal car, a prize of prizes, loot of loots. Trouble was, as soon as the excitement died away some, they both knew the car was a piece of shit. Neither really wanted to keep it, and yet almost at once they were fighting over it.

Tony was king of the kids. Even then he was the biggest, the toughest, the fastest, the practical joker who fought them all, beat them all and crowed in delight over his prize. He carried a special rock in his pocket. He knew how to use it too. He struck the first blow this time (preempting the action was his trademark): a good hit, enough blood to send any kid in his right mind screaming. Besides, David was only little and yet . . . Well, this little kid turned abruptly into some kind of frenzied fighting machine. There just didn't seem to be any stopping him. But the real shock came when Tony looked up from his whimper of defeat to find David in tears too and destroying the little car piece by piece with the same meticulous fury, that same fraying tightrope of control—mind teetering on the edge of implosion—that he'd plainly turned on the books in his apartment.

So Tony had cheered up at once and offered his hand in friendship; all the way back then, at seven years old, he had no doubts that he'd won the war if not the battle. Nothing had changed since. He kicked his way through the shredded pages. "Me?" he said. "*I* get angry: I beat up some bitch on the street like a regular guy. You? Know what you remind me of? Remember that guy what cut off his own arm with his penknife? 'Course, his hand was caught in rocks or something, and he was gonna die if he didn't do it. Not you. You just do it for fun." He leaned against the wall and glanced around the room again. "There's got to be a better way of getting kicks even for a screwball like David Marion. Besides, it's a cruel waste of money if you ask me."

"I didn't ask you."

"Speaking of money, you worked out the plans for that jewelry store yet? Not much time left."

"We'll have to put it off." David slumped into a chair at the table, pulled a pack of cigarettes out of his pocket, lit one.

"What's that supposed to mean?"

"Exactly what it sounds like."

"I hate it when you joke about the mighty U.S. dollar. Some things are sacred, you know."

"No joke."

"You been moonlighting on me?"

"Worries you, does it?"

"David, even you have to pay the rent."

The way they worked it, if they could break into a secured premises on the basis of floor plans and the name of the firm employed to do the securing, something was seriously wrong. If the owners agreed, they hired David and Tony to install a new system or refurbish the old one. David's apartment served as office; he and Tony were the only staff. They were good at what they did. They were fast. They were cheap. Business was picking up every day. They didn't even have to advertise anymore—nor did they need the Herndon & Freyl endorsement that had got them going. The only cause of friction between them in this was that David was the main player just as he had been in the relationship ever since the long-ago fight over the little metal car out of a garbage can—always excepting the prison years, of course—and Tony found a secondary role harder to take with every passing day. Even the business itself had been David's idea; he was the one with a real feel for security systems, for the overall picture. Okay, so Tony's role was crucial. No business can function without a front man, and he was all mouth and persuasion, the perfect foil for what David planned and put together. But there were times when he had to fight to keep himself from showing the resentment he felt.

He eyed David suspiciously. "You been to see old Mrs. Freyl

again?" No response. "What'd she want *now*? Signed confession?"

"A little detective work," David said. He saw no reason to tell Tony that her aim had been to turn him into a killer-for-hire.

"You?" David shrugged. "You're kidding me. She hired *you*? This is for real? Aw, come on . . . Now, there is a first-rate joke. I got to hand it to you. That *does* make me laugh. I didn't think you had it in you—setting somebody up like that. Especially *her*."

David was abruptly tired, and his voice took on an edge of exhausted wonder. "How could this place look so enchanted to me two years ago? I hate the sight of it. I hate everything in it."

"Well, so, you're leaving. Got yourself a new house in the west with the rich folks. Leaving all us poor folks behind. Look at them packing crates. How come you got to start on packing so early? You been getting ready for weeks."

David went over to the open window to shut out the cold. The swirling paper settled; he took a plastic bag out of a drawer and, cigarette still dangling from his lips, began to clear handfuls of litter off the floor.

"Nah, that can't be it," Tony said, watching him. "I got it backward, didn't I? You're the fall guy—*you*—not the old bitch. She can't be wanting you to find the bad boy what hurt her baby darling, 'cause she's got you all fitted up for that role your own self. Know what I think? I think maybe her and me got something in common. It's like if you're going to play a joke on somebody, you got to make them think everything's just fine or it won't come out as funny. Know what I mean? You got to sucker them into walking through the door that's got a bucket of pigs' piss hanging above the doorjamb or, say, eating the cookies you made with ExLax instead of chocolate chips. They got to *trust* you. They got to think you're their friend. So she plays nice and makes out like she's hiring you. What do you figure she *really* wants? I bet she didn't expect you to take nothing for it."

David only shrugged.

"I'd sure like to a seen that," Tony went on. "One day she *knows* you're gonna take her money and get out, and you throw it in her face. The next day, she knows you *not* gonna take it, and you . . . What the fuck. I guess you got her dancing on that one. I might even have to admit it myself. How much you squeeze out of her? Huh?" David glanced up at him, then back. "Okay, so it's none of my business. But life's got to go on, David. Hear me? First thing, you got to get the heat back on in this place. Take a shower. Change your shirt. We can grab a sandwich at Cockran's. You got a week left on the east side. You can't just stop living until the days are up—or until that old woman gets you to crap in a pot with Saran Wrap stretched beneath the toilet seat. Hey, I ever tell you about the time I pulled that one on—"

"Not now."

"—that dumb old nigger at Cockran's?"

"No!"

"Okay, okay. But we got to sit down and talk sense about this jewelry store."

"Don't crowd me, Tony. I don't like it."

"Nobody's crowding you. We got us a good thing going. We got to take care of the good things. Both of us. Me and you together." He watched David pack the plastic bag. "That old hag really is screwing with your mind," he said. "That part of it ain't no joke, David. You're being had. I done it too many times myself not to know it when I see it."

David had just come from the bank, where he'd cashed Becky's check after a flurry of telephone calls and the consternation of a furious bank manager. He put down the bag, took a thick wad of bills out of his pocket and peeled off a few. "This ought to hold you for a while," David said, holding out the notes. "It's just the kind you like: blood money. The very best."

"You think *that's* what I'm talking about?" David began scooping up paper again. He moved with an easy grace that had always fascinated Tony, efficient, clean, not a single wasted gesture. For years Tony had struggled to imitate it, but his sheer size—the extra bulk of muscle he carried—somehow managed to get in his way. "You and those books," he said, and there was real despair in his voice. "I used to *know* you. You used to be someone I could talk to. Not anymore. Who are you anyhow? *What* are you? I bet you don't know any better than I do, and I don't know nothing. Those guys with their money and their *books* . . . Don't let her do this to us." David worked on as though Tony wasn't even in the room. "I can't just stand around watching some old woman cut your balls off. I know you think you got her. You're wrong. She's the one's got you. She's got you strung out to dry." Still David said nothing. "You hear me, David? I'm talking to you."

David took the money out of his pocket again and handed the entire wad to Tony. "Paper the walls with it."

"Listen to yourself, David." Tony was backing away, shaking his head, his hands held palm outward in refusal. David shrugged and put the bills back into his pocket. "You're turning into some kind of a manservant for the lady of the manor. What the fuck am I saying? Manservant? You're her personal whipping boy. She's laughing at you, friend. She's thinking, 'That one sure is a meat-head. He sure is a yo-yo.' That what you want her to think? Is it? Huh?"

David finished filling the bag. Tony watched him tie it at the top, get out another, begin to fill it. "You got nothing to say to me? Nothing at all? What's going to happen to you anyways? You can't just shut up every time somebody asks you a question you don't like. Questions ain't going to go away just because you want them to. What do you expect me to do? Let them hurt you even if I know how to stop it? You want me to just walk off and forget about it?"

David sighed irritably. "That would be a start."

Tony slammed the door behind him.

As soon as he was gone, David stopped filling the new bag and stared around at the remains of the small library he'd collected; there was still a light sprinkling of torn pages over much of the floor, and he hadn't even touched the heaps clustered in corners and caught under furniture. Most of the books had been new; a great deal of his cut of the money from the business had gone on them. But the rest had been his history, the only part of his past that he didn't see as a waste of time. One was that first law book Hugh had given him as a reading primer; he'd hidden it in his cell for years. Another was the novel that had told him how people on the outside act when somebody dies. Now there was nothing. Emptiness. The void. And the void extended right inside his head too. It had taken hours to do this. He'd wakened from his dream of the Monaghans and started in almost at once. Clearly he had. And yet, like Tony, he'd had to reconstruct what he'd done from old memories.

Because he did not remember a single moment of the hours that this much meticulous destruction had taken. He remembered the waking, and he remembered picking up Stephanie for the visit to the graveyard. Everything in between was a blank.

14

THE BUILDING THAT HOUSED HERNDON & FREYL—NOW Herndon Freyl, & Zemanski—occupied a third of the block and showed up in daylight as solid, impressive, ornate. Yesterday's snow was piled up on cornice and moldings; it frosted the metal scrollwork of a front door too elegant even to carry the firm's name on a discreet brass plate. Inside, there was a stately hush. The ceiling was high. The floor was marble; David's footsteps reverberated as he walked across it in the course of his first official act as Becky Freyl's enforcer.

The uniformed security guard inside his mahogany enclosure knew him well. So did the receptionist who sat behind the large desk at the far end of the lobby. They'd both seen him come and go for the past two years. They did feel a slight tremor admitting him today, a hint of uncertainty; only a week before, he'd been confined to a police cell suspected of Hugh's murder; the story had made all the newspapers. Not that either the guard or the receptionist really thought he could be guilty, but still it added something to seeing him again, especially since everybody in this building was aware of his record. Maybe Becky hadn't concerned herself all that seriously with his past until Hugh died, but no group of legal people would have been likely to remain ignorant of such fascinating details for even as long as it had taken Hugh's circle of friends to dig up the story, and several in this building had actively contributed to David's release from South Hams prison; he'd been a regular visitor ever since, and however much the partners disliked and disapproved of him, the lower echelons of staff, even the maintenance arm of it, felt a little proprietary about him, a little protective—enough to overcome all but that last shred of a qualm.

"Good to see you back, David," the security guard called out.

David nodded a greeting. "Bertie's here today, isn't he?" Bertie Wannerman was the secretary-cum-assistant hired by Becky to replace Stephanie; he was male, middle-aged, with a whining wife and three teenage sons: no threat to the stability of the Freyl household in any shape or form.

"Yeah. Poor bastard," said the guard.

"Oh?" said David.

"They didn't exactly kick him *up*stairs."

" 'They'?"

"Whatever."

"Zemanski?"

"Shoved the guy down on the second floor with the kids." The guard shook his head. "Poor bastard," he said again.

"I'm so sorry about Mr. Freyl," the receptionist said when David reached her. "We are all devastated." She was as elegant and mannered as the building; doubtless she meant what she said, but it came out as though she was a social secretary issuing an invitation to a garden party.

"Yes," said David.

She checked her screen. "Mr. Wannerman is in 2401."

The elevator was a cage that matched the metalwork of the outside door; it occupied a glass-encased well in the middle of the massive staircase so that there was the sense of being wafted up through the flight. David got off at the second floor, the very floor of cubicles he'd visited in his nighttime search of the premises. On working mornings like this one, it was closer to a busy department store. Everything looked as solid as it ought to, even the partitions that cut the large floor space into its rows of cubicles. Young data researchers rushed up and down the aisles. Small clutches of them gathered here and there, half inside this cubbyhole, half outside that one. Most were barely more than boys and girls, just out of college. Their talk had a childlike excitement to it, a playground animation. Their training was in hard sciences, engineering, medicine, accountancy, areas with which lawyers are rarely more than casually acquainted, even though their cases often involve such material. The kids were hired to seek out inconsistencies in the masses of correspondence that touched on these various fields and that their bosses did not have the background to spot.

Bertie Wannerman had been a chemistry major years ago; that had been the excuse for sticking him here. He'd been given the first cubbyhole in the fourth row, not a bad position, all things considered, close to the fire escape and the bathrooms. He sat at his desk, his head buried in his hands.

"Bertie?" said David.

Bertie jerked to attention. "David! You scared me half to death."

"What is this?" David gestured at the bare little space.

Bertie followed the gesture with his eyes. "I don't suppose you could call it a promotion."

"No."

There was a burst of laughter somewhere off to the right. "I guess I'm getting old. Maybe I smell old. You think I smell old? Zemanski doesn't want me anywhere near him."

"I need your help," David said.

"I wish more people did." Bertie's face softened, and he gestured at the only other chair in the space. He'd stretched his sparse red hair into painstaking strands across a freckled pate. "Sit down. Sit down. Welcome to 2401." He sighed. "Of course, I can't really complain, can I? Seven's a lucky number, and 2401 is seven cubed times seven." Bertie's wife read him the astrology page first thing in the morning; he couldn't have faced the day without it, and he had a small library of books on numerology. "Even the digits add up to seven, and seven represents perfect order. It's the number of the planetary spheres and the Deadly Sins—the Cardinal Virtues, too, of course. Think maybe Zemanski did me a favor after all?"

"No."

"It's also the symbol of pain. Did you know that?" David shook his head. "Zemanski's always been too eager. My wife says his tan comes out of a bottle. She says his back is hairy and he has to get it waxed every eight weeks."

"Did Hugh seem to be worried about anything, Bertie?"

"You looking into this mess?" David nodded. "Well, thank the Lord for that. How could anybody do something like that to him? The police are either stupid or corrupt. I told them all kinds of

pends on the surface touched, the skin of the person who did the touching and, in the case of a bloody print like the one in David's file, the investigator's skills in enhancing what was visible and photographing it. Even if the prints are relatively clear, there is a great deal of controversy over just how many markers—points of comparison—constitute a firm identification. South Africa calls for seven. The Netherlands insists on twelve. The United States and England leave the number to an expert's discretion.

The negative of the print in David's file had been poor to begin with, and it had suffered damage in its years of jostling among the loose pages of the unbound murder book where it did not belong. I doubted that even the relatively new computer art of fingerprint enhancement could bring out enough markers to distinguish it from my own fingerprints.

"What about Fourier transforms?" Jimmy asked.

"It's too damaged," I said impatiently. Fourier transforms stretch the gray scale of the image to produce greater clarification; they are a standard part of fingerprint identification armory.

"Filters?"

"Tell me something I don't know, Jimmy."

Jimmy paused a moment, somewhat torn, I think, between the desire to show off his expertise and the worry that I might lay claim to insider knowledge that was rightly his. "You got the original, right?" he said, reluctant still. "Well, there's this guy in Chicago, he's worked out a special algorithm for scanning the image off the film. He sets the parameters after and plays with a bunch of other algorithms like the rest of them, but it's that kick back at the starting gate that changes things. I bet he could get you maybe seven markers. Maybe more." I shrugged, and Jimmy laughed. "You don't believe me, do you?"

"Few people would dare to call you trustworthy."

"He just sold his new toy to Argentina."

"Argentina?" I had a bite of salad halfway to my mouth. "Lucky man."

Argentina leads the world in fingerprint analysis. Their program began as a method for identifying the students, journalists, priests, nuns, young children and others who disappeared from the face of the earth during the years of the military junta. If Argentina was interested, there certainly was something to be said for the technique.

But confirming the fingerprint as David's only undermined a possible attack on the grounds that the prosecution had presented it even though it was unidentifiable.

◄◦►

David climbed the four flights from the researchers' floor and Bertie Wannerman's ignominious cubbyhole to the senior partners' floor at the top of the building. An open foyer greeted him here and a desk with receptionist much like the desk and receptionist downstairs in the lobby. This person was also Becky's choice, and again she was definitely not Hugh's type. Her role was the standard one of dragon at the gate, protector of the top brass in this legal firm, and she performed it with an evangelical zeal. David nodded to her as he passed just as he always had, and she watched him disappear into the law library beyond.

The heavy oak tables that had been scarred and gashed during Hugh's murder were nowhere to be seen in the long, grand corridor of a room. The arched windows at both ends lit up only collapsible card tables. The oak ones were valuable pieces, historic ones. They'd once stood in the Old Capitol; Lincoln himself spent many midnight hours bent over them, law books open in front of him and piled all around him. Adlai Stevenson had one of them moved to the Governor's Mansion so that he could spend his own midnight hours working on it. Both oak tables had gone off this morning to a specialist restorer in Pennsylvania, and the library was bereft without them; it was empty, soulless.

The door to Hugh's office—now Jimmy's office—was at the far end where the building allowed that panoramic view of the Capitol Complex laid out in all its glory; David opened the door without knocking and found Jimmy in the act of running his hands over the polished surface of Herndon's old desk as though it were a prize heifer at the state fair. He'd known of David's presence in the building within minutes—this building was *his* fiefdom now—and there was pleasure to be had in a new chief's greeting to an old chief's much disliked protégé.

"Hiya, David," he said. "Come to see me in my new home? Take a pew. Take a pew."

The books that had not yet been sorted or shelved on David's nighttime visit to this room were in place. Jimmy's hideous filing cabinet was topped with a sculpture that seemed to be a football player in a dash, although it was difficult to tell because the ball he was carrying somehow managed to serve as his head too.

David walked over to it. "You didn't have this before," he said.

"What a beautiful piece, huh?" said Jimmy. "Very rare. It looks even better here than it did in my home."

It was the same chunky statuette that Hugh's daughter, Helen, had considered using to bash in Jimmy's head on the night of David and Tony's job at the bonded warehouse near St. Louis; David scanned it with distaste. "I have a couple of questions," he said.

"Yeah? Any reason why I should answer them?"

"A personal favor."

"Since when do I owe you favors?"

"Not me. Mrs. Freyl."

Jimmy laughed. "You're kidding."

"No."

"How the fuck did you manage that?" Jimmy rapped out an appreciative tattoo on Herndon's desk. "Hugh dead less than two weeks, and you got the mother all sewed up." David's gaze was steady. "Well, I really got to hand it to you. That bitch hates your guts even more than she hates mine—although, in your case, I guess I got to say *used* to hate them. So what's she want out of me?"

"She'd appreciate it if Mrs. Hardcastle put together the pleadings for the cases Hugh was working on during the last year, a list of his clients, his appointments schedule for the last six months and copies of the firm's telephone records. I'll pick them up on my way out." Mrs. Hardcastle was the dragon at the gate.

"Now you *are* kidding me."

"No."

"The client list is privileged. I can't just hand it out like wieners at a ball game."

"I also need a written report from you in regard to—"

"No way."

"—what he was doing for each of his clients."

"What is this anyhow? You playing detective or something?"

There was a flash of anger across David's face. "Get Mrs. Hardcastle to put that material together."

"Oh, come on, David. I already had a guy in here fishing through Hugh's stuff. The DA and I chose him together, but he

didn't find anything interesting. You got to realize Hugh wasn't
doing all that much anymore: four, maybe five cases."

"Just *get* the material."

Jimmy switched on the intercom. After all, Becky was important to his future, seriously important, whether Hugh was dead or
not. If she'd hired David to sniff around for her, well, then David
had to be viewed as important—at least for the time being. Jimmy
saw himself as a man roaring along the road to success, a good-
looking hunk of beef and smart as hell, a man destined to marry
Becky's granddaughter, Helen, and go straight to the top of the tree
in this town. He was going to be a Freyl. He was figuring on running for mayor one day. Why should such a person have to come
to terms with a loose canon like David Marion? The day would
dawn when he didn't have do things like this anymore. It *would*
come. He *knew* it. In the meantime, though, something had to be
done to gloss over the jabs here and there that showed, well, maybe
a little too clearly just what his feelings were. He smiled at David
as he gave Mrs. Hardcastle instructions to dig out the information.

Perhaps David didn't see the smile. Perhaps he paid no attention
to it. He was glancing over the wall where Jimmy's legal degrees had
displaced Hugh's. Pride of place went to a framed photograph of
Jimmy with Senator John Calder, clearly taken at Hugh's funeral;
the senator had his arm around Jimmy's shoulders, an older man of
power comforting a younger power-to-be on a loss to them both.

"You don't miss a trick, do you?" David said, indicating the picture with a nod of his head as Jimmy switched off the intercom.

Jimmy tilted his chair back on its hind legs and stretched his
hands behind his neck. "Why doesn't Becky get herself a real detective?"

David shrugged. Becky could hardly hire a licensed detective to
go in search of somebody to kill. "What did the police talk to you
about?" he said.

"What's she want to know that for? Suppose I don't *feel* like
blabbing it to you?"

"You wouldn't be standing in my way again, would you,
Jimmy?"

"Okay, *okay*! Keep your shirt on." Jimmy straightened his chair,
rattled despite himself and his newly elevated position. "What's the

matter with you anyhow? Can't you take a joke? They were pretty disappointed—kept getting unhappier every minute I was with them. I mean, how could I know anything that would contribute to anything? Killing off lawyers is hardly my territory."

"They ask you if he had any enemies?"

"How the hell would I know about enemies? Hugh would have talked to you a lot quicker than me if somebody was trying to push him around. This whole thing has just got to be one of those opportunistic situations. A screwball or an addict who just went nuts, and chewed up Hugh in the fallout. It's one hell of a shame—isn't anybody who'd say otherwise—but it's the only rational explanation. Otherwise, *none* of it adds up. No forensics either—nowhere to start, nothing to start *with*. That's what the cops told me. They're pretty sure already they're not going to get anybody for it. It's going to be rough on Becky. People like her have a real need to watch somebody swing."

David got up and turned to leave, and Jimmy steeled himself to tend to the fences between them that still needed patching. "Hey, why don't you come around for a drink?" he said.

David turned back. "A drink?"

"Yeah. What do you say?"

"I just might take you up on that."

15

POLICE FILES THAT GO MISSING AS DAVID'S HAD, DO
sound suspicious to outsiders but, as I told Stephanie, anybody working
on old cases runs into the problem all the time. People who carry out official duties are far more fallible than they like to let on; so are their filing systems, computerized or not, and paper seems to have a tendency to
get lost even without all this help. But I could not hold that argument
with any serious conviction when we failed to turn up copies of David's
murder book either at the district attorney's office or the public defender's office. Furthermore, as Stephanie argued, somebody could easily
have pillaged David's police file at any time before I took those copies of
it—along with the original negative of the fingerprint—and the same
somebody (or some other somebody) could have engineered the file's
abrupt disappearance afterward.

And yet why bother? So far as I knew, David was not important to
anybody in a position to cover up details of his arrest and trial, nor was
there any hint of a reason to cover them up. Stephanie and I began an
inquiry into David's past.

The first people we contacted were the Monaghans, since regular letters and visits from them were a part of his prison record. We went to see
them together. They lived in a middle-class section of Springfield between the two sets of railway tracks, a small, neat house hidden down a
flight of stairs behind a high privet hedge that must have been in bloom
because it smelled of honey. They greeted us warmly, fussed over which
chairs we were to sit in, then brought out coffee and cookies. Stephanie
guessed that they were both in their late seventies. They told us that
their son had settled in Omaha and their daughter had gone to live in
Montana when her children, their grandsons, were nine and ten.

"That's what gave us the idea," said Mrs. Monaghan. Stephanie told me she was as apple-cheeked as an ad for chocolate cupcakes, round, bright eyes, a dumpling of a woman, who looked as spirited as she sounded. "I adored those kids. I doted on them. But Montana? When was I going to see them? Christmas only? Maybe summer vacations? Bud here—that's Mr. Monaghan—he was still running his roofing business, and we couldn't go gallivanting off whenever we wanted to. So I said to him, 'Let's foster a child.' We entered the program, and they brought us that beautiful boy. He was only eleven at the time."

"Did they warn you about him?" Stephanie asked. "I mean, he had a pretty bad reputation."

"Sure they did," Mr. Monaghan said. Stephanie described him to me later as well-knit and tall with long hands and unexpectedly mischievous eyes, probably very handsome when he was young—he still had that ease about him that beautiful people develop—and he had clearly been something of a tough kid himself. "They said he was trouble. They said he'd robbed stores and hijacked cars and dealt in drugs—pretty good, I thought, for a kid that little. They told us he'd steal from us too. They even said he was a murderer in the making, but we never had any trouble with him. Well, maybe a little at first, until he got used to us. He didn't like school much, but I couldn't see what was so wrong with that. Seems only natural to me. I hated it when I was a kid. Besides, how could he like it? It bored him to tears."

"And did he steal from you?" I asked.

Mr. Monaghan hesitated. "Like I say, we expected it. He didn't know any better. He'd had a real hard background."

"Tell me something," I said then, abruptly curious. "You don't happen to know if he could read or write, do you? Back then?"

" 'Course he could read and write," said Mrs. Monaghan. "He was the smartest boy I ever saw. I hate to say it, but he was much brighter than my grandsons."

"You are certain that he could read?"

"They told me he couldn't, just like you. They said he probably had dyslexia or something else wrong with him. It wasn't true. Not a bit of it. I figure he just thought it was fun, running rings around them, keeping them guessing, because he used to read Bud's newspaper out loud to me while I was ironing. I knew more about what was going on in the world while David was with us than I ever knew before. There was hostages in Iran. See? I even remember what he read me about. Some Arab tried to kill the pope and somebody did kill the president of . . . well, of someplace. I still remember him sitting at that big red table in the kitchen with his dark head bent over the paper. He always had that real pretty hair, so black you could almost see blue in it even in summertime when all the other kids went blonder."

"How'd you find out?" said Stephanie.

"What do they know about David?" said Mrs. Monaghan. "You tell her, Bud." There was pleasure in Mrs. Monaghan's voice. "You tell it better than me."

Mr. Monaghan laughed at the memory. "The three of us used to walk to the supermarket to save on gas and bus fares," he said, "because business wasn't so good in those days, and David used to run on ahead of us, then run back, then run off behind us the way we'd come and run double quick to catch up again. One time, I was holding his hand, and out of the blue he said, 'Make sure you're serious. Jeep Cherokee. The truck.'

" 'Something you heard on TV?' I said.

" 'Yeah. But I don't want a Jeep Cherokee. When I grow up I'm gonna buy me one of them old cars—one of them Chevy Impalas. It's got the biggest horsepower of all.'

"And then Maggie said, 'Bud, look over there.' And right in front of us was an ad for a Jeep Cherokee. At the top it said, 'Make sure you're serious.' At the bottom it said, 'Jeep Cherokee. The truck.'

" 'Probably remembers it from TV,' I said.

"But Maggie, she wasn't going to let it go at that. 'Oh, look, Bud,' she said, pointing to another billboard. 'It says we can get the curtains cleaned before Labor Day for only $14.95.'

" 'You're stupid,' David said.

" 'I am not,' she said. 'I want my curtains cleaned before Labor Day. You're going to meet my grandchildren on Labor Day, and I want everything perfect.'

" 'It's "carpets" that they're gonna clean for $14.95, and it says "for Christmas"—not "before Labor Day." You're stupid.'

"Maggie and I burst out laughing. 'Davy, my boy,' I said, patting his shoulder. 'You've just been rumbled.'

"He looked really surprised. Then he got angry and sulked the rest of the way home, but he never pretended he couldn't read after that. If there's any mercy in heaven, he'll get that Chevy Impala one day."

"I'd sell my soul to get David out of prison," Mrs. Monaghan had said to Stephanie and me as we were leaving. "He doesn't belong there. I don't care what he did. People give in too easy. They get scared off too easy. Standing up to the big guys is what caught my eye about Bud here, first time I saw him. It's what I liked best about David. He wasn't going to let them beat him. Not then, not now. What's the matter with people anyhow? You treat a boy like he was treated, what do you expect? If they'd let us adopt him, none of this ever would have happened."

"Why do you suppose they didn't?" Stephanie asked. "I mean, let you adopt him. You seem like the perfect people for him."

Mrs. Monaghan sighed heavily. "I don't know. I really don't know. We fit all their requirements."

"They must have given you some reason."

"Yeah, well, they said we couldn't control him. They said, if we could, he'd go to school and stop thieving. But they didn't even give us a chance to explain that to him. Maybe it wouldn't have made any difference—I don't think he was doing much stealing anyhow—but they could at least have given us the chance. Poor little kid. He had it all figured out in his own head. I know he did. The fates or God or whatever had him marked down as one of the damned. Only eleven years old, and that's what he thought."

It was no more than ten o'clock in the morning by the time David left Jimmy's office at Herndon & Freyl—or rather Herndon, Freyl & Zemanski. He dropped the files of Hugh's case pleadings at his apartment and headed west again. He had an appointment with Allen Madison, president of the Springfield Federal Bank, one of the worthies at Hugh's wake—one of that elite circle who'd sniped from a safe distance—and one of the people who'd refused to speak to David before Becky's interference. David's presence in the banker's offices on a bright winter day was not welcome. Welcome? It was an insult. He would never have agreed to receiving this disreputable person for anybody but Rebecca Freyl; he'd been furious at the injustice of it from the moment he'd found himself committed to it. Now, with David in front of him, he was seething.

"I cannot imagine why Mrs. Freyl wishes you to examine her son's accounts," he said.

"It's none of your business."

The banker stiffened. "How dare you speak to me like that?"

Three large windows looked out into a landscaped yard beyond the office. There were trees and shrubbery and a statue of Ronald Reagan, the only United States president actually to be born in Illinois; the great Lincoln made Illinois his home, but he came from Kentucky. Allen Madison liked to refer to Reagan as his cousin Ronnie. They'd both been born in tiny northern Illinois towns, and Madison had spent years tracking down the second cousin of a cousin once removed who just might have linked them. He'd even resembled the ex-president once, faintly anyhow, but puffy jowls and broken veins on his cheeks—Springfield's famous weakness, too much booze over too many years—had buried any Reaganesque affability except when he was in the best of moods. This morning he was in a bad mood—a *very bad* mood.

David had anticipated something much like this—and got pleasure out of seeing it. What he hadn't anticipated was a tension in the man that came across as fear, which was puzzling; the banker was safely in his own plush and roomy office with armed guards on duty just on the far side of the door. Maybe David's presence rattled him as well as outraged him. Or maybe he'd just found out that his wife was sleeping with his friend the broker, something that had seemed to David all too obvious from the way those two stood together at the wake. Or maybe he was just so in awe of the great Rebecca Freyl that any request from her frightened him.

On the wall behind the president hung his degree from the University of Chicago Business School alongside various civic awards with rosettes and embossed symbols. Pride of place went to two framed photographs, one of Madison's dog, a huge, hairy creature of indeterminate parentage and a grill over his muzzle; the other was of Madison shaking hands with Senator John Calder. David buried his uncertainties in abrupt amusement.

"Is a picture like that obligatory?" he said, indicating the photograph.

"My fondness for Bozo is none of your business."

"You don't really call him Bozo in the privacy of the Sangamo Club, do you?"

"You may not approve, Mr., uh . . . but dogs have names even as you do."

"Not the dog. Calder."

"I *beg* your pardon?" Despite himself, Madison swung around to look.

"You and Calder. Jimmy's got one of them hanging behind his desk—himself with the great senator instead of you, of course."

Allen Madison could hardly bring himself to speak; his cheeks went from pink to puce. "I shudder to think how you persuaded Mrs. Freyl that you are qualified to undertake the task at hand—or for that matter, any task remotely approaching it."

"I want Mr. Freyl's records for the past three years."

◄○►

Maybe the tension David sensed in Allen Madison was only a figment of his own imagination, but the banker's doubts were as reasonable as they were impolitely expressed. A grasp of accounting hardly fits the profile of an east-side murderer who'd spent most of his life behind bars, even one with the advantage of Hugh Freyl's tutoring behind him.

On the other hand, prisons sometimes offer the occasional CPA if that's the kind of thing that interests a man. Not that David had been interested. Why should he be? Accountancy sounds so tedious. And yet everybody knows that an accountant was responsible for putting Al Capone behind bars, which ought to lighten the image a little. What a lot of people don't know—and what's more fun—is that usually it's the other way around. If the local church fund gets caught bamboozling the parishioners, they blame it on the accountant, and the accountant goes to jail. The Gaming Commission is indicted on fraud charges, and who goes to prison? An accountant. It isn't that they're innocent pawns; they know precisely what they're doing, and the pay is very good. It's just that they're expendable. The world is crawling with number crunchers willing to fiddle the books if the money is right, but it takes somebody special to figure out how to make the money that creates a need for fancy footwork in the first place. Think of Enron; most of the guys at the top got off clean with their millions. Or was it billions?

During the mid-1990s—about halfway through David's sentence—some strange convergence of the stars brought four accountants into the cells of South Hams State Prison all at the same time. They stuck together, and mainly they were left alone to tend the library, do the prison accounts and train successors in these jobs. Training other inmates took up an increasing amount of time, and one of the accountants—he was known as Professor Flaam—set up a special course to be held in the library, which was manned by the four accountants and their trainees. This course had official approval, but since prison officials are as bored by accounting as the rest of the world, they didn't bother to find out that its unofficial title was *Shenanigans*. The first lesson opened with what the Professor called "The Schlicit Agenda":

> *Why bother with financial fraud?*
> 1. *It gets you lots of money.*
> 2. *It's easy.*
> 3. *You won't get caught.*
> *Lesson One: Begin by stealing a handful of credit cards.*

The Professor was a short, bald, excitable man of complex principles who would have skinned his grandmother for a nickel but would have treated that nickel with the delighted and delicate respect his grandmother deserved and never got. He'd been adviser to the city of Springfield on its $2 billion a year municipal bond underwriting market; he got caught taking bribes in return for giving investment bankers in Chicago a piece of the action. He conducted his prison classes striding from one side of the small library room to the other, gesticulating with short, plump arms as he drew comparisons between the way an African stalks a bushbuck and any American with half a brain can stalk a fortune: study the habits of the prey, secure your escape route, strike quickly, leave no trail of blood for the lions to follow. Once you get the knack, it's kind of like picking a lock—only easier to get away with.

When you've stolen your handful of credit cards, get cash advances to their limit and beyond if you can. Buy yourself an airplane ticket with some of the money—do *not* use a stolen card for this (the lions might catch the scent)—stuff the rest in a suitcase, carry it off to Panama, bank it under a false name. Then go home and start again.

Inside a year, you're rich.

As to the technicalities, follow-up lessons included identity theft (and other easy ways to steal credit cards), Illinois's riverboat casinos (and other easy ways to get cash advances on stolen cards) as well as the charming semilegality of smuggling raw cash (sadly lost in the wake of 9/11).

Flaam saw at once that David was smarter than most. Just to test the aptness of his pupil, he set a bogus estimate in an interim financial report. David plowed through pages of income and expenditure and rousted out the phoney much as he might have rousted out some kid hiding behind a garbage can in a neighborhood gang fight. From there, Flaam led him into the forests of what's called "creative accounting" in the trade. That's what puts accountants behind bars when they're not as wary as an African with his bushbuck.

The records with which President Allen Madison of the Springfield Federal Bank presented David were no challenge to someone with Professor Flaam's genius behind him. David was finished before the end of the lunch hour. But neither Hugh's private accounts nor Herndon & Freyl's professional accounts showed up the irregularities he knew how to spot. Payments in and out had followed much the same pattern for several years, and the bank's accounting methods had remained the same for all that time. If Hugh had the financial troubles that Bertie Wannerman suspected, they weren't apparent here.

Later in the afternoon, David saw Hugh's broker, another of the worthies from Hugh's funeral, the very one who was spending two afternoons a week with the banker's wife at the St. Nicholas Hotel. He was almost as angry as the banker too. Again David sensed a tension that would have passed for fear in prison; again he dismissed it. As before he was troubled and irritated by his unreliability in assessing people who'd never lived behind bars; he'd once been an expert in fear and yet seemed useless at spotting it on the outside, while he had no doubts about the liaison between the broker and the banker's wife despite eighteen years without women.

David's final visit of the day was to Hugh's accountant to check his tax records. They revealed no more than his bank statements or investments had. The accountant was not an elevated enough person to have attended Hugh's funeral—just one of the horde that worshipped from afar—nor elevated enough to have a photograph like Madison's of himself shaking Senator Calder's hand. And that was puzzling too, because he was the one who should have been most in awe of Becky, and yet he showed no sign of the tension in the others.

◄◦►

David called Stephanie as soon as he got back to his apartment.

"Oh, David, I feel so sick," she said.

"I'll take you to a doctor."

"I hate hospitals."

"Is there some friend I can call?"

"Don't want to talk to anybody—except you, of course."

"Let me see what I can do."

He frightened the clerk at the motel desk into giving him the manager's name and telephone number. The manager's uncle was a semiretired internist who lived not too far away; David insisted that he be called in at once.

People forget that flu kills tens of thousands every year, some of them as young and strong as Stephanie, and that a plane trip drives the infection deep. Besides, to be sick away from home, alone in a motel room in this town of too many memories: Stephanie couldn't bear to look at those heavy suitcases she'd carried off the plane, much less open them. As for David, he knew—he *knew* this even though he was completely wrong—that if he pressed her too hard, she'd never let him know what was inside. So he turned reluctantly to the heap of records and files that Jimmy's hatchet-faced receptionist had given him.

David fought his way through list after list of telephone calls as well as Hugh's appointments schedule; he worked until early the following morning, and not so much as an intriguing coincidence or grouping of calls or clients showed its face. The next day he made a start on Hugh's current legal cases. Hugh's lessons had included forays into the law, and David knew that papers like these constituted maps of the shark pools of the world. After all, a corporate lawyer's job is to ensure that the sharks strip every last shred of meat from every last bone. But mergers, bankruptcy, reorganization and dissolution of corporations, contracts, cash-flow, finance and such arcane subjects as arbitrage and equilibria: David found them as dull as telephone records.

A day and a half of steady work—broken only by an hour at Cockran's to share a sandwich and a beer with Tony—and still he found nothing. By late afternoon of the second day, a few unsorted piles remained, but he could not bring himself to start on them. He put through a call to Stephanie in the hopes that her flu had subsided enough for her to talk to him about what was in her suitcases. The moment she answered he knew it was out of the question. She'd developed a harsh cough that interrupted almost every sentence and made her breathless. She said that the motel manager's uncle, the semiretired internist, had told her that another degree of fever, and she'd have no choice about going to the hospital. The most she was up to was cable reruns of *Cagney and Lacey,* but her head hurt too much even for that. She had yet to make it through an entire episode.

As before, David's inexperience in the world outside bars kept him from suggesting that he pick up the suitcases from the motel and make a start on them alone. Why would she trust him to take away something that belonged to her? Why would anybody? Besides, if he pushed, he might scare her off. Only a fool would take the risk.

Instead, he put through a call to Justice Samuel Clark. As soon as he hung up the phone, he called the airport and reserved a ticket for the evening's flight to Washington, D.C., via Chicago, due to leave in a few hours' time.

◄◌►

With the exception of the Monaghans, the picture that emerged of David as a child brought to mind a Dickensian street urchin, scavenging for life in an alien and forbidding landscape. I had had no idea how much so many of our children suffer—and how much suffering they cause.

After Social Services said the Monaghans were incapable of controlling him, they sent him to foster families who gave bitter reports of
theft, insubordination, obstruction, vandalism, fighting, unprovoked violence and delinquency of practically every other known variety. A member of staff at a group home where he had been an inmate had more of
the same to offer. A fellow inmate at the Juvenile Detention Center at
Washoga—tracked down by a young researcher from the second floor—
told us David was the central figure in a smuggling ring that supplied alcohol, cigarettes and various assorted drugs to South Hams State Prison,
only a few miles away. Nobody in charge ever figured out how to pin it
on him, which even all these years later provoked delighted glee in the
fellow inmate. We were not able to talk to the wife and mother of the
people David had killed—she was in a hospital undergoing lengthy treatment and tests for some unspecified ailment—but we tracked down a
couple of social workers who had so disliked and mistrusted him that
they could hardly bring themselves to speak of him, even though they
admitted that he had been very badly treated over the years.

The first person we talked to about the double murder itself was the
owner of the car that David had been servicing when it happened, the
man who had walked in on the blood-soaked garage scene and stumbled
out again, screaming for the police. Stephanie and I went to see him. She
told me afterward that he was small and round, in his mid-fifties with
cheeks so full that the lenses of his glasses pressed them back and made
the skin beneath them sweat.

"Pretty impressive to own a car that two guys got murdered under,
don't you think?" he said to us. "Me and my wife figured we'd get good
money for it." He laughed. "We were right."

"It must have been a terrible shock at the time," I said.

"Christ, I lost my lunch and damn near pissed my pants. I never saw
anybody dead before, and those two in that pit . . . Most god-awful mess
I ever encountered—makes me feel nauseous just thinking about it. What
did you say their name was? Fisher?"

"Birds, not fish."

"Huh?"

"Fowler: a hunter of birds rather than fish."

He laughed. "Yeah. Right. Chuck Fowler. That's the name. Imagine
forgetting that. I never thought I'd forget that name, 'cause that's just
what I used to think back then—see?—that there's not a single car me-

chanic on the face of the earth that isn't out stalking some dope of a car owner, and that guy Fowler really used to make me feel like a poor little chicky bird. Funny thing is, I don't remember anything about calling the cops. I know I did 'cause they told me so and they took me to the hospital with the kid. He was beat up pretty bad himself." As Stephanie and I were leaving, he added, "People are weird, know what I mean? The kid, he was a good mechanic. He was the only one I trusted out of the three. Not that I trusted him much. He must have cornered the other two guys or something—planned it out step by step. He wasn't any bigger than me, and those two: they were real bruisers. No way he could a totaled them otherwise."

After we left the car owner, we interviewed the doctor who had seen David at the hospital. Our photocopies of the Springfield Police Department's official record reported that "Subject (David Marion, juvenile) had suffered extensive cuts and abrasions. At Methodist Permanente Hospital, Cecil Bennington, MD, attended and certified Subject able to answer questions." Stephanie found out that Dr. Bennington was still on the staff of the hospital—head of Urology by that time. At first he did not remember the case, but hospital records turn out to be somewhat more reliable than police records; when we arrived for our appointment with him, he had David's brief file on his desk.

"From what you tell me and from my description," he said after scanning the file, "I would be inclined to say that the boy's injuries were consistent with the police report . . . Wait a minute. I do remember this kid. Sure I do. There are some people . . . good-looking boy. He'd plainly been in a bad fight. There were a couple of pretty deep scalp wounds."

"Should he have stayed in overnight?" I asked.

"Hard to tell."

"Why do doctors never say what they mean?"

"Let me put it this way. If this boy had been your son, you would have screamed until we ran extensive tests for concussion and managed to ease the pain he was in. But kids like these: they carry scars you wouldn't believe, and the first time they get the medical care they need is in the morgue." The doctor took in his breath. "Somebody should have seen him again. I told the duty sergeant—what did you say his name was? Wellwood?—to bring him back in a couple of days so we could take out the stitches."

"And?"

"Says here it never happened."

He checked the page again. "Apparently I got my secretary to follow up. I guess I really was intrigued. I have no idea what they told her, except that . . ." He checked the file once more. "What it says here is that he was no longer in the cells. They certainly shouldn't have kept him there. He'd have been transferred to a juvenile facility—and got medical attention soon after he arrived."

But what little photocopied material we had in our possession left no doubt about the matter: David was still in an interview room in the Springfield Police Department on the very day that Dr. Bennington's secretary called.

"Did he seem rational to you?" I asked, thinking of Stephanie's point about the possibility of some kind of momentary insanity.

"I'm not a psychiatrist." The doctor sighed. "I do remember thinking that he needed a priest more than he needed me."

"Because he'd just murdered his foster father and brother?" Stephanie asked.

"Jesus. Is that what he'd done? What the hell, that's got to be it. He was awful young to go around killing anybody. Why would a kid as young as he was do a thing like that?"

So here was another person puzzled by the apparent lack of motive that nagged at me. But more important to the case, the doctor had entered the first substantive questions to our unanswered list: If David was in police custody, why had Sergeant Wellwood not taken him back to the hospital to have the stitches removed? If he was no longer in custody, how could he have confessed in a police interview room? Or, put another way, why had the police told the hospital he was not in their custody when their own report stated that he was? It is true that simple administrative error could explain these discrepancies just as—at a stretch—it could explain the loss of David's records from three separate agencies and two departments in one of them. The police clerk to whom the doctor spoke could have misread the checklist of prisoners in the cells. The doctor's secretary could have called a few days later than David's file said she had.

But add these questions to the missing files and it became impossible for me not to believe that there was some pattern to what had gone on.

16

THE TRIP OUT OF SPRINGFIELD AIRPORT WAS TO BE DAVID'S
very first in an airplane; the timing meant that he was scheduled to
fly on the same sixteen-seater that had brought Stephanie to Springfield, a routine night return to O'Hare Airport in Chicago.

These are *real* planes, these old ones. This is what flight is all
about. Cross a windy, open airfield to a shaky, ladderlike set of
stairs up to a tiny door in a fragile fuselage—no more than tinfoil
picnic plates tacked together like a cereal box trinket—the ceiling
inside so low that a man as tall as David had to half crawl his way
down the aisle to get to his lone seat. No doubling up here, much
less tripling. He was on his own with a private porthole window beside him, the door to the cockpit open and the airfield a sea of black
in front of him. The pilot entered; a steward shut the tiny doors,
one to the outside and one to the cockpit. The propellers clunked
into action: a tremor of movement, a juddering and the taxi began.

To a first-time flyer, even a big plane picking up speed feels as
flimsy as this one looked to David; even in jets, that initial judder
develops into a violent shaking that tosses passengers deep into
their seats. The engine sound rises steadily in pitch as though the
entire structure is preparing to explode. Then comes the extraordinary, gentle intake of breath that is liftoff. It's a kiss of life. Afterward, everything is calm, quiet. A glance out the window shows
that the lit-up airport below has made the abrupt drop into insignifi-
cance that it has always deserved.

It doesn't matter that the movies, television, books have supplied hundreds, even thousands, of previews. A first flight is a magical experience. Nothing touches the reality, especially in an old

propeller plane. Nothing prepares a person for the ecstatic freedom of being airborne. The trembling wings that had worried Stephanie just added one more element of zest to David's excitement as did the splodge of lights down below—all that remained of the town of Springfield. The towns and cities along his flight path were no more than smatterings of light that came and went in a lazy fashion.

Fog closed in before he reached the great metropolis of Chicago; he could make out nothing of it except a luminous glow that gave no hint of its size and power. He should have spent no more than forty-five minutes in O'Hare. The delay in the flight to Washington came in dribs and drabs, first ten minutes, then half an hour, finally stretching into three full hours start to finish, all of it spent at that massive thoroughfare of a place where Hugh had gone blind. No sane human being wants to spend three hours of his life there. David could have seen a little of the city in that time, although he had to admit that he wasn't particularly interested. Not anymore. He had just acquired a liking for towns as seen from the air, where they were as remote and quiet as the sky.

The flight he took out of Chicago to D.C. was a leap of half a century in the development of aviation and much more what the movies promised: pretty stewardess, little bottle of whiskey, plastic-wrapped food—a pale replica of the thrill that comes with a sixteen-seater prop plane: a second flight and David was already a seasoned traveler. His glimpse of the capital told him only that it was another blur in the heavy cloud cover beneath him.

A uniformed chauffeur appeared discreetly at his side as soon as he reached the rotunda of Dulles International Airport.

"Mr. Marion?"

"Yes."

"I will take you to Justice Clark, sir. Your luggage?"

David indicated his briefcase. "You're looking at it."

"May I carry it for you, sir?"

"I think I can manage."

The Supreme Court justice's eccentric visitor—luggageless and dressed in a leather jacket and jeans—followed the chauffeur to a limousine, where the door was opened for him very, very respectfully, every bit as novel an experience as the flight out of Springfield had been.

"You will find food and drink in the cabinet directly in front of you, sir," the chauffeur said, tipping his hat as David climbed in.

The chauffeur kept his eyes on the road as he drove; he said nothing more. The highways and countryside through the car windows could have been Illinois at night, but the first light of dawn was just breaking over the landscape as the limousine drew up to the wall surrounding the justice's house; there was dense forest on the other side of the road. The morning mist let through only glimpses of the property itself. Even so, the scale and the money on show made David uneasy just as Hugh's house, cars, offices always had. He concentrated on what he could see of the security of the place and was impressed.

Despite the alibi that had wholly excused him in Becky's eyes, this was his first view of Samuel's system. It was the first time he'd visited this part of the country for any reason. How could it be otherwise? He'd never been out of the state of Illinois before.

◄◦►

Almost as soon as the police picked David up two weeks ago, he'd sensed that they had nothing solid against him; he knew a local attorney who wasn't afraid of Becky and would have sprung him within hours. Even so, his only telephone call had been to Samuel. The thought of Samuel's intervention in her strong-arm tactics had been too good to miss. Besides, he knew they could only hold him legally for forty-eight hours without a charge—or over the weekend in this case. So he'd waited patiently in his cell for Samuel to return from an incommunicado weekend. And yet who would have expected the man to drop a full-blown alibi at David's feet? especially such an ill-founded one? On the other hand, who in the Springfield Police Department would dare to pry into a tale spun by a Supreme Court justice?

Sex had played a part in all this. One prison mug shot of David and Samuel's untroubled heterosexual life was never going to be the same again. "Oh, my God, look at the way he smolders," he'd said to Hugh. The revelation didn't lead to embarrassing encounters in public toilets or beatings-up in bathhouses; Samuel would never have received the appointment to the Supreme Court if anything like that had gone on. There wasn't even a sudden interest in other men. All that mattered was this one, just David Marion, convicted murderer, but the passion Samuel felt outstripped anything he'd known *could* exist. He couldn't even figure out what it was at first. As soon as he did, he hated it. He hated himself for feeling it and for failing to quash it—he tried with every ounce of his strength to do just that—and all too often he hated David for provoking it in him. Sometimes he fell to his knees and thanked God that David was safely locked away; that way there was no hope of the consummation that tortured him, nor was there any possibility of the inevitable rejection. Besides, he always knew where David was. Always. The moth was stuck through with a pin and could be studied at leisure, indulged in private, like any other specimen in a collection. So Samuel had written to his secret love—unable to keep the entirety of his feelings out of his letters—and waited like a starstruck schoolgirl for the responses.

Anyone who thinks sex is not about power should pay attention to the caste system that ruled the maximum security facility of South Hams prison—and still rules many others like it. The whole population was male; and yet only a small group carried the distinction of being real men, the power figures within the gangs that divide prisons along racial lines. The larger proportion—whether members of gangs or not—were for all practical purposes not men at all. They were women, slaves, objects for pleasure or labor or sale: "galboys," "punks," "bitches." The operative pronoun was "she," and the operative demeanor toward "her" ranged from profound contempt to the indulgent condescension with which David regarded Samuel's sexual predilections. David had been aware of them from the beginning of the correspondence, and he'd used them to his advantage; he knew full well that they were a major reason why Samuel would want to make Becky squirm.

David had been a member of the prison elite. He'd had to fight for position as all the elite did—bitter, violent, bloody contests—and few members of the top echelons in any society ever lose the sense of high caste in their own minds, no matter where they find themselves afterward. Even so, he was on Samuel's turf now, and the rules were different here. As soon as he arrived, a servant took him to an elegant upstairs bedroom that looked out into a sea of fog and promised something spectacular when the sun came out. The bed was one of those French sleighs made of solid mahogany; he'd been prepared to find Samuel in it and was relieved that it was empty. So far, so good. The walls were lined with books, floor to ceiling, over the windows and under them. So were the walls of the bathroom where he showered and shaved. But a good part of the tension in him as he walked downstairs an hour or so later came from not yet knowing which rule book—if any—Samuel was going to follow during the long day they were to spend together.

In warm weather, French doors opened onto extensive lawns and landscaped gardens. On this wintry morning, Samuel was in a solarium off the dining room, a glass domed structure where a plumbago vine bloomed. The pale blue flowers—each small, stellate, delicate, the mass of them vulnerable, overladen, clinging to the far wall for support—brought Helen to mind in her pale blue dress at Hugh's funeral party, raising her glass from across that wide foyer to toast David as her father's murderer. The terra-cotta table in front of Samuel was set for breakfast for two.

"Good morning, David," Samuel said, putting down his newspaper, getting up and reaching out his hand to shake David's. "So we meet at long, long last."

"Yes." David was clipped and cautious.

"I'm so sorry about the circumstances. I truly am—and probably more than you can guess, but it's really such a pleasure for me to have you here. I've waited way too long to thank you in person for your wonderful letters. You did receive copies of the book, didn't you?" David nodded. Just after the title page of *Clark on Prisons* came the dedication: "For David, who knows."

"I'm also sorry about the delay at O'Hare," Samuel went on. "There's nothing more irritating than an unnecessary three-hour wait in an airport. Did you get any sleep at all?"

"Enough." David pulled out a pack of cigarettes and lit one.

"Oh, dear, I really would prefer it if you didn't smoke," Samuel said then. But a member of a prison elite does not give in to the nagging of a galboy; the cigarette stayed where it was. Samuel shook his head in appreciation of what he mistook for meaningless defiance in so tiny a sphere when the stakes were so high. "On the other hand, you know that as far as I'm concerned, you may do anything you like anywhere you like. I owe you too much to insist on conformity. Now, sit down and have something to eat. Coffee? Tea?"

Samuel was a heavy man, not really fat—not yet—but in need of weight-watching and a careful diet. In some men, too much flesh is a virtue, and Samuel was one of them. Newspaper columnists often remarked that he looked more like a judge than anybody who had ever sat on the bench; his white mane of hair, heavy jowls and a jaw almost as square as George Washington's appeared again and again in articles about the Supreme Court. He was the one the photographers always wanted. Living near the original George Washington's Mount Vernon estate—this house on the Potomac was only a few miles downstream—might have seemed to be gilding the lily and yet somehow, for Samuel, it made him all the more the embodiment of the great traditions of the country: every American's image of a fair, thoughtful, equitable man, straight as a die in word and deed.

And in many ways he was precisely that, not only in his public life but in the privacy of his home. Despite his passion for David, he loved the companionship of women, and was well known for it. He was also a well-known family man who remained fond of and loyal to his wife of thirty years even though she bored him; usually he missed her when she went on her annual trek to Mexico. This time he'd missed her only until the call came in from David, and then he'd rejoiced that she had another week yet to run in the artists' colony of Ajijic. Even so, he hadn't expected to spend a sleepless night waiting for David or feel a jolt of adrenaline when he heard the limousine arriving. Nor had he expected his heart to pound and his hands to start trembling when he heard what he knew were David's footsteps on the stairs. He'd had to take eighty milligrams of a beta-blocker just to calm himself enough for breakfast; he'd dreaded this meeting as much as he yearned for it. He'd avoided it for all this time—the entire two-year period that David had been out of prison—for fear of precisely what he was experiencing now. Why wouldn't this inexplicable obsession call a halt to itself? He didn't want it. Nobody wanted it. Clearly David couldn't care less. But here Samuel was, sweating in his chair despite beta-blockers, just because David was sitting opposite him.

"You probably want to know why I dreamed up that tale about your visit to me on the night Hugh died," he said.

"I certainly hadn't expected it."

"Damn Becky anyway. What's the matter with her? twisting policemen's arms to make them hold you until after the funeral? She's probably been aching for your blood since she first laid eyes on you. It was wrong to keep you locked up through Monday. If you were an honest citizen, you'd sue them for it."

"That doesn't tell me why."

"I'm sorry?"

"Why the alibi?"

Samuel shook his head. "They'd have lifted Illinois's moratorium on the death penalty especially for David Marion. Springfield is a vengeful town. I couldn't let them do that—not to you."

The morning's fog cleared for a moment and a pale ray of sunlight fell on the plumbago, one of those unexpectedly scentless varieties despite its lavish appearance. A maid in a black uniform brought orange juice, poached eggs, a basket of pastries, jam. She poured coffee from a silver pot and withdrew; a somewhat uncomfortable silence fell over the table as David and Samuel ate.

"Perhaps you'd better tell me where you really were that night," Samuel said, as he refilled David's coffee cup.

"What night?"

" 'What night?' The night Hugh died. What other night would I want to know about?"

"It was stupid to take a risk like that. I could have been anywhere."

Samuel refilled his own coffee cup. "It was worth it. I enjoyed myself. I really did." He paused. "At least I *hope* it was worth it."

"Nobody saw me."

"Were you at your apartment all night?"

"The Monaghans gave me dinner."

"Did they? Well—God almighty—then *they* saw you. Why didn't you mention this on the phone when I talked to you at the police station? It would have been an awful lot simpler to build a story around them."

"Even the best people get old. They have to struggle to remember which day is which."

"And I bet they'd say whatever you wanted them to say."

"Probably."

"You left them at what? eight? eight-thirty?"

David nodded. "Too early to keep me out of the time frame."

"And then?"

"I ran."

"Where?"

"What difference does it make?"

"Did anybody see you?"

"I doubt it."

Samuel studied the murderer whom he loved more passionately than he'd ever loved anybody in his life and who, in his own mind (and many other people's), was responsible for his seat on the Supreme Court—those letters that had turned *Clark on Prisons* into the stunning indictment that it was—the muscular forearms revealed by sleeves rolled up a couple of folds, the permanently angry eyes, the planes of the face.

"We'd better get to that material you brought, hadn't we?" Samuel said.

The maid took the coffeepot and their cups into Samuel's study. The inside of Samuel's house—the entire building—had something of the quality of Hugh's study, except that there was none of Becky's Japanese delicacy on show, nor any sense that the tabletops would be irrevocably stained if a glass was put down without a coaster. The walls everywhere, like the walls in the bedroom and bathroom allotted to David, were lined floor to ceiling with books. A few abstract paintings in moderate sizes hung here and there over the shelves. Windows looked out toward the Potomac to the east; this morning they showed only the shifting mists that had greeted David. So did the windows to the south, where on clear days there were long views over wetlands of cow clover and buttercups and, a couple of centuries ago, fields of tobacco. Samuel's study faced west; here, heavy velvet drapes framed an interplay of fog and sunlight that revealed glimpses of landscaped gardens. The chairs were leather, deep, sybaritically comfortable. David laid out the papers from his briefcase on a low table between himself and Samuel.

Samuel could contribute little to David's review of Hugh's bank accounts, tax records, investments, but he was interested in Bertie Wannerman's thought that there might have been some kind of financial trouble, especially in terms of Jimmy Zemanski's speedy takeover and his apparent discomfort when questioned about Hugh's enemies.

"I need to know about these shadier sides of business," David said.

"Whose business?"

"Hugh's."

"There was no such side."

"Sure there was. He was a lawyer."

"You've got him all wrong, David." When David only nodded, Samuel sighed and went on, "You mean like that bank account in your name?"

"What about it?" But David had not expected this question. The alibi, yes. That had to be clarified, and he still had no indication of what Samuel was going to demand in return for it. There were some other things too, things yet to be raised. But not *this* question. Hugh had told him about the account more than a year ago, but he hadn't said anything beyond that. He rarely discussed money— probably a leftover from his English education—and David got the impression that nobody else knew about the bequest. He'd just assumed Samuel would find out along with the rest of Hugh's circle, and one of the reasons he'd taken this trip so soon was that he figured he'd better get to Samuel before the will was read and troublesome suspicions roused.

"Probably you are unaware that the account is separate from his formal estate," Samuel said. "All you need is the account number, which I am to give you, and a copy of the death certificate. It's a good, sizable sum. And you're right. Of course you are. Hugh was . . . well, an interesting man, definitely an *interesting* man. Here he was renowned for his absolute probity, and so every once in a while he could toss aside the petty legal restrictions and nobody suspected anything—except you, of course. He liked playing games, even with the IRS. It amused him. He used to get a kick out of not declaring offshore accounts—God knows why—and he couldn't think of anybody he knew who would know what to do with them when he died—again except for you. Always except for you."

The jaw clenched beneath those cheeks, and Samuel's heart turned over in his chest.

"We're going to have to be careful, David. If anybody finds out about this account, it provides a powerful motive. Put that together with an alibi that could slip sideways if a credible witness turns up and a history of . . . a history of murder, two members of a foster family and then . . . Oh, David, why in God's name didn't you stop there?"

David's gaze was steady, unwavering.

◄○►

I did not dare reveal to Stephanie that I knew David was responsible for a death in addition to the two that had resulted in his life sentence.

Partly, I felt I was to some degree at fault; if I had not insisted on transferring him from Marion to South Hams, this third murder would never have happened. Partly I was afraid that knowing about it might dampen her interest in him and cast a pall over our pursuit of his past. She and I had come to feel like children on an Easter egg hunt. We crept off to lunches so we could discuss what we had learned; we held late-night telephone conversations. As our enthusiasm grew, a number of people from Herndon & Freyl joined us. We had a common cause that entertained and excited us all. We were having fun. Besides, the third murder was clearly an isolated event from a good many years back; I did not believe that it affected the overall picture of the man now. I know full well that this excuse can be discredited. But there was another one, far more important to me: I kept quiet because I could not find it in my heart to condemn him this time.

It is probably best if I explain what happened as it was told to me. My informant was frightened that David would kill him too. I think he hoped I might intervene on his behalf, although I have no idea how I could have done such a thing without revealing him as my informant and thereby putting him in precisely the peril he feared.

The key to what he told me is this: In prison you meet your attackers.

When David was about thirteen years old, a couple of foster homes and a group home away from the Monaghans, he was arrested for trafficking. He was tried—a slender child handcuffed throughout the proceedings with no more than a bored court-appointed attorney at his side—and sentenced to six months at the Bootmaker Youth Center. The term was short because evidence was almost nonexistent. I am not claiming that David was innocent. I assume he was not, but young as he was, he was already adept at covering his tracks. What he did not bother to hide was his insolence. Judges like to see docility and remorse, not defiance and anger; David was dispatched, still handcuffed, to serve his time.

The juvenile sector of the penal service is grossly overcrowded and underfunded all over the United States for the simple reason that unwanted children have no political power and without political power, funding stays low. One can only hope that not many institutions sink to the level that made Bootmaker notorious. Certainly food is inadequate and poor in many of them. Quarters tend to be cramped and dirty—even filthy. At Bootmaker, the boys were not just hungry; they were malnourished. Insects and rodents infested the washrooms, the dining hall, the dormitories, even the beds themselves. Violence and drugs were everyday matters. The difficulty with a place like this is that once it starts a downhill slide, it gathers speed because nobody wants to work under conditions like these, especially at the meager salaries on offer. When David arrived at Bootmaker, it was at its nadir. The staff, with the exception of the principal, were people whom no one else would hire, not fast-food chains or slaughterhouses or nursing homes or even other youth centers. Even so, staffing levels were such that no applicant was turned down. Put a scavenging crew like this together with a population of vulnerable, incarcerated young people, and the result is sadly predictable.

We all try to deny it, but the urge to defile is an integral part of the human psyche: the first bite of a gingerbread man, the first ski tracks through virgin snow, the first flag on the moon. I assume the same impulses drive pedophiles. David was a good-looking boy. There still seems to be a strange kind of purity to him; Stephanie says his skin seems to glow with it as though all that anger in him sterilizes his spirit, keeps it clean of the dross that infects the rest of us. At any rate, he had not been in Bootmaker more than an hour before a group of the staff descended on him.

The principal of Bootmaker was a man by the name of Derek Poole, and all the boys feared him. This was not because he was large or strong or imposing; he was none of those things. But he was shrewd, and shrewdness always rules when it is combined with a vicious streak. Also he was an exception to the staffing rule in that he could easily have found himself a job elsewhere; he alone worked at Bootmaker because that was where he wanted to be. Only at an institution like that could he enjoy a steady supply of young boys as well as a group of staff members who shared his interest in them.

Mr. Poole interviewed new boys in his office in the presence of a social worker. When the social worker left, the boy's indoctrination began. First on the agenda was a shower. I know little of the opening attack on David beyond the fact that he was in the shower room when six full-grown men under Mr. Poole's command beat him senseless in the course of getting down to the business that preoccupied them. A considerable number of boys underwent the same initiation; from Mr. Poole's point of view, the virtue of the location was the ease of cleaning up afterward. There was often a good deal of blood. If the victim was lucky the other boys ministered to him; they did so in David's case. But what was different about him was that as soon as he managed to get to his feet, he shook off the others and found his way, half staggering, half running, to Mr. Poole's office on the ground floor of the administration block.

It must have been quite a scene. The office was a sizable room with grilles over the windows, metal filing cabinets, a metal desk. Mr. Poole sat behind it, a bespectacled, schoolmarmish man to look at; two other staff members—and my informant—were with him at the time. In front of him stood a violently abused and badly beaten child, naked, unsteady on his feet, blood still oozing from his nose and ears, too out of breath from his ordeal to speak. And yet this child faced him as wild-eyed as a rabid dog—and apparently as oblivious to consequences.

"A boy who does not knock before entering will be sanctioned," Mr. Poole said, very prim, as though the social worker were still present.

David struggled to find his voice. "I see you outside this shit hole, you're dead."

He was assaulted once more right there and then.

But David's sentence at the Bootmaker Youth Center came to an end, and he was released. Ten years passed before he saw Mr. Poole again. This time it was across the exercise yard of South Hams prison: as my informant had said, in prison you meet your attackers, and men like Mr. Poole tend to be put away sooner or later. Older people almost always look the same to the young no matter how much time goes by, while young people change so rapidly that they are wholly unrecognizable to anyone who has not watched them develop from puberty through to adulthood. David recognized Mr. Poole immediately; Mr. Poole had no idea who David was.

The balance between guards and prisoners at South Hams prison was delicate and carefully orchestrated. It had to be. After all, without the tacit agreement of the prisoners, a prison cannot function. There were parts of the complex that guards did not patrol for days at a time. One of these was the shower block, which gave the act a true poetic justice. Another piece of poetic justice was the bait: two other prisoners brought Mr. Poole there on the pretext that he would find a willing young man waiting for him. They left him alone with David.

David worked in the kitchens, where he had access to knives. Inmates in the machine shop made and sold knives and picks to order. Lengths of pipe were readily available. But in prison, killing with the hands is considered an insult to the victim; Derek Poole was beaten to death—killed with the hands—just as he and his cronies had beaten the boys in their charge. He lay in the shower block for several hours before his body was found.

Prison murders are almost never solved. This one was no exception.

"Suppose the Springfield police found out about Poole," Samuel said to David as they sat across from each other in the book-lined study of his Mount Vernon house. "If I know, other people do. There's always the man who told Hugh about it."

And looking at David, his fear of what he'd done on impulse ten days ago abruptly swamped him; he twisted in the coils of it. He'd never done anything like it before—told outrageous lies to the police to free someone he'd fallen in love with, perverted the course of justice for the sake of a ridiculous, uncontrollable urge. The shame of it was terrible. So were the all-too-possible consequences. The slightest hitch, and his life was over, finished, and yet even in his terror he could not take his eyes off David.

"Nobody can find a shred of anything to tie you to Hugh's murder," Samuel went on, his breathing uneven, his face going hot, then cold, then hot again. "Not a hair. Not a scrap of skin beneath the fingernails. They're desperate. They'll take whatever they can get. If they find the person who told Hugh about Poole, they'll get you for that. Suppose somebody saw you leaving the Monaghans? or saw you running after that? Do I tell the police I only dreamed you were here with me? I do dream about you. I wish I didn't. I wish it with all my heart, and yet dreaming about you is the greatest pleasure I have in life. You know what I don't understand? David, I don't care *what* you did, whether it was to Hugh or anybody else. I can't even bring myself to care *why*. But somehow I've dug a ditch and trapped us both in it, and it is not what I intended—not what I intended at all—whether you killed my closest friend or whether you didn't."

There's a famous old story about a priest who says, "If I didn't believe in God, I'd rape, murder and steal." For the staff at Boot-maker Youth Center—as for the staff at Marion Federal Penitentiary and South Hams State Prison afterward—God was suspended. So was the Law. So was any other moral imperative. It's just the way of the world. But what about the prisoners? For them, injustice on such a scale strips the flesh off the bones—bares the nerves so that a puff of air scalds like boiling oil. No wonder inmates are wolves. No wonder murder is the only solution to any transgression, however large or however small. Two years ago Samuel would have been dead already for this lover's speech of his that revealed weaknesses—as well as dangerous knowledge of David's past—that could easily destroy David as well as himself.

But two years can be a long stretch in a life, and David was a quick learner. Priorities are different in the world outside bars: in polite society, no matter how severe the shock to the system, you get out *before* you kill.

"Oh, don't take it like that," Samuel cried, getting up, scrambling after him out of the study and across the large open hallway, an awkward figure, too portly, too dignified for scrambling. He slipped on the stairs going up the grand flight to the floor above, pulled himself to his feet, followed again. "You'd hardly have come here if you'd killed Hugh yourself. I wish he'd never told me about Poole, but he did. I can't forget that. How could I? You couldn't expect . . . Hugh was closer to me than any human being alive. I miss him desperately, and I'd do anything to have him back. Absolutely anything—except hurt you. It's just that if something goes wrong, I don't know how to handle this. It's not like me to be stupid. I guess I just don't have enough experience of it, and I don't know whether I can shield you from the stupidities I've committed on your behalf. I don't know how to begin to tell you how sorry I am. Clearly you could have managed far better on your own without my meddling. But I *have* meddled—and disastrously. It's done, and now all I want is to protect you from the mess I've created."

Just outside the door to the room where David had spent an early-morning hour after his arrival—where he was heading to collect his few belongings—he turned. The brief moments that it had taken to get here had not been enough to get control over what had to be controlled if he was to achieve what he'd come here to achieve. And yet he had to know what Samuel knew—if anything. He *had* to know.

"The guy who told Hugh about Poole died years ago," he said.

"Did you kill him too?" The question was ripped out of Samuel before he could stop it. "Forget it," he said at once, stumbling over the words as he'd stumbled up the stairs. "How could I say that? Please forget it. It's none of my business."

But the control was slipping again. "Give me a few minutes," David said, pushing past him. The cold outside helped.

Samuel's estate was even larger than it had looked from the front. David paced it off as he ran, calculating it at somewhere between twenty-five and thirty acres although it was difficult to gauge with any accuracy because the bridle paths that crossed it took him in a meandering route through banks of evergreens and brilliantly colored stems in yellow and red, and from there into dark and shaded copses, then out again to open fields—the fog lifting completely for brief, snatched glances of the grandeur of the Potomac River in sunlight. If David was right about the acreage, the high perimeter wall would have to have been in the neighborhood of three-quarters of a mile long. He checked the gates as he passed them and the CCTV system. In half an hour, he returned to the house.

A manservant David hadn't met before showed him to the baronial dining room, where lunch was to be served and where Samuel waited with a glass of wine. He rose, greeted David much as he had that morning, offered him wine, poured it out, all as though the incident that had sent David on his run had never happened. The meal was simple—slices of cold meat and a salad—and throughout it, they discussed Samuel and Hugh's lifelong friendship: the summer vacation when they'd met as little boys splashing in the warm waters of Lake Michigan, the summer vacations afterward that had knitted together the years of letters while Hugh went to school in England, together full-time as law students and roommates at Yale.

They must have made quite a pair in law school, out on the prowl for girls before Samuel had even the faintest inkling that a man could rouse in him feelings that no woman ever had. Back then, his hair had been as dark as his eyes: Welsh ancestors, maybe, or maybe one of those Irish families with Spanish or Jewish blood. Clark is a name that could have come from anywhere and meant anything. Because the green-eyed Hugh had been nearly blond in those days, their classmates had dubbed them "the best of dark and light"; there's nothing to beat the assurance that comes with old families and old money.

It was two o'clock before David and Samuel went back to the study and the pile of papers from David's briefcase. They quickly reviewed the three decades during which Hugh's law practice grew and Samuel made his way toward the Supreme Court. Then they went on to Hugh's current cases. They were as thorough as the time constraints allowed—but found nothing that either of them could make out as suspicious enough to call for further investigation. David was just closing the last of his notebooks when the morning's housemaid in black appeared, this time with a tray of Scotch, an elegant siphon in silver-mesh cladding, a bucket of ice, glasses. She set the tray on Samuel's desk, drew the heavy drapes over the windows—it was dark outside by now—and lit the logs in the fireplace.

"I'm afraid I haven't been much help," Samuel said, getting up to make the drinks. "Scotch?"

David nodded. "You never really answered my question about Hugh and bending the rules."

"Didn't I?"

"It's the kind of thing that makes enemies."

"Greedy friends too."

"Like me, you mean."

Samuel laughed. "No, I didn't mean that. Not this time, but the Freyls can always bring pressure to bear when it counts, David. You know that." Samuel wasn't thinking of David's enforced long weekend in the police cells before Hugh's funeral but of the difficult years that had led to the release from South Hams prison; Samuel and Hugh had been in constant contact toward the end of that time, and there had been a number of maneuvers that would hardly qualify as kosher. He tried to imagine how Hugh would have wanted him to react to David's probing—and could not. He handed David a Scotch on the rocks and sat down opposite him.

"What about Hugh's women?" he said by way of diversion. "There are always jealous husbands lurking in the wings."

"Too long ago."

Samuel laughed. "No, David. *Not* long ago. There were women all over him after he went blind." Samuel laughed again at the query on David's face. "I have to admit I was curious too. I never understood it myself, but whatever it was about those green eyes of his was more so *after* he lost his sight than before. And whatever it was, it had always gone well with that precise mind and courtly manner—a little at odds with it: an unresolved conflict between the legal mind and the man's body and what seemed to be a bemused pleasure in the conflict it provoked in himself. Very appealing. Even so, a blind man is a blind man. No amount of political correctness is going to change that. I met a couple of his lovers, and I couldn't resist asking.

" 'So what's a blind man got that interests a beautiful girl like you?' I said to one of them. This one *was* beautiful too—I wasn't just flattering her—and smart as they come.

"She thought a moment, then she said, 'Nobody would argue that *looking* is what sex is really about. So think how the blind explore their world—and then think of your body as *being* that world. Then there's the relief of not having some guy obsessed with my face and the way I walk. I don't mean to say I don't get a kick out of being told I'm sensational. I like it. I like it a lot. But—oh, dear—I'll take being touched the way Hugh touches me over being ogled any day of the week.' She turned a dazzling smile on me. 'I'm a convert. If he dumps me, I'm going to set out at once and find myself another blind man.' "

Samuel got up, poked the fire into flames, sat down again. "How many women were there after Stephanie left?" David asked.

"Do you know, I think it's entirely possible that he turned them all away. At least he never mentioned anybody. How could she have done that to him? I met her several times, and she didn't seem like that kind of a person. It tore him to pieces."

"What about the three or four years he was with her?"

"I got the impression that other women ceased to interest him."

"So we're talking maybe five, maybe six years."

Samuel nodded. "Something in that region."

"Too long ago," David said as he'd said before.

"What is it with you and the past? People carry grudges, you know. Things hang on. Old loves. Old jealousies. Childhood rivalries."

David stared at Samuel, then shifted his gaze to the fire. The fireplace was imposing, marble, in scale with the house. The wood was dry, the logs big. Flames snaked up the back of the hearth and threw out warmth across this large room. Not long after David's conviction, a couple of Marion inmates had doused a guy from a rival gang in gas and set him alight: that was the only time David had seen a fire burn as fiercely. He looked back at Samuel, shook his head.

"The past is a waste of time," he said.

David's flight back to Chicago was due to leave at midnight. After dinner in the baronial dining room, he and Samuel sat together as before in front of the log fire in the study, Samuel with a brandy, David with a beer. The lighting was as soft and luxurious as the chairs they sat in. Mozart's *Dissonance* played in the background. David wasn't sure whether the music gave him pleasure or pain, but he realized that he was holding himself rigid against it.

"Turn that thing off," he said.

Samuel went over to the bank of knobs that controlled the sound system, and the room was absolutely quiet for a moment— not even a crackle from the fire. With his back still turned to David, he said, "The idea of employing you to look over the security system here wasn't off the cuff, you know. I'd been thinking about it for some time."

"You don't need me for that."

"You're the best in the business. Hugh told me so."

"What you've got here looks more than sufficient."

Samuel sat down again. He swirled the brandy in his snifter but set the glass back on the table without taking a sip. "Why didn't you confirm for Becky that you'd been here on the night Hugh died? It wouldn't have hurt for her to hear it from you."

"It wouldn't have helped."

"I think maybe somebody—" Samuel broke off, shook his head. "I don't know how to say this." David waited. "Everybody knew how close Hugh and I were. Everybody." He stared down into his brandy, moved the snifter a little to the left on the table beside him, then a little to the right. "But why Vivian? Why *her*? What am I supposed to do without Vivian?"

David stared into the fire. "Vivian," he said. It wasn't a question.

"The name means 'full of life.' Did you know that? It used to give me pleasure to think she would inherit my money when I died."

17

I KEPT SAMUEL INFORMED OF THE INVESTIGATION STEPH-
anie and I were conducting into David's past, just as he kept me informed of
his progress with *Clark on Prisons*. During one of our conversations, he asked
me what I thought of sending his daughter, Vivian, to interview David on
videotape. Yale University Press planned publication in October, less than a
year away; Samuel's editor had gently broached the idea that the book just
might create a buzz even in Washington if he could add a touch of what they
referred to as "personal interest." What they meant—as Samuel and I agreed—
was the injection of a little sex that would appeal to a wider audience than
the legal ramifications of male-on-male rape and prostitution.

A nice girl's view of a dangerous man behind bars would fit the bill
perfectly. We both thought the idea had a charm—as well as a black
humor—that was all its own: a modern twist on the ancient fairy tale of
beauty and the beast. Vivian was very pretty.

At the time, she was working for her doctorate in anthropology at
Washington University in St. Louis. People fascinated her: how and why
they worked together, what happened to them under given circumstances,
how they came to believe this or that. She was two years younger than
Helen—they had played together as children much as Samuel and I had—
and she was a good scholar if one of a different turn of mind. Helen was a
straight-A student; once physics caught her interest, all the others seemed
to follow naturally. Vivian couldn't be bothered with anything that was not
alive and breathing. Mathematics did not interest her unless it touched on
the movement of populations. Physics did not interest her beyond its forays
into genetics. But biology, sociology, psychiatry: she excelled in them all. As
an anthropologist, her particular interest lay in the development and functioning of isolated societies, which is to say that she was superbly qualified

for the job of interviewing David in the cut-off hothouse of a prison. Samuel and I also agreed that as well as enlivening an all-male text, she just might provoke David to an interest in what Stephanie and I were doing on his behalf. I was coming to find his indifference to our efforts as irritating as his early indifference to my lessons in literacy.

Springfield is a short two-hour drive from St. Louis; Vivian's studies at Washington University meant that she often came to Sunday lunch at our house; she certainly livened up those occasions, especially since Helen was at Columbia then. Vivian was enchanted by the idea of studying South Hams State Prison. She prepared for it carefully; she read a full-scale history of the prison as well as numerous formidable texts on the U.S. penal system, but Samuel decided against giving her his manuscript for fear that it might taint her reactions. The Sunday after her meeting with David, she came to lunch. It was early winter, and over Lillian's roasted chicken, Vivian described—with great excitement—how the visit had gone: the high prison walls, the elaborate entry procedures, the contempt of guards for visitors as well as inmates, the barrenness of the place, the ingrained filth, the ceaseless racket of voices—shouting, laughing, cursing, even crying—and the never-ending clank, slam, rattle of metal doors that jars the nerves every time, the smells of sweat, Lysol, cheap food, sewage and unwashed bodies, the ugliness of everything—as though deprivation of beauty was an integral part of the punishment being meted out—and the sheer nastiness of a system that separates people by panes of dirty glass and makes them talk to each other through low-quality microphones that cut off syllables and make voices sound tinny.

"Nothing in those books prepared me for it," she said. "Nothing."

"You and Samuel should be ashamed of yourselves, Hugh," my mother said, ringing the bell for Lillian to take away our plates. "Sending a young girl like Vivian into a place like that to see a man like that. What could he have thought of her? Suppose you do get him released, which I sincerely hope you do not, he's going to make assumptions that might put her in danger."

"You know, now you come to mention it, that's one of the oddities," Vivian said, and she did sound puzzled. "I'm usually quite good at what guys think of me, but this one overreacted to practically everything. Sudden noises seemed to jolt him. Even unexpected shifts in conversation seemed to cause some kind of visceral response. I couldn't tell if any of it had to do with me or what I was asking or—I don't know—with anything at all that was going on at the time."

"He's a savage," my mother said. "You can't expect him to respond like a normal person."

"I really don't think that's it." Vivian had always defended her opinions; it is one of the reasons my mother was so fond of her. "He seemed to be in some kind of hyperalert state that was independent of me or anything else."

"He is not long out of solitary," I said, "and the reactions you describe are the usual ones, especially if there has been some form of drug treatment. From your description I would guess that they had him on antipsychotics."

"Oh, God, don't tell me he's crazy. It would break my heart."

I shook my head. "The use of antipsychotics is common at South Hams whether or not prisoners actually need them."

"I don't believe that, Hugh. Not for a minute."

"Really? Why not?"

"Prisons are full of unbalanced people. You've read the studies yourself. People like that are going to need medication to function on even a minimal level. It's natural for them to complain, but that doesn't mean they don't need to be treated."

"Let's forget the mentally ill—"

"But that's the whole point, isn't it?"

"—for a second. What do you expect to happen when you put perfectly normal people in a cage? Just think about it. Only the meek are going to acquiesce without a struggle. The rest are going to be angry, and the strongest are likely to turn violent and rebellious. It's just the human spirit—and a prison's duty is to break it. Chemicals are very effective."

She thought a moment. "No, no. It won't work. There are psychiatric evaluations, regular state checks. The material is very well documented."

"Psychiatrists sign prescriptions without examining patients. This is pretty well documented too. State investigators are poorly paid and understaffed, turnover is high, all of which makes abuses easy to hide. As for prison wardens who supply university sociologists with information, they are no more likely to give details of chemical punishments than a modern dictator is likely to discuss torture chambers beneath his palace. But I can certainly tell you one thing: a person's recovery after such treatment can be very hard on the body, and looking at you would be a shock to the system even if he had been in an ordinary state."

"No, I really can't . . ." She paused, thought again. "How sure are you?"

"I doubt you could get access to South Hams's medical records, and I doubt they would reveal much if you did. But now that you have seen the situation for yourself, I am certain your father will want you to read what he has to say. You might also try reading some of the essays prisoners themselves write."

"Daddy agrees with you about this?"

"It forms a major part of his argument."

Perhaps Vivian's greatest asset as a scholar was her ability to take in alternative views. "He should have told me what he thought. You should have told me, Hugh. If you're right—"

"I am," I said.

"—it's got to be stopped."

"Your father's book is likely to have a very considerable impact."

"A book! Who pays attention to books?"

"What else do you suggest?"

"You know what I think?" she said then. "I think you should draft Daddy into your plan to get David out of there. I don't know how much I believe about the rest of what you say, but he's not the boy who killed those people, not anymore. He shouldn't be in that place at all. I didn't really understand what a remarkable thing you'd achieved until I saw him, but he's . . . I mean, it's incredible. It's a true metamorphosis. You took an out-of-control loser and transformed him into somebody who could really contribute to society. All you have to do is hear him talk. I don't know how in hell you did it, but we'll all be the poorer if we don't get him out."

"Vivian, my dear, those are my thoughts precisely."

"I want to help too. What can I do? I'll do everything I can."

"So you were impressed?"

"He's so very, very intense, isn't he? I mean, even aside from solitary and whatnot?"

"He frightened you," I said, responding more to her voice than her words.

She laughed. "That was the best part of it."

◄◦►

David could usually recall conversations almost word for word, and yet he remembered not a single exchange of that interview with Vivian. He had no idea what she'd said or what he might have said in response. All he'd wanted to do—all he'd been able to do—was look: dark eyes that caught the dull prison light and turned it into sunshine glancing off water, dark hair, heart-shaped face, dimple in the chin, a smile in the voice and a body somehow both fresh and luxuriant beneath a severe navy blue suit. She'd dressed like that in deference to the prudery that respectable people adopt when they're near convicts, but she belonged in red. He saw her in red. He remembered her in red, even though he knew it was wrong.

She'd come on Friday; on Saturday, she wrote him. His hands trembled as he opened the envelope and unfolded the sheet of paper. "Dear Mr. Marion, I want to thank you for so kindly agreeing to talk to me . . ." It ended, "Yours sincerely, Vivian Clark." A very formal note, the kind of thing she might have written to an old schoolteacher after morning coffee in a church hall: he pored over its every word, its every punctuation mark. It did not call for a reply.

Almost all prisoners file for appeal soon after sentencing unless they'd pleaded guilty, as David had. And yet he had grounds for appeal. He'd known that right from the beginning—but he'd made no move. He'd refused to explain why to the few people who asked—Hugh, the prison committees that helped prepare appeals, the occasional inmate—because in his own mind, prison was where he belonged. There was wild confusion around the area of his thoughts that guarded this strange commitment to dying behind bars—and guarded it fiercely—but he had stuck by it, paying as little attention to Hugh and Stephanie's efforts as he had to anyone else. All that changed as soon as Vivian's letter arrived. He knew there were still legal mechanisms open to him; Hugh had told him so, but at best the law is grindingly slow. He had no time. He began at once and feverishly to fill in the details for a plan of escape that he'd worked on until now as just one more of the puzzles he'd used to distract himself in solitary. Years ago he'd memorized prison blueprints stolen by an inmate who rented them out for the equivalent of six months' prison pay. He knew the air duct system and how it connected to the sink and stool in his cell; he could plot it out in his mind step by step. He knew how to carry out what's called a maintenance chase—work on the plumbing—that would take him up through the roof and then out on the security wall. And yet Vivian

so obsessed him that he couldn't bring his mind to focus on the crucial details of timing or the precise route across to the outer fence
and down to the parking lot below where cars waited just begging
to be hot-wired.

◄○►

There was an unexpected tension in David when I saw him not long after
Vivian's visit. It was as though his mind was off to one side of whatever
subject we were talking about; nothing I could do seemed to bring him
back into focus.

As I was about to leave him, he said, "That confession."

I stopped packing away my books. "Yes?"

"I really can't tell you whether I said anything or not."

I knew how difficult it was for David to ask for help; the ground was
very delicate. "Did you have something along the lines of a blackout?" I
asked.

There was an uncomfortable pause. "You might call it that."

"What would you call it?"

He got up from the chair he sat in and began to pace the room. "I
think the cop who questioned me wrote it—signed it too."

"Which one?"

"One of the ones that came later."

"How many were there?"

"Three, maybe four."

"And you think one of them just made it up?"

"Like I keep saying, I don't know."

"But that is what you think?"

"Yes."

"Why did you not appeal your sentence, David?" I burst out. "What
could have been in your mind?"

"That's not your business."

"If it is not mine, whose is it?"

"Mine." His pacing picked up speed. "I was fifteen years old. Isn't that
enough?"

"No."

"What do you think guys like that do to kids like me?"

"I want to hear it from you."

"Why?"

"Were you coerced? Is that it?" I could almost feel him give me one of those angry glances of his, but he said nothing. "What has changed your mind to tell me even this much?" I said in exasperation. There was no response. "David?"

The pacing stopped, and he took in a breath that seemed to sear his lungs. "I want out," he said, and then rushed on. "You said once you'd represent me. Or you implied you might if I asked. Will you?"

I began packing my books again. "Of course I will." So Samuel and I had been right to send Vivian to see him. She had clearly given him some sense of what he was missing. There was no other explanation. "Since talking about it seems to be so difficult for you, I suggest that you prepare something on paper for me. Write it as though it were a memoir not of your own experiences but of the experiences of someone you once knew. If you were coerced we will need evidence to prove it: names, detail."

He gave a derisive snort. "Who's going to believe it?"

"I am."

"Yeah. Sure you will."

"Oh, David, you do not make it easy for me, do you. Whether I believe you or not is immaterial. If I can see a way to make a case for you—any way at all—I will do everything in my power to free you. I promise you that."

David tried to concentrate on a brief for Hugh, but he could not. All he could think of was Vivian. Even though her letter had called for no answer, he spent every waking hour composing one in his head, draft after draft. Nothing satisfied him. In desperation, he dashed off a note asking her if she might consider corresponding with him. He had no way of knowing it, of course, but by this time Vivian had become an ally. She replied at once and much less formally. She told him she'd thought a lot about her half hour with him, and she asked—he had to read the sentence half a dozen times before his brain would agree that his eyes had recorded the message correctly—if she could come to see him again.

A week later, and she sat opposite him beyond that glass barrier.

"Hugh tells me you've decided to help in getting out of here," she said. She wore beige and tan this time, muted still but lighter than the severe navy of before.

"Are you here as his errand boy?"

She hesitated. "Does it matter?"

"It might."

"I guess . . . You kind of catch me off guard, Mr. Marion. I guess I'm—"

"David."

"—I'm not quite sure why I've come, except that I want to help."

"Why?"

"Because I sincerely believe that you don't belong in a place like—"

"I'll do anything you ask."

"Then we *can* get you out," she said delightedly. "I *know* we can. One way or another. But you must promise me—"

"Anything."

"Obey the rules religiously. Keep a low profile. Stay out of trouble. Can you promise me that?"

He'd have cut off his fingers knuckle by knuckle if he thought it might please her. Even so, he said, "Only if you promise to visit me regularly."

"It's a deal."

"And write to me."

"Will you write back?"

"That's a stupid question."

Vivian put her hand against the glass barrier. David frowned in puzzlement. The only physical relationship David had had with anybody in all the prison years was violence. South Hams didn't allow football or any other contact sport. When she didn't take her hand away, he slowly raised his and matched it to hers, thumb to thumb, then finger to finger, the first gentle touch in all that time— and separated by a barrier of glass.

As he left the visiting area, dazed, aglow, heart racing, he passed a maintenance crew carrying toolboxes; he took no notice of them. But an hour is a very long time in a prison, plenty long enough for prison walls to turn from a way of life into the ancient torture of pressing that crushed its victim under a pile of stones. That's when he saw a straggler from the crew, bending over to tie a shoelace. Before he gave it a single thought, he'd waylaid the straggler, knocked him out, exchanged clothes, picked up the toolbox and walked across the yard wearing cowboy hat and sunglasses as though the place belonged to him. He went straight up to the picket officer at the back gate tower and said his job was to install video surveillance equipment; he seemed so sure of himself that the picket officer let him pass. Sometimes only the rashest of plans will work. Once inside that back gate office, he'd have been able to control the perimeter gates. But it was not to be. The rest of the maintenance crew realized what had happened before he'd even got close.

He was sentenced on the spot to an indeterminate period in what turned out to be the total blackness of South Hams's now-infamous hole, communication privileges of any kind withdrawn along with all daylight. Which is to say that this madman's attempt to see Vivian resulted only in his not seeing her or anything else for the rest of the time he spent in prison—except in his imagination, which she never left. He knew nothing whatever of the developments in the effort to free him. But seven months later he was out of South Hams as well as the hole, both at the same time, and only ten days after that—his eyes still so sensitive to daylight that even inside the house he had to wear dark glasses—he heard a light tap at the door to his east side-apartment. And there she was. Or so it seemed.

The first few steps into the world outside after a lifetime of prison walls are a bewildering experience. Stone walls create a half-life where every emotion except rage and fear is lost in a gray mist and the range of every sense is reduced to an aimless damnation like Sisyphus rolling his rock up the mountainside. Food tastes of nothing, smells are sweat, excrement, boiled cabbage, Lysol. Textures are coarse; everything visible is ugly; the only green and growing things are mold and weeds. Once outside, ordinary objects overwhelmed David. Trees along a street, cars, groups of shoppers, kids on skateboards bombarded him like mortar fire on a battlefield. The simplest, most everyday sights were surreal, as though he'd stepped into Salvador Dalí's world of melting wristwatches lit up by blasts of psychedelic color and sound from some cosmic disco through which occasional voices slipped and slid like God or the devil whispering into the ear of a schizophrenic.

And in the midst of all this stood Vivian. Much more likely she was a hallucination. He shut his stinging eyes. He pressed his hands against them, but when he opened them, she was still there, and he was mute, speechless, frozen to the spot before the reality he had dreamed of so often.

She smiled at him. "I suggest we begin with the introduction," she said, just as Hugh had said of the *American System of Criminal Justice* by the great jurist Cole.

"Begin?" he said stupidly.

She stepped across the threshold and closed the door behind her. Keeping her eyes on his—or on what she could see of them behind the dark glasses—she raised her hand, palm forward, just as she'd raised it against the glass barrier in prison at the end of that second visit, just as she'd raised it again and again in his dreams of her during the months that followed. He raised his hand too and matched it to hers—no barrier of any kind between them now—thumb to thumb, finger to finger, flesh to flesh.

Among other things, anthropologists study sex and sexual practices all over the world; a convict who has lived only among men for eighteen years is just a man from an alien culture in a domestic bed. Vivian was eager and patient at the same time. She was a good teacher, thoughtful, imaginative, forgiving. David? There are intensities and intensities in a life, more of them in his than in most, but he'd never experienced anything approaching this.

And yet it was in the weeks and months afterward that the real war inside him began. Resistance is a disease of the mind. Just as Hugh had told Vivian, prisoners like David—rebellious, violent prisoners—were chemically restrained at South Hams; chemical restraint had been heavy during that last stay in the hole, when the unfamiliar passion for escape from the blackness of his filthy underground bunker had reeled out of control again and again, something that rarely happened before. The diagnosis was irrelevant: paranoid schizophrenia, acute confusional state, whatever. Treatment was neuroleptics: Haloperidol, various phenothiazines and thioxanthenes. Dosages were high. There are official-sounding, medical words for the effects: toxic psychosis, torticollis, dyskinesia, oculogyric crisis. The reality they hide is well beyond the imagination of the most avid watcher of televised bloodlust. Prison guards attack with truncheons, but they attack from outside a man's body. These drugs are guerrilla terrorists; they attack from the inside. Delirium, seizures, hallucinations, night horrors, bizarre visions are only part of it. Agonizing muscle spasms arch the body into a backward bridge. Uncontrollable trembling and involuntary jerking make an Olympic feat of buttoning a shirt. The eyes glaze and roll upward. There's so much pain, it's impossible to tell where it starts.

To stay sane in prison, an inmate has to keep a good, clear distance from himself at all times; these drugs strip him of the ability to keep any distance at all. They drive him into the very depths of himself. They suffocate him in his own entrails, where no healthy man ventures without extreme peril.

Vivian fell in love with this strange being from another culture, and she reveled in it as lovers do, in the fizz of life and the enchantment of a world that has only two people in it. But David had no idea what was happening to him. It wasn't just that he knew only enough of the warmth that most of us take for granted—of the generosity of spirit we expect as a part of our daily lives—to distrust it. Above everything he feared loss of control, and he couldn't control his reaction to her at all. The turmoil she provoked in him brought to mind only those ferocious antipsychotic attacks. When he managed to tear his attention away from her—which wasn't often—other women were a glorious relief. If they became more than that, he just walked away. That's what a free man does, isn't it? walks away? In some way that he could not fathom, Vivian had managed to put him right back behind bars—and on heavy chemical restraint at that.

He wrestled with the emotions that invaded him the way Jacob fought with the angel. And just like Jacob, he lost. For his entire life, his only approach to something he could not control had been to strain every fiber of his being to crush it. He knew no other way.

◄o►

"The verdict was a hit and run," David said to Samuel as they sat around the fire in Samuel's study, David with his beer, Samuel swirling his snifter of brandy.

"Do you believe that?" Samuel said, not looking at him.

"I see no reason not to."

"I'm so sorry that the two of you never became friends," Samuel said.

David and Vivian had kept their relationship secret from every-body except Tony, who could hardly escape knowing since he and David used David's apartment as an office. David's reason for se-crecy was every long-term convict's reason: never tell anybody any-thing. Vivian's had been fear of upsetting her father, whose love of David had become as painfully obvious to her as her own; she was, after all, a professionally acute observer of human nature. Samuel didn't even know that they had met each other after David got out of prison. His impression was that David had not really liked her very much; if she went to Sunday lunch at the Freyls, David did not. She had not dared let anyone see them together, certainly not Becky.

She'd died in the early hours of the morning on a litter-strewn sidewalk around the corner from one of those all-night liquor stores cocooned in metal mesh only a short distance from David's apart-ment: across the street, down a block and around the corner—the way David had usually returned from his midnight runs. These days he ran back from the opposite direction, the same way he set out; he went out to the supermarket for beer and cigarettes. There'd been a light drizzle the night she died, and she'd always feared dying on the street in the rain. At least it had been quick. Even so, the police hadn't been called until daybreak. Maybe nobody realized that she was dead until then, rather than just another homeless drunk bundled up in dirty clothes. Maybe nobody cared. Maybe no-body even noticed. But it was almost nine o'clock before the police got there following their usual roundabout route to the east side in the hopes that the incident would disappear altogether before they arrived on the scene. Homicide detectives carry a backlog of cases—half a dozen to a dozen of them—and yet another case brings every single one of them to breaking point. Much simpler to dismiss Vi-vian's death as a hit and run. Which it looked pretty much like any-how. Driving did get crazy on the east side: street gangs, drunks, dope heads. They figured the car would turn up sooner or later.

Samuel employed his own detectives at once, but what chance

did they have? As a matter of principle—with a long and venerable history behind it—people in that part of Springfield wouldn't talk to *any* detectives, not even police detectives with warrants; private ones might as well forget it before they start. Exhaustive efforts turned up not a single witness. Forensic evidence was too compromised to be useful; by the time the Springfield police had arrived on the scene, Vivian had been stripped of everything salable— watch, jewelry, purse, shoes. Samuel's detectives did manage to locate the car in a car graveyard, but they might as well not have bothered. It was an ancient Chrysler stolen from a cheap rent-a-car agency several days after the last legitimate customer had brought it back. Nobody had cleaned it in years. It stank of rotgut and vomit. Steering wheel, seats, floor were so covered with prints, fibers, hairs, bodily fluids of all varieties and from so many sources that there was no hope of determining which—if any of them—belonged to the thief.

"She would never have gone out to the east side on her own," Samuel said to David in desperation. "Never. Somebody lured her there. I know it. What *else* could she have been doing? Studying the primates of Springfield in their native habitat? At two in the morning? No, no. There was a new guy in her life. Her friends told me so, but I knew it anyway. She had a glow on her. Why wouldn't she tell me about him?" David only shook his head. "Whoever it was, she didn't tell her friends either. Maybe she didn't think we'd approve."

"She could have been right about that."

"He lived on the east side. I'm certain of it. It's the only reason she would have gone there. The *only* one. I think she must have tried to tie him down. Silly girl. She was pregnant, did Hugh tell you? She'd found out about it that very day."

David hadn't known about the baby, but he knew perfectly well that Vivian had been on her way to his apartment when she died. Even so, not a flicker crossed his face. He never bothered to hide anger; he knew its power too well. But the harsh lessons of his childhood included not only silence in the face of authority; just as important was that a show of pain—however severe the wound—is a show of weakness, and weakness only provokes further attack. Fortunately, news like this doesn't come often. The technique is the same simple one that kept him from striking out at Samuel earlier in the day—why are the simplest things the hardest to perfect?—hold absolutely still until the last tremor of the quake dies away.

He kept his eyes on Samuel's. "What are you trying to tell me?" he said.

"You *think* you know something. I don't mean *you*," Samuel hastened to add. "I mean me. You think you understand, well, not much, but *some*thing. And it turns out you don't understand anything at all. My grandfather's best friend was a Kosher slaughterer. A *sochet*: that's what they're called—the men who kill the big animals, steers, sheep. Did I ever write you about him? Butchery is a sacred art. It calls for a sacred knife called a *chalaf*. I never saw one, but it must be a hell of a brute: a full eighteen inches long. There's no point on it because the blade is what has to do the work, and it has to be perfect—razor sharp, not the tiniest flaw or nick—because a single stroke must take it straight through the trachea and the esophagus to the jugular. The Torah says, 'You shall not eat any blood, whether it be fowl or beast,' and if death is slow, the blood is harder to drain afterward. The butcher hangs the carcass up to bleed, strips the arteries where any blood might pool, soaks the meat and salts it to get out every last drop."

Samuel ran a hand over his eyes. Unlike David, he'd never learned how to hide pain, especially when it was like this. "First Vivian, then Hugh. Blood is what gives meat its flavor and moisture. That's what makes it *meat*. Take away what a man loves and you take away whatever it is that makes him the person he is. You take away his will to live. The butcher—the *sochet*—used to refer to the process as a 'bleedout.' "

"A bleedout, huh?"

"People do the strangest things to appease their gods."

"Pity the Lord if all it takes to impress Him is tasteless beef."

The fire crackled in the hearth. Samuel ran his hand over his eyes again. "Maybe I'm nuts. Maybe I'm cracking under the pressures of this job. People do. Sometimes I think that's all it is . . . and yet, I can't escape the idea that someone could easily be trying to . . . I don't know who. I have too many enemies. I get death threats practically every day. It comes with the territory. But *this*? I'm frightened, David. I couldn't bear it if something happened to you." David had no idea how to respond to such a comment. He was a man whom people were afraid *of;* with the exception of the Monaghans, he'd never known of anybody who was afraid *for* him. "A year ago," Samuel went on, "there were three people in this world I loved: Hugh, Vivian and you. Two of them are dead. You're the only one left."

They sat in silence, and the minutes ticked by until it was time for David to leave for Dulles Airport.

"Will you be careful?" Samuel said then.

"Nobody's coming after me."

"David, there's always somebody. If I've learned nothing else from this job, I've learned that there are vipers in every nest." David shrugged. "Are you packed?"

"Yes."

"The chauffeur should be waiting for you."

They walked outside together. The night was as clouded over as the night before when David had arrived. The chauffeur opened the door to the limousine as they approached. David half got into the car, then turned back and held out his hand. He wasn't even sure why he made the gesture. Samuel shook his hand, then retained it in both of his.

"Just promise me you'll watch your back, David," he said.

18

I CAN'T REMEMBER WHY I MENTIONED JIMMY'S FINGER-
print expert to Stephanie—it had really seemed to me to be of no particular relevance—but she was full of enthusiasm at once.

"Suppose the fingerprint isn't David's. Wouldn't it be wonderful if it
wasn't?"

"I do not think it would make any difference."

But she was not listening. "Maybe that's why they dumped it so un-
ceremoniously into the box. Put that together with files that walk off by
themselves and get lost . . . This whole thing stinks, Hugh. I bet it's just
some cop's print."

"David's escape attempt has not helped at all."

I have to admit that I did not know the extent of David's punishment
until much later. Prison authorities informed me that his attempt had resulted in the equivalent of a lockdown without communication privileges
for an indeterminate period: "no human contact" is the phrase. I knew
nothing of total darkness for months on end. If I had, I would have filed a
habeas petition at once alleging a violation of the Eighth Amendment
that should have protected him from such cruel and unusual punishment.
South Hams is an old prison, remote from cities and the media, custom
built a century ago when light deprivation was fairly common; the facility
had been turned into a punishment chamber for the most intractable
cases: a sterile white box with canned air, electronic voices and twenty-
four-hour fluorescent light. This is easily enough to drive a person out of
his wits, and way too many of today's prisoners end up insane in precisely
these conditions. When it came to David, the prison staff locked him inside the chamber and flipped off the power supply so that he spent the
entirety of his final months in total darkness. The state was as unaware of

his treatment as I was until I exposed it when I found out about it in the course of David's release. But even now, even though I know it was true, I find it impossible to believe that such tortures could have persisted into this day and age. Punishment by dark cell confinement in an American prison: it simply never occurred to me.

"Oh, damn the man," Stephanie said with something akin to a moan, "why couldn't he keep his promise to Vivian and be a good boy? Why couldn't he have done that?"

I shook my head. "If only he had written a statement for me before that absurd attempt at escape, we might have something to work with. As it is, we have nothing more than that the last time I saw him he implied he had been coerced."

"What about not getting checked over again? you know, by that doctor who said he was pretty beat up? That's got to indicate something, doesn't it? Isn't that neglect? The cops didn't follow medical advice. Sounds like neglect to me."

"He could easily have been checked at some other hospital. We have nothing to indicate he was not."

"Goddamnit. I don't know what or how, but I am going to find a solid piece of evidence in his favor. I swear it. Somehow or other we've got to get him out of that place."

A few weeks later she came running into my office.

"Remember that print of David's?" She was bubbling over. "The one we sent off? To the lab in Chicago?"

"Stephanie Willis, I did not send any print to anybody."

"I know. I know. But you don't mind, do you? You couldn't mind. Especially since . . . I've been reading up on prints. Okay, so there are only the three types, but it's so easy to mix them up. Lots of them can look like they have whorls in them until you get enough markers to differentiate—"

"Stephanie!"

"Oh, Lord, I do wish you could see this. David's prints are a mishmash of patterns like everybody else, but here's the thing: his whorls are two double loops and an accidental. Remember?" There are three basic types of fingerprint patterns: arches, loops and whorls. Each breaks down into subcategories. A whorl can be a plain whorl, a central pocket loop, a double pocket loop or an accidental. "I must have seen a dozen sets of David's prints by now," she went on. "And the one that's come back from the lab: it's still pretty messy . . . Hugh, you can see a plain whorl in it now—as clear as day. If it's got a plain whorl in it, there's no way anybody could claim it's a double loop or an accidental. Maybe we'll never know whose that print is, but it couldn't possibly be David's."

"Maybe you are right. Maybe it does belong to one of the policemen who arrested him."

"Could we prove it?"

"Probably not—not enough markers."

"I'm so pleased with myself I can hardly bear it. I deserve a medal, don't I?"

I could not help laughing. "You deserve everything there is on offer."

"Is it enough, Hugh?"

"For what?"

"People reopen old cases, don't they? Couldn't somebody take another look at this one?"

I shook my head. "The conviction came about on the basis of a confession. A wrongly identified print would not have affected the outcome." She sighed so wretchedly that I added, "It does reinforce suspicions raised by missing records and conflicting information. I do agree with you about that."

The morning after David arrived back in Springfield from D.C., he went to the Freyl house to search Hugh's home office and his bedroom suite. Going through a dead man's relics is a disconcerting job at the best of times, but this one was made far worse by Becky, who insisted that Lillian oversee his every move.

"I'm real sorry, David," Lillian said when Becky left them alone. "She figures you going to steal the silver or something."

"I know," he said.

"I can do some dusting. Polish that silver. You just pretend I ain't here, okay?"

There was little legal work to be found, but there were full copies of everything to do with Hugh's teaching activities, methods, equipment, background files on his pupils, past and present, as well as his notes on each of them, including David himself. Hugh had taught no more than three or four each year, but he had taught for a quarter of a century; the paperwork filled a filing cabinet. David paid no attention to his own records, although he recognized many of his reactions in the notes about others: frustrations and angers, boredom and the occasional breakthrough. But no threats emerged, outright or veiled. Nor did any worrisome resentments. There didn't seem to be any clearly disturbed personalities on show either, and no pupils had been recently released who might have posed a potential danger to anybody.

"The police performed an entirely adequate search," Becky said to David. They were sitting in her private rooms after a search that had taken most of the day. Becky's furniture was delicate, old—nineteenth-century Japanese lacquer and copper-wire sliding doors—as carefully feminine as Hugh's rooms were carefully masculine; she'd drawn up the designs for both herself. "I do not complain of their thoroughness—only of their lack of intellect and the restrictions placed on them by ill-thought-out legislation."

"What did they find on the body?" David asked.

Becky was at once affronted. How dare he refer to Hugh as "the body"? By what right? The days were telling on her badly. She was thinner and paler. Her husband's death had been a blow, but she'd been totally unprepared for Hugh's. Such a painful, ugly death too, such a demeaning, disgusting conclusion to the life she'd prized above all things in the world; it was the kind of brutish end David had meted out himself. It was the kind *he* deserved—not Hugh.

Becky was known for the precision of her mind; her attention to detail was legendary. She knew a good question when she saw one, and she knew David's question was a good one. She also knew that he was just covering bases, just being as thorough as the police before him. She should have been impressed. She *was* impressed, and yet . . . Well, why hadn't she thought to ask the question herself? How could she be other than affronted when this low person, this acknowledged murderer, was the one who asked it instead?

"Watch, change, keys," David went on when she didn't answer. "They must have given you a list."

"Of course they did. There wasn't anything interesting on it—nothing unexpected at all. I told them so, and now I'm telling you."

"Do you still have it?"

"Of course I do."

"I'd like to see it."

"Why?"

"Why not?"

Becky opened the drawer of her desk with a jerk, rummaged a bit, then handed him a sheet of paper. David scanned it quickly. "Where's his cell phone?" Hugh had used a cell phone for all personal calls.

"How should I know?"

"He usually had it with him. Is it here in the house somewhere?"

"It couldn't be. He *always* carried it. A most annoying aspect of modern life this . . . thing that makes idiotic noises in a man's pocket at all the wrong moments. Those fools just forgot to list it." Becky was more irritated than ever. Here was one more element she hadn't noticed herself.

"Do you know if they found it?"

She pursed her lips: if she hadn't noticed it was missing, she could hardly have asked the police about it, could she? But she refused to say as much to David, who could not fail to have been aware of it already.

"Check to make sure," he said, getting up to leave. "Was it an Internet account?"

"What difference would *that* make?"

"Nothing would show up except on his credit card statements. The police could easily have missed it."

Yet a third element she'd failed to catch herself.

David spent the evening at the Pair-a-Dice with Hiram Draper, Lillian's eldest, chauffeur to Hugh for many years. It was Saturday night, and the Pair-a-Dice was jumping: bright lights, loud music, laughter. Groups of ten crammed themselves into booths designed for six; the raw wood tables in the center of the room were just as packed. Waiters and waitresses pushed their way through the crowds, trays balanced at shoulder height and piled with steaks, french fries, salads, drinks, coffees, desserts. The smoking section, where David and Hiram sat, was a little less crowded but not much.

Hiram's skin was as white as David's, but nobody would have mistaken him for white; the nose was too broad, the mouth too full. He was fat, amused, far smarter than he looked. He could have become any number of things; all he'd ever wanted was his wife ever since he first laid eyes on her when they were both sixteen: he was a family man through and through. He'd suggested he and David meet at the Pair-a-Dice instead of at home for fear that talk of a murder, especially this brutal and intimate one, might unsettle his wife and daughter.

While they ate, Hiram told David about his new job. Becky had fired him on the day of Hugh's funeral, and he hadn't had any idea what he was going to do with himself. At his wife's urging, he'd taken a post office exam, passed it with flying colors and been offered work as a motor vehicle operator picking up and delivering vast quantities of mail every day. The pay was $10,000 more a year than he'd been getting from Becky, and prospects for promotion were good. He just might be going up in the world despite himself.

"You look right worn out, David," he said as a waitress took away their plates.

The past few days of fruitless quest had told on David; so had the unfamiliar experiences, a first plane flight and a visit to a Supreme Court justice. He thought he might even sleep the night to come. There wasn't much more paperwork he could do to probe into Hugh's finances and legal practice until he'd checked the files from Stephanie's suitcase.

"You must have been the last person to see Hugh alive," he said.

"Yeah. I guess so—excepting the guy that killed him."

"You drove him to the office as usual?"

"Yeah."

"Why wasn't Athena with him?" Hiram shrugged. "Didn't she usually go with him at night?"

"Yeah."

"But not that night."

"I told him to take her. I *told* him."

"Any idea why he didn't?"

"He said she was getting too fat. She kept eating sandwiches out of wastepaper baskets." The waitress unloaded two cups of coffee, milk, sugar from her heavily loaded tray. David took a cigarette out of the crumpled pack in his pocket, lit it and waited for Hiram to speak again. "Them secretaries was always bringing dog biscuits around for her on top of all those leftover lunches. The kids downstairs bought her toys all the time, dolls and rag balls and I-don't-know-what-all.

What's Athena going to do with toys? Them kids, they don't understand nothing. Some dogs like toys. I guess they do, anyways. Athena
ain't one of them. She sure does like her food, though."

"Could there have been any other reason for leaving her home?"

"Can't think of nothing." Hiram shook his head unhappily. "If
I'd a just had the *sense* to insist . . . Supposing he fell or something,
all alone there like that. That's what I said to him. Supposing he got
sick. He just laughed at me. No, sir, he wasn't going to bring her no
matter what I . . . Then he went and told *me* to leave him alone.
Made a joke about that too. Said I ought to go home and worry
about my own self. I had a kind of a cough. Wasn't nothing much. I
shouldn't have left. I *never* should have left."

"He sounds quite buoyant from your description."

Hiram looked up. "You're right. Know that? I kind of forgot
about it after . . . I remember thinking to myself that he was real
happy, know what I mean? He'd been kind of down in the mouth
for a real long time, ever since that Stephanie left. Not that night.
That night he was in a real good mood, like something wonderful
was just about to happen."

"You think he was planning to meet someone?"

"Could be. Thinking about it now: just could be."

"Any idea who? Could he have been planning on going out?"

"It'd have to be somebody he knew well if he was going out.
Otherwise he'd a taken Athena with him." Hiram studied David a
moment, then shook his head. "I didn't think nothing of it. Just glad
he'd picked up some." Hiram shook his head once more. "I guess I
just wasn't thinking much at all."

◄○►

David and Hiram stood outside the Pair-a-Dice for a few minutes—
the formalities between people brought together by a tragedy—and
then set off separately to their cars. Traffic was still reasonably
heavy, and David wouldn't have paid any attention to the battered
Ford behind him as he pulled away from a red light if he hadn't
caught a glimpse of it on his way to the restaurant.

Even so, he only registered the oddity of the coincidence. No more.

19

STEPHANIE TELEPHONED DAVID AT ABOUT NINE-THIRTY
on Sunday morning.

"David, I have to get out of here."

"You sound awful," he said.

Her voice was gruff and feeble, both at the same time. For the
better part of a week, her world had been confined to occasional visits from the motel manager's retired doctor uncle and the few feet
that separated her queen-size bed from the bathroom in her room.
"Ah, come on. I sound great, and if I stay in this room one more
day, I'll go stark, raving—" She broke into a harsh cough.

"Go back to bed," he said when she quietened.

"Come on, David. There's a good boy. Let me take you to that
lunch at Norb Andy's. An evil drink like a chilled martini is the
very thing I need. Doctor's orders. He really did say that. He's a
nice old guy, this internist. His wife peeled a little bowl of grapes for
me. I'll meet you downtown. Besides—you see?—I can get through
a whole speech without coughing. It's just lack of practice."

"What time?"

"Is twelve-thirty okay for you?"

"I'll pick you up at twelve."

"No, no, no. I'll meet you there. I've already ordered a taxi. I've
been dreaming of that martini for days."

"I'll pick you up at twelve."

"You shouldn't argue with the sick. It's bad for them."

"I'm seeing Lillian in an hour. I'll be at your motel as soon as
I'm finished there."

Lillian's house was on the east side of Springfield, not all that far from David's apartment, and yet the feel of the neighborhood was entirely different. Respectable people lived there. There were no refrigerators rusting away in front yards. Front paths were cleared and salted. Lawns beneath the snow were trimmed and neat. But since the snow had melted off the roofs, the houses couldn't help revealing themselves for what they were. This was junk housing, quick and cheesy prefab jobs, tar-paper siding, thin walls, hollow-core doors, foundations crumbling after only eight years. All of it had been overpriced; mortgage terms were extortionate. Forget talk of equality. Forget the parade of black female judges in TV programs and the endlessly changing, tangled euphemisms that range from "African-American" across "Afro-American" to "Person of Color." This is how it really is. This is the underdogs' ghetto of a U.S. state capital where racism is in the blood.

And yet the people who lived here were rich by the double standard. One of Lillian's daughters had her own office in the Centennial Building. Another owned a small chain of clothing stores. As for Lillian, maybe she answered the Freyls' door and cooked Becky's dinner, and maybe she wasn't paid what she was worth—not anywhere near—but the pay was regular, and it had been for thirty years. Besides, her youngest son still lived with her, and he brought in good money. And as Hiram, her eldest, had told David, he looked to be going up in the world: federal civil service job with the U.S. Postal Service and a federal pension at the end of it.

But it was a mark of the profound divide in this town that no Freyl would admit in public to setting foot in this living room where David sat with Lillian.

"David, you eat one of them blueberry muffins," she said.

"That's an order?"

"I made them special."

David nodded. "It's an order," he said, and the amused pleasure in his voice was so rare—so unexpected—that Lillian laughed.

"Whatever happened to your mama?" she said.

"I don't know."

"That the truth?"

David nodded again. "I wanted to ask you about Helen."

Despite the ghetto, despite the painfully obvious inequities, Lillian's loyalties ran deep, and she was not pleased by the question even though she had been expecting it ever since he'd arranged to come and visit her this morning. "What's Miss Helen got to do with it?" she said irritably.

"I'm just looking for patterns—or the beginnings of them."

"She don't have nothing to do with Mr. Hugh's death."

"What's she need all the therapy for? Twice a week, isn't it? That's a lot of therapy."

"Her mama done died right in front of her. Ain't that enough?" Before David could answer, Lillian pulled her ample form out of her chair. "You need more coffee in that cup."

He watched her make her way to the kitchen. The house was smaller inside than it looked from the outside, but this room—the best room, the living room—was warm, bright and sunny despite winter cold and shoddy construction. There were smells of Sunday dinner to come, and he could hear Lillian tending a roast while she made more coffee. One Sunday a month, family gathered on Sundays; there would be near enough to a dozen around the table: Lillian, her youngest son, her own mother—very aged now—one or two of her other children with wives and husbands, a smattering of grandchildren.

"I need to know Hugh better," David said when Lillian returned. "I need to know the family better. Maybe somewhere in among them—maybe just in the process of looking—I'll run across something."

She handed him the fresh coffee, sat down again, shook her head. "David, these ain't bad folks. Lot of bad things happen to them, but they ain't bad. I guess I been with them too long not to like them. You get so as you like practically anybody if you stick around them long enough. Even so, these ain't bad folks."

"I know."

"So what are you saying to me, huh?"

David spread his hands in a gesture of despair. "I'm not accusing anybody. I'm not even hinting at accusations. But look at it this way. A guy has to be patient to kill the way Hugh was killed. He has to enjoy his work. He has to plan it well and control it at every stage. The risks are enormous. The longer you spend torturing your victim, the more likely you are to leave traces—or get caught before you can get away."

"Ain't got *nothing* to do with Miss Helen. No way."

"Suppose somebody she knows—or has encountered—bears her some grudge that works its way out through her father. Killing a man that way is a statement. Somebody's saying something."

" 'Bout her?"

"It's possible."

Lillian relaxed just a little. "She ain't never told me nothing about therapy."

"She's been seeing therapists ever since her mother died?"

"Lord, no. She wouldn't talk to nobody way back then. Not for years and years. Not her daddy. Not her grandma. Not me. Nobody. Certainly no *doctor.*"

"But didn't you just say it was her mother's death that—?"

"Now, you listen here at me, David Marion. I ain't going to let you trick me into saying things I don't want to say. Bad stuff hangs on in a life. You know that. Besides, them potatoes need watching." She got up again.

This time David got up too. "I'll bring the dishes," he said, picking up the tray of coffee cups and cake plates.

"Guess I can't stop you."

He followed her into the kitchen, set the tray on the counter, then leaned against the doorjamb to watch her with her pots and pans, the steam rising, the clatter of dishes, the promise of a family get-together ahead of her. "Whoever did this knew Hugh's comings and goings," he said. "So whoever it was knew how Hugh lived and how he worked—or found out from somebody else."

She stopped and turned to him. "You mean Dr. Berry?" Dr. Berry was Helen's therapist.

"I wouldn't think so, no."

"Lord knows how come anybody figures a cold fish like that could help Miss Helen."

"It probably depends on why Helen went to see her."

"Pretty smart, ain't you?" Lillian said. She brought out a huge bowl of cooked prunes, turned her back on him with cold determination and concentrated on pitting them. David took off his jacket, rolled up his sleeves and helped; he was as deft at pitting prunes as he was at picking locks, and she laughed delightedly despite her irritation. "Where'd you learn to do that?" she said. "I ain't never knew a man could pit prunes that fast."

"Prison kitchen."

"You do the cooking?"

"Some of it."

"Lots of knives in a kitchen."

"Not many lug wrenches, though."

"And just take a look at you now. Your mama would be real proud of you, know that?"

They finished the prunes in silence. Lillian found a sieve; he took it from her and began to press the pulp through it.

She watched him a minute, then said, "I don't figure Helen has a very good time with much of anything, poor little girl. It's true what I say: she's never been quite right since her mama died. When she was a child, she used to cry and cry and cry. I used to hold her in my arms till my shoulders was soaking wet. I never knew a child to cry so much." Lillian took the prune puree from David, scraped it into a bowl of chilled whipped cream and folded it in. Prune whip was a speciality of hers. He'd eaten it himself at the Freyls' table. "There was this one man she liked. He was kind of old for her, and she . . . I don't know nothing about nothing, but they had to take him off to the hospital in an ambulance. Miss Helen . . ." Lillian trailed off.

"Miss Helen?" David prompted.

"It weren't no better than he deserved," Lillian said, bristling again, although not at David this time. "He was greedy. I'd a cracked his skull myself if I'd a had the chance. Miss Helen got the chance. He spent a couple of nights in the hospital whining at the police. They was falling all over themselves laughing. It got all kind of hushed up on account of Miss Helen agreed to go see that Dr. Berry regular."

"How badly was he hurt?"

"If it'd a been me, he'd a been in a lot worse shape." Lillian had no intention whatever of telling David that concussion was only a part of the picture. There'd been a good ten stitches in the man.

"Are there other boyfriends now?"

" 'Course."

"Anybody special?"

"She always got somebody special—*several* somebodies special."

He could see the gates and guards on duty again in that profile of Lillian's. "What about Jimmy Zemanski?" he said.

"What about him?"

"Something's going on there, isn't it?"

"Mr. Hugh's job ain't enough for that man." Lillian spit out the words. "He wants the daughter too. He figures if he can get Miss Helen, he can get his picture on the society page."

"That's what he wants?"

"He's greedy just like the other one. They is *all* greedy. They don't give a—"

The front door to the house slammed open to interrupt her with a bang and a blast of cold air. That's the trouble with life outside prison. There's no order to it, no continuity, nothing to rely on. The rules keep changing.

"Mama?" The voice was high-pitched, tense, perfectly suited to the woman who rushed into the kitchen dragging two small boys behind her. "I got to leave Eddie and Tommy with you while I get some of my—" She broke off as soon as she saw David.

The bigger of the two little boys let go his mother's hand at once. "Hey, who is this man?" He walked—a confident strut, hands on hips—in a circle around David. "You play ball?" he said to David.

"What kind of ball?" said David.

"Any kind of ball."

David considered the question and the boy asking it. His answer was sober, careful. "I guess that's the kind I play best."

"Not as good as me, I bet. I bet you anything. I'm the best that ever was. *Any* kind of ball: I play best."

"He isn't staying to dinner, is he?" Lillian's daughter said, eyeing David suspiciously.

Lillian glared at her. "Says he can't stay today. Says he's going to Norb Andy's for lunch. I ain't asked him about *next* week."

"Mama, you can't—"

"David, how about next Sunday?" Lillian interrupted.

But she could see reluctance in his face, not snobbery, not that. What she saw is the reluctance of a foreigner—a man with a very poor idea of what a family means or how it functions—asked to intrude on a ritual he knew he could never understand. He was already disturbing it, had already upset this daughter whose name he didn't even know, had already intruded even though he was no part of anything here, was barely even an onlooker.

"Don't you pay no attention to this girl of mine," Lillian went on. "She's just naturally sour. She's exactly like *my* mama. Thing is, Miss Helen is coming next week. Mrs. Freyl is letting me have another Sunday off special, and you can talk to her then. I'd feel a whole lot better if Miss Helen has a chaperone when the likes of you is sniffing around her." Lillian laughed and patted his chest. "Or maybe you're the one needs a chaperone."

20

DAVID'S ROUTE FROM LILLIAN'S HOUSE TO STEPHANIE'S
motel took him east to west again; downtown Springfield, even with
clear skies and a Sunday morning lull, looked more fake than ever
to him. A sham town: dirty snow clung to Carmel-style structures
and ugly block buildings much as the dust collects on the plastic
flowers out at Oakland Cemetery. Of course, all evidence of dirt
stopped abruptly at the edges of the little Lincoln quarter, already
spick-and-span this morning (an electronically controlled vacuum
plow especially designed for the purpose) and shining with Disney
World artifice in the midst of the filth.

Stephanie's motel was out near the White Oaks Mall; it was one
of those Best Westerns with the ugly yellow crown for a logo and ar-
chitecture that belonged to supermarkets, but there are far worse
places to battle off a bout of airplane-exacerbated flu. She was waiting for him outside the office with one of her suitcases. She lugged
it toward him as soon as the Chevy pulled up.

"Have you decided to change motels?" he said, taking her suitcase from her and putting it in the trunk.

She shook her head. "I want to show you this stuff."

"You ought to be lying down," he said as he started the engine.

She settled herself firmly against the door. "Just take me to
Norb Andy's. It'll make me feel better just to be there."

They drove back to the center of town in a silence that was punctuated only by her coughing spells. When they reached the structures
that form the town's praetorian guard around the Capitol Complex,
Stephanie said, "Do you plan to stay on in Springfield? after all this is
over? You'd be a success wherever you went. I know you would."

"Cities look much alike to me."

"You haven't been in all that many, have you?"

"I've flown over both Chicago and D.C."

"You've flown over . . . Are you teasing me, David Marion?"

Driving alongside the Capitol Complex itself, it was harder to forget that Springfield is the capital of a rich and powerful state. Maybe Chicago has the edge on crime and culture, but Springfield is where the deals are done. Senators, representatives, Speakers, governors are made here, even presidents of the whole union. The place crawls with lawyers, lobbyists, reporters, scroungers, fraudsters too; and a lot of the politics that goes on, goes on over the tables at Norb Andy's.

David parked no more than a hundred yards from the door.

"Could you get the bag out of the trunk for me?" Stephanie said.

"Not exactly trusting, are you?"

She laughed. "After I'd been working for Hugh for a year or so he said to me one day, 'At last you're learning to be a little suspicious.'"

Norb Andy's window seemed to try for a nautical feel, but there was no heart in it. Open the door, though, walk down the steps, and the mood changed. It was night down there. Rooms meandered off in various directions, and they looked—they really did—as though real people went there to eat and had gone there for generations. The walls were dark; the general impression was the bustle of a Village joint in New York City, although Sunday was not a big day and a number of tables were empty.

David and Stephanie found a booth; he slid her suitcase in beside her. She ordered a martini on the rocks and a horseshoe sandwich, Springfield's claim to culinary fame and Norb Andy's speciality, a concoction of hot cheese, toast and meat.

"What about you, David? Aren't you hungry?" He shook his head. "You ought to eat something. How about pastrami on rye? You like that. I know you do. Hugh told me so. It's the only thing you ever told him you *did* like to eat."

"Bring me a beer," he said to the waitress.

"Any particular kind?"

"Whatever you suggest."

"*And* a pastrami on rye," Stephanie added as the waitress left. Then she turned to David. "If you don't want it, it can sit there while you admire it. Why do you always drink beer? It has no taste."

"Precisely why I like it."

The drinks arrived almost at once. Stephanie raised her glass and clicked David's; she looked pale, drawn, weak from her days in bed. "To the murderer and the ruiner of domestic arrangements. Oh, Lord, I hate to think where I'd be this very day without Hugh Freyl. Goddamnit."

"He called you on the night he died."

She looked at him in shock. "He what?"

"I went over the records before I saw Lillian this morning."

"I can't believe . . . No, no. You're wrong, David. There wasn't any message. He'd have left a message. I know he would have."

"Perhaps he didn't get the chance."

The telephone call had been logged at 8:33 P.M. Becky had given David a copy of the postmortem, which estimated the time of death at a couple of hours on either side of nine-thirty; the state of the wounds on the body indicated most had been inflicted before death. Stephanie knew none of this, although she sensed that David had withheld details, and she could not bring herself to press for them. But this final telephone call came as a bad shock; she took a swallow of her martini, shuddered with the impact and leaned back in the booth.

"He told me going on retreat would get me into trouble one day," she said. Every year she spent a week in a cloister on the Russian River, a cool, calm place with stone-covered walkways, no telephones, no television, no clutter. It wasn't religion that drew her; her body seemed to crave an annual period when life was simple and orderly—when somebody else made all the decisions.

"You'd better change your number," David said, but he could see she wasn't hearing him. "Listen to me. The police didn't find the cell phone. They still can't find it. They didn't even know he carried one."

"Oh, how I'd love to have heard his voice. Just once more. I *loved* hearing him talk."

"Are you going to change that number or not? There's no way of telling who has the phone now."

Stephanie was only half aware of David. She'd tried so hard.

She'd known from day one that she couldn't forget Hugh. She just had to learn to live without him. She'd set out to construct her days as though each one were a trek into an alien land not unlike her Russian ancestors' trek into the frozen territory of the Kodiaks and the Aleuts—except that there was no prize to be found at the end of hers: wake up, dress, cook breakfast, eat, brush teeth, drive to work. She was back in hospital administration, leading people through insurance forms and claims; she could do it without a single thought entering her head, which was good because then she wasn't likely to find herself somehow diverted to Hugh. Lunch. Back to work. Drive home. So far so good. But the evenings, oh, dear God. Hugh had told her about how hard they were after Rose died. He'd quoted Victor Hugo to her: "I am a widower, alone, and the evening is upon me."

And yet Stephanie knew that if Hugh had called her, it meant that David's assessment just could have been right, that Hugh hadn't wanted to get rid of her, that Becky had jockeyed for position—and won. At least it *could* mean that. But there was no pleasure in the thought; an abrupt desolation came with it and took her breath away, vacuum in the middle of her chest where her heart ought to be, dimming of the vision as though she was going to faint. None of it need ever have been. They need never have lost all those days. Two years of days and nights—and those evenings that had been so very, very difficult. Worse, if she hadn't left, he'd have been with *her,* not alone at his office being . . . No, don't go there. She finished her martini hardly aware she was drinking it. Another appeared in front of her.

"Why is it always too late?" she said, more to the new drink than to David.

"It's just the way of things." His voice was gentle.

"What am I going to do, David?"

"Help me find out who killed him."

◄◦►

"There's an article in here about time limits for appeals," Stephanie said to me one morning, bursting into my office and rustling her newspaper at me. "I didn't know there were limits. Are there limits?" I nodded. "Sixty days. Is that right?"

"From the original sentence, yes." I was standing in front of my desk, feeding a contract into the scanner.

"But, Hugh, David's sixty days were up a generation ago. Where's the mercy in a system like that? Make a guy jump through hoops, then make him go over it all again before he's had a chance to catch his breath. Not that it matters. Not for David. He's going to rot in jail for the rest of his life. It's all for nothing. There must be hundreds like him. Thousands. It's monstrous. Jails must be littered with them. Why didn't you tell me? You should have told me."

"It is only the filing that has to come within sixty days. Samuel handled quite a few appeals on cases like David's, and some dragged on and on. It took him two years just to locate the court records in one of his cases. There was another, a capital case, I think, where he ended up spending a full eight years to complete the brief."

"Are you saying that David just didn't file?"

"People who plead guilty generally do not appeal because they cannot."

"But if he was forced to confess?"

I sighed. "I guess the real answer is that I just do not know."

"Aren't there guys in jail who help other guys do stuff like that? I mean, okay, so maybe he didn't have the skills to do it himself back then, but couldn't he have got help?" I nodded. "Well, damn it all, he's not stupid, Hugh. He's far from a sack of potatoes. What could have been in his head? For sixty days he doesn't file, and suddenly the whole thing's meaningless."

I took in my breath. "The simplest explanation is that he did not appeal because he was guilty as charged, and he knew it."

I heard her slump into the chair beside me. She seemed in such despair that I reached over instinctively to put my hand on her shoulder.

But a simple, physical reaching out like that—the only meaningful communication at times like this when no words will serve—is the privilege of a sighted person. I remember waking in the middle of the night once many years ago when Rose was at her mother's—this was when I could still see—and making sweeps with my arms to locate the bedside lamp. I ended up knocking it over: hardly a dignified maneuver. It was exactly the same with Stephanie's shoulder; if I wanted to put my hand on it, I had to find it first.

"Is there something you need?" she said, suddenly concerned at this hand that was waving around in her general direction.

"I was looking for your shoulder." I laughed, embarrassed at my attempt as well as at my awkward failure.

She took my hand then, and it was the first time I had ever touched her—or she had touched me—in a way not connected to my blindness. I had not expected this, although I had hoped for it many times before, so much so that I found it difficult to make my voice work again. I doubt I made much sense when I succeeded.

"Maybe you are right about David," I said. "Maybe it is meaningless in the end, but if you go far enough toward the end, everything is meaningless. One way and another David himself forced me to see that all those years ago after Rose died. He also forced me to see that houses have back doors as well as front doors." I was afraid that she might let go of my hand if I stopped talking, so I babbled on. "That is not entirely accurate, is it. He forced me to see that I was just an ordinary mortal like other mortals and had to use the back doors in my personal life just as I had learned to use them in my . . . "

But somehow I could not quite remember what I was saying.

"You think there's some other way to get him out, don't you." She got to her feet and stood beside me, still holding my hand in hers; there was excitement in her voice. "Something other than an appeal? Some special kind of appeal? Maybe something that doesn't qualify as an appeal? Maybe something that isn't strictly legal?"

"So many things seem possible right now."

"I don't care if we have to break every law in the book," she burst out, abruptly furious all over again at the idea of keeping a changed man like David in prison for something he'd done as an out-of-control teenager many years before. "Keeping him locked in a cell by himself, not allowed to talk to anybody, nobody allowed to talk to him: it's something out of the Spanish Inquisition. I thought we were supposed to be an enlightened century. What's the matter with people who don't think anything of doing that to a man for months on end? How can he stay sane in there? The very idea of it makes me teeter on the edge, and there's no sign whatever that they're going to let him out."

I made a huge effort to concentrate. "We are going to need more material. If only I had been able to see more of the file on him . . . maybe if I could get some glimpse of why he did not appeal before the time limit ran out. Maybe somebody was threatening him. But given so little to work with, I think the most promising approach is to find a way to challenge that confession." I could feel her breath on my face, and the words began to wander off in some direction of their own. "And I would very much like—oh, more than anything—for you to come with me to . . ."

But the most unexpected of complications get in the way of the blind in the important matters of life. I had released her hand gently, and as I spoke (whatever it was I was saying) I guided my fingers up along her arms to her shoulders. A slight quiver went through her that somehow ended up meaning that I had my arms around her. Even so, I had only a general idea where her face might be—a better idea certainly than I'd had about her shoulder, but not better enough.

A bump of noses. Left a little. Down a little. Oh, Stephanie.

Stephanie scanned the room of Norb Andy's that she and David sat in as though it were an alien planet. People laughed. They talked. Just as though nothing ever came to an end. She suddenly noticed there were tears rolling down her cheeks; she brushed them away angrily. "David, I really . . . I only worked with guys like you. You know, Hugh's teaching. All that other stuff he did—mergers, assets, bankruptcies . . . I don't know anything about it. Boring, boring. I really don't."

"I was never certain what your role with him was."

"It doesn't matter anymore."

"Everything matters."

"I kept track of dates, appointments, pupils, progress. I handled the reports to various authorities and helped figure out ways to translate his ideas into methods a blind guy could use with a seeing pupil. We spent a lot of time persuading wardens into letting him do what he wanted. They used to put up all kinds of stupid barriers— invent regulations, pretend they'd misunderstood when they hadn't. They really resented him, everything about him, what he did, who he was. On top of all that, they felt that dealing with a blind man— even a Freyl—was beneath them. I know that part of it hurt him, but he got a real kick out of outwitting them." She stared down at her drink as she had before. "I just got angry."

David took a pack of cigarettes out of his pocket, lit one and waited for her to continue.

"What fascinated me was his pupils' pasts and their personalities, why they did what they did, the details of it, what might have happened if they hadn't got caught, what they might do when—or if—they got out. I read everything I could find. Hugh was interested only insofar as things like that affected how he could get them to learn what he needed to teach them. Except when it came to you, that is. You were different right from the beginning. He called me a couple of times in the middle of the night with some thought or other—nothing to do with him and me, just about you. But what I'm saying is that I was no part of his legal work. I didn't really pay any attention to it until one day . . ." She shrugged and lapsed into silence.

"Go on," David prompted.

"I walked into his office and found Jimmy Zemanski bending over him. Not that there was anything unusual in that. They worked a lot together, and Hugh's signature had to be on all kinds of papers, but this time there was something . . . I don't know. Jimmy's shoulders took a jolt when he saw me. I couldn't figure it out. I was just another face to be found in and out of offices, sometimes on the fringe of a conference. He never paid any attention to any of us. So I thought: 'A bad night maybe? a hangover or something?' I hate to say it, but Jimmy's one of those guys who brings out the worst in me. All of a sudden I heard myself saying, 'Getting him to sign away the family silver?' "

The expression on her face was the sheepish one of a good girl caught with her hand in the cookie jar. The fierce independence of Hugh's early years as a blind man had never diminished, and he hated any hint that he could not deal with his own affairs. It was one of the few areas in his life where his sense of humor failed him.

"Damn Jimmy," she went on. "I couldn't believe I'd said such a thing. I still can't, and I felt so awful I almost missed the critical part. Jimmy's neck went red the way it does when he gets mad. And I thought, 'So what's *that* for?' I knew perfectly well that he wasn't worried that I might have hurt Hugh's feelings. Not Jimmy. All I wanted was to get away from there before I blurted out something else I shouldn't, but Jimmy gave me one of those looks of his like he and Hugh had hold of some special boys' toy that girls were too stupid to play with. At the same time Hugh made some reference to the

Follaton lease. So I figured, all right, I'll show them. I'll learn all there is to learn about leases. If I can put up with the boredom of administration at Memorial Hospital, I can put up with leases. I figured I might as well start with the Follaton. At least I knew it was current. I asked a friend of mine—she worked in one of those nasty little cubbyholes on the second floor—if she'd let me take a look at it. She said she'd dig it out, but . . ." Stephanie shrugged.

"She couldn't find it."

She smiled at him. "You're almost dangerously smart, aren't you?" A little color had come to her cheeks, but her voice was still harsh despite the gin, almost a basso; she coughed to clear her throat. "I figured maybe Jimmy had taken it home or something. He did that quite a lot. I forgot about it—leases really do sound boring to me—but I just happened to run across him in the library one day a month or so later. By that time, I'd got to the point where a single glance at the man was enough to set me off. I didn't even think. 'Tell me about this Follaton lease,' I said. 'I'm getting interested in property law.' And guess what? His neck went red again. I'd completely forgotten about the earlier business—his neck going red in Hugh's office and all that—and I might well have forgotten again, but he had to go on and give me a lecture about the sanctity of the attorney-client relationship. I mean, how stupid can you get? So I wasn't on the staff—not properly speaking—but a lease is hardly a confidential document. Anyhow, the way he was talking, it was clear that *he* had remembered the incident in Hugh's office even if I hadn't. I couldn't figure out how come. It's just not the kind of thing that sticks in the mind of a guy like that.

"So I looked up the Follaton property. It turned out to be more of a complex than a building, a hell of a place in downtown St. Louis, one of those state-of-the-art palaces made out of mirrors, maybe twenty stories high. It takes up a whole block, and it's set back from the street on all sides by maybe fifteen feet, trees and shrubs, just to show how much cash they can throw away on land. I bet the mirrors are supposed to fill employees with pride as they watch themselves approach—know what I mean?—oh, wonderful me to be a part of a fairy tale like this. A two-story-high entry into a grand lobby of brushed chrome and some kind of marble in dove gray, and out of the midst of all this muted splendor, the company logo blazing like the star that led the kings to little Jesus. Everything—absolutely everything—*screamed* money. And the security! Guns and uniforms that belonged . . . I don't know . . . in the White House or something. One look at the checkpoint, and I turned tail and left." She took a drink of her martini. "The best I could do was a Net search on the place when I got home: a really elegant Web site too, lists of all kinds of assets and stuff. Then I went through the board members."

"And?"

"Hugh turned out to be a director."

"What's the company?"

"Uniplex Advanced Something. Bunch of initials."

"You sure about that?"

Stephanie considered. "Yeah. UACI. The logo was so snazzy. It flashed in orange and red."

"There's nothing like that in his list of directorships. No hint of it in his portfolio or his tax accounts. There aren't any payments from it into his personal accounts or the firm's account."

Stephanie cocked her head at him. "David, I know you're a miracle worker, but how on earth would you know about Hugh's finances?"

While the waitress set down a horseshoe sandwich and a pastrami on rye, David explained that Becky had called him in, hired him to find Hugh's killer, given him the authority to look at all files and interview anybody he wished.

Stephanie stared at him aghast. "She didn't."

"She wants something."

"Revenge."

"That too."

"I thought she thought you killed him." David shrugged. "She's changed her mind?"

"Looks kind of like it."

"I always figured her as the kind who'd cling to a decision no matter how wrong it was." Stephanie poked at her horseshoe, this midwestern species of Welsh rarebit with slabs of meat lurking inside.

"You can't eat that thing," David said, taking a bite out of the pastrami and rye that he hadn't wanted.

"It's really good. You'd like it." She cut into it, chewed, swallowed, then smiled—a brave attempt if not a wholly successful one.

"Zemanski takes files home, does he?"

"To hell with Jimmy. I want to know about Becky."

"Tell me about the files."

"Oh, come on, David, be nice to me. I'm sick."

"The files."

She sighed. "They all take them home." She took another bite of the horseshoe. "This Uniplex lot—UACI—sounds pretty big. It listed assets of over $420 million."

"What's the rest of it stand for? The other initials?"

She thought a moment. "Uniplex Advanced . . . something. Let's see. I think maybe Uniplex Advanced Ceramics . . . probably the *I* stands for Industries."

"What *is* that?"

"What is what?"

"I never heard of 'advanced ceramics.' "

She looked a little taken aback. "It's got to be some kind of pottery, doesn't it? I just assumed . . . Maybe they started out making dishes and diversified. They certainly don't have anything to do with that kind of thing now. I checked their assets. They have factories in several states that develop and process funny-sounding things like . . ." She licked her fingers to clear off a little smear of cheese, pulled the suitcase up onto the table, opened it and extracted a glossy pamphlet with a Navy ship at sea on the cover. " 'Thermal Management for Platforms.' And this one"—she picked out another glossy pamphlet—"has something to do with 'Acoustic Signature Reducing.' Then there are mines in California and places like Colombia and Tanzania and Pakistan that produce stuff I'd never heard of like . . . let's see"—a third pamphlet—"beryllium-aluminum. Then I ran across a couple of companies that said straight out that they were doing research and development in fields like torpedo warheads."

"Platforms could be missile platforms, I guess," David said. "I haven't any idea what beryllium is."

Stephanie peered at a note she'd made on the pamphlet. "Some of it goes into nuclear weapons," she said. "Yeah, I remember. I looked it up on the Net. Would you be horrified if I had another martini? Could you drink another beer?"

David signaled the waitress, who had been watching him covertly all this time and came running. Stephanie laughed.

"What?" he said.

"Do you always have this effect on girls?"

David looked at her blankly and ordered the drinks. The waitress stood rooted to the spot a moment, staring at him; she was very young—long blond hair—and her mouth was a little open. Stephanie glanced from one to the other with an amused smile. The waitress caught her eye, blushed furiously and jostled her way back toward the bar to fill the order. Stephanie watched her go.

"Hugh's directorships are pretty conservative," David said. "He's trustee of a couple of charities and a private foundation or two, all connected with the family. He's on the board of his mother's opera house and the art museum. There are a couple of corporate directorships—family interests again—but nothing remotely connected with the arms industry."

Stephanie turned back to him. "I didn't dare ask him—especially what with all that prying I'd have to explain—but I couldn't just let it alone either. The way Jimmy was acting made it all look so sleazy. Hugh didn't like sleazy. Another thing: all these assets have acronyms that are mostly the same letters—UACI—all switched around. I kept forgetting where I was and which one was which. I don't see how even board members can keep track of them."

David nodded. "This begins to sound familiar."

◄◦►

David's lessons with South Hams's rogue accountant, Professor Flaam, took him from the tangled forests of creative accounting into the overcultivated orchards of corporate fraud where there's money for a song, for dirt, for dog shit—money for anybody and everybody who's smart enough to put out a hand and let plums drop into it. But David didn't go there willingly, not at first, anyway. Like most prisoners who become literate inside, he was heavily influenced by radical ideas, Marx, the Russian nihilists, the Weathermen, the Black Panthers, almost anybody who fought this system that offered up its caged prisoners as playthings for sadists. To him, one rich man plundering another was just another sign of generalized rot on the outside.

But one day as he was walking past the accountants in the exercise yard, the Professor was saying, "What the hell, gentlemen, you know Flaam's cardinal rule: 'Helpless people plus money equals' "—he paused for effect— " 'a very fine business opportunity indeed.' "

David squatted down with the group at once. "This rule," he said. "Social Services fit into it?"

"Social Services runs on money just like everything else," the Professor said cautiously. David was almost as out of place in the accountants' clique as he was among Becky Freyl's funeral guests, although for the opposite reason. The young, dangerous and violent are the Becky Freyls of prison society; David was somebody to be feared and placated by middle-aged, white-collar criminals with weak stomach muscles and no interest in fighting.

"What part of Social Services are we talking about?" the Professor went on.

"Foster kids. Adoption," said David.

"How big a caseload?"

"Sangamon County."

David was eleven years old when Social Services had torn him away from the Monaghans. At the time, he'd seen conspiracy everywhere, as children do; later, he'd come to accept it as just one of fate's nastier whims. This was the first hint he'd had that he might have been closer to the truth at eleven than he was all these years later.

Flaam knocked at pebbles on the ground with a short stick and considered the question. "Handling a lot of kids is a pretty big operation: offices, *accountants*"—he glanced over at David and ventured a smile—"administrators, auditors, lawyers, negotiators, doubtless assessors of some sort or another, child psychologists, doctors. The bigger the operation, the more power it has. The more power it has, the more money it has. The more money it has, the more money it can get. So how to pull cash out of the ground?" The question was rhetorical. Flaam mused on it, then continued. "Old people, sick people, disenfranchised people, prisoners, poor people, ignorant people: all of them spell easy cash. Children? They're flotsam and jetsam in an adult ocean. Hence the answer has to be, yes, it is more likely than not that we're talking fraud at one level or another."

"Where's the money coming from?" David asked.

"Federal funding," said one of the other accountants, a lanky black guy in spectacles and a turned-around baseball cap.

"I think that is a safe assumption," said Flaam. What he meant—what was clear to everybody, including David—was that Baseball Cap had merely stated the obvious.

"I had four Social Security numbers," David said then, "and not one of them was mine."

"Did you indeed." Flaam drew a line on the ground with his stick. "One Social Security number is legal. Two could be a mistake." He drew a second line at right angles to the first. "Three is definitely suspicious." A third line. "But *four* Social Security numbers for *one* boy . . ." He completed a square on the ground, studied it a moment, then shook his head. "Every time they place this boy with a new family or whatever, there has to be money in it: administration, assessment, negotiation. Every time they place *one* boy, the federal government pays out for the *four* Social Security numbers attached to him. Sounds good to me."

It's always a shock for a man to find out he's been used. So it hadn't been fate or the devil or any other evil cosmic force that had taken David away from the only people he'd cared for and the only ones who'd wanted to adopt him. It hadn't even been conspiracy. He'd just been one more faceless statistic in a bureaucratic power game, just a pawn for a bunch of civil servants scrabbling in the government coffers. His response was abrupt and angry.

"A kid gets adopted, and funding stops," he said. "That's got to be how it works."

Professor Flaam nodded. "One boy out of the system is bad enough if you're looking to build up a power base—but to lose federal money for all four Social Security numbers?" He scratched out the square he'd drawn in the dirt. "Under these circumstances, Social Services would be crazy to allow an adoption if they could think of any way to prevent it."

◄◊►

"Confusion protects money" was another of Professor Flaam's rules, and it was the one that came to David's mind when Stephanie mentioned the jumble of switched-around letters of assets belonging to the corporation that occupied the Follaton buildings in St. Louis.

A fraudster covers his tracks just as a runaway convict does, throwing out false scents, backtracking on himself, assuming false identities, heading for a stream to block the dogs. Strings of related companies sharing the same initials in their corporate titles—precisely what Stephanie had found in her research—is a red flag to anybody in the know. It's a time-honored method of introducing the chaos that puts off trackers, either government or private.

"What else have you got in that suitcase?" David said to Stephanie. They were still at their table in Norb Andy's, sandwiches and drinks finished by now, table cleared, cups of coffee in front of them.

"A Net search I did put Hugh on the board of another corporation," she said. "This one's called UCAI. At first I didn't even notice that the A and the C were reversed—I figured it was the same site—then I realized it was too small to merit a mirrored palace, not many assets, only a year or so old back then. Want to guess where it rented space?"

"The Follaton complex?"

She nodded. "One of a couple of small buildings off on one side. I'd noticed it when I was wandering around there. I mean, speak of a poor relation. This is church mouse and fat cat, the church mouse kind of cowering behind the main building and trying to pretend it isn't there."

"What about Zemanski?"

"Jimmy?"

"Is he on the board of any of these things?"

"Should he have been? It never crossed my mind. I really don't know what to make of this material. I never did. I bet you'd be able to figure it out at once."

There was a pause. "You're willing to let me take a look?"

"Oh, David, if I can't trust you, who can I trust?" She put the pamphlets carefully back in the suitcase, shut the clasps and shoved it toward him. "Besides, there's hardly anything definitive here, corporate reports, quarterly statements, stuff like that. And then, well . . . see, there are records of . . ." She laughed self-consciously. "Don't take this the wrong way, will you? I'm afraid I . . . well, I started keeping track of what Hugh signed and what he didn't."

"You did *what*?"

Stephanie gave him a sheepish smile. "I bugged him." Before David could say anything, she rushed on. "I just couldn't bear the idea that Jimmy might be tricking him somehow. It wasn't all that hard to keep track of the paperwork. I used one of those nursery things. You know what I mean, that little gadget that lets you hear the baby when it cries."

◄◦►

Lunch at Norb Andy's was as much as Stephanie could manage. David dropped her at her motel, went back to his apartment and spent the rest of the afternoon going through the material in her suitcase. Most of it concerned UACI, the company that owned the mirrored palace she'd seen on the other side of the Mississippi in St. Louis; she'd interspersed annual reports, computer printouts and glossy brochures with notes on what she'd heard through that baby monitor. David could see why she'd felt the need to explain before she showed them to him; the notes were clearly more in the line of speculation than fact. One day Hugh was supposed to have signed seven documents and ended up signing eight; on another, a contract already signed had been redrawn and signed again.

But Hugh's name did appear on the board of this UACI company in which his own records indicated no financial interest, just as she'd said; that alone called for serious looking into.

Toward evening he began an Internet search. He found stories about UACI from quite a way back—some of them the same accounts Stephanie had printed out and included in her suitcase—its growth, its brilliant prospects, its power, its steady rise in the stock exchanges. It was still booming when she left the Midwest, as promising an investment as anybody might wish, and it had gone on booming until only a few months ago. Then out of nowhere— none of the usual warning rumors—the bubble burst. Overnight UACI went broke. In itself, this is nothing remarkable. An astonishing number of companies just as promising go bankrupt every year; fortunes are lost, bank loans defaulted on, pension schemes down the drain, stockholders stripped of life savings. An article in the *St. Louis Post-Dispatch* covered details of this one's bankruptcy; at the end of it, David noticed a reference to assets sold off at bargain-basement prices only weeks before the collapse.

So there had been warnings of disaster after all.

That's what really caught his attention, the sale of assets. That's when he got too strong a whiff of a scam to ignore: it was the church mouse who'd done the buying, the small company across the street from the glamorous main structure, the one that had looked as though it would be hard-pressed to pay the rent much less appropriate massive assets even at knockdown prices. How had it raised the cash? Why had it been able to secure loans large enough? And yet it had. A recent story in the *Post-Dispatch* reported the steady growth of its fortunes and mentioned in passing that an early investor had been the Springfield Federal Bank, Allen Madison's bank, the same Allen Madison who had seemed inexplicably tense when David talked to him about Hugh's bank accounts only days ago. The story ended with a paragraph on this rising star of the business world in its new building. And this new building? The very premises vacated by the bankrupt, the mirrored palace filling a whole city block. On the face of it, the transformation was a true American rags-to-riches miracle.

But where did Jimmy Zemanski fit into all this? Nothing in Stephanie's material even mentioned his name. Net searches turned up no tie between him and either company, bankrupt or newly powerful heir. Not long after eleven—a dark, cold night—David set out for the lake and Jimmy's large house on its edge.

21

IT WAS NOT UNTIL STEPHANIE AND I BEGAN SEEKING IN earnest for ways to release David from prison that I found myself with uncomfortable thoughts about what such a future might bring. Getting him out was a long shot—no matter what route we chose or how many manipulations of the law we were prepared to allow—but suppose we were successful. What then? His life before prison was hardly a reassuring preparation for the world outside. What had happened during the prison years . . . well, there was the third murder that I did not dare reveal to her. Nor did I feel I could tell her just how much my role as a teacher of prisoners had taught me about the conditioning such men encounter.

A boy as young as he certainly had not belonged in Marion, not even if his offense had been a federal one. He should have been sent to a youth correctional facility or a young offenders' wing of a penitentiary. We think of ourselves as an enlightened society, and yet every state of the union has mechanisms that allow teenagers to end up in adult high-security prisons. At least he had spent his few months at Marion before the infamous lockdown, but it was already the repository of many of Alcatraz's former prisoners. Violence was a daily reality. Murders were routine, serious injuries even more so: such barbarisms formed the internal regulatory system of prison life. We are social creatures, and our societies have similar overall structures no matter where they occur, in a maximum security prison or on the west side of Springfield. There is always a small elite that rules the majority and often reduces them to a state all too often indistinguishable from slavery. Marion was simply a particularly violent version of the pattern. Most prisons are, and while South Hams State Prison was something of an improvement over Marion, it was still a place where men went to bed at night with steel plates and JCPenney catalogues tied to their chests to protect them while they slept.

A system like this brings most full-grown men to heel within twenty-four hours of arrival. How could a mere teenager have been expected to protect himself? Someone as young as David was then—fifteen going on sixteen—was fair game for anyone and everyone. Yet one more harsh reality I had not realized until I became involved with the prison system myself is that juveniles like him are often sent to such places as added punishment: self-indulgent jurists in overheated robes entertain themselves with the consequences in their beds at night. But I was not the only one who sensed the aura of threat that David carries around with him. No mere visitor can distinguish which prisoner is of the master class and which is a minion, but David's reputation reached even an outsider like me. When he was still only a boy right at the beginning of his sentence, few inmates were foolish enough to attack him or to try to claim from him what they viewed as their right. The authorities had been equally cautious early in his prison life, and they remained so. Guards went after him only in groups.

This is to say that the dark side of David was darker than I could guess at, and it had been for all the time of his imprisonment. No matter how hard I tried, no matter how many books I read, no matter how many prisoners I dealt with, I could not imagine what an environment like that would do to a person, especially one who had grown up in it, for whom it represented the only known setting for adult life. I had struggled, maneuvered, tricked, inveigled—done everything I could think of—to create a civilized being from material I did not understand, to neutralize prison-engendered dangers that I could only guess at. In this I felt I had succeeded far better than I could have hoped, and I longed to let him breathe the air of the world outside. A prison is death. I wanted to give him life. And yet, few people could control this man when he was behind bars; those who could, needed truncheons and torture to do it. What would happen if he got out? Who would control him then? Could I? Could anybody? I could see that the training I had given him might well serve him only as camouflage, an elegant and unexpected façade over what amounted to a primal force subject to no laws. People would be very unlikely to guess the truth until it was too late.

So there was fear in the prospect of his release as well as excitement. I do not deny that, and yet I pushed it to the back of my mind while Stephanie and I intensified our search for a way to let him loose on society.

◄◦►

It was past midnight, and Jimmy was still crouching in a dark corner of his living room, his hands clasped in his crotch, his face sweating, his heart racing—slamming in his ears. He hadn't been like this since he was a little kid and his mother beat the crap out of him.

The way Jimmy saw it, it all began with the two New York sharks last month, a couple of weeks before Hugh's murder. They wanted to see Hugh, said it was an emergency, reluctantly accepted an appointment with Jimmy instead, then walked into his office and handed him a copy of the bankruptcy file for Uniplex Advanced Ceramics Industries. Just like that. He sure as hell hadn't expected it. Thank God all the legal work bore Hugh's signature. Thank God jealous old Becky had got rid of Stephanie Willis. Nosy bitch. She could have screwed up the whole works. Jimmy figured he handled the sharks well. Not a tremor crossed his face despite the shock, and they'd scared him. They were *very* classy, New York classy—the best—ruthlessly young, as cold as the weather outside and as smooth as ice in their handmade suits, Italian shoes, Ivy League accents. They were what Jimmy had wanted to be at their age—what he still wanted to be.

"I'm afraid I can't help you," Jimmy had said to them. "Mr. Freyl is away until the week after next, and unfortunately I'm only one of the partners."

Thank God for Hugh's vacation too. The luck of the timing had been truly extraordinary. (Jimmy was beginning to see a new interest in God. Maybe there was something to be found in church after all.) A couple of weeks would probably give him time to figure some way out of the mess. The sharks said they represented Galleas Industries Incorporated.

"I'm sorry, gentlemen," Jimmy said, "the name means absolutely nothing to me." Then he added (a nice touch), "What are advanced ceramics anyhow?"

The question was fair enough. He'd never been sure. All he knew was that they played an important part in snazzy military hardware and that he and his cronies at Uniplex had sold fifteen, maybe eighteen million dollars' worth of them to Galleas. Of course Uniplex went broke before any of the material could be delivered—although comfortably *after* they'd collected a ten million dollar down payment from Galleas. Not that they had any ceramics or whatever for sale in the first place.

After all, how could they? They'd already sold the plant that manufactured the stuff.

Risky? Hardly. Jimmy didn't believe in risk. It scared him as much as those predatory kids would have if Hugh hadn't been so conveniently off in Michigan. No, no, this kind of manipulation is candy from babies. Everybody's doing it. Strip the cash from a hundred deals, scatter a paper trail so screwed up nobody can make sense of it, file for bankruptcy and hey, presto: "Sorry, guys," you say to the punters, "every penny's gone. Whoosh! Just like that." All that's left is to gather up your cut and dance yourself off to your own stretch of sunny beach somewhere. Jimmy thought of the U.S. bankruptcy laws as his government's kindly gesture to imaginative entrepreneurs like him.

The only real question was why a couple of sharks were following up at all. Galleas's ten million or so is pocket money. Nobody reputable cries over such a piddling amount. Nobody reputable sends out a deputation even when the amounts are worth crying about. Reputable corporations just swallow their losses. Our sainted government doesn't even blink when it gets skinned. (Jimmy much preferred government contracts; after all, "The Consortium," as they called themselves, was set up to handle just such deals.) Which means what? One of those Manhattan mobs? Or one of those nasty little countries that butchers everything that moves? So what was supposed to happen to Jimmy when these guys finally talked to Hugh?

Jimmy had wrestled with that one day and night. Then Hugh went and got himself murdered, and Jimmy fell to his knees, a born-again Christian in two seconds flat, "Glory be to God. You exist after all." He'd gone to church that very Sunday. He'd given his humblest thanks to the Supreme Being who made mobs and nasty little countries so dumb: kill first and ask questions later. Jimmy had been let off the hook.

Until tonight, that is.

And yet he'd only half noticed the sound at the door when he heard it, an odd sound when he thought about it now, crouched in his corner, the sweat still running down his neck, a strangely gentle sound. But as soon as the front door had opened—as soon as he felt the draft from the night outside—he'd been on his feet, adrenaline pumping, breath coming fast. How could they have guessed? It's true that there were papers all over the place after Hugh's murder, but there wasn't much to be found at the offices at best. What little there was of it was buried in boxes of paperwork that reached from floor to ceiling; a team of accountants would need a month just to get started—and even then they'd be fishing blind. You have to know what you're looking for to make sense of a mass of material like that. He'd heard his front door shut. He'd heard footsteps in his hallway.

There was a moment of frozen indecision before he'd bolted for the kitchen and the back door—but a moment's indecision is too long when the stakes are as high as this. Somebody had already been standing behind him.

"Scared you, did I?"

He'd swung around to find David there, briefcase in hand, and his relief had been so great that it took him a moment to realize what had happened. David couldn't have got in unless he'd disabled the alarm system and picked the locks on the front door. After the visit from the Galleas guys, Jimmy had started setting the alarm even when he was at home. That must have been the source of the gentle sound, a metallic sound now that Jimmy came to think of it: David disabling the alarm. And then the guy just stood there like breaking into somebody's house at midnight was a perfectly normal thing to do, no apology, no uneasiness, no hint of embarrassment: scare the crap out of the owner and act like you're on some dainty social call. First Galleas, and now . . .

Jimmy was as big as David. Sure he was. He'd played football at college, but he was alone, damn it. He was *alone*. "How did you get in here?" he said, but even he could hear a tremor in his voice.

"You asked me over for a drink. Remember?" David had said,

sitting down in one of the Eames chairs shipped in from Houston only a month ago, his briefcase in his lap. An original Eames, worth a small fortune. "What is it with you lawyers?" David went on. "Security was one of Hugh's failings too. I can't understand it. How can such intelligent men be so stupid?"

Only Jimmy sat in that chair. Nobody else was allowed. He gathered his ragged courage around him. "Get out of my house." It was as close to a snarl as he could manage.

"I have to look at the contents of your safe. It's over there, isn't it? behind that ugly painting? You guys always put it in the same place. Amazing. It must have crossed your mind at some point or other that the first place you think to put it is the first place a guy like me is going to look for it."

"You want to look at my . . . ?" The artist was the newest sensation in Chicago; Jimmy had paid $200,000 for this one oil. His fear escalated abruptly. The thing is, see, only fools trust their business partners. Jimmy wasn't a fool. He kept—had kept—a little insurance. His policy was—had been—a sheaf of carefully selected papers right where David said it was, and a guy as smart as David . . . There were bank statements and contracts that charted the otherwise impenetrably complex transfers of assets, cash, inventory before the bankruptcy as well as all kinds of other things, including capital infusions from investors that had been abruptly renamed "loans" to be repaid to, well, to Jimmy for one. Which is to say, there was evidence of bankruptcy fraud, tax fraud, wire fraud, mail fraud, plenty to justify violence in the FBI to say nothing of a team of hit men from Galleas. Jesus, a week of sifting through this carefully selected documentation, a week collating it and . . .

What *was* it about David anyhow? Just looking at him set Jimmy's twanging nerves into some kind of frenzy, and yet all he'd been doing was getting up from the most elegant chair in the room and strolling over to the most expensive painting as if he were the host and Jimmy were some clumsy guest out of his social depth in his own house. David glanced behind the picture, took it down and shook his head in disapproval at the metal door he found beneath.

"If it's stupid to put *any* safe here," he said, "it's even stupider to do it with *this* one. It's as much an open invitation as your alarm system." He pressed down on the safe's handle and began to wobble the combination wheel. "But what *am* I going to find when I get it open?"

"You can't just walk in here . . ." Jimmy said, finding a semblance of a voice at last. "Stop at once! You can't *do* that."

"You're going to find interrupting me a little difficult. The forces aren't any more equal between us than they are inside a cheap lock like this—or any lock for that matter."

There had been techniques other than accounting to learn in South Hams. David had found out that there's more to opening a lock than smash and grab. There's a Zen to lock picking. There really is. That's what the real artists say anyhow. "Think lock." Don't *look* at it. *Listen* to it. *Smell* it: if the oil smells fresh, you adjust accordingly because a newly oiled lock doesn't respond like a dry one. Use your hands and tools to *feel* out the mechanism. Precise tolerances come in thousandths of an inch. Over such tiny distances, metals behave like springs. As the metal responds pin by pin to the tool inserted in it, the map of the lock is transferred to the brain of the picker.

Advanced lock picking is a state of mind.

"A little pressure on just the right spot, man or lock," David said, "and the resulting imbalance tells me exactly what I want to know. The bolt . . . slips into the notch . . . There! One of the numbers is thirty-seven. Now . . . just a moment"—he'd turned the knob—"it's the third number, isn't it? Only two numbers to go, and we're home."

David's back had been to him. Jimmy reached a tentative hand toward the telephone.

"What a good idea," David said, not turning around. "We can both talk to the police about what you have in here."

"They won't . . . They . . . You . . . What do *they* care what you're stealing?" But the tremor in Jimmy's voice had been too close to a sob. Those papers would tell the police as well as David that the Consortium's dealings just might have resulted in Hugh's death. "They'll put you away for years. Do you hear me? *Years!*"

"We can serve our time together." David had continued wobbling the combination discs as he talked. "On the other hand, you have to bear in mind that even if I let you make that call, a squad car will take maybe ten minutes to reach here. They rely so heavily on security systems like yours that they don't patrol this part of the lake with any great sense of commitment. You ought to mount a residents' protest. Of course, you might be lucky, but this is a very simple safe—no more than a five-minute job. That should give me, say, five minutes' leeway." He'd turned to face Jimmy. "Do you suppose you'll be alive when they get here?"

Jimmy had already been scared out of his wits, but the anger-whipped control that fought its way across David's face so terrified him that he fell against a table, knocking it sideways. Less than five minutes later, David took a clutch of papers out of the safe and packed them into his briefcase. And to think that only this evening Jimmy had been free and clear: clear in Galleas's eyes—whoever or whatever they were—and free of the one person who could expose him. His teeth were chattering. He tried to say something as David was leaving, but no words came.

"You never gave me that drink, did you?" David said, turning back to face him. "Don't worry. I'll be back for it—sooner rather than later if I find anything in this material that connects you with Hugh's death."

He'd shut the door behind him as he left, and Jimmy had sunk into this corner where he crouched still.

⟨∘⟩

On Monday morning, Stephanie awoke as exhausted as she'd been when she left Norb Andy's the day before. Some of it was hangover from a complicated flu. She knew that. Some of it was too many martinis. But the lion's share was grief, and she couldn't even bring herself to answer the telephone when David called. She hadn't expected it to hit her again. Not like this.

And why does grief have to settle on the silliest things? She thought Hugh was wonderful to look at and wonderful to go to bed with. He made important comments and brilliant observations. She loved the lines that scored his cheeks and gave way to dimples when he smiled. She loved the way his hands explored her body. She should never have taken David to lunch at Norb Andy's. That was stupid. Really stupid.

Because all she could think of now was lunch at a table not all that far from the one where she'd sat with David when Hugh told her that he'd feel strange if he ever had to walk around Washington Park on a Sunday afternoon without a chorus of "doggy doggy doggy woof woof doggy" following him as though he were the Pied Piper. She'd laughed and laughed. Maybe he'd said funnier things, but the bemused, amused quality on his face had never seemed more charming to her. He was a little embarrassed—a slight flush on his cheeks—as though he wasn't sure what her response would be and couldn't quite understand why he was telling her about it in the first place.

How could such an innocent, insignificant memory have turned into an instrument of torture? She couldn't staunch the blood. She couldn't salve the agony of it. The thing about Hugh . . . A man with modestly crossed eyes has to concentrate hard to see you. It makes him look as though he's fascinated by you, anxious to please you and yet a little fearful that he might get it wrong—and that's sexier than practically anything else. Michelangelo's *David* is a little cross-eyed, and scholars seem to wonder why so great a sculptor would have included so unexpected and unnecessary a flaw in a study of the perfect man. But how can a man be perfect if he isn't fascinated by you? if he isn't trying to please you and a little worried that he might not be succeeding?

Hugh couldn't see at all and kept trying to make out her face even so, kept trying to *see* her every reaction even though the task was hopeless.

Motel rooms are as indifferent as the dead, which ought to be balm to someone as overwhelmed as Stephanie felt by this memory. But why remember "woof woof doggy doggy" at all? Why not remember the profundities or the languorous hours upstairs on her own bed? She paced from soulless motel bed to blank face of TV and back again, trying her damnedest not to think at all. Yet at the same time she was afraid to let go of her thoughts, afraid that she might forget too much and that her dreams of him would become less frequent—and they were rare enough as it was.

And yet the idea of dreaming about him always brought David to mind.

◄o►

I may have worried about David's ability to function in the world outside the fiercely enforced laws and brutal atmosphere of a prison, but Stephanie didn't.

"He's going to be absolutely fine." She said it several times.

Stephanie owned a small clapboard house on the north side of town, where there are still some old buildings. This one had a living room cum dining room and kitchen downstairs; upstairs there had been three small bedrooms that she had combined into a single large one dominated by a bed—although perhaps the domination of the bed is just the way I think of it now. She had told me she loved pillows in brilliant colors; a collection of them decorated her bed, pillows made by Kodiaks and Aleuts—mementos of her unusual ancestry—with a few South American ones thrown in for variety. The walls were white; the windows and doors were raw wood darkened with age. So was the staircase leading to this room of many memories. From her descriptions, it must have been a very handsome place.

One night—we were lying among the many pillows—she said, "You've got to stop worrying about David. Only today . . . Oh, I forgot to tell you about it, didn't I? This afternoon I talked to this woman—"

"What woman?"

"You probably know her. She grew up here and married a chemistry professor at Chicago." I shook my head. "Curly hair, pert little nose, sassy smile—very pretty—the kind of person you'd expect to see as the boss's secretary and you might be suspicious about just how she managed to keep her job. She is the absolute opposite of what you expect from a top political analyst for the *St. Louis Post-Dispatch*."

"The *St. Louis* . . . ? You cannot mean Florida Evans Powell."

"That's the one."

"I always imagined her with a beard and a black belt in karate."

"One of those ghastly foster families of David's mentioned her, so I e-mailed her and it turned out she was right here in Springfield spending a couple of days with her parents. She told me she'd been a classmate of his during one of the short periods when he went to school. Eleven years old. Maybe twelve. Seventh grade, I think. She said he had a cocky walk the other kids envied, and he didn't give a damn what anybody else thought or did. He didn't seem more interested in her than he was in any of the others, but one day when she was sitting at a table in the library—she was a good student and I bet she was a really cute little girl—he sauntered past, paused a moment, then turned back, leaned over her and said:

" 'Dreamed about you last night, kid.' "

I laughed at the sheer incongruity of such a comment ever having come from the edgy, explosive character I knew.

"Anybody who can say things like that"—Stephanie was laughing too—"is going to do just fine on this side of the bars. Don't you think?"

usual in the process—just old-fashioned theft followed by money laundering—and there's a lot more of it around than most people tend to think. Mafia accountants keep track of their share of similar goings-on in a very straightforward way: two sets of books, one for the IRS, another for the organization. The organization books are what put Al Capone behind bars. The papers in Jimmy's safe would do the same for him and the rest of the Consortium if the FBI ever got hold of them.

David had been surprised and delighted to find out that Allen Madison, president of the Springfield Federal Bank, was a member of this manifestly crooked and mystery-shrouded organization—the very man revealed in Stephanie's material as an early investor in the takeover of the mirrored palace. Hugh's broker, another of the stuffed shirts David had visited in search of Hugh's finances, was also a member. Perhaps that's why David had sensed some strange tension in the two of them, something that he could identify only as a very much out-of-place fear. It just might make sense since the broker had provided him with a list of Hugh's directorships—a list that hadn't included the bankrupt company, and yet Hugh's signature was on Jimmy's paperwork as executive director just days before the bust. It wasn't hard to imagine a flurry of telephone calls and a hurried conference. Only a day or so after David called on those guys, he'd first spotted the battered Ford.

But the thought didn't hold him long. What good would following him around do for the Consortium? Respectable businessmen scratch each other's eyes out for money every day, and they rarely murder guys like Hugh for it. They don't have to. They just hire a firm of even more expensive lawyers and cook the books some new way. They don't follow guys like David around either, especially when they think he couldn't possibly be qualified to catch them out if there was anything in Hugh's private papers to catch them out with—and there hadn't been.

But that brought him uncomfortably back to Tony's point that he ought to have his head examined. He hated that. He hated anybody saying it. He hated the thought even skirting the edges of his mind. And yet the truth of the matter was that the Consortium was no more than a long shot—a very long shot at that—and there wasn't anybody else. He saw no validity in Samuel's worries about the deaths of Hugh and Vivian putting him in the frame as the next victim; he'd put the whole idea down to an overfed ego the moment he heard it, and he still did. Which left him tangled in his own thought processes, turning a fluke of coincidence into a conspiracy or tailoring something he'd seen in an imagined plot: those terrifying twists and contortions of the brain that haunt convicts, especially ones who've spent as much time in solitary as David had.

He ordered another beer and turned resolutely to the TV.

◄o►

Back at his apartment, he began on a file from the Zemanski safe that looked as though Jimmy might have attached some special interest to it. It wasn't any thicker than the others, but the word "Galleas" printed on the cover had been underlined three times. David glanced through it. At first it seemed much like the Department of Defense contracts, except that this time it was a commercial company: an order placed that was never going to be delivered and a huge down payment paid that was destined to get lost one way or another during a convoluted trek around the globe. But tacked at the end of it was a brief report on the visit from the two Galleas representatives including the gist of the conversation.

Jimmy hadn't even tried to hide the sense of threat.

And what a relief it was for David. He leaned back in his chair and lit a cigarette from the butt of the one he'd been smoking. A threat like that gave credence to the tensions he'd sensed as fear in Hugh's banker and broker. Jimmy had doubtless informed other members of the Consortium of the visit from the Galleas sharks, and they all knew how ruthless Becky was. They might well have thought David was connected as much with the sharks as with her—which gave them every reason to be scared. They also had reason to want to find out where David was going and what he was doing, what he knew, what he might have guessed: hence the battered Ford. But it needed proof. There was still the possibility that he'd just misread the banker's and broker's faces.

He spent most of the night on Internet searches of Galleas, and shortly after seven the next morning, he put through a call to Samuel Clark. Samuel had given him a private number in case the police picked him up again or he needed help for any other reason. The conversation was long, over an hour. David took several pages of notes. As soon as he hung up, he booked a flight to New York, scheduled to leave early that evening; then he called Becky. At eleven, he set out for St. Louis.

The trip to the Mississippi River always began as an unexpected disappointment. In daylight, Illinois's minimalist landscape was cornfields crushed under a vast swathe of macadam with small towns scattered off to the sides like Coke cans tossed out of car windows. At the Illinois border, East St. Louis was barely the scrag end of an industrial town. But then comes the Mississippi itself, which never disappoints. For so massive a river, it's narrow where it separates East St. Louis from St. Louis proper, but still it's a vast, impassive expanse of water beneath the rush of traffic. On the far side of the bridge stands the Gateway Arch, a giant stainless steel parabola rising some 630 feet high, a soaring, heart-stopping creation glistening up into the sky no matter how familiar it's become—and how debased. Eero Saarinen borrowed the idea from Le Corbusier who'd designed it for Moscow's Palace of the Soviets, and it really is a charming irony that almost as soon as the arch appeared, that ultimate capitalist machine McDonald's swallowed it whole and spat it out as American hamburger.

The arch looms so high over the city that David could see it as he parked his Chevy near the mirror-sided construction of the Follaton complex. Glass doors led to the two-story-high lobby where pale gray marble took over when brushed chrome ran out. When Stephanie had come here, the bankrupt's logo, UACI, had flashed in orange and red above the muted lobby; the present logo flashed just the same, the only difference in the easily missed shifting of the A and the C to read UCAI. Otherwise, everything was exactly as she'd described it, including security tight enough to satisfy any government building. Armed and uniformed guards manned the checkpoint that David approached.

"Mr. Bagley," he said to them. "The name is Marion. I'm here on behalf of Mrs. Rebecca Freyl."

The guards checked David's driver's license, made a telephone call, issued him a visitor's pass.

The elevator David took—one of a bank of four—was a brushed

chrome and mirror cube that matched the lobby and the outside of the building. It let him off on the twentieth floor, an intensely quiet place with huge leather chairs and full-size trees in pots beneath panes of glass in the high ceiling. A receptionist waved him to a seat. Annual reports decorated the low marble table in front of him, pale gray like the lobby, and he flicked through the pages as he waited. "Univers Chemical & Analytical Industries": so that's what the switched letters of the logo stood for, no more Advanced Ceramics—at least not in the company name.

"Mr. Bagley will see you now, Mr. Marion," the receptionist said a few minutes later.

Mr. Bagley's office was large and as moneyed as the rest of the building. The vast desk he got up from was completely clear, not a paper to be seen on it. The man himself was as polished as the mirrors outside, youngish—early forties—steel-rimmed glasses, healthy complexion, graying temples, Hugo Boss suit. He shook David's hand and ushered him to the end of the room where a massive sofa and massive chairs looked out through a vast window wall to the Gateway Arch and the Mississippi beyond.

"Please sit down, Mr. Marion," he said. "Now, what can I do for you?"

David said that Becky had become personally interested in the operation and that he had come as her representative. Mr. Bagley smiled, leaned back and launched into a discussion of mining opportunities in Colombia and Tanzania and U.S. Navy contracts in Germany, much the same profile as the bankrupt Stephanie had investigated before this one began swelling to its present glory. David studied the room while Mr. Bagley talked. Diplomas and family photographs decorated the interior walls alongside trophies representing major deals and company milestones: those endlessly confusing acronyms, ACI, UIA, UCAC. A brass rack held three hard hats as testimony to Mr. Bagley's work on various mining projects.

"I read all this in your annual report," David interrupted after Bagley had been talking for five minutes or so. "There's quite a lot of overlap with the bankrupt Advanced Ceramics corporation, isn't there?"

"It's not really overlap, Mr. Marion. We bought a number of their assets. We drive a hard bargain when we get the opportunity, and I'm afraid they weren't in the best of positions at the time." He shook his head. "It always makes me feel sad when a good company goes down."

"As far as I can see, the two of you just shifted places. You were out and they were in. Now they're out and you're in."

Mr. Bagley studied him. "Mr. Marion, I'm happy to talk to you about this company, but I'm really not in a position to talk about another one."

"Thank you for your time," David said, getting up.

Mr. Bagley got up too. "I understood Mrs. Freyl had some questions."

"No."

They walked to the door together and shook hands again. "What did you really come here for?" Mr. Bagley said then.

"Information."

"Oh, come on, Mr. Marion. I haven't told you anything you didn't know already. There must be some aspect Mrs. Freyl would like to explore further. Otherwise, you've been wasting your time—and mine."

David glanced around him. "Okay. The bankruptcy that got all those nice assets for your company must have run into—let's see—maybe hundreds of millions?"

"Probably."

"How much of that did you manage to stuff into your own pockets?"

The fear on Mr. Bagley's face was replaced almost immediately by shock and outrage, but it was the fear that David had driven all this way to see. Here was the product naked, raw, uncomplicated—a stench of fear that any convict would detect, however hard he found reading faces on the outside—and it provided the confirmation he needed of what he thought he'd caught wind of in Hugh's banker and broker. David nodded his appreciation, opened the door and, leaving it open behind him, walked out through the expansive reception room to the elevator.

23

IT WAS NEARLY MIDNIGHT BY THE TIME DAVID WAS RID-
ing in a taxi from Kennedy Airport into the city that never sleeps.
Manhattan glittered ahead of him, an amazing sight for the first
time in a life. The movies don't prepare a person for this reality any
better than they do for a first flight in an airplane. A fantastic network of lights—it looked to David from the distance like a chain of
jewels—turned out to be the lights of FDR Drive shining into the
East River. The streets beyond seemed shoved underground by the
mass of buildings that soared on and on upward—that plainly
closed over somewhere out of sight way overhead—and squashed
the ground beneath with such force that steam boiled up from it.
The traffic could only scuttle along at the bottom protesting, loud,
frenetic even at this late hour. There was grandeur here of a kind
and on a scale he'd never imagined—the city is a gauntlet thrown
down to God Himself—and it went a long way toward preparing
him for the glory of the Plaza hotel.

He'd booked one of the Central Park suites, and there was a reason for the extravagance just as there had been a reason why his
ticket out of Chicago was first class—and not because the information in the bag he carried was worth a fortune either. This time he
was assuming some watchers—New York watchers who'd stay with
him until he left town—and he knew exactly who they would be if
they were there; Samuel had emphasized that appearance was
everything. The flight was no problem. Two years of running a
business on the outside and a good grasp of the Internet made buying a first class ticket not all that much of a challenge. David hadn't
needed Samuel's help with the hotel either despite his inexperience

in such matters. One of the first real novels he read in prison was F. Scott Fitzgerald's *The Great Gatsby*. He still remembered lines that sounded to him then like pure fairy tale: " . . . we all took the less explicable step of engaging the parlor of a suite in the Plaza Hotel." So David had taken that step himself—more explicable in his case than in Gatsby's—and the hotel's lobby lived up to the city that contains it: vast, chandeliered, encrusted, carpeted, polished and shining, an arrogant, insolent, shameless opulence.

They didn't call them "parlors" anymore. This came as something of a disappointment; they were "living rooms" now, and "living room" doesn't have quite the same ring to it. But it was only a momentary lapse. A sedate flurry ended in a liveried boy carrying David's suitcase to a suite so impressive it had a marble fireplace that didn't work. It had its own chandelier too, dangling heavy from the ceiling, and this *did* work; David flipped the light switch several times just to make sure. Inside the closets were hangers covered in padded satin. A cautious trip to the bathroom revealed wonders of plumbing he couldn't even identify. *Gatsby* was a summertime book. That party of Plaza-goers opened the windows to heat and dry summer smells from the park, and David more than half expected this city's semidivine powers to extend to providing even that.

But what blew in on him was air as freezing as Springfield air. He shut the windows and sat down to work at a carved and fluted desk; tomorrow was going to be difficult at best. He opened the Galleas Industries file from Jimmy's safe and stared at the first item: a copy of the original contract signed by Hugh for an $18 million consignment of "Ceramic Chest and Back Plates" to be shipped to Kirkuk. But what could $18 million worth of ceramic plates be *for*? It sounds like a comical order, as though the people of Kirkuk must have some strange custom of dressing themselves up in dinner dishes like Tweedledee and Tweedledum in *Alice's Adventures in Wonderland*.

The Internet is the best research tool in the history of the world. Ask the right question—any question on any subject—and the answer just falls into your lap. Of course, phrasing that question can sometimes call for art as well as ingenuity, but Kirkuk and advanced ceramics are easy topics. Kirkuk turned out to be a Kurdish stronghold, the center of Iraq's oil industry, connected by pipelines to ports on the Mediterranean. Advanced ceramics are a modern substitute for metal and a stunning improvement on it in all kinds of ways. They're stable at higher temperatures, lightweight and incredibly tough. They don't corrode. Maybe old ceramics were brittle; these aren't. Given such sterling qualities, it's not too surprising that they play a huge role in modern warfare. The radar-evading skin of the Stealth fighters in the 1991 Gulf War was made from them. In the 2003 Gulf War, a major use was in precisely such body armor as Galleas Industries had ordered. And what amazing armor it is; on top of its extreme light weight, it can stop multiple rounds from a thirty- to fifty-caliber machine gun at point-blank range. But it's expensive—fiercely expensive. In a six-month period, a single supplier can easily invoice the U.S. Department of Defense for $100 million of it, and the department has many such suppliers.

But only ground forces in heavy combat need ceramic body armor, and only governments have the legal right to raise armies. A *business* had no aboveboard reason to buy such stuff. The Galleas Industries Web site had looked to him much like other company Web sites: a short history, an abstract of a recent corporate report, an outline of their corporate structure, links to subsidiaries. They did have extensive oil interests in the Middle East, although nothing indicated they were involved in the war machine of any country. But following links from site to site, David ran across a mention of the company in a *Washington Post* story on mergers between business and the mysterious Mafia-like structures that play more of a role in international trade than anybody wants to admit—and raise their own armies for large-scale enforcement operations just as legitimate governments do. That was when he began to see just how much of a hornet's nest Jimmy had stumbled into.

He'd also turned up a CNN profile of Christina Haggarty, a leading figure in Galleas; she'd played a central role in his long conversation with Samuel Clark this morning. CNN began with unadulterated flattery—Christina was both beautiful and brilliant—and yet the profile had ended with speculations on her company's connections to shadowy peers in the crime world. Then by sheer fluke—a click on one of those innocuous-looking references that people follow when their concentration strays for a moment or two—David had run across an academic study so dry and stilted that it was virtually unreadable (which was probably why its author at Galleas Industries from her father, who had died the year she received her degree from Harvard Business School, leaving her with great power in her hands at the tender age of twenty-six. He'd been a legend in the financial world, ruthless, ambitious, imaginative. CNN compared her to the first Queen Elizabeth; the reporter said she was a lion's cub with a lion's heart and she even had the queen's red hair. A business rival was quoted as saying she was as terrifying as Elizabeth too, a Machiavellian ingenuity, an icy clarity of mind and something of the same royal disregard for the laws that bind ordinary mortals. Rumor had it that her initiative was behind Galleas's expansion into the oil-producing lands of the Middle East and that she ruled her territories there like fiefdoms.

Even in her tastes as a woman, Christina resembled Elizabeth; they both liked the rough, and David caught her eye the moment he entered the restaurant. Duchesse was a place for jewels and the most elegant of handmade clothes like the ones she wore herself. Not that there was anything wrong with his gray suit and gray knitted tie in raw silk, but to the rich and worldly, both were all too obviously off-the-rack and over-the counter. They hardly belonged here. And yet he wore them with an angry contempt and a natural ease that made origins irrelevant, that were all too reminiscent of the way that panther at the zoo wore its coat. Which is to say that he could have been wearing anything, anything at all, and still catch the eyes of a number of other diners—men and women both—as well as Christina's. She'd watched him for perhaps a full minute before she realized she was looking at David Marion; the dossier her staff had put together so quickly over the past twenty-four hours was complete with prison mug shots.

He approached her in the wake of the maître d'.

"Ms. Haggarty?" he said when he reached the table.

"Mr. Marion," said Christina. The handshake was as formal as Duchesse, which overlooked the East River with the Brooklyn Bridge in the distance: the very first example of steel in a suspension bridge when it was built a long, long time ago. The maître d' pulled out a chair for David with a flourish. David sat, caught sight of the bridge and stared out the window at it, transfixed for a moment by the glory of that extraordinary span, and the faint beginnings of a smile played at the corners of Christina's mouth.

"It was the longest bridge of all for years and years," she said. "You know, when they started, they figured they were putting up the eighth wonder of the world—that's what the papers called it back then—and they went right ahead and used defective wire rope in the cables. There's nothing so pleasing as old-fashioned graft, is there?"

"They take it down and start again?"

She shook her head. "Just wrapped it up in reinforcement. At the core of all that beauty and strength lurks the old cheap and cheesy wire. Makes it even more beautiful somehow, don't you think?"

"No."

"Oh, come now. Walt Whitman said the bridge completed Columbus's mission. Hart Crane said it was the affirmation of the divine wholeness and unity of all history. What's either assessment without a little sin at the heart?"

"I hate disorder." A waiter with the wine list stood hovering impatiently. David glanced at him, took the list, opened it. "Any preferences?" he said to Christina.

"I don't know what I'm going to eat yet."

"The rack of lamb?"

"Sounds good to me."

Christina waited impatiently to see what would happen next. An introduction through an eminent Supreme Court justice, the promise of insider knowledge of the UACI bankruptcy and a background that belonged to some character out of *A Clockwork Orange* or *Papillon*: David added up to a delicious unpredictability in a setting like Duchesse. No New York restaurant is considered first-rate unless the waiters are hideously rude to the clients, and these waiters were the rudest in all Manhattan. Furthermore, only French was spoken here; no member of the staff admitted even to understanding directions given in English.

David scanned the list. "La Turque 1990," he said. His French sounded comfortable if accented with what's known as "British schoolboy" (after all, Hugh had learned his own French in England). He handed the wine list back to the waiter. Then he added, *"Carré d'agneau pour deux."*

"Well, well, well," said Christina. "You're a man of many surprises."

David spread his hands in a gesture of self-deprecation that he'd learned from watching Hugh. Becky's dinner table every other Sunday for the past two years had taught him the general rules of battle; during his conversation with Samuel Clark, he'd taken careful notes.

"I would suggest the rack of lamb," Samuel had said. "It shows a fine balance between simplicity and elegance. Order it *bleu.* The wine . . . Let's see. You could try . . . No, no. How about a La Turque 1990? I know it's on their list, and it'll impress her. Check its background on the Net just in case she asks. Now, to the ritual of the wine tasting."

"Ritual?" David had asked.

"At Duchesse it's as rigid as any Japanese tea ceremony, a matter of timing, performance, elegance, knowledge. Wait until the sommelier has poured a little for you, lift the glass to check the wine's color, swirl it—are you writing this down?"

"Yes."

"Sniff it, take a sip, roll it around in your mouth, swallow—"

"You're putting me on."

"After you swallow, pause a moment, then nod."

"That's stupid."

"Go over it a couple of times with a glass of water. I kid you not, David. Any deviation marks you out as a barbarian."

Sitting across from Christina and watching the sommelier make his way toward the wine cellar, David rehearsed the steps in his mind. "So you flew in from Springfield yesterday, did you?" she was saying. "That's a pretty long way for a man like you to come for a talk about a sleazy piece of corporate fraud in which, so far as I know, he played no part. I gather you haven't been on an airplane half a dozen times in your whole life."

"It's not the fraud that concerns me."

"Oh?"

"I want to talk about Hugh Freyl."

"The murdered lawyer?" David nodded. "What about him?"

"He wasn't your man, Ms. Haggarty."

"You do get right down to business, don't you."

"Am I rushing you?"

"No, no. I like it." Christina glanced out at the bridge, then glanced back. "Most men over lunch are cats spraying a wall in the yard. I had to go to Kuwait a few months ago, and the wall-spraying went on for nearly two hours. Not a single issue could be discussed until each male's territory was clearly marked out. Women save so much time." The hint of a smile played about her lips again. "So do you, of course. Are you going to tell me how you come by this fascinating opinion?"

"What's important from your point of view is that I have the critical paperwork."

"That's what's important to us, is it?"

"Yes."

"Then I guess you'd better tell me about it."

"I have a copy of a UACI contract with Galleas that ties up in an interesting way to records of the sale of the subsidiary that handled all orders for ceramic armor. I also have some records tracking the down payment."

"Sounds to me as though somebody's getting ready to blackmail somebody." She rested her chin in her hands. Her eyes were a soft gray. "Whatever your loyalties or convictions, your Mr. Freyl certainly had an important role to play in our involvement with the company."

"I know."

"We first contacted him in—"

"Just about two years ago. February fourth."

She shook her head. "I don't understand why you've come to us."

"The delegation you sent out interests me."

"You mean Nicholson and French? How dare the UACI creditors demand $8 million for an unfulfilled order?"

"It's the law."

"Not for me it isn't. I should have handled the deal myself. My colleagues were overly impressed by Hugh Freyl. A man with a distinguished pedigree like that—and an equally distinguished career—shouldn't lend his name to such an affair. It's misleading."

Her face showed no sign that she was aware of the irony in what she said, so David said nothing. The sommelier appeared at the table and showed him the bottle of wine; he read the label and nodded as Samuel had taught him.

"*Monsieur?*" the sommelier said. This word in precisely this tone signaled the wine-tasting ceremony that even now David only half believed could be for real. And now that it was actually upon him, the order of the steps was somehow upset in his mind—even though it had been perfectly clear to him only five minutes ago. Sniff first? or sip? Why do either?

"Just pour it," he said to the sommelier in English, his French abruptly deserting him too.

The waiter frowned. *"Pardon, monsieur?"*

"If we don't like it, we'll send it back."

"Monsieur?" The tone was close to a snarl.

"Just pour the wine." David's glance of barely suppressed violence so rattled the sommelier that he obeyed despite himself.

Christina lifted her glass. *"Santé,"* she said. Guigal's La Turque 1990 is spicy and tannic, complex and fruity. "It's a Côte-Rôtie, isn't it? You must have learned a very great deal about France in your studies." David shrugged his indifference, and she set down her glass. "Tell me, if your Mr. Freyl wasn't the—what shall we call it?—the guiding hand behind UACI, what was he?"

"Fall guy."

"You're wonderfully blunt."

"There's no way around it."

They made a fine couple, these two, and yet there was something disturbing about them. Christina on her own would have slotted seamlessly into a restaurant where the walls were hand-painted, the glass imported from Murano, the staff exquisitely trained. But with David across from her, a dissonance entered the equation. It had nothing to do with his suit either, although the turbulent edginess on his face was clearly part of it. She seemed to catch, reflect, exaggerate him; he did the same for her. Together they brought to mind the spiny threat that gives a rose its special allure and turns puffer fish into a sought-after delicacy. Perhaps this was not too surprising. After all, here in this honeyed atmosphere, a major player in a criminal empire and a professional killer sat together at table over a rack of lamb that was rare enough to spill blood onto their plates.

The word "professional" in regard to David had meaning too. Becky had given it that, and while Christina knew him only as an amateur in the field, she was one of the few who knew the extent of his experience. Prison scuttlebutt—her researchers had readily tracked it down even in the brief period allowed them—confirmed what Hugh could never have guessed; David's kills were by no means limited to three. There's a righteous, moral testament for people like him. It comes from Mickey Cohen, the very mobster who buried Johnny Stompanato with full military honors not two hundred yards from Hugh Freyl in Oakland Cemetery: "I have killed no man that in the first place didn't deserve killing by the standards of our way of life." So it was with David. Within a couple of days of arriving in a place like Marion, a boy of fifteen is either whore to an older inmate or his murderer. There is no in-between. David had been fully aware of this from the time he was small. All street kids knew it. His first priority on arrival at the federal penitentiary was a knife; no more than a few hours after his transfer from the county lockup, he'd acquired a slender, six-inch blade whittled out of plastic—a "shank" is the word for it—that fitted neatly inside a sock.

As for the transfer Hugh had arranged from Marion to South Hams State Prison—the kindly act intended to place a vulnerable David in a more hospitable atmosphere—it had required a repeat performance.

Things didn't stop there either. They couldn't. Prison is a gladiator school; it teaches men *how* to kill, and the best gladiators rule all the others. They don't get caught for the simple reason that they're too important to the stability of the regime. With them in charge, an administration can control the inmate population. With them in rebellion, the administrators can be dead before they know there's anything to worry about. Which is to say David was not just a killer but a very good killer, and nobody ever pinned a murder on him despite the many times he ended up in solitary or the hole or the punishment cells for one infraction or another.

All this Christina knew, and yet not even she guessed the extent of it. What escaped her was something that had crouched in the dark recesses of his mind ever since he killed his foster father and foster brother—and it was the only thing about his skill that frightened him. He enjoyed it. He even knew the very moment he'd realized this uncomfortable truth about himself: Hugh's first visit to Marion Federal Penitentiary, when he'd made it clear that he was going to have David moved into another prison whether David liked the idea or not. David had stared at him, speechless with dread because he knew what such a move meant that he was going to have to do. Then abruptly—Hugh was talking some inane liberal guff about boys in prisons—dread gave way to the thrill that a born fighter feels on the eve of a battle. Strategy and tactics: how to lay the ambush, what weapon and how to use it. But most telling of all, there'd been a fore-taste of the triumph that comes with the kill itself, that ecstatic mo-ment when the control goes and a man is truly free.

"You can't mean you see no reason to live anywhere but Spring-field, Mr. Marion," Christina was saying. She leaned across the table to study him closely. "You do mean it though, don't you. You're enough of an alien right there in your own hometown." She took a bite of her lamb, chewed it contemplatively. "What is it you really want from me?"

"Just tell me about Hugh Freyl."

"I'm afraid I know all too little."

"He was blind. He was beaten to death. Somebody was making a very clear statement about something. The question is, what was the something?"

"Ah, I see," she said, eyeing him up and down, and by now her smile was broad. "You want to know if we . . . ?" She lifted her eye-brows.

"Yes."

"Galleas doesn't operate that way, Mr. Marion. It's not that I don't believe in meting out punishment where punishment is due, but it's hardly Galleas policy to torture blind men to death. It's inef-ficient."

"I see."

"It's not the way we do business, Mr. Marion."

"The way you do business sounds pretty rough to me."

"It is *not* the way we function."

A waiter cleared their plates. Another waiter swept away crumbs. A third took David's order for cheese and a second bottle of wine.

Then Christina said, "Let me assure you that we're anxious to help you in your search in any way we can. We've been hurt too, and we have resources you couldn't possibly tap."

"My only interest is Hugh Freyl."

"Our interests aren't all that divergent. What we're looking for is the central figure."

The structure of the secret Consortium wasn't revealed in the files of Jimmy's that David had reviewed so far. Hugh had been listed as executive director of the bankrupt UACI. His name was on the board of the daughter company now operating out of St. Louis, the company his banker, Allen Madison, had put money into; both Allen Madison and his broker, Piet, were on the board. Everybody listed as a member of that board was implicated, no matter who actually signed legal documents for the corporation. So David figured Hugh was a stooge for someone *not* on the list. Jimmy? Couldn't be. Jimmy didn't have the guts. Also, the only other file David had read carefully dealt with a government contract, and Jimmy didn't have the right kind of contacts to lobby the appropriations committees that hand out defense contracts.

"This is important to me," Christina was saying. "I've taken a personal interest in the case. I would not have agreed to meet you otherwise. It's true that I *dislike* being wrong, but I find it literally painful to be"—Christina seemed to struggle even with the phrase—"taken for a ride."

David was amused, and it showed.

"If there's a connection between the power structure and Mr. Freyl's death, will you let us help?" she went on.

"I'll welcome it."

"That's what I like to hear." She lifted her glass. "Meantime, I propose a substantial stipend—as an assurance of our goodwill, if nothing else."

"No."

"No?"

"That's not the way *I* do business."

At last Christina's smile broke into a laugh—and it was a laugh of pure pleasure. The cheese was perfect, the second bottle of wine even better than the first and the staff were cowed and cooperative, as befits a conquered people. When David and Christina had finished their coffee, she said, "I could use a man like you. Sometimes a person is less of an alien in an alien place. If you ever want to try out the idea, come to New York."

"I'll bear it in mind."

"Oh, dear, that's a very formal response. 'I'll bear it in mind' always means 'no,' doesn't it?"

David paid the bill; they picked up their coats, and as they walked out into the blare and the frenzied restlessness of New York streets, she said to him, "May I ask you a question?"

"Go on."

"Do the Monaghans have any idea at all about the—how can I put this?—the *complexity* of your prison life?"

The Monaghans? She really had done her homework on his past; David nodded his appreciation. He also knew she was talking about the murders that were no part of any official file anywhere. "Blackmail?" he said.

"Oh, dear no. Only curiosity. You interest me. You really do. How long have you been working with Tony Schama?"

More impressive homework. "I've known him a long time."

"I see." Christina paused. "Tonio Liberty Schama. Quite a name—no doubt about it—but Mr. Marion, you're an educated man."

"I've known him a long time," David said again.

"I suppose he isn't fully acquainted with the details of your past either?"

"No."

"You could do better, you know."

"That depends on what 'better' means."

"So it does. So it does," Christina said as they shook hands; it was as formal a gesture as their greeting two hours before. Then she gave him a teasing smile.

"I'll bear it in mind," she said.

24

THE MAN CALLED HIMSELF JOHN DOE. I SPOKE TO HIM only because he said he had information about David's case, and yet he seemed reluctant to go any further over the telephone. When I suggested we meet, he began to withdraw altogether.

"Look, I'm beginning to think I'm a real dumb jerk to be talking to you at all."

"You choose someplace discreet," I said. "I will be wherever you say whenever you say."

"I don't know. I just . . ."

"Why not Washington Park?"

Then he said, "I don't even know what I'm scared of. Maybe nothing."

"Would it help to know that I cannot identify your face?"

Athena and I waited for him on Sunday morning in front of the carillon. Springfield's carillon is the fifth largest in the world; sixty-six bronze bells hang in it, all of them cast at a three-hundred-year-old bell foundry in faraway Holland. There are few bell towers even approaching this caliber in the United States, and the noise it makes is glorious but very, very loud up so close. That afternoon the ringers were practicing for a concert. I realized Mr. Doe had kept his date with me only when I felt the tension in Athena.

"You know, the one good thing about being blind," he said—or rather, he shouted over the bells—"is being able to take your dog with you wherever you want."

"Mr. Doe? Is that you?"

"Yeah. Kind of, anyhow." He squatted to stroke Athena (I know this because she stiffened in her harness). "How come you been asking around about the Marion case?"

We set off along one of those winding paths into the park. As soon as the bells receded enough for normal speech, I said, "My assistant has a very sharp eye. Something in my files on David worried her, and it worried me because it worried her."

"Just kind of intrigued, huh?"

"You could say that."

"Figure you can get him out?"

"There are anomalies, and he is an unusual man."

"He's trouble."

"That too."

I told him how and why I had encountered David, and he remarked that he knew something of the early history because he was a retired policeman. I saw no reason to tell him that I had assumed he was connected with the force from the outset. The moment I realized what his interest was, I thought of the gossipy clerk down at the Springfield Police Department's Old Records Division; she would have bored the first person she encountered at the coffee machine with this blind man's requests for an old murder book.

"Look, I know it sounds corny," he said. "But, goddamnit, we're supposed to be the good guys and . . . See, it ain't right what was going on there."

"Before he was arrested? Afterward?"

"After, mainly."

We walked on for a moment in silence. "Are you going to tell me what went on?" I said.

"Sometimes the good guys get overeager. Know what I mean?"

"I can guess, Mr. Doe, but I would prefer not to."

"Supposing you ask me a question or two I can answer with a yes or a no." We sat down on a bench and again he leaned over to stroke Athena. Again she tensed herself against him. "I'm usually kind of good with dogs," he said unhappily. "This one sure don't like me much."

"It's not you, Mr. Doe. She is a professional on duty. Rather like a Secret Service agent."

"Yeah?"

"You must meet her in her free time one day."

"Friendlier, huh?"

I nodded. "A question that can be answered with a simple yes or no?" He grunted an assent. "Did you know that one of the pieces of evidence against David was a fingerprint on a lug wrench and that this print was not David's?"

"Yeah."

I could feel Mr. Doe becoming uncomfortable already, and what went through my mind was that Stephanie was even more remarkable than I'd thought. I could hardly wait to tell her about this. "Did you know that David had signed a confession?" He said nothing. "Mr. Doe?"

"Can't answer that."

"Why not?"

"Don't fit the terms of this here agreement of ours."

"Not a simple yes-or-no question?"

He sighed. "Nope."

"Suppose I rephrase it. Did you know the record states that David signed a confession?"

"Yeah."

"Was a confession presented to him to sign?"

"How the hell could he sign nothing?" Mr. Doe burst out. "He was beat up too bad. He was bleeding all over the joint. Ah, look, I'm sorry. I shouldn't a shouted. I hate this. I hate what you're asking me. I hate what I'm telling you. All of it."

"The record says he confessed."

"Sure it does. What do you expect?" The carillon went entirely silent for a moment, then started up again.

"Before you say any more, I have to tell you that I know who you are."

"I figured it wouldn't take you too long."

"Your name is Wellwood, isn't it? I remember you from the transcripts of your interview with David. You were a sergeant then. Doubtless you did not remain a sergeant long."

"Nope. Never made lieutenant."

"I'm sorry to hear it."

"Yeah."

"It's an unusual policeman who can get as much as you did from that boy."

"Couple of sentences ain't much to show for an hour and a half," he said. We walked on for a few minutes. "I told the guy defending him," he burst out then, and I could almost hear a sob in his voice. "I told him. I wrote it down for him in black and white—handed it to him myself.

Burned like hell it did, but I gave it to him with my own two hands."

No wonder he had been so cautious with his information. I could hardly have read David's records and not know who had defended him. "You are talking about my old friend John Calder, aren't you?" I said.

◄◦►

There are people who lead charmed lives. Senator John Calder was one of them. *Everybody* said he was going to be Illinois's next governor. The elite of Springfield, the guests at Hugh's funeral, simply assumed it. So did the media, who had mobbed him even at a time like that when he was officially mourning his friend. People in the street adored him. Perhaps his bad boy's smile and small boy's enthusiasm hadn't been on show at the funeral itself—after all, the dead man was Becky Freyl's son as well as his friend—but they were his trademarks. He was one of those people who could arrive at a cocktail party in his honor, disappear upstairs for half an hour with his host's ten-year-old son and a train set, then come back down and listen—as though it was the most fascinating conversation on earth—to a pompous magnate who droned on forever. He'd laugh at stupid jokes, take the hand offered him in both of his to shake it, assure the guy that these amazing insights would be top priority tomorrow. When the party broke up, the magnate would make out a $2,000 check to the Calder campaign—sometimes even a $20,000 check to the joint reelection committee that backed him—and slip the money discreetly into a Calder aide's pocket.

And this future governor was so much the embodiment of what every red-blooded American male wanted to be. He could shoot and hunt and fish. He'd boxed a little and sailed some. He kept four mutts in varying sizes and walked them as a pack; he drove a Special Forces–issue Land Rover and indulged a passion for single malt Scotch. His young and pretty doctor wife worked at one of those major teaching hospitals in St. Louis, and while she bought some of her clothes at Neiman Marcus, her personal secretary swore she made a few of them herself. She even bought her towels at JCPenney.

Or rather, some people lead charmed lives *most* of the time. Which leaves the occasional slip from favor. The senator's father had lost the family fortune. John still couldn't believe such a calamity had happened. To John Calder? *The* John Calder? There's nothing more appealing in a man than a tragedy overcome, but his misfortune had actually done him the damage that added a touch of vote-winning vulnerability to his strong features. Things used to be so simple, so certain. Now if anyone gave him an unexpectedly hard time, doubts and complexities came flooding in to muddy the picture. Like today. Today he was being interviewed by a notoriously difficult journalist from Chicago, and he was far from at his best anyhow. Last night . . . Well, last night was *rough*.

Worse, his aide had warned him. "Turn her down, Senator. Three positive interviews are more than Ms. Pickles has ever meted out. This is number four. The odds are way too high that she'll roast you this time."

John had brushed this excellent advice aside. "Come on, she likes me. Everybody likes me. Even you."

And then the journalist said right out of nowhere, "What do you figure, John? Are you a giggly drunk or a sloppy one?"

"I'm not any kind of drunk at all," he said irritably before his aide (or his own well-honed good sense) could intervene to stop him.

"Look at the bags under your eyes. I'll bet just about anybody that you hung one on last night. Come on, tell little old me, happy drunk or weepy drunk?"

At the last interview they'd laughed together over a fine single malt. They'd clinked glasses. They'd both drunk a little more than was strictly prudent, and the interview that appeared had painted precisely the picture of him that he liked best, principled, forceful, with just enough spice and humor to lighten the mix. So he laughed this time as he had then and said, "Well, if you're going to press the point, I suppose you could say I tend toward the sanguine."

" 'Sanguine' huh?"

She gave him a pained expression; that's when he should have known that the bitch had decided before she left to meet him that she'd present him as a man who'd gone as far as he was likely to go. "Hey, you don't look any friendlier than you sound," he said. "Where's my old drinking companion got to?"

The pained expression only deepened. "Gimme a break, John. I covered your first landslide to the legislature. I covered the state senate campaign you lost. I read the stuff you put out as God-on-wheels behind the death penalty while you sat on your ass and nursed your wounds: crime on the streets, terrorism abroad, blah, blah, blah. Another landslide to the Senate. Wrote about that too. Major force on defense appropriations . . . See?" she said, turning to the aide. "You're only a piece of machinery and you're already asleep."

Painful accuracy was Georgie's trademark; the aide was young and very stern but . . . well, other human characteristics were scarce. Sex? The hair was long and held at the back in a kind of a bun and the face was delicate, but the suit was manly as well as trim and tweedy. Blue shirt, mandarin collar. "Unless you can confine yourself to the senator's career"—even the voice hinted at computer simulation—"I will have to terminate this interview."

"You remember that guy," Georgie said as though the aide hadn't spoken. "Lemme see . . ." She rummaged in her purse. "David Marion. You defended him, didn't you? I had a look at the case. Nobody mentioned a single word about you in all this stuff about Hugh Freyl's murder. How'd that happen, huh?"

There was a pause. "Hugh and I grew up together."

"Yeah, sure," she said. "That's rough, but what about Marion?"

"So that's going to be your story, is it?"

"How come nobody mentioned the connection? Seems kind of funny to me: famous senator defended murderer who got out and killed senator's old buddy."

"You know I can't talk to you about the case, Georgie," he said, turning away from her. She waited. She knew he would go on; she could feel it in her bones. "Just look at the number of troubled kids we have on our streets. We all know they're there, and look what we feed them. Glorified violence. The murderer as hero. Blood in Technicolor. How come we're surprised when they turn vicious on us? Just *look* around you. Kids are turning into jungle predators right in front of our eyes. It's been going on for at least thirty years, maybe fifty. They're more than just predators. They're super predators. Georgie, we've tossed up a mutant gene: the murdering child who kills without thought and without remorse. Is there anything in modern life more terrifying?" The senator faced her again, and he did not have to play at the depth of his feeling. She could see it on his face—and was impressed despite herself. "Maybe worst of all: there's nobody to blame but ourselves. You know how rarely

public defenders win cases—it turned out to be a far more depress-
ing job than my youthful optimism allowed me to think—but having to defend super predators was a major reason why I quit that
side of the bench."

"What are you telling me? You'd have thrown Marion to the
wolves if you could have?"

John shook his head, regret of the past, sadness for the future, a
man who hadn't lost sight of the things that really mattered: this
time even his aide was impressed. "Just tell me what we've done
about the problem in all this time. We've dilly-dallied and shilly-
shallied. We have violent, unrepentant criminals on our streets—
they just happen to be young—and we say, 'Oh, they're really sweet
little boys and girls deep inside. They're just expressing themselves.
They'll grow out of it.'" He sighed heavily. "So people keep on
dying, and families never get the satisfaction of seeing the killers
punished to the full extent of the law. Maybe if we'd instituted a
death penalty for murderers no matter what their age when the
need first showed itself all those years ago . . ." He shrugged.

"Freyl might still be alive?"

"You said it. I didn't."

"And yet he's the one who went and got Marion released."

John sighed again. "I argued with him about it. I fought him. It
was such a crazy idea. Why? What good could come of it? Hugh's
mother was equally adamant. He wouldn't listen to either of us."

◄o►

Sergeant Wellwood and I walked in silence for quite a while; the bells
died out. I knew he was worried, and I was not entirely certain what had
upset him.

"I think maybe I said enough—more than enough," he said.

"Because John Calder is a friend of mine?"

"I don't know. Maybe. I'm real sorry if I've hurt your feelings."

"I like the man, Sergeant. He is charming and astute, but I am not
sentimental. I have no illusions about him. People do not become politi-
cians unless they are corrupt at one level or another. John would not give
a second thought to it if undermining me suited his purpose. As it stands,
I am much more useful to him if he treats me gently and respectfully."

The silence settled over us again. We turned back. Then the sergeant said, "Jesus, retired ten years, near enough anyhow, and still . . . God-damnit, not making lieutenant still churns me up inside. Every time I think of it . . ."

"I know."

"A guy like you?"

"Even a guy like me."

"Aw, come on. You don't know what you're saying."

"If I catch myself off guard, I resent going blind in much the same way, and that's nearly a quarter of a century ago now."

An abrupt breeze brought us the sound of bells again even though we were still quite a way from the carillon. "Calder caught me in the hall-way one afternoon," the sergeant said, "and thanked me nice and friendly-like for my information. Said it was real important for me to come forward but he didn't think what I was saying was 'substantive.' I said, 'Oh, yeah?' And he said, 'In this case, I'm afraid not.' I just stood there staring at him. I mean, come on, so maybe I'm just a dumb cop, but the kid's lawyer—his own lawyer—is telling me a forged signature on a confession isn't 'substantive'?"

"So the confession did carry a signature?"

"Yeah."

"And you know this signature was not David's."

"They handed him over to me right after they brought him in, and he was already pretty beat up. I got him to the hospital, and they patched him up some. Even so, I don't know how much of it happened before they brought him in, and how much—"

"Before?"

"At the garage. Anyhow, when I finished with him, I know they was taking him to Allandale."

"Allandale? Robin Allandale?"

"Yeah."

"Is he the one—?"

"Yeah."

People make complaints against the police all the time. It is normal and expected, a part of the job. It is even understandable: the police complain about the people they arrest; people complain back. Allegations are routinely dismissed unless a pattern develops that nobody can deny. In Lieutenant Allandale's case, complaints of undue force mounted up over the years. The authorities paid less attention than usual because his father was sheriff of Sangamon County, and the word of a sheriff's son carries weight. But he became involved in a street beating, ostensibly resisting arrest; unfortunately for him, a CCTV camera caught the incident: clearly a case of undue force. The lieutenant was reprimanded. Three more reprimands followed in quick succession. Not long afterward, an attorney swore out an affidavit stating that he had visited his client, found evidence of torture, photographed it and submitted it to a medical expert. The expert supported the claim. Lieutenant Allandale was charged along with his cohorts Sergeants O'Hara and Sanchez. Other cases appeared in the course of the proceedings against them, some of them very shocking: shattered cheekbones and kneecaps, broken jaws, ribs, fingers, cigarette burns and electrical burns, internal injuries. When a jury convicted the three men—it was one of the most public trials that Springfield has ever known—the headline in the *Illinois Times* ran: "Justice at last: Springfield's police torture ring feels the lash."

Allandale was sent to South Hams State Prison. He was killed within days of his arrival, and I have to admit that the first thing that crossed my mind when Sergeant Wellwood mentioned the name in connection with David was that David might have been the killer. On the other hand, South Hams must have been full of Allandale's victims; sending him there was a death sentence. Almost any inmate—or any group of inmates—could have been responsible, and I had caught wind of no rumors that implicated David. The carillon bells in Washington Park started in on one of those elaborately pretty eighteenth-century tunes, light entertainment for the rich and the bored.

"How badly did Allandale hurt the boy?" I asked the sergeant.

"Ah, Christ, I don't know. Allandale . . . He got a real kick out of that kind of thing. There's a lot of electrical stuff you can use if you know how, but Allandale kind of preferred body contact. They ended up calling in a vet from down the block."

"A vet? Are you serious?"

"They couldn't take him back to the hospital, could they? Hospitals keep records. Vets don't got to write down nothing—not if the patient is human. They'd been at David for, I don't know, maybe four or five days, and they got scared he might die on them. See, guys usually break pretty quick, especially young kids like that. You slap them once and they start crying for their mommies. After that, it's free sailing. You write out a

like this one. David sighed irritably. He feared the jumpy
[..] Tony suspected in him. He feared his own fear of them.
[..] a man can manage his terrors in a place like Marion, he ought
[..] able to defeat them absolutely on a pretty, tree-lined close on
[..] est side of Springfield. And yet as David passed the Honda, he
[..] see the driver still inside. Who sits in the dark for nothing?
[..] He turned into the four-lane highway of the boulevard. Then
[..] versed back into the close. The Honda was just pulling away.
[..] screeched into its path and stopped short. There was a mo-
[..]'s pause before the Honda's driver threw open the car door and
[..] running. He knocked furiously on the Chevy's window. He
[..] a chunky man in his fifties, in pretty good shape for a man his
[..] dark-eyed, gray hair cropped within a half an inch of his skull.
[..] face was clearly visible in the light from the streetlamps, proba-
[..] Hispanic somewhere not too far back.

David rolled down the glass.

"What in hell do you think you're doing?" the driver cried.

"I don't like people following me."

The driver seemed genuinely taken aback. "You don't like . . .
[..] think I'm doing *what*? What's the matter with you? Why would
[..] llow *you*?"

"What are you doing here?"

"I *live* here. What do you expect?"

"Prove it."

"Are you out of your mind? Why should I?"

"Prove it," David repeated.

"Jesus, I'm so goddamned tired I can hardly . . . Oh, to hell
[..] th it." The driver turned and aimed his remote at the garage of
[..] e house in front of which he'd been parked. The garage door
[..] eaked itself open. "Satisfied?" David studied him a minute, then
[..] lled up the window without a word. "You know what you are?"
[..] e driver called after him as he drove away. "You're paranoid.
[..] hat's what."

◄◦►

[..] ockran's was as smoke-filled, noisy, barren as usual. As usual,
[..] ony was at the bar, his back to the door. David slid onto a stool be-

confession, close the books, call the mommy and everybody's happy. But
this David . . . Allandale was getting more and more hyped up, and the
kid wouldn't say nothing. Not a word. So Allandale starts wanting a
signed confession, not just any old confession."

The carillon's pretty tune played on, growing louder as we approached the bell tower itself. "You've never spoken to anybody about
this?"

"Allandale was a cop, see?" the sergeant burst out. "Maybe he was a
shit, but he was a cop." There was an uncomfortable pause. "What the
hell. I don't know. Maybe we all stayed out in the sun too long or something. Nobody gave a rat's ass what happened to that boy David. Not
Calder. Not me. Not even himself. Maybe that was what's saddest. That
boy felt guilty. He didn't say nothing much, but I got the sense . . ." The
sergeant paused. "I don't know. Maybe guilt ain't quite it. Maybe it's like
the only thing that scared him was what he done. He certainly wasn't
scared of me. He wasn't even scared of Allandale. Kind a like he'd caught
sight of something deep inside himself that maybe he hadn't known was
there before and . . ." The sergeant trailed off again.

". . . he felt he deserved whatever they meted out to him?"

He sighed once more. "Yeah. I guess. Something like that."

25

IT WAS AFTER TEN IN THE EVENING BY THE TIME THE LIT-
tle sixteen-seater plane from Chicago, final leg in David's return from New York and his meeting with Christina Haggarty, landed at Springfield Airport. He picked up the Chevy from the airport parking lot and drove to the east side as preoccupied as he had been when he left Manhattan.

If not Galleas, then what? Or who?

Because he didn't doubt Christina Haggarty. He was good at assessing other killers; it was a part of his own skill in the trade. She didn't use her own hands as he did. Of course she didn't; she gave orders from a boardroom. But her style was unmistakable from the way she conducted business: orderly, efficient, cool-headed. A bullet behind the ear would have been a likely method of choice. Hugh's murder was the reverse: messy, risky, emotion-charged. Besides, David knew from what she said that she would have wanted other potential threats to find out about the price of betrayal—and be warned. She'd have left her mark on the scene.

He parked the car beside a low bank of filthy, week-old snow, climbed the stairs to his apartment, opened the door, flipped on the ceiling light. The place was empty. Absolutely empty. There was not a packing crate to be seen. No bed, no chairs, no anything. He leaned against the wall, took out a cigarette, lit it and gazed around at the bare space that had been his home for two years: shadeless bulb, dirty windows, stark walls. Then he threw the stub on the floor, ground it out with his shoe, flipped off the light, locked the door behind him, got back into the Chevy and headed west.

He turned into Jefferson Place, a tree-lined close just off the

four-lane highway of Grover Cleveland Boul across town from his apartment. Cast-iron str row lit up the clean-swept roadway and side windows of two other houses—one next do street—threw out bright pools onto tended a ground. He parked the car at the curb. A sh neath a deciduous tree—rough, raw sketch of against the sky—brought him to an elegant fro solid wood. He fished in his pocket for keys and

This time the flip of a switch brought on so ing. There was an entryway with closets th doors; the room beyond was large and open; its stone fireplace banked on either side by double out onto a patio that could be visible with switch if he wanted it. His packing crates were was his sofa bed, the big round table, the chair: which was lying on its side, a desolate reminder He checked to make sure Stephanie's suitcase a ski's files had made the journey, then he left, lo hind him. He drove slowly back along the privat Place, from this day forward his official address the business he and Tony ran together. That's wh Honda parked in front of the last house before the highway beyond.

Either Tony was right, and his mind had mad of its own or the Consortium really had decid tailed—and had hired somebody very professiona true that there were lots of black Hondas around, mistake cars in the dark. Even so, David could have was the same one he'd seen at Springfield Airport t when he picked up the Chevy. It was a markedly cle car, the Honda, a world away from the battered For ken taillight that he'd thought was following him be New York. Not that David knew much about follow Tony's point about the Ford sounded reasonable: it use on the east side where nobody would notice i would have stuck out like raw sewage—rather as h did. The Honda, on the other hand, slotted neatly in

close
nerve

If
to be
the w
could
Why
he re
Davi
men
came
was
age,
His
bly

You
I fo

w
th
cr
ro
th

T

side him. Jason, the bartender, nodded a greeting. The mirror above the bar had smears across it where he'd made a halfhearted attempt at cleaning a day or two before.

"Give me a Scotch," David said, lighting a cigarette.

"You off the beer?" said Jason.

"For tonight."

Tony kept his eyes forward. "You been a hard man to find today," he said to David.

"I had things to do."

"You did, huh?"

"Yes."

" 'Things to do.' Kiss my ass. You just plain forgot, didn't you." Tony swung around to face him. "So who's got to move house for you? Me. That's who. You arranged it yourself. Said today had to be the day. *Had* to be. Remember? You ordered the truck. Remember that? What did I do? I done exactly what I said I'd do. I was *there.* That poor old lady of mine was having a real bad day too. She needed me to stay there with her, but did I let you down? No, I did not. Her regular home-care was off sick, so I had to get me on the phone and hire a private nurse for her—fifty-eight bucks an hour for five fucking hours and *nothing* in return, not a single . . . Ah, come on, David, what are you doing *now*?"

David had taken out his wallet; he tossed $300 onto the bar. "That ought to cover it," he said.

"I didn't say it was your problem. I didn't say *nothing* like that, and you know it. Besides, it's too much. What do you expect me to do? Make change?"

David shrugged. "Keep the change," he said. His tone was precisely the one he'd used when he'd tipped cabdrivers in New York.

"Don't you ever say you're sorry about *nothing*? Don't you think you at least owe me some kind of a apology or something? You got to the point where if you got a problem, you think all you got to do is shove money at it." The bartender set David's Scotch down in front of him. "What's the matter with you anyways?" Tony went on: "Forgetting something like that? You never forget nothing, and here you're forgetting the stuff that's so fucking important you're going to drop the way you lived for your whole life long. Put that together with all that stuff about guys following you . . ." Tony shook his head. He poked at the $300—it still lay on the bar where David had set it—as though it were a half-dead mouse. "Them rich guys really done a job on you, David. They got you packaged up just like chicken soup. Cute little can. Neat, cute little label on it. Open it up, and what you got inside? Ain't nothing but cat piss. You can't remember what you're doing and you can't remember your old friends when they're doing it for you. What is that, huh? Holes in the head? Too much prison shit in your veins? I'm telling you, David, I *know* you, and you're a man been selling off his soul in job lots since the day you got out. You forgetting who you are and where you come from. We're not good enough for you no more."

David didn't counter the charge because he couldn't. He was out of place in his snazzy new house on the west side of Springfield, and he knew it. He didn't understand the people who lived there; he didn't want to understand them. The trouble was, he was as much of a stranger in the east. It had taken him nearly all this time to realize he didn't belong there either. As Christina said, he was an educated man; he had learned to want—even to need—the trappings that come with such an altered state of mind. But there were other elements too, and there was no way even to approach an explanation that would mean anything to Tony. Tony had adapted quite well to the dislocated life of foster child in many homes. Within weeks, he was either out altogether or he'd come to dominate the family who'd taken him in. Except for the Hunters—and for all David knew, even with them—he ruled the families as harshly, absolutely, gleefully as any petty monarch until he managed to get caught dealing or carjacking or whatever and sent away for another stay in some juvenile detention center. Once inside, he ruled the other boys the same way he ruled the foster families outside—except for a couple of months of one stretch when David was with him—and he enjoyed it.

David's experience wasn't at all like that. The moment he was in the door of a new foster family, he wanted out. It didn't matter who the family was. All he wanted was to get away from them, but what he wanted most was a place that nobody else had ever lived in before him. The idea had grown on him gradually until he came to hunger after it, and this west-side house was in a fresh new development. He would be the very first person to live in it.

Tony watched David's face in the barroom mirror, and despite the lack of expression on it, he had a pretty good idea what was going on. David always did think too much. He let a few surly minutes go by, then he said, "I love you, David. You know that. You're the only guy outside of the Hunters that I ever did love. So I forgive you. What the hell, I'll even get off your back. I promise. I know you got troubles of your own. Hey, come on, lighten up, huh? After all, I had some adventures with your furniture. Some fat old woman said she was going to call the cops less of which I could prove you hired me to move you. That had me stumped for a moment. I sure didn't want to carry all that junk back across town and hoist it up five flights of stairs. So I put a pencil behind my ear, called her "ma'am" and showed her your signature on the bill."

"That do the trick?"

"She watched me the whole time from behind her curtains— had her hand hovering over the phone." Tony laughed. "If that's what you want—fat old ladies checking up on your every move— well, who am I to stand in your way? But you sure as hell owe me a couple of drinks."

"I owe you far more than that."

"Then start paying up, friend. Start paying up."

In America, the citizen is king, even the citizen who finds himself in prison. When he petitions for a writ of habeas corpus he is asking for permission to create his own private court. It is not only as lawful an assembly as any court in the land, it's a true royal tribunal in that it takes precedence over the state and sits in judgment of it. If the writ is accepted, David Marion, convicted murderer and yet citizen king can order the state to produce evidence of the injury it claims he caused. If he can demonstrate to a judge—for one like David, this would probably be a lower court judge—that the case against him is fatally flawed, he has the absolute right to dismiss it.

The origins of this glorious law date all the way back to 1215, to King John and the Magna Carta; Article 39 was the very first curb on a sovereign's power, institutionalized nearly five hundred years later in the Habeas Corpus Act of 1679. American colonists fought the Revolutionary

War in large part to reclaim this very right for themselves; the Constitution guarantees it to us all. Of course it was only a dream, then as now—more of a dream now than ever before. Even so, it is a dream that can be brought before a court.

Stephanie and I were propped up on the pillows of the big bed in her house one day when I said to her, "You know, it has been one of my lifetime ambitions to present a habeas case."

"It's David you're talking about, isn't it? One of those back doors you mentioned?"

"Not exactly."

"But it can be made into one?"

"Winston Churchill wrote that the true measure of a civilized society is how it treats people accused of crimes."

She raised herself up on an elbow, and I could feel her studying my frown for clues. "Oh, dear, so it's not going to be easy?"

"The route would have been a good deal more straightforward ten years ago."

"You're saying it's a gamble."

"It is certainly that."

"Risky?"

"Depends on how we go about it."

"Oh, Hugh, this is going to be fun, isn't it? If the thing's still on the books, you can turn it into whatever you need. I know you can. What is it anyhow?"

There are many famous cases, and changes have occurred in the law and the Constitution itself as a result of them. In 1858, the government signed Ponca territory in Nebraska over to the Sioux and drove the Ponca into Oklahoma. This was one of the infamous forced marches that shocked foreign correspondents of the time: men, women, children stripped of tools, seed, household goods and whipped like cattle into a single-file herd to walk all the way across Kansas. The Ponca died in droves. Many more died when they reached the unfamiliar and inhospitable new land. Their chief, Standing Bear, and about thirty others returned to Nebraska in defiance—only to be arrested and thrown in jail.

John Webster and A. J. Poppleton, two country lawyers with high ideals, helped the chief petition the court with a writ of habeas corpus. The government response? It sounds like something out of a Nazi handbook. Their case rested on the premise that the Ponca were not human beings within the definition of U.S. law. If they were not human, they could not be citizens. If they were not citizens, they had no right to bring suit. This is the kind of thing that makes us hang our heads in shame; only the courts allow us to lift our gaze again: the decision went in favor of the Ponca. Which is to say that a writ of habeas corpus is the means by which we bestowed the official title of "human" on the people we found in this country when we arrived.

Standing Bear and his thirty followers were released. Their land was restored to them.

"So that's how come I have the same rights as you," Stephanie said to me.

I shook my head. "I am afraid you are a woman before you are anything else. You had quite a while to wait. Some might argue that you are waiting still."

The hours I spent with Stephanie at her small house constituted a magical period in my life. An aura of youth, hope, adventure bathed the relationship. Simple things took on a glow that I had assumed was long dead. From the time I was a small boy until I lost my sight, mornings had been my favorite time—hardly a characteristic that endeared me to Rose, who woke with a depressive's dread of what lay in front of her. Stephanie seemed as delighted at the prospect of a new day as I had been once, and slowly I began to feel that way again. It was as though I could see the first rays of dawn myself, just by the pleasure I could feel surging through her when she woke in my arms. The afternoons and evenings had a blessed quality too, work punctuated by lunch at a restaurant and ending in a drink, dinner, love, sleep. Who needs concerts and cocktail parties? We seemed sufficient unto ourselves, and we talked about everything, wonderful conversations: gossip, books, the meaning of truth, the best way to plant basil seeds. Weekends were especially charmed; somehow she turned them into relaxed, easy times that ranged from the big bed with its many pillows to a bottle of wine and back to the bed again.

"Habeas corpus sounds just like an appeal to me," she said as we lay among the pillows. "What's the difference?"

"Nothing outside the record is admissible on appeal. A habeas petition is a way of raising issues that do not appear on the record."

"How about time limits?"

"Only for federal cases. This one would start out as a state petition, and there are a number of detours around state limits. If we lost, we could then move to a federal court. Allandale's torture ring certainly violated David's constitutional rights. So did our esteemed Senator John Calder in failing to follow up that information about the confession. So did the prosecution."

"When do we start?" She was already getting up. "What do we have to do?"

"Come back here," I said, grabbing her before she could escape me, pulling her back. "First things first. A step at a time."

Legal cases are mountains to climb. Each move has to be hacked out of the rock face—and the body of the climber hoisted up its couple of feet—before the next one can be considered. But the overall plan of ascent went like this:

One, submit a habeas writ to convince the court to review the charge of first-degree murder against David.

Two, persuade the court that the conviction was unlawful—that the confession was forced, the evidence flawed and due process not accorded in his original trial.

Three, work out a deal with the prosecutor to reduce murder in the first degree to what's called in the tangled obscurity of legalese "the lesser included of voluntary manslaughter."

And finally, argue that the years David had already spent behind bars were enough to fulfill the debt that society demands of him.

"Will it work, Hugh?"

"You can never tell what a court is going to decide."

"If it does work, I suppose the prosecution goes right ahead and appeals, and we start all over again."

I shrugged. "Unlikely."

"He's really got a chance? Can we do it? Can *you* do it?"

"It just may turn out to be a little tricky."

"But you're going to try?"

"Why not?"

In fact, it was as sheer a mountain face as I had ever contemplated. Sergeant Wellwood's information made a good enough case in law, but there are literally hundreds of habeas writs with foundations just as strong or even stronger, and they get nowhere.

◄o►

The Monaghans' house was the only house on Cooper Street with any hedge at all, much less a six-foot privet hedge. Mr. Monaghan kept it perfectly clipped; he was very proud of it. Except in spring-time, when he let it bloom and straggle until it was finished, its cor-ners were precise right angles; its top was accurate to the green bubble in his level. He and his wife were reclusive people with a very private approach to life—David had known this for nearly a quarter of a century—and yet every time he saw the hedge he thought of his panicky street kid's reaction to it: they'd grown it only to hide away from the neighbors whatever evil they carried on behind it. He parked, opened the gate and walked down the long flight of steps to the front door.

Most of the time he loved these visits and looked forward to them with a delighted, innocent anticipation; they were a home-coming, a magical event—something he'd never expected to have once in his life, and yet he'd experienced it again and again. Each time he arrived they greeted him as though he was the person they most wanted to see. They'd supported him just that way throughout his prison life, as steady as his own heartbeat, presents every Christ-mas—books, cigarettes, cash—six visits a year, a letter every month. One of the rare pieces of personal advice he'd asked of Hugh was what he might get for them in return, which is how he'd come to understand about the ritual of Christmas gifts. And his first Christ-mas attempt as a free man had been a silk shawl for Mrs. Mon-aghan, shantung with wide beige and tan stripes. She'd put it on at once and wore it often; she swore it was her favorite piece of cloth-ing. But presents outside of Christmas? The small elegant packages, one in each pocket of his leather jacket, irritated him. They embar-rassed him. He wished with all his heart that they weren't there. He'd probably paid too much. Or had he paid too little? Should he have wrapped the packages? Put cards on them? The Monaghans ir-ritated him too. What were they so kindly *for*? If they were just nor-mal people, he wouldn't be in this position.

Not long after he'd got out of prison, he'd installed a security system for them; it was that job combined with the glaring flaws in the system at Herndon & Freyl that gave him the idea for the busi-ness he and Tony ran. But the Monaghans had no more sense than Hugh did when it came to such matters. They practically always forgot the chain, and sometimes they even left the door unlocked. He rang the bell as he always did—he never used the key that they'd insisted he keep—and waited nervously, his mind circling those little packages and the minefield of presenting them.

The door flew open. "Davy!" cried Mrs. Monaghan, pulling him into her arms. No one else called him Davy. Hearing the name this day unsettled him even more than it usually did. It had always had the sound of the person he might have been—and that person would know all about giving presents. But she'd thrown the beige and tan shawl around her shoulders to answer the door: at least he'd got that one right. "How nice of you to come and see us. How *are* you? Come in. Come in. Don't stand out there getting cold."

"The door wasn't locked," David said, glowering to cover his unease.

"Let me have your jacket. Can you really be warm enough, wearing just a jacket? It's absolutely frigid outside. Bud will be so pleased. We were talking about you just now, and here you are!"

"You ought to keep that chain across."

"Oh, stop nagging. Come and sit. You'll have dinner with us, won't you? Plainly this was destined. I've made the pork you like and there's always way too much for just the two of us. I don't know *why* I do that. My mother always made too much salad, and I do exactly the same thing with pork."

She was leading him into the living room, which always reminded him of the tattered *Saturday Evening Post*s from the prison library, a homey Americana from another age. The overstuffed furniture was covered in a knobbly material and decorated with doilies that Mrs. Monaghan's grandmother had tatted nearly a century ago when she was learning household techniques at Springfield High School. The fireplace mantel held photographs of the Monaghan children and grandchildren; David was there too as though he'd been born into the family just like the others. More family pictures decorated the walls along with portraits of Lincoln and Vachel Lindsey, the homegrown poet who'd killed himself in Springfield, swallowing Lysol and stumbling down a grand staircase in front of his horrified family.

"The best people get out of this damn town," Mr. Monaghan said once; he had a tendency toward black moods. "The ones that stay behind end up like Lindsey. If they're lucky," he'd added, his mood blackening further. But this evening, he was in fine spirits. He shook David's hand, slapped him on the back, asked him how he was and what he'd been doing, sat him down and gave him a beer while his wife busied herself with the pork in the kitchen. The TV news was on, and David explained—talking over the noise—that he'd been in New York. Mrs. Monaghan appeared at the kitchen door at once, wiping her hands on her apron as though it were a dishcloth.

"You haven't!" she said. "Really? New York? What was it like? I've always wanted to go to New York." There was a sizzle from the kitchen. "No, no, don't say a word till I get this stuff on the table." She disappeared. "Don't tell *him* either," she shouted from the depths of the oven. "I must hear everything fresh."

As soon as the roast was on the table and the two men seated, she said, "So tell us about New York. Is it as exciting as it is in the movies? What's it like?"

"Big," David said. "Somehow I hadn't figured on it's being so *very* big."

"Start right at the beginning. How come you went there in the first place? Oh, you make me wish I was young."

So David explained that the trip had been in connection with a job he'd been given; he let the Monaghans assume it was another security installation, an out-of-state, one-off job. He described his flight to New York—giving it the excitement of that first sixteen-seater prop plane to Chicago when he was on his way to see Samuel Clark; he told them about his arrival at Kennedy, his impressions of Manhattan streets, the Plaza, Central Park, Brooklyn Bridge. He left out Christina Haggarty because that was business and he left out actually staying at the Plaza as well as eating at Duchesse because such things brought to mind the packages that nestled in his jacket pockets—that even from the hook in the hall-way seemed to be burning holes through the leather—and involved social rituals more impenetrable in the telling than in the experiences themselves.

But he spoke with a freedom and an ease that he had with no one else, not with Hugh, not with Tony. There'd always been a tutorial formality between him and Hugh, and despite all the years he and Tony had known each other, conversations between them tended to mark out territory that had been marked out again and again since they were children; even the silences that punctuated their talk amounted to a kind of macho hand-wrestling. This was basic stuff to any east-side male, but it hardly allowed for much leeway. Besides, the food was never as good when he and Tony ate together. It wasn't as good at Hugh's house either. Mrs. Monaghan's pork was roasted in thyme and mace; she used Madeira for the dark sauce that went with it: a simple dish but rich and full—like the character of the woman herself. She asked him questions with great excitement. She praised him for taking the trip in the first place, for describing it so well, for having had such wonderful experiences. She patted his hand and told him he was brilliant as she always did.

"You never say grace anymore," said David, the thought suddenly striking him. They sat at the big round table in the kitchen where he'd first eaten with them, oh, so very long ago when he was only eleven years old and hating everything in sight. In those days they'd always said grace; they hadn't said it once since he'd got out of prison, and he hadn't been able to bring himself to ask why until this very minute.

Mr. Monaghan looked fixedly down at his empty plate. Mrs. Monaghan studied David a minute, then bit her lip. "We thought you expected it, Davy," she said.

"Me? Why?"

"They said we had to be good Christians or you'd feel threatened. We had to go to church and we had to say grace. We were supposed to make you say prayers too, but somehow we just couldn't go that far." David shook his head; he'd certainly guessed at the corruption in Social Services by that time, but he hadn't realized the extent of the state's sanctimony. "It wasn't so bad," she said. "We got a book out of the library and did a little memorizing." There was a pause, and she added, "Sometimes you have to, well, kind of bend the rules to get what you want, and we so much wanted you. You aren't too disappointed in us, are you?"

At the time, so many years ago, David had been caught between a state that bordered on panic and a fierce physical hunger for the dinner he smelled in the Monaghans' kitchen. But all he could think of was the street kids' lore that the religious ones were always the worst, and his mind was scrambling in its darkest corners for hints of what might await him here.

"You scared me half to death," he said.

Mr. Monaghan laughed. "You certainly didn't *act* scared," he said.

"I was terrified."

"We kind of figured you might be."

"I've been scared ever since I can remember," David said. It was a statement of fact like his height or weight, and he thought uneasily of the small packages in his jacket pockets.

"Me too," Mr. Monaghan said. He tapped his plate gently with his fork. "Me too," he said again. "But I'd say you're the most unscared-*acting* person I ever knew. Man and boy: you seem scared of nothing. Know what I think? I think anybody who isn't scared is just plain stupid."

"That's a prison motto."

"More meat, Davy?" Mrs. Monaghan said.

And the words tumbled out despite him. "I bought you a keepsake," David said.

"From New York?" David nodded. "For me? Oh, goody. Let me see at once. I can't wait." Her cheeks were ruddy with pleasure. David got up and fetched his jacket from the hallway. He took out one of the small packages and handed it to her; it showed a delicate green world compass and the word "Rolex" in the lower left corner with a little crown on top. She looked up at him and smiled.

"Open it," he said.

Inside the protective outer layer, she found a small hardwood box. "A Rolex box," she said. "Oh, this *is* lovely. I'm going to put my watch in it right this very minute."

"Just open the box," David said, his voice tense as he awaited judgment on his gift, his whole body taut. He was still standing, and she glanced up at him uncertainly, then slowly lifted the hinged top of the box and peeped inside. On a cushion pillow was a watch that read ROLEX OYSTER PERPETUAL. She took it out, turned it over in her hands, studied it back to front, held it up to the light. A woman's Rolex is a handsome enough design, both delicate and strong although not as clean in its lines as the man's version. "Oh!" she said

on an intake of breath. "I've never seen anything so beautiful in all
my life." She got up impulsively and kissed David on the cheek.
Somewhat reassured, he took the watch from her and put it on her
wrist.

Again she held it up to the light. "It looks just like a real one,"
she said. "How can they do that?"

"It *is* real," David said. "It's white gold."

"White what?"

"I didn't like the platinum."

"It's—" She broke off, laughed, studied the watch as she had before. "It's the prettiest thing I ever saw. I never thought I'd be wearing . . ." Then she frowned. "But Davy, you don't really mean it's
real, do you? Real ones cost thousands. Even *I* know that. People
like me don't wear watches that cost that kind of money. I don't
know just *exactly* how much—but thousands."

And the bars of the cage slammed shut. How could he have
made himself so ridiculous? Why hadn't he just forgotten the whole
idea? put it out of his mind the moment it occurred to him? A Rolex
did cost too much. He'd made an attempt at this ritual of gift-giving
and messed it up entirely. When was he ever going to learn?

"Did it . . . cost you *thousands*?" she said timidly when he didn't
answer.

"Yes."

She looked up at the angry confusion on his face—and misinter-
preted it. "David, you did *buy* this watch, didn't you?"

David had no doubt that what he was seeing in both the Monaghans' faces as they scoured his for clues was that extraordinary
fear *for* him, not *of* him. So the tension in him eased off, and he
shrugged. "It was just sitting there on the counter," he said. "Right
out in the open. You wouldn't want a pretty thing like that to go to
waste, would you? Nobody will miss it."

Both Monaghans went pale, and there was a moment of dead silence. Then the strangest thing happened. David, who had not
laughed in years—who was famous for never even smiling—broke
into laughter. "Come on," he said, "it's okay. This job: a very rich
woman hired me to do it. She's paying me far too much, so I figure
what she really has in mind is that you ought to have an absurdly
expensive watch."

"It's the truth?" Mrs. Monaghan asked, her voice tremulous, pleading.

"God's truth. Cross my heart and hope to die."

She let out her breath and sank back in her chair. "Well, thank the Lord for that." Then she kicked his foot under the table. "How dare you scare me like that, you rascal?"

"So where's *my* Rolex?" said Mr. Monaghan.

"Just wanted to make you ask," David said. He pulled a matching package out of his pocket and set it on down on the table.

26

EVEN AFTER HE'D BEEN LIVING IN IT FOR SEVERAL DAYS, David's new house remained much as it was when he'd got home from New York. Empty boxes of Domino's pizzas and cartons from various Chinese outlets filled the garbage can under the sink in the kitchen; the plates used for them had been dried and put away. The only evidence that he had actually moved in was a bowl that served as an ashtray and the thick cigarette smoke that hung in the air.

It was early Saturday morning, and the double glass doors on either side of the fireplace revealed the patio and a wintry woodland beyond, a rare feature in this town. The sun was bleak and slanting; it cast shadows across the big round table between him and Stephanie, creating a kind of skyline—a low, disorderly east side of Springfield skyline in this very orderly west-side development—from stacks of glossy brochures, cash flow statements, balance sheets, inventories, tax claims, printouts of articles and analyses from the media. These piles of paper were growing taller sheet by sheet as the two of them sifted through the contents of Jimmy's safe and the suitcase she'd carried off the airplane, interspersing what they found with the results of Internet searches that explained obscure references, verified dates, filled out background material. They'd been at work ever since he got back, both of them strung out on coffee and adrenaline.

The contents of her suitcase showed the public face of the pre-bankruptcy UACI, complete with inspiring mission statement: "To provide Advanced Ceramics that surpass the expectations of each client and each shareholder." The annual report reflected a healthy, thriving corporate structure that broke down into companies responsible for mining, transporting, storing, processing, manufacturing and selling weapons-grade advanced ceramics as vehicle and body armor, visors, shields, missile sheathing and missile platforms and a list of other items that didn't really seem military except in the fine print.

Jimmy's safe was the dark side of that rosy picture, the shadowy world of a junior-league Enron in the days before its collapse. By now David was growing familiar with the manipulations that led huge cash borrowings, product sales and subsidiary sales through elaborate banking routes with zigzagged paths back and forth across the globe; he was beginning to see a pattern in the chunks of money that disappeared entirely or reappeared as assets of the onetime church-mouse company that had mopped up whatever was most profitable before the bankruptcy. It was an elaborately orchestrated confusion according to the dictates of the great Professor Flaam of South Hams State Prison, almost as though its creators had learned their techniques at his feet just as David had. By now Jimmy's papers left no doubt that the bankrupt had spent most of its final months running up debts it had no hope of paying off and collecting on goods and raw materials it did not have in inventory, had no intention of acquiring and hence no intention of supplying to anybody: the very maneuver that had brought the Galleas sharks on their visit to Herndon & Freyl.

But an answer to the critical question—if Galleas had not killed Hugh, then who had?—was only a little closer than it had been when David and Stephanie had sat down to the big round table. They'd put aside thoughts of official government involvement, whether the United States or any of the several African or Middle Eastern countries involved, on the grounds that such people are used to writing off losses. Besides, the messy method of Hugh's death pointed to a kill for personal reasons, not an execution. The strongest possibility remained the one Christina Haggarty favored: Hugh had uncovered the fraud—which would explain his interest in old files and his secrecy about them—and was getting too close for comfort to the central figure behind it.

The one clue to that closeness was a file that Jimmy had titled "Number One Fund Papers." It consisted of records of payments to various people for "Consultation," members of the boards of various of the subsidiaries in amounts ranging from $100,000 to $500,000, each stapled to a page of a balance sheet from one of a dizzying array of subsidiaries, partnerships, alliances that the old corporation sprouted in its final years. In each case, the balance sheet included a matching reference to an account marked "NOF," presumably for "Number One Fund."

"But what was Jimmy getting out of it for *Jimmy*?" Stephanie said to David, pushing her chair away from the table. She was still pale and wan; even this early in the day all she wanted was a warm bed and sleep.

"He's hardly going to put material that incriminates him in with all this."

"He must have been getting something."

"Who cares?"

"I do."

"Why?"

"Damn it, I want some idea what Hugh's closest associate was doing all this *for*."

"Okay. A chunk of money comes in, gets shifted back and forth: not difficult to divert it straight into Jimmy's pocket. And then if I'd been in his shoes, the first thing I'd have done was buy stock cheap back at the beginning, watch it go up and sell just before the crash. He knew they were going to go bust years ago. He'd have made millions on it. I'm sure they all did."

"That's insider trading?" David nodded. "You'd have done it? Really? Your very own self?"

"Somebody offers you money, you're stupid not to take it."

"Oh, come on, David, we can't be as low grade as this. I don't even get the principle here. I can't see how the thing actually works either. I mean, precisely *how* do you do it? *Why* don't you get caught? Why does it work at all?" But before he could answer, she rushed on. "That's hardly the point, though, is it? I mean, they're a bunch of sad, sick bastards if you ask me. The one truly meaningful thing that comes across in all this"—she waved a contemptuous hand at the papers—"is betrayal and greed."

David got up and went to the doors onto the patio. He ran his fingers over the glass. At the far edge of the patio beyond there was a row of flower pots with fluted sides. The agent had told him the gardener planned to fill them with daffodils in spring and red geraniums in summer: daffodils and geraniums to be tended for the pleasure of a murderer. David couldn't explain this to himself. He couldn't explain the free market either. How could he? Even Professor Flaam had to struggle with the subject.

"Well, now," he'd said, "I tell you. Guys like me, we're just like priests teaching acolytes in seminaries. How do you explain God? Do you say He's the unmoved mover? set the whole mess in motion and forgot it? Or do you say he's around all the time like the screws and the smell of shit from the latrine? All you know for sure is that He's a devious bastard, and it sure seems entirely in keeping with His sense of humor that the cleanest scientific model anybody can think of for the deep and mysterious workings of the free market is the cigarette trade right here in South Hams prison. Everything's fluid—every complication stripped away. There's no government to interfere. Users feed an addiction and entrepreneurs accumulate wealth."

David kept his eyes on the patio. "This particular fraud is called a bleedout," he said to Stephanie. "Basically, anyhow. Jimmy and his friends added some trimmings of their own that lower the level somewhat."

Bleedout was a word David had known long before he'd heard Samuel Clark talk about the kosher butchering of large animals, that ritual draining of meat to satisfy the laws of the Torah. He knew it even before he'd heard it from Professor Flaam. One of his many foster families had run an intensive farm up near Bloomington. His foster father had liked to claim that he could ream an ounce of blood out of every pound of live bird weight without a single bruise showing on the flesh: that's called a bleedout too.

"The trick is to bleed the company dry while it's still functioning," David said, "but make sure it looks healthy right up to the minute the last drop is gone. Last January, Uniplex Advanced Ceramics reported a comfortable profit of $450 million."

"Are you saying none of it was real?"

"—and in February, it went broke."

"It doesn't make any sense, David."

"Oh, yes, it does."

"Then how . . . ?" She shook her head. "Maybe we should forget chickens and corporate assets. Maybe we should concentrate on the man. I mean, look at Hugh's life. It's as though God Himself was trying to bleed him dry. Who's he supposed to be anyhow? Job? First he goes blind. Then he loses Rose. Then all his friends betray him. So many of these guys were his *friends*—and all of them must have been willing to sell him out. What's the matter with people? What's the matter with *us*?" David only shrugged. "David, it's a serious question."

"If there's money involved, nobody can be trusted."

She studied him a minute. "Do you really believe that?"

"Yes."

"What a barren world you inhabit." He shrugged again. "You can't even trust yourself."

How could David reply to that? How could a word like *trust* possibly apply to his view of himself? Forget money and people. Money's easy, clean, external, something to be used, manipulated, ignored according to will. As for people, they do what they do; you make your choices in regard to it. The only serious enemy is the mind inside a man. It can slip sideways and sabotage him, and he doesn't even know it's happened. Just take the Honda. David's St. Louis visit certainly let the Consortium know he had an idea what they'd cooked up. They had to be worried—clearly they did—but he still couldn't believe they were worried enough to put a tail on him. And yet he'd looked out for the Honda and its owner more than once in the past few days. Neither had been visible. Under different circumstances he'd have checked the garage of the house the driver had opened with a remote control. He'd have checked the house itself. But everybody's vulnerable. Everybody has an Achilles' heel. For most people, it's the fear of death. For David, it was that old prison-engendered terror that his mind had slipped sideways one afternoon when he wasn't looking—that he'd gone crazy and didn't know it.

"I'm beginning to think it ain't no joke anymore. You really ought to have your head examined." That's what Tony had said about the battered Ford.

The Honda's driver had called after him, "You know what you are? You're paranoid."

So David hadn't checked the garage that he'd seen the driver of the Honda open. He hadn't checked the house that went with the garage either, and he turned back to the table and the piles of paper that were penetrable—that if nothing else, were rational in their disorder.

The sorting, collating, filing, reordering continued.

◄∘►

By midafternoon Stephanie was too tired to continue; her throat hurt. She slept on David's bed, fitfully at first, then deeply; by the time she woke it was after dark, and she felt much better. On top of that, she'd figured out the technical part of the secret that had puzzled her so about the bleedout: those vast loans that had plumped out UACI so nicely and then simply disappeared into thin air with the bankruptcy.

If she concentrated on just the one person, say Allen Madison, president of the First Bank of Springfield, she could put aside all the complicated stuff about balance sheets and simplify things greatly. So she supposed he wanted an Aston Martin worth $100,000 but didn't have the cash on hand to buy it. Obviously his bank would lend him the money, but banks want to be repaid—even his own bank—and she assumed Allen would have no intention of paying back his debt. Instead he'd set up what's called a "special purpose vehicle."

The phrase "special purpose vehicle" began life meaning a truck rigged to perform some special task like lifting up an engineer to repair telephone wires. It's much the same in business. The sole purpose of Allen Madison's would be to shift money around so that nobody could trace it, a financial maneuver that needs only two things to make it entirely legal: a registered name and somebody else's guarantee to back a tiny 3 percent of the capital. So suppose he calls his special purpose vehicle Bozo in honor of the great hairy dog that adorned his wall and suppose he persuades his cousin to pledge the first $3,000.

The cousin runs no risk because not a single penny will actually change hands. And yet on the basis of this minute, half-imaginary pledge—and Allen's impressive financial reputation, of course—the first bank he contacts is more than likely to hand $97,000 over to Bozo.

The next step is for Allen to take control of the money himself. So he draws up a contract to sell Bozo a can of dog food for $100,000, fully covering his cousin's $3,000 and the bank's $97,000. This might sound like a great deal to pay for dog food, but there's nothing illegal about any price, however outrageous, if the seller and the buyer both agree to it.

All that's left is to pay back the bank with somebody else's money so Allen can keep the $100,000 in his own pocket—a process that turns out to be very like the old lady who swallowed a spider to catch the fly that wiggled and giggled and jiggled inside her. He sets up a second special purpose vehicle that he calls Athena in honor of Hugh's guide dog. Athena needs only a pledge for $3,000 from some *other* cousin and a loan of $97,000 from some *other* bank; she buys Bozo's expensive dog food so that Bozo can pay off the first bank when the loan falls due. Then to pay off Athena's debt, Allen sets up a *third* special purpose vehicle . . .

If chains like this grow to hundreds of deals in length—each deal a little different in timing and phrasing and money—almost nobody can follow the trail. Every step is legal; only the intent to defraud turns it into a crime.

Meantime, Allen owns an Aston Martin for the price of a can of dog food. It's all a conjuring trick, a house of cards so fragile it even lacks the bottom tier; special purpose vehicles like this were a major device in making Enron so very, very rich—and they were what scattered bankruptcies all over the landscape when the house of cards collapsed.

But Stephanie could find no place in any of it for the mysterious file Jimmy called the "Number One Fund Papers" that showed millions of dollars ending their long journeys in private bank accounts of board members for some unspecified variety of "Consultation."

She got up from David's bed and took a shower in his bathroom. Back in the living room, he was still bent over papers, a cigarette dangling from his lips. Even though she felt much better—even though at last she understood something about the internal workings of the Consortium—she couldn't bring herself to sit down at that table again. She rinsed out the bowl that served as an ashtray, put the pizza boxes and Chinese cartons in the garbage can in the garage, stared out the windows. Only then did she go back to the table and flip disconsolately through some of the few remaining unsorted files from Jimmy's safe.

That was when she ran across the envelope entitled "Trivia." There were several sheets of paper inside.

"David?"

"Um."

"This is . . . interesting."

"Um?"

She began to read, " 'Know all men by these present that I, James Emmanuel Zemanski, of Springfield, Illinois, have made, constituted and appointed, and do hereby make, constitute and appoint Hugh Freyl of Springfield, Illinois—' "

"Give me that. What *is* it?"

"A power of attorney."

He took it from her and read it carefully. "Why does Jimmy hand over control of his money to Hugh? It ought to be the other way around."

Powers of attorney can be strange documents. Stephanie's first experience with one came when her father persuaded his aged great-aunt to sign one so she couldn't leave her house to her thirty-seven cats. Which is odd because a doctor had to be present to testify that the aged great-aunt understood what she was signing—and yet the document wouldn't be necessary if her head had been functioning properly in the first place. Years later at Herndon & Freyl, Stephanie had heard lots of gossip about powers of attorney— lawyers' offices are full of them—serving all kinds of purposes.

"It's pretty smart," she said to David. "What it means is that Jimmy's name doesn't have to appear anywhere. Anything goes wrong—anybody catches on to the fraud—and it's all Hugh's fault. His signature is on all the important papers, whether it's the Follaton lease or the Galleas contract or some special purpose vehicle. Officially Jimmy doesn't know anything about anything. He's just a lawyer in a law firm."

David read the document again. "Nobody ever said Jimmy was stupid."

"You did, you know."

"Only about locks and safes."

"He's even got a sense of humor buried in there somewhere,

don't you think?" She cocked her head at the notation on the envelope—"Trivia," written in Jimmy's hand—then scanned the next page. "But listen to this, David Marion. 'Know all men by these present that I, John Calder . . .' "

◄◦►

Police departments run on grapevines almost as vigorous as a ladies' sewing bee, and I didn't have to wait long for John to make contact after my supposedly secret carillon meeting with Sergeant Wellwood. He asked me to his house.

Hiram drove me the few miles from the center of town out to Lake Springfield. The lake is the biggest reservoir in the state, built nearly three-quarters of a century ago at a time when social consciences ran almost as high as the passion for a water view and a place to sunbathe. The rich built houses on the largest and best stretch of shoreline; the rest of the acreage was to remain the province of the less well-off. But nothing ever works that way. Inch by inch, year after year, the rich squeezed out the less rich. The Calder property takes up what was once a modest neighborhood and is now a private park enclosing a monumental structure of glass, steel and rough oak, extremely handsome so Stephanie told me, and a tourist attraction all on its own.

There was a party in progress when I arrived; even so, my old friend, the senator from Illinois, met me at the door in person.

"It's good to see you, Hugh," he said. "Come in. Come in. It's been too long—way too long."

Except for me, the Freyls have been a politically active family for two hundred years; my mother has actively supported John from the very beginning of his career. She likes his politics. She likes his table manners and his old and eminent medical family, even though she laments their history of financial ups and downs. John brought them all back from the brink, himself included, with his own efforts only a few years ago. "A man like that does honor to the party," she says. I see little reason to argue the point, but I have never run across a successful politician who was not ready to sell his honor fast enough to shock a Mafia boss. And yet John is more charming than most, an amusing dinner guest, a thoughtful host, an attentive friend. I've known him since we were boys together.

He offered me his arm and led me to his study. It is something of an art, leading a blind man, gentle guidance, nothing obtrusive or intrusive, rather like beau leading belle onto the dance floor of a nineteenth-century ball. John seems to do this kind of thing as instinctively as Stephanie does. His extraordinary physical ease with people—a pure animal warmth as deceptive as it is beguiling—is one of his most powerful weapons as a politician. He shut the door behind us and offered me a chair, which I took. He offered me a drink. This I refused.

"Aren't you drinking?" he said. "My old auntie used to tell me, 'A little bit of what you fancy does you good.' She was Danish, married into the Bloomington Calders."

"Not this evening."

"You haven't suddenly gone on the wagon, have you? not Hugh Freyl?"

"Let's forget the social chitchat. You haven't summoned me here for that."

" 'Summoned you'?" The hurt in his voice was as earnest as his touch was deft. "I didn't 'summon' you. What's the matter? Is something wrong?"

"Please, John. Spare me."

"You look so angry. I hope I haven't done—"

"David Marion."

There was a pause. "Yes, of course. Dear God, you're good at making me feel clumsy."

Stephanie told me that John has aged pretty well. His bad-boy face has taken on that pulpy look that comes from too much liquor over too many years, but he has a full head of curly hair that's graying at the temples in true statesmanlike fashion. Gray temples lend gravitas—"gravitas" was her very word—to the impish smile that has already won landslides in Illinois. He certainly looked like being our next governor until my visit that evening. Who knows? If I had not found out about his role in David's case, he might well have had the potential to win voters across the country as well.

"It all happened so long ago," he said.

"Um."

"Hugh, I thought I knew what was important. I thought I could change some things. Sometimes I still think that." It was raining that evening, a gentle, steady fall. The blind love the rain. Sighted people tie the moments of their lives together with a landscape that flows from one vista to the next; only rain gives the blind a continuum like that, and I listened to the pattering on the window until the silence between John and me had stretched to an embarrassing length. "Come on, Hugh, be fair."

"You see, that is precisely what bothers me. I cannot establish how the concept of 'fair' entered into the conviction of David Marion."

"He beat two guys to a pulp. He was guilty as sin."

"That is not the point."

"You really are mad at me, aren't you."

"I know I cannot prove you were behind the disappearance of David's files after I saw them, but removing them was not . . . How can I put this? It did not show your usual acumen in character judgments. You could easily have found some way around the compromising aspects, but you probably would not have had to. Only when the records walked off did the case begin to catch my attention."

He sighed. "How much have you got?"

I opened the file I had with me. "Plainly you know about the witness who has already given me a statement. You probably also know he is willing to testify in court that as soon as he had interviewed David, the boy was handcuffed behind his back and led to another interrogation room. David's subsequent interviewers were O'Hara, Sanchez and Allandale."

The details that came out of the trial that convicted all three men of "excessive force" had read like the kind of interrogations that were routine during the black days of Saddam's reign. The damage "Springfield's police torture ring" did to the reputation of departments all across the state can still be felt.

John said nothing.

"My witness says they beat the boy—using fists and feet mainly but not, I gather, exclusively—and repeatedly suffocated him. A typewriter cover over his head. Interesting, isn't it? the inventiveness of the human mind? Who would have thought a typewriter cover could be so versatile? They prepared a confession and repeatedly tried to force him to sign it even though in those days nobody much cared whether or not a confession was signed. When he would not respond, the, er, interrogation began again, and again. And again."

John rattled the ice in his drink. "You know I feel really sorry for Norton Wellwood. I gather he never was able to come to terms with the fact that he just wasn't up to the job of lieutenant—sees enemies everywhere. If I were you, I'd take what he has to say with a grain of salt."

"Oh, I do, John. I do. And I have to agree with you that I would have difficulty building a case if he was my only source of information. But as you know, you were a little late in your destruction of David's police records, and I have what has become the only copy. Even though it is patchy, it contains valuable insights in addition to its corroboration of Sergeant Wellwood's story. As a matter of fact, I am blessed with so much information that I find it hard to decide just where to start. Let me see." I rifled through the papers. "Suppose I begin with the statement that David's blood was splashed on the bodies. The record mentions tests, and yet there is no data. Curious, don't you think? Apparently David's blood was all over the garage pit, again passing mention of tests, again no data. This constitutes suppression of crime scene test results, a violation of the Fourth, Fifth and Fourteenth Amendments to the—"

"Hey, Hugh, I already know the Constitution."

"The lug wrench was awash with blood and various other human remains. The one partial print is definitely not David's and yet the state claimed that it was: falsified evidence. According to the doctor who examined David soon after he was arrested, the wounds on him indicated that he had been hit with some kind of metal instrument or instruments. Such instruments could easily have been wielded by the dead men, and yet they disappeared from the scene and were never found: critical physical evidence destroyed."

John got up and walked across the room. I heard him making himself another drink. "Won't you change your mind about a drink? I've got a seriously good single malt here."

I shared John's passion for single malts; for years we had conducted a modest competition to find the best one. "Thank you, no," I said.

"It's not far off Laphroaig, maybe a little lighter on the gunmetal. I think it just might be—"

"John, we have known each other too long for this."

He sighed. "Okay. Okay."

"You did not apply for a handwriting expert," I went on, "even though you had been informed by a policeman on active duty that David's confession bore someone else's signature. You did not apply for an investigation into any of those strangely missing pieces of evidence. You entered a guilty plea without considering the evidence of torture when—"

"Hugh, hey, hang on a minute. I didn't have evidence of any such thing."

"Really?"

"Of course not. What do you think I am?"

Pages in the file I had open on my lap were annotated in Braille. I found the one I wanted and handed it out to him. "Here's a report from a physician by the name of Bennington. He examined David an hour or so after his arrest: the boy had plainly been in a fight, and he needed medical attention, but he was walking and talking. And yet a few days later, his condition was so grave that someone asked a vet to check him."

The intensity of the smell from John's Scotch told me that his new drink was minus the water. I could hear no ice in it either. He took a swallow but did not say a word.

"I find myself thinking of that vet, called away from tending a cat with the flu or a dog with mange," I said, "to be ushered down to the cells for a half-dead boy vomiting blood. Why did nobody call an ambulance? Or take David to the hospital? The vet was so horrified he could not forget about it, not in twenty years. He even remembers the precise time of day. Allandale told him he was looking at a 'street gang revenge' that had to be kept secret: some nonsense about a risk to the lives of police informers. He did not speak out despite his suspicions only because you assured him it was the truth." I handed him another piece of paper. "Here is an affidavit from him to that effect."

The rain intensified outside while he scanned the document. "That's it?" he said.

"My photocopied records state that you paid your one and only pretrial visit to David on that very day, not long before the vet arrived." I am sorry to say this was a simple lie—or at any rate, a bluff. Sergeant Wellwood had told me of the first visit, and I was guessing that the first was the only one. John did not demur. "You are the person who called in the vet, are you not? What were you doing there yourself? A little odd, don't you think? The boy didn't ask for a lawyer." There was not a sound from John. "Let me tell you what I think might have happened. Somebody at the station called Sheriff Allandale and said his son was beating a suspect to death. The sheriff called you to put a stop to it and clean up the legal mess it left behind. Poor John, you must have been scared to death by what you saw, and you are not indifferent to another's pain. This is probably a failing in your character as a politician. It must have been a very large favor you owed to go to such lengths." Still John said nothing. "As I remember it, Sheriff Allandale was not above a spot of blackmail when it suited him, and then there were rumors of sticky fingers and a pension fraud scheme. At any rate, to repay your debt you kept the boy alive and maneuvered him into prison quickly and quietly. As you can see, a petition charging ineffective assistance of counsel could be very—what is the right word?—uncomfortable for a man in your position."

He took in his breath and let it out slowly. "What are you thinking of? the validity of the conviction? So where would attacking that get you? Clemency maybe? Getting the sentence commuted?"

A state governor has the unchallengeable right to commute sentences, and Illinoisans have more reason to be aware of it than Americans from any other state. Only a couple of years ago, the outgoing governor redeemed a career of almost unadulterated corruption by commuting the sentences of the state's entire population on death row, a full 164 prisoners awaiting lethal injection. However beneficent and laudable such a move was, it was not popular. The public has always relished a good hanging. Perhaps these days they cover their bloodlust with righteous indignation, but no governor in his right mind would be likely to commute David's "life without parole" to a specific sentence that I could argue down; the move toward harsher treatment for convicts is way too powerful for that. Which is to say that the thought of a pardon had occurred to me, but I had dismissed it.

"I have something else in mind," I said.

John thought a moment. "You're a weird guy, I always said so. But you wouldn't have come here tonight if you were fool enough to bother with a habeas petition."

◄◦►

It was eight o'clock at night and pitch-black outside David's house.

"Isn't there something we can do about this?" Stephanie said to him, tossing the Calder power of attorney down on the table.

"What do you have in mind?"

"Can't we confront him? Can't we . . . ? I don't know. There must be *something* we can do."

"We'd never get to him."

"We could try."

"Even if we cornered him in a broom closet, he'd have some kind of explanation. I don't know what, but he'd be ready."

She sat down with a sigh. "You're right. Of course you are. He'd only say Herndon and Freyl was in charge of some case he was a party to or . . . maybe he and Hugh once owned some property together or he was sick, and Hugh handled his finances for him."

"You'd use a power of attorney for all those things?"

Stephanie nodded. "David, there *has* to be some way we can get him over this. He's got to be in it for the money, so he has to have bank accounts somewhere. So maybe we could . . . there's no way we could get into those, is there? What about that Number One Fund? Maybe our figures are wrong. Maybe he needs a lot more to run for governor than we thought."

David glanced up at her and turned back to the papers on the round table. "Try a couple more searches. There just might be an article tying him to one of the defense contracts in Jimmy's file."

Stephanie watched him for a moment, his head bent over, smoke from his cigarette curling up across his cheek, his attention implacably focused on the rows of numbers in front of him. But she could think of no other way to distract him—or herself—and she sat down to the computer with a sigh. She turned up a Calder speech in the Senate justifying higher spending: "We are hurtling into an age of warfare that will require unimaginable speed and complexity, where the dangers to personnel will be terrible beyond present understanding, where the consequences of failure may spell the end of liberty for us all—and even life on earth itself. This is not science fiction. It is truth."

A moving speech: he got a standing ovation for it. She also found out that Calder sat on the Senate Appropriations Committee, which was pushing for an extra $40 billion in research and development. So at least he helped put money into the kind of thing UACI sold.

She switched off the computer. "Damn it all," she said, "I can't bear this a minute longer. It's going to take weeks to find anything this way—if there's anything to find. How can you sit there so calmly?" She watched him light yet another cigarette from the stub of the one he took out of his mouth; he'd been chain-smoking ever since he got back from New York. "Does that help?"

"Help what?" he said.

"Smoking: does it help you concentrate? Let me have one." He shook a cigarette out of the pack for her and lit it. She took a drag, grimaced. "David, that is *disgusting*. How can you *stand* it?" She stubbed the cigarette out and rubbed her hand over her mouth. "Can't we at least dig a TV out of this mess?"

"I don't have a TV."

"You don't . . . ? What's the matter with you, David Marion? How do you ever find out what's going on in the world?" But she was only ranting, and he didn't bother to answer. "I've really got to get out of here," she went on. "I'm starving. Besides, I'm going to die of asphyxiation in this place. Where do you usually go at this time of night if you want to go out?"

"No place you'd want to go."

"Oh, good."

"Why don't you order another—"

"If I ever *see* another chicken velvet or another Domino's pizza I'm going to go crazy. I'm going to die in fits on the floor, and you'll have to clean it up all by yourself. I want to get away from here. I want to go *out*. *And* I want to go where you go. I bet it's somewhere I could never go on my own."

He pushed his chair away from the table. "How about Norb Andy's? Or the Pair-a-Dice?"

"Do they have a TV at this other place?" David nodded. "How about sandwiches?"

"If they're past their sell-by date."

"What more could anybody ask?"

They drove to the east side and Cockran's. Stephanie's eyes lit up the moment she saw the exterior with its spluttering neon sign and half-broken letters that made it shift from "Cockran's Bar and Eatery" to the cryptic "Cock B Eatery."

"Absolutely perfect," she said, taking David's arm as they went inside.

She'd certainly miscalculated one thing, though: the smoke was so dense that the edges of the room weren't wholly visible. Even so, she gazed around delightedly. The clientele were mainly black, a few white faces, a Hispanic or two, all men except for a whore drumming up business. The television blared; nobody was looking at it. Tony sat at the bar as he always did at this time of night; he had a newspaper open in front of him, but the banter going on be-

"Lot of us around here know him a little too close up."

Stephanie unwrapped her sandwich. "He defended David," she said, a little cautiously, not sure how much Tony knew.

"That's what they call it, huh?"

"Not too inspiring an example, I'm afraid."

"Lady, he even let them set *me* up. Not all that hard probably, since he couldn't remember rightly what I was charged with."

"What were you charged with?"

Tony shrugged. "Playing a joke. I mean, it was stupid. I done lots of things, and most of the time they don't even bother to press charges."

"Yeah?"

"Yeah."

"How come?"

"How come what?"

"Why don't they press charges?"

He laughed. "Suppose I get acquitted. They couldn't have that, could they? It'd be a blot on the high conviction rates that get them guys elected. They either let you off or set you up. It's the only way they can calculate the odds. So this time, they set me up. They get me for a *joke*. They fingerprint me. They get my DNA on file. What am I supposed to be? A terrorist or something? What's the matter with a world that can't take a joke?"

"What kind of joke?"

"You won't like it. Ask David here. He hates my jokes. He don't have a sense of humor."

"Tell me anyhow."

David was staring fixedly at the TV, an extra measure of his irritation apparent in the clench of his jaw that overrode that stifling indifference. Tony noted it with delight and gave Stephanie a roguish smile. "I was working in this paper factory, and the manager was a real shit. They got in a big order one morning and had to get it out that very afternoon, so I snuck a couple of beehives in through the back door and super-glued them to the warehouse floor." Tony laughed and slapped his hand on the bar. "Ain't that something? You really should a seen it: eighty thousand little stingers whizzing everywhere and everybody jumping up and down and running around and screeching and yelling. The best part of it was that the bastard manager turned out to be allergic to bee stings. But, I mean, what the hell. How was I supposed to know that?"

Stephanie was a little taken aback. "He wasn't hurt, was he?"

"They carted him off to the hospital." Tony reflected a moment.

" 'Course, if I'd a known he was allergic, I'd a glued down twice as many hives."

She was beginning to feel that maybe David was right, maybe Cockran's wasn't an experience she wanted—certainly Tony had lost his charm for her—and there was a somewhat uncomfortable silence.

Then Tony said, "I sure as hell didn't deserve a couple of months inside for ADW."

"What's that?" she said.

"Assault with a deadly weapon. See what I mean? Bees ain't a deadly weapon. I done far worse things than that. And now that fucker Calder is going to run for president. Imagine that. John Calder in the White House."

This time the silence was stunned. "You're kidding me," she said. "You can't mean that."

Tony grinned and poked David's arm. "What you been doing all this time, huh? Come on now, tell your Uncle Tony. He sure does like a story of true romance."

"Is this true?" David said.

"Don't you know *anything*? All over the TV tonight. Nothing else on the news. Couldn't you even take five minutes off to get a paper or something? Going to reform the legal system. Going to put all us bad guys behind bars where we belong. Going to make America great again. That's what he says. You and this Stephanie here sure must a been going at it hard."

"Governor, maybe, but *president* . . ." There was wonder in Stephanie's voice. A presidential campaign would probably eat up every penny in the file Jimmy had called the Number One Fund and come back for more.

Then she shook her head. "He wouldn't *dare*."

"You just watch him," Tony said. "He can do whatever he fucking pleases."

◄o►

John was right. Of course he was. I would never have bothered to go all the way out to his lakeside mansion for the lost cause of threatening to file a habeas petition. I had dismissed this most admirable of remedies the moment it had crossed my mind.

It is true that Americans fought for the right of habeas corpus. They died for it in their thousands. It is a rock of our society, a foundation stone, and it has been officially suspended only once in our entire history as a nation: by Illinois's own Abraham Lincoln during the Civil War—an irony I could not escape as I sat with John. People in the streets of Springfield, like people in the streets of every other American city, assume that habeas stands now as it always has (with its one short exception). They may not know its name or its history, but the sense of invulnerability it gives us is a defining trait of the American character; most of us really believe we are the citizen kings that this ancient writ alone gives us the power to be. We are famous throughout the world for living as though no tyranny can break us, as though we carry in our physical makeup—in our very being as Americans—the weapons to protect ourselves from any injustice imposed by mankind.

The trouble is, this power is illusory. John knew it. So did I. For all practical purposes habeas corpus no longer exists in the United States. It is extinct.

The reasoning behind this nationwide extinction is precisely the same as the reasoning behind the futility of an appeal for clemency in the state of Illinois. Perhaps the man who lost to the present governor emptied Illinois's death row as his last official act, but the backlash made the public ever more vengeful. "Getting tough on crime" wins votes. Freeing convicted people by the eight-hundred-year-old principle of habeas corpus, however obvious the innocence of the person convicted, is no more popular than commuting death sentences. Both lose elections. It is as simple—and as sad—as that. These days, most courts, state and federal, throw out habeas petitions without so much as a cursory examination of the facts.

But John was now in the position where most of the favors were owed to him. There were numerous judges in his debt. Stephanie and I had dossiers on three of them.

I got up from my chair opposite his desk. "I want David Marion out of prison," I said. John got up too and offered me his arm as he had before. I took it, and we walked out of his study. His guests were laughing and talking in the rooms beyond. "I suggest Judge Julius Roxon. He is one of those men who can never be satisfied with what he has, and he already owes you far more than he will ever be able to repay."

John chuckled and patted my hand fondly. "You know, Hugh, I've misjudged you for a lifetime. I'd never have guessed that dirty tricks were part of your repertoire. I find the idea quite exhilarating. After all those years of putting you right in the same bracket with Honest Abe Lincoln, I find out you're not any purer than he was. And he certainly wasn't all that pure, was he. So . . . let's see . . . who's been telling tales out of school? Could it be . . . ? I know, you've been talking to that eminent justice Samuel Clark."

I had to laugh. I really do admire John's shrewdness. He can almost smell a political maneuver coming at him, and he was as right this time as he usually was. Samuel and I had plotted out every step of this evening's interview; in fact, he was the one who suggested Roxon as the most likely candidate.

"How the hell did Clark get on the Court anyhow?" John went on, fulminating with the humorist's mock anger that was another of his charming traits. "One boy in a bed—our murderer, say—and he's violated God knows how many laws in how many states. What's the matter with the gutter press these days? Don't they know how to dig up dirt anymore? What's the matter with the Court's selection process? Have the rules changed since I looked last? Are unconvicted felons welcome?" He paused. I could have been alarmed for Samuel, but I was not. John was a very shrewd man—and a very penetrating one—but he was only fishing. I knew it, and he knew I knew it. "Hugh, my old friend—I hope and trust we're still friends—this is straightforward conspiracy, you know. He has as much to lose as I do."

"No one has as much to lose as that." When John did not respond, I said, "There is a rather well-known journalist named Georgie Pickles"—I felt an abrupt tension in him—"Ah, the name is familiar. I understand she is very interested in your career."

"Hey, Hugh, a deal's a deal. Have I said I wouldn't deal? Roxon's an asshole. I'll get a kick out of scaring him a little. But, uh, tell me, you haven't been running home to mommy with these tales out of school, have you?"

"One of my mother's greatest pleasures in life is writing checks for campaign funds. I would not dream of upsetting her with details that might spoil her fun."

He sighed—relief that he could still rely on the Freyl money and the Freyl name—but the tension in him did not ease. "Well, thank God for that. You had me scared there for a minute."

"I am afraid I am going to frighten you more. I have not betrayed your secrets to her, but she will write no more checks to get you elected. Provided we avoid this monumental scandal, you should be able to enjoy the couple of years you have left in office. After that, your career is over. I really do not think it is in the interests of the country for a man like you to run for governor."

We had reached the front door by this time. John's guests sounded raucous up this close, and there is a strange, sad quality—reminiscent of the moan of a train whistle across the prairies—about people enjoying themselves unawares while their host is being threatened in deadly earnest by one of his oldest friends.

"Well, well, well," John said, patting my hand again, although I could not say that there was much fondness in it now, "ain't life a corker? I've already said I'll be a good boy and talk to Roxon. I'll do it first thing to-morrow. That good enough for you?"

"There's more."

"Now what?"

"Sentence for the escape attempt to run concurrently with—and end with—David's term of solitary confinement."

"Tried to escape, did he?" I nodded. "This is dumb, Hugh. The guy's dangerous. He's a public menace—should have got the needle years ago. Okay, okay, damn you. You got it. Now run along home like a good boy, huh?" I shook my head. "Jesus, what are you going to hit me with now? Drawing and quartering? crucifixion?"

"As I have said, you will not run for governor."

"Quit the kidding."

"No joke."

"Jesus, Hugh, cut it out. Haven't you kicked me around enough for one night?"

"If you try to run, I will air this material publicly."

There was a long pause. I could feel him studying my face. "You mean this," he said then, withdrawing his hand from my arm.

"I do."

"Who the fuck do you think you are?" he burst out. "You come here claiming the moral high ground . . . I hate the way you do that. You've always done it, ever since we were kids. One of these days it's going to get you in real trouble, know that? You can't pressure an elected official of the government into agreeing to suborn a judge—and go straight on to diddle the electoral system. Lincoln? Hell, I was thinking too small. Way too small. You figure you're God Almighty Himself. You figure you can hand out the spark of life and take it back—pass judgment on anybody. Last I looked that's what was called hubris. It's what melted Icarus's wings and brought him down."

"If I had wanted to damage you publicly, John, I would have handed the material over to Georgie Pickles this evening instead of to you. I can still do so if that is really what you prefer."

"Blackmailers end up in dark alleys with their heads bashed in."

"Only in stories. In real life they get what they want."

◄o►

When David and Stephanie left Cockran's, he caught a glimpse of a car he could have sworn was that black Honda even though it was a couple of blocks away and most of the body was hidden by a corner liquor store. Only the front fender was visible—and that's absurd. Nobody can be certain a front fender at that distance belongs to any particular kind of car, much less a particular model, especially at night where streetlights are broken. And yet he knew it was a Honda. He knew it was *that* Honda. As he drew away in the Chevy with Stephanie beside him, headlights appeared in the rearview mirror. He knew those were the Honda's too, even though a rearview mirror at night reveals nothing of a car except the twin spots it throws out to light its own way. How could anybody say a given set of spots belong to a black Honda? or a battered old Ford for that matter? South Hams prison was bursting with nutcases. Some of them arrived crazy, schizophrenics, psychotics, manic-depressives. The rest were driven crazy inside. The way it works is this: fear trickles into the brain and cracks it open from the inside precisely the way scrap collectors funnel water into metal artillery spheres so that freezing can burst them into salable fragments.

"Something the matter, David?" Stephanie said after they'd been driving for a few minutes.

"No."

She swung around to look out the rear window. "Think maybe somebody's following us? like in the movies?"

"I don't think Calder has the backing to run for president," he said, overriding her. "You just might have a point about the Number One Fund and campaign funds."

"Where do you suppose the rest of them get it? Are they *all* dirty?"

David shrugged. "Try another search tomorrow. If we assume enough contributions to fund a presidency, there has to be some way for these companies to put money behind him."

"I suppose they list things like that somewhere," she said unhappily. "How do you contribute vast sums to a guy like that anyhow? I mean, we got to be talking a huge amount of money. You can't just write him out a check, can you? Hand him a wad of cash?" Then without any transition, she went on, "Your friend Tony thinks we're in bed together, doesn't he?"

"He's a limited guy."

"I don't think he approves either."

They drove in silence for a few minutes. The night was cold enough for icicles to form on telephone wires; they glistened in the Chevy's headlights. There wasn't much traffic. David checked for the Honda a couple of times, trying each time to stop himself from doing it, but the road behind him had taken on an opaque indifference anyhow.

"Haven't we got enough to confront Calder now?" Stephanie said as they approached her motel.

He shook his head. "Tracking down a couple of payments would help."

"We could get to him through Becky, couldn't we?"

"If you can find something, I'll see what she has to say."

"Tomorrow?"

"We don't have enough. Not to confront Calder. Not to present to her. I have to talk to Helen tomorrow anyway."

"You're not thinking she might be part of this, are you?" said Stephanie, turning to him in surprise.

"No."

"She blamed Hugh for her mother's death. Did he ever tell you that? She kept dropping hints—even accused him openly a couple of times. Why do kids *always* do that? It's like some kind of emotional acne. You going out to her place to see her?"

He shook his head. "Lillian's house. Lillian wants to be there when I talk to her. You'll be all right on your own for a couple of hours around noon tomorrow, won't you? I shouldn't be long."

Stephanie laughed. "I'm pretty sure I can manage it. If I get tired or bored or hungry I'll call a taxi." As he let her out in front of her motel, she said, "Same time in the morning?"

"I'll be here at eight o'clock."

"Good night, David." She gave the car door a fond pat.

He watched her take a few steps toward the motel entrance, then he called out after her, "Double lock your door tonight, huh? Make sure the windows are secure."

She turned back. "You didn't really think anybody was following us back there, did you?"

27

WHILE WE WERE WAITING FOR RESULTS FROM MY VISIT
to John Calder, Stephanie said she thought she ought to visit David's foster mother, who was by this time out of the hospital, to give her some
warning of what might lie ahead. I have to admit I thought the idea a little foolhardy, but Stephanie insisted that David's release might otherwise
come as a terrible shock to a sick woman. I could not let her go alone;
sick or not, the woman was all too likely to be hostile. I made an appointment for us both.

Hiram drove us to an area of town close enough to where David lives
now. There were cracks in the sidewalk outside the house. I had hold of
Stephanie's arm; with her beside me, there was no need for Athena. She
knocked on the door. We waited a few minutes without movement from
inside, and we both began to grow restive.

"I gather she is virtually housebound," I said to Stephanie. "Clearly
some species of degenerative nerve disorder. The person I spoke to assured me that she never goes out."

"A nurse?" Stephanie said, knocking again.

That's when the thought struck me. "It was a strange conversation. I
had the feeling I was missing—"

Sounds from beyond the door interrupted the thought that I wish I
had finished now. But it is too late for regrets, isn't it?

"Mrs. Fowler?" I said when a draft of fetid air announced that the
door was open. "Ellie Fowler?"

"You're the . . . guy who . . . called?"

The voice was slow as well as hesitant, and it was dull in tone—none
of the organ-pedal resonance that characterizes normal voices. The words
were faintly slurred too, and yet there was no hint of alcohol about her.

"You might . . . as well . . . come in," she said.

I could smell that this was a desolate place. Mrs. Fowler guided us through the rooms—down a mean hallway, through a door—at a pace that was as slow and hesitant as her speech. The walk seemed to have winded her.

When we came to a halt, she said, "I got to . . ." She stopped mid-sentence for breath. "Got to . . . sit down."

"Are you too tired this morning, Mrs. Fowler?" I asked. "Would it help if we came back another day?"

"Coming back won't . . . improve nothing."

Stephanie tells me that despite the strange voice and a degree of weakness serious enough to make a complex job of helping her into a chair, Mrs. Fowler was a beautiful woman: dark blond hair around an oval face, slightly almond eyes, straight nose, short upper lip. Even at fifty years old there was early-summer lushness to her.

"Was David Marion the only boy you fostered?" Stephanie asked her, thinking (as she told me later) that the mere sight of this woman at thirty would have driven a healthy teenage boy into a frenzy.

"Stupidest thing . . . I ever done."

"Oh, I know how you must feel—" Stephanie began with a rush of sympathy.

"Lady, you don't got . . . no idea."

"No, no, of course not, but I can imagine—"

"I'm dying, lady . . . How good are you . . . at imagining that?"

"I am so very sorry to hear it, Mrs. Fowler," I said.

"What the fuck . . . do you care? That kid . . . destroyed my life . . . more than eighteen years ago."

There was an awkward pause, and I said, "Eighteen years is a long time."

"He's a animal."

"Some people change."

"Ought to be put down," she spat at me.

Stephanie and I were both as soothing as we could be. Mrs. Fowler pushed our efforts aside. In an attempt to ease the way, we asked about David's time with her family, what he had been like when he first came to them, how he had changed in the interim, whether there were friends, why he had refused to attend school. To all these questions she would say only that he was an "animal" who "ought to be put down." Stephanie told me that Mrs. Fowler's face lost none of its beauty as she spoke; there was no ugly curling of the lip or distortion of the features, just a heightened color and a heightened brilliance to the eyes.

So finally I said, "Mrs. Fowler, you really do not have to talk to us about him. All we wanted to do—"

"Nobody cares . . . what I think. Nobody's said nothing . . . to me. Not in . . . the whole . . . fucking time." Mrs. Fowler struggled a moment to marshal the affronts of eighteen years into a single outburst. "Look at me," she cried. "He's the . . . one done this. He's the one . . . made me into this."

Again Stephanie and I tried to be as soothing as we could. Again Mrs. Fowler pushed our efforts aside. Stephanie said later that looking at this kind of misery—and knowing how ghastly the future was going to be—made the old Eskimo solution of death on an ice floe seem civilized and humane. Legend has it that freezing brings warmth and a sense of pleasure after the initial pain. Even if legend has it wrong, there are few deaths that are as merciless as the agonies modern society visits on people like Mrs. Fowler.

"You pretend to go all . . . mushy on me . . . you come here . . . to tell me . . . you're getting that animal out! Ain't you? Don't you . . . dare deny it."

"I would not dream of denying it," I said.

She gave an abrupt burst of laughter—sudden, sharp, inappropriate to anything. "Ever see a . . . wolf in . . . the night? Ever see its . . . eyes glow? Wolves . . . they'll attack anything. Don't matter if . . . it's bigger and stronger. They wait and . . . wait. All they want . . . is to kill. When the moment comes . . ."

She stopped, and her labored breathing went on so long this time that Stephanie said, "You mustn't tire yourself anymore, Mrs. Fowler, we can see ourselves out."

"Look at me, lady!" Mrs. Fowler cried. "What are you doing . . . helping a animal like that? What . . . about me? What kind of life . . . have I got? Why ain't I got you . . . and your blind man . . . and all his money . . . and his big car . . . helping me out? That animal . . . he gets free, he kills people . . . He'll wreck your life just like he . . . wrecked mine. Look at me! Don't I deserve . . . better than this?"

◄o►

Lillian began setting the table in her dining room with the help of two of her grandsons at eleven-thirty on Sunday morning. The dining room was larger than the living room where she and David had coffee the Sunday before, and it was very much the family room of the house. The photographs on the walls told the story: a baby on a blanket, gatherings of schoolchildren, a proud college graduate in mortarboard and robes, weddings, family groups with two generations, three generations, four generations, and finally a lone gravestone. But it wasn't just any old gravestone. It was very special, and it set the family off from all the others on the east side. Here lay great-grandfather Aloysius, groom to Abraham Lincoln at the Governor's Mansion in Springfield, who had died protecting the great man from a mad dog and was rewarded by a grave in Oakland Cemetery—to this day, the only dead black man alongside the dead white and mighty like Hugh Freyl.

But Lillian's dining room, although it was the largest room in the house, was barely large enough for the twelve diners expected today; some squeezing was going to be necessary. No matter. There was excitement in the air. Something interesting and unexpected might happen. The tablecloth on the long, narrow table was the peach-colored one, Lillian's best, ironed on the table itself so that not even a crease marred its smoothness. The napkins were flowered in red and blue. The room was filled with smells of cooking from the kitchen, where a leg of lamb rested in the warm cupboard above the refrigerator. Gravy waited off to one side of the stove along with peas and beans in their pots. Apple pies were ready to go in the oven as soon as yams and marshmallows finished their twenty minutes more.

David was the first guest to arrive. Lillian threw open the door when he knocked.

"You come right on in here, boy." She embraced him, let him go, looked him up and down as she ushered him inside. "What you got in that paper bag, huh?" He handed her the bag with several bottles of wine in it. "Now, ain't that nice? It's just exactly what we need. I'm going to get me some—"

"You got a mitt?" cried the older of the two boys, catching sight of David, running to him in delight and tugging at the baseball bat he carried behind his back. "You got hardball?"

"Softball," David said, taking it out and handing it over along with the mitt.

"I ain't having no baseball in my house," Lillian said. "David, you take that boy and Tommy out to the street out back." The older boy ran outside at once, slamming the kitchen door behind him. Lillian caught the younger one mid-flight. "You got to help Tommy here to put on his boots first. He ain't no good at that. Keeps putting them on the wrong foot."

David hesitated a moment, uncertain that he could have heard her correctly and yet absolutely certain that he had and so puzzled, even a little troubled that two young children should be entrusted to someone like him without any question.

"You do as you're told," Lillian said to him. "And don't you break none of my windows neither, hear me?"

It was a strange, unsettling experience for a man who had spent so long separated from the vulnerable to help five-year-old Tommy into his boots, the child's fragile arm around his shoulder for support. Then outside, Tommy playing shortstop, David pitching to Eddie, who swung hard, missed and cried "Strike one!" with all the enthusiasm of a fan for the opposition. The second swing made up for it. The ball flew high—Eddie did have a real feel for the bat, just as he'd said himself, extraordinary for so small a boy—and David ran backward over the icy road surface to catch the ball, not an easy feat and perhaps not his most graceful maneuver, but one that gave him a kind of exhilaration he hadn't even guessed at since he was Eddie's age himself.

By the time Lillian called them in to dinner, the other guests were assembled around the table: the grim-faced Florence, mother of the baseball players and Lillian's middle daughter; Lillian's mother, an aged woman with a hearing aid and an expression so sour that it put even Florence to shame; Hiram, Lillian's eldest, Hugh's chauffeur for so many years, probably the last person to see him alive and David's Pair-a-Dice companion a week before, Hiram's fat wife, who taught economics at Springfield High School, and their giggly teenage daughter with her yappy little dog, one of the kind that's all hair and malice. Last to arrive had been Lillian's moody youngest son and his new girlfriend over whom he hovered protectively, even though she plainly needed nobody's protection—and certainly not his.

In pride of place at the head of the table sat Helen.

David could see that she was not comfortable there, although he was not at all certain why. He did not know that the occasional Sunday dinner at Lillian's was a tradition that went back as far as Helen could remember and that she'd long been resigned to the role of visiting dignitary for whom the tablecloth must be brought out of storage and ties must be worn. She would have loved to play at being a real part of this family, to change her Sunday eminence with Lillian, who sat halfway down the table among her children today but headed the table on all other occasions. For reasons Helen could not explain to herself, she felt more at home in this house than she'd ever felt at her grandmother's despite all the snobberies that told her she shouldn't even be here, much less enjoy the experience.

She had noted the empty guest of honor's place to her right, usually reserved for Lillian's mother, but it had never crossed her mind that it might have been reserved for David. At first she was too shocked by his appearance to speak, and as Lillian pointed him in her direction she rose partway out of her chair. "What are you doing here?" she said to him.

Lillian put her hands on her hips. "You set yourself right back on down, Miss Helen," she said. "This is my house and I asked him here."

"I don't think it is a very good idea," Helen said carefully.

"Miss Helen, you *set*. Hear me?"

Helen sat, but reluctantly, and there was an uncomfortable silence.

"Open them bottles, David," Lillian said to break it, "and pour us out some of that wine. I'm bringing in the meat right now. Florence, you get the plates. Mrs. Hiram, I need you for the vegetables."

Lillian carved the meat and handed out the plates. Peas, beans, yams, gravy made the rounds. David poured the wine, a red wine, not distinguished enough to be daunting but rich enough for the meat and handsome in the glasses Lillian had bought one by one over the last ten years or so, crystal glasses for Christmas and weddings, glasses that had to be washed separately and buffed. A pocket of tension remained at the head of the table, but the others talked

and ate animatedly, all except for Lillian's youngest son and his girlfriend. They were too wrapped up in each other for food or words;
Lillian had carefully placed them on opposite sides at opposite ends
of the table, but it was to no avail. They sensed nothing and no one
in the room except each other and the absurd barrier of a table that
divided them.

There was a pause when David got up to refill glasses, and suddenly Hiram said, "I told Mr. Freyl to take Athena with him that
night. I *told* him. Supposing he fell or something. It's dark. Supposing he got sick."

"Hiram, you never *was* good at *nothing*," Lillian's mother said.

"Oh, mama, he was top of his class," said Lillian. "You know he
was."

"Exactly. Now look at him. He don't even have no—"

"You said he seemed quite happy," David said, cutting across
the old woman as he filled Hiram's glass.

"Yeah, I guess so."

"Nobody happy is going to let you bully him into what's
right."

David had arrived here dressed as formally as Lillian's family—
the very suit he'd worn in New York to meet Christina Haggarty—
but his baseball game outside had brought him out in a mild sweat
that a warm house couldn't disperse. His face shone with it. It bur-
nished the muscles of his cheek and neck, and Helen's glass was not
yet empty. She swallowed what remained.

"Me too," she said to David. "What's this about being happy?"

"Just something Hiram mentioned." He leaned sideways across
her to fill her glass. "Truce?" he said.

"What for?"

"The duration of lunch."

"I have nothing to say to you."

"Around my table," said Lillian, mother hen in full command of
her chicks, "everybody got to talk nice to *every*body."

"I talk how I want," Lillian's mother said, the corners of her
downturned mouth turning down even farther.

"Sure you do, Mama," Lillian laughed. "That what you want to
act like, Miss Helen?"

Helen said nothing, but the tension around her didn't ease.

Everybody felt it except Lillian's youngest son and his girlfriend, and yet they were the only ones who dared escape. She announced that she had a headache.

"Can't you wait till after dessert?" Lillian said irritably.

They couldn't. Plainly they couldn't. Not one of the apple pies—the youngest son's favorite—had reached the table when they ushered each other out of the room, already locked together. By the time the last of the wine was drunk, and the rest of the guests felt free to leave, Lillian could see that Helen was not entirely steady. Besides, it was colder outside than it had been when she arrived. The roads were icier, just as they had been on the day Helen's mother died.

"David," Lillian said, "you got to take Miss Helen home."

"No," said Helen.

"Ain't nobody else can take you. Hiram's got Mama. Florence got the kids. You can't drive yourself, hear me?"

◄○►

The Sunday afternoon streets of downtown Springfield were stark, bleak, ugly, a wasteland of sleet frozen into ruts on the road itself and spewed out on pavement and up on sidewalk like horseshit from the olden days. Raw telephone wires swung in the wind, coated with ice that glistened in the orange light from arc lamps. It was barely three o'clock in the afternoon, but the day was darkening already, that dull, monotonic gray that means it's going to snow again. Roads in conditions like these call for extreme care from Springfield drivers, who crawl along them, leaning forward in their seats, faces so close to the windshield their noses almost touch it. Not David, though. He handled the Chevy with an offhand ease, instinctively aware of its rhythms, changes, internal connections and hence of the surface beneath the wheels. He had the same affinity for mechanical things that some people do for animals and for much the same reasons: machines don't scheme, plot, wait until you're down.

Beside him Helen sat tense and wary despite too much wine. She strained to capture the contempt for him that she wanted to feel. Maybe she was just too tired. Maybe she was . . . Damn it, she hated being scared, and she wasn't even sure what was scaring her. She couldn't pin it down: a sense that there was something just beyond the edges of her marginal vision—something that slipped out of sight the moment she turned her head. Besides, the road frightened her. So did the dark day and the ice. It was the twin of the day her mother died; the road had looked just like this. The snow had been just as dirty. And here she sat beside a man who would not have hesitated to kill her if it suited his purpose. Was that it? Was that what frightened her? Not that she was afraid of being dead, but the process of getting there . . .

Dear God, why could she never get rid of the smell of her mother's blood in winter?

"We need to talk," David said.

"Why?"

"There are things I need to know."

"What about?"

"Your father."

"That's no concern of yours." And yet she knew it was his concern. Becky had told her so.

It was all so complicated, her feelings about David. The thing is, she could remember the very moment she first knew he existed: a walk through the woods with her father in midwinter, just like now. It had been the year after her mother died, not long before she went away to school—a full year of growing further and further from everything that had been close to her before, only half alive, only some leftover part of a human being, shut away behind an impenetrable glass wall where no one could hear her, no matter how loud she screamed, unable to reach out past it to anybody or anything. Her father, her best friend, school, even Lillian: what difference did it make? What difference did anything make?

Then on that winter's walk, David appeared in the conversation, and she'd sensed the heat of him at once, young as she was. She'd even felt the vague stirrings of something, not sex—not yet, anyway—maybe just a reason for staying alive. After that, after she'd gone away to school, she'd demanded stories about him in letters and more stories as soon as she got home on vacations. He'd become her secret brother. She had rights over him—how could anybody deny it?—and yet when she'd asked about his crime, Hugh would say, "I don't pay much attention to what the men are doing behind bars." If she pressed (which she often did), he'd laugh and say, "Come on, Helen, leave the poor boy a few secrets of his own."

So she'd found out herself just as many of Hugh's friends had found out. She'd searched the morgue at the *State Journal-Register,* and knowledge is liberating. It truly is. A murderer is not a brother, certainly not *her* brother. She studied David's neck (so near to her in the car) because she was something of an expert in men's necks; as she had always said, elegance and power make a dangerous combination—never to be trusted. She had undressed him mentally over the Freyl dinner table more than once to trace this neck to its origins deep in the muscle of the shoulders (and beyond, of course). The pity of it was that reality so rarely measures up to imagination, although leaning back in her seat she saw that the hair curling over his collar was as vulnerable as curls on a Renaissance cherub's head.

"Cigarette?" he said, offering her the pack, one hand on the wheel.

"I'll do it. You watch the road." She took a cigarette and put it in her mouth. He offered her the car's lighter. "Keep your hands on that wheel, damn it."

But she let him light the cigarette for her. While he lit one for himself, she stared fixedly out at the road, still four lanes wide and lit with arc lights even though there were residential properties on either side. This near highway formed an impenetrable moat between the middle classes who had crept right up as close as they could to the rich and would never get any closer unless they robbed a bank or died and went to heaven.

"You want to tell me where you were the night he died?" David said.

She tossed her newly lit cigarette to the floor and stubbed it out. "I most certainly do not."

"Your grandmother says that the innocent are always eager to help clarify matters. That's all I'm after: clarification."

"It's none of your goddamned business."

"I could hazard a guess."

"Do what you goddamned please."

"Maybe I should ask Jimmy."

She stared at him, genuinely taken aback. "Maybe you should . . . You arrogant prick."

And yet there was no smugness in the voice. There was no smugness on his face either. No triumph. Not even the hint of a sneer. There was no expression at all. It was as though she hadn't touched him any more than the ice on the road had interfered with his driving.

28

THE ACTUAL TRANSLATION OF HABEAS CORPUS IS "YOU have the body": the body in question was David's and the holder of the body was the warden of South Hams State Prison. My writ in effect petitioned the court to order the warden to bring David before it for the purpose of reconsidering the conviction that kept him behind bars. It was the best brief I ever wrote, and I was genuinely sad that I would never have the chance to argue it. In fact, I need never have written it. I could have alternated pages from the Song of Solomon with pages from *Winnie-the-Pooh* and submitted them instead; the result would have been the same. The petition went to Judge Julius Roxon—I sincerely hope John did get some pleasure from bending the man to his will—and the court granted it. There was not a single leak to the press, nor a single murmur from them.

On a frozen winter Monday no more than two weeks later, I arrived at the courthouse with an assistant paralegal from my office (a blind man needs other people's eyes in court). David's case had been slipped into the docket first thing in the morning; there was no reason for anybody to connect the name of an obscure felon named David Marion with the eminent John Calder who had defended him a generation ago. Without that connection, nothing going on in court that day was interesting enough to attract the attention even of a cub reporter on the local paper. The charge against David was murder in the first degree. Judge Roxon was to preside over what is known as a bench trial: no jury.

David had been transferred from South Hams prison to the county jail the night before, the first time he had been out of solitary confinement in many months and the first time he had been outside those thirty-foot-high walls since he was a boy. That morning he had come to court with a busload of other inmates, placed with them in a holding tank in the basement, then transferred alone to a smaller cell until the court was ready for him. The judge, the prosecutor, my assistant paralegal and I were waiting in the courtroom when the bailiff brought him up. I knew David had arrived from the sound of shackles, and as soon as he stood beside me, I recognized that familiar bristle of anger.

"This will not take long, David," I said, hoping to reassure him.

There was no reply.

Stephanie had told me that Judge Roxon is a very fat man, that beads of sweat trickle down his forehead from a thin swatch of brown hair that looks as though he has dyed it with shoe polish. I never would have guessed the hair, but I could smell the sweat even from my distance across from him, and he wheezed when he spoke in the way only very fat men do.

"This is Criminal Case number, uh, 86-1215," he said, an opening ritual he would repeat a dozen times and more before lunch. "Identify yourselves for the record."

I spoke first. "Hugh Freyl, Your Honor, for the defendant, David Marion."

The prosecutor said, "Your Honor, I am Louis Rae MacMahon on behalf of the people. Your Honor, I believe we have a disposition in this court." Lou MacMahon had been in the DA's office for years; Stephanie once described him to me as tall and thin with a mournful Easter Island face.

"Get on with it," said the judge.

There was a rustle of paper. "The people are willing to accept a plea to two counts of voluntary manslaughter, necessarily lesser included offenses to the counts charged. Defendant would be sentenced to"—Lou rustled some more paper—"to eleven years on the first count and three years on the second for a total of fourteen years. He will receive credit for time served. The reason the people are offering this disposition is that the original trial was eighteen years ago, and it may be difficult to locate the necessary witnesses. Further, the homicides do appear to have occurred during a sudden quarrel. Therefore, both factually and practically, the charges of voluntary manslaughter are appropriate."

"Voluntary manslaughter, huh?" the judge said to me. He prided himself on running his court his way.

"Yes."

"That what your client wants?"

"Yes, Your Honor."

"Take off the glasses, son," he said to David. "I hate them dark glasses—never allow them in my court."

"I am afraid he cannot," I said.

"Ah, come on, Counselor, what's that supposed to mean? 'Course he can."

"He has come directly from solitary confinement in total darkness," I said. I had learned about this only moments before when my paralegal and I had talked to him briefly in a holding cell outside the courtroom. I made no attempt to hide my outrage. "His treatment was, as I am certain you are fully aware, in contravention to his rights under the Eighth Amendment—clearly cruel and unusual punishment."

"In the dark, huh?"

"Yes, Your Honor," I said. "The glasses are medically prescribed until his eyes get used to daylight. Otherwise he risks going blind—like me."

"Well, that's a new one—doctor saying a guy got to wear dark glasses to court. You got any proof of that?"

"I can easily supply it, Your Honor."

There was a tense moment, but nobody in this court wanted to face a delay. The judge wheezed and addressed himself again to David. "You gonna contest the charges, Mr. Marion?"

This time the moment was charged rather than merely tense. I held my breath and prayed that David would answer.

"Mr. Marion, glasses or no glasses, you got to say something," said Roxon.

"Come on, David," I said irritably. "This is no time for heroic gestures."

"No," he said through his teeth.

"Speak up, son," said the judge. "How are you pleading?"

"No contest."

I gave a sigh of relief, and the judge got on with his eccentric court. "You saying he didn't really plan on killing that woman, Counselor?" he said to me.

"Men," I said. "Two men."

"Whatever."

"No, Your Honor, he did not."

"How long did you say he served?"

"Eighteen years, three months and six days."

"Well, I'd say eighteen years is a long time, wouldn't you?"

"Indeed I would."

The judge shifted his weight to address the prosecutor.

"All happened a hell of a time ago, didn't it, Lou?" he said. "Kid was awful young at the time."

"Yes, Your Honor," said the prosecutor. "It is agreed that Mr. Marion receive credit for time served and be released forthwith."

The judge turned his attention back to me. "You happy with that, Counselor?"

"Yes, Your Honor."

"I don't got to remind you that Marion's a convicted felon. You better make damn sure he stays out of trouble."

"I will do my best."

"Now get him out of the building before I change my mind."

I waited on the first floor of the courthouse while the bailiff took David back to the holding tank, processed him out of the system, exchanged his prison blues for a white paper uniform and brought him back to me.

"Now what?" David said to me.

"It is over, David," I said. "It's time to go home."

I had expected triumph, delight, relief from him. Or at a pinch, confusion and bafflement. Maybe even fear of the unknown. For him, the release was abrupt and wholly unexpected. His escape attempt had cost him all communication privileges with the outside world; he had had no idea that freedom was more than the remotest of possibilities until he was removed from the dark of the hole at South Hams to the county jail less than twenty-four hours before. I had come to know him well over the years, and there is always that undercurrent in him, rather like the tingle-shock of static electricity when you touch metal on the coldest winter days. Even so, the abrupt fury I sensed in him—exactly as it had been on the first day I met him all those years ago—took me completely by surprise. At what was it all directed? the universe? God? me? everything and nothing?

I thought again as I had before, "Rage is the nuclear core that powers the boy—physically as well as mentally."

And then I realized I had one part of the answer I had been seeking so long: when he loses control, he kills people. This he knows.

◄o►

Helen's rooms were a studio within the boundaries of the Freyl complex, off by themselves a little, a separate entrance via a separate drive. There was the feel of a tree house about the place as she and David approached it; pines and firs hid the rise in the ground so that the roof seemed perched in the treetops. It was not until they were almost on it that the building itself appeared; he parked the Chevy in the clearing in front. Ice hung in branches that creaked a little above the two of them as they climbed the flight of raw redwood stairs to the front door.

"You're coming in," she said, although she had no idea why she said it or why he was with her still or whether she wanted him to come in or whether she dreaded it.

"Yes."

She unlocked the door into the foyer, tossed her heavy winter coat to the floor—he took his off and carried it with him—led him into a large room beyond, sat in a bentwood rocking chair and waved him to the sofa opposite her.

David glanced around him. There was forest outside—or what passes for forest in the middle of a town—shadowy dark greens in the semi-twilight of this overcast afternoon, rough trunks and dense undergrowth protecting a patchy tarpaulin of old snow: the treehouse promise brought to life. An entire wall of the room was windows, long, narrow panes divided by strong redwood moldings and looking out into the winter landscape. Another wall was solid books; in front of the books stood a desk with a computer and piles of papers on it. A third wall held marble and oak kitchen utilities.

But the fourth wall . . . However delicate Helen's mental balance may have seemed to him in the past, David could not have expected anything like this.

Prints of pictures by the Spanish painter Francisco Goya covered this wall from floor to ceiling, and they made one hell of a wallpaper. Here in a light and airy live-in tree house were the *Disasters of War*: death at its harshest, the atrocities that no one admits to but that Goya saw with his own eyes. Beneath them ran a tableau of night horrors from his "Black Pictures": tormented figures blending into one another under the direction of an indistinct, hooded figure.

The pictures shocked David. It wasn't their subject matter; he'd seen them before in books, years ago, longer ago than he could remember. The thing was, one day a fellow prisoner—the guy had been reading a book on psychology—said to him, "Think of a sheet of white paper." So he'd thought of a sheet of white paper. Then his fellow inmate said, "Now imagine yourself on it." And what David had seen was not any David Marion he'd ever imagined before. He saw himself as one of the Goyas, the first in a line of blindfolded men tied to posts. All the others were dead, shot, executed. What wasn't clear to him was whether the first man, the one that was himself, had already been executed too or was still waiting for it to happen.

Helen brought very few people back to her house. She watched David carefully as he scanned this wall, but the stoicism he'd learned so well in prison meant that he seemed to her as unfazed by it as by the kitchen or the forest outside.

"You listen here, Mr. David Marion," she said irritably, "I don't have anything to say to you about anything. Do you understand me? Not about anything."

He turned his back to her to study the books on her shelves. She watched him, angrily aware that from this angle, his shoulders just might live up to her imaginings. The back too: those triangular muscles that fan out from beneath a man's arm and run almost to his waist are the *latissimus dorsi;* she'd looked them up in a medical book once, and she could see them tense beneath his jacket as he moved. The moments ticked by.

"If you want answers from me," she burst out, "you're going to have to give a few yourself first."

"That sounds fair enough."

"I want to know about those people you killed." He said nothing. "Well?" she went on.

"Is that a question?"

"Of course it's a question."

"I'm sorry," he said, but he didn't sound sorry and she didn't know precisely what he meant. Sorry that he murdered? Sorry that she'd asked about it? He sounded bored, which infuriated her.

"Don't just sit there," she said. "I want facts. I want to see the picture. Either tell me or get out."

"Another Goya for your collection?"

"You just . . . killed them? Just like that? No provocation? Nothing?"

David turned to look at her then, and to her delight she saw that he wasn't bored at all, that what she'd mistaken for boredom in his voice was fierce control over a confusion of emotions that had grown too great for his face to hide them. "It depends on what you mean by provocation," he said.

"I don't care what you mean by it. Give it any meaning you like."

"For some of it there was provocation. For the rest—" He broke off.

" 'For the rest'?" she prompted.

"I don't know."

"What am I supposed to make of a comment like that?"

"Whatever you will."

"Oh, no. No, no. I'm afraid that won't do. I won't accept it."

"I can't tell you what I don't know."

"Okay. Then I want details."

"There's no point in details. They don't matter anymore. It's past. Finished."

A gust of wind slapped the tree branches against the window. "The past is *never* finished," she said bitterly, and the bitterness was pure, not even a tinge of sarcasm to soften it. "I can tell you that. Never. You can pretend whatever you want to pretend. You can talk however you want to talk. You can run as far and as fast as you can run—and still you'll find it clinging to your body like sweat. Wipe it off your legs. It clings to your arms. Wipe it off your arms, and it blinds you."

The blue-green fabric of the forest around this room of her house exaggerated the greens and blues of her eyes. Why did he forget every time he looked away from her that she was graceful as well as beautiful? Why did it always come as a surprise? It was true that there was a brittle stiffness in her manner, but the wintry resistance around her mouth was wholly out of keeping with the warmth in her eyes, and the drape of her arm over the chair was pure summertime. And there was more to it than that. Much more. Just as she'd come to feel that he half belonged to her; he'd come to feel that he'd watched her grow up, observed her from an enormous distance and through binoculars as other prisoners watched sparrows and starlings, charting nesting times and flight ranges. Hugh had told so many stories over the years. The summer birthday party when she wore ribbons in her hair, the fall off her horse that had dislocated her kneecap, her triumph as school valedictorian: these things were David's memories as well as hers, his past as well as hers.

"Tell me," she said. "Can't you see? I need to know." He turned to look at her. "I *need* to know," she repeated, and there was a desperation in her voice that he could not deny.

They'd come after him in the pit. Both of them. Chuck, who was mid-forties and a bruiser. Jackson, the son, full-grown at seventeen, as big as his father, bigger. They thought they had David trapped there. How could he get away? He didn't really start growing until he got to prison, and he couldn't have been much over five foot seven. They were both huge compared to him. Much stronger too.

"You raped my mother," Jackson had said.

David was stunned into speech. "Ellie said that?"

He remembered the shock of the oil pouring out onto the floor of the pit when his foster brother's exultant first blow struck the pan out of his hands. David rarely dropped things, and in that moment's consternation they caught him in the face and the stomach at the same time. He doubled over. But they hadn't counted on the edge that such confined quarters gave him. They hadn't expected him to be gauging his advantage even as he straightened up, even before he was fully aware that both of them were attacking him: *he* could maneuver; *they* couldn't stand up straight.

That's when it happened. That's when his story stopped short in an eruption of white light, with the air sucked out of his lungs and a roar in his ears. The shock wave that breaks away from ground zero in nuclear explosions annihilates everything in its path—and both the Fowlers were in David's path. He'd felt nothing when it was over. Not pain. Not numbness. Just nothing. The sight of the two bodies, quiet, meaninglessly ugly, sprawled in a stew of blood, flesh, brains and black engine oil: this sight had touched him no more than the lug wrench in his hand. He'd crawled out of the pit.

Now, all these years later, he sat in this handsome room of Helen's and didn't remember how he came to be sitting down at all.

He got up and walked to the window; the forest outside was beginning to grow darker.

"Lucky you," Helen said in a half whisper.

"What?" He assumed he'd heard her wrong.

"That's what *I* want. I want to *feel* that. *Alive*. Just like that. Just for a second. I'll trade all the rest for a split second of what you had."

"That's not what it's all about."

"You don't mean that."

"No."

"You had it all. Life and death. All at once."

"Yes."

She was staring at him, her lips parted; even facing away he knew this. She got up from her chair, went over to him, took the cigarette from his mouth, stubbed it out. She studied him a moment, then traced the tip of her finger down the line of the neck that had meant so much to her for so very long.

"Do you want to go to bed, David?"

◄◦►

David's first weeks out of prison were almost as strange an experience for me as they must have been for him. He was for all practical purposes a blind man, completely lost in this seeing world beyond prison walls. It was not just unfamiliarity either; without dark glasses and if the day was bright, his eyes were almost as useless as mine. In a certain sense there was a blessing in this; I was his guide, a literal example of the blind leading the blind, and because his inability was to some degree physical as well as mental, I found I could teach him in much the same way as I had been taught by my instructors at the Lincoln Center where I had spent so important a six-month period of my life and where I had learned how to function all over again like a child.

He too had to learn the simplest things from scratch, the most elementary techniques of a civilized society: get on a bus to go downtown, watch the traffic, cross the street, buy a toothbrush, count his change, choose clothes in a store, try them on, order a cup of coffee in a café, wait at the table for his bill, go to the cash register to pay it: things that the rest of us take entirely for granted from the time we are small.

And that is only the beginning. Prison is enforced childhood; David had never even glimpsed an adult's autonomy. That is to say that for much of today's world he had not even the aid of memory; either he had been too young to need such techniques when he went to prison or they had not yet been invented. What did a fifteen-year-old boy in the 1980s know about getting cash out of a wall? cell phones? the Internet? DVDs? There were not even any computers available to inmates at South Hams prison. I gave him a temporary job at Herndon & Freyl as a personal assistant, where I could teach him such modern technical skills and pay him enough to keep himself until he found work. These were only the simplest of matters. The more difficult tasks had all the quality of Herculean feats to a person of his inexperience in the ways of the world. We had to seek out an apartment for him to live in. He had to open a bank account, not an easy job at best for a man with a prison record and no credit rating. We shopped for a bed, dishes, blankets. We bought him a car, an old Chevrolet Impala, the very car he had wanted when he was eleven years old and living with the Monaghans.

But even all this constituted only the least part of what he had to learn.

A long-term prisoner comes from a world where violence is so constant, so relentless, so meaningless that the world outside baffles him. Even hidden behind dark glasses, he finds our landscape too loud, too bright, too busy. He reacts to the slightest noise as though it were the crack of a gunshot, interprets the most insignificant gesture as a death threat, sees every new face as an enemy. During David's first few weeks of freedom, Athena stayed at home for a well-earned vacation, and I took his arm so that I could check at the source the sudden flares of anger I could feel in him when someone inadvertently crossed his path, looked at him askance, brushed against him in the street, expressed surprise at his innocence of modern life or made some comment about it that passes for a minor irony in this outside world but in prison would call for immediate and brutal retribution.

It is one thing to visit the panther in the zoo with guards and guns at your command should the ground rules shift in some way that does not suit you. It is altogether another when the panther becomes your daily companion. Yet I enjoyed the sense of danger David carried with him; I sunned myself in the frisson he caused in other people, in the charge I could feel in the air the moment they caught sight of him.

And I enjoyed his belief in me in ways I find it hard to explain. There is something magical, moving, deeply touching in being treated gently by such a one.

◄o►

Not long after midnight Helen woke with a jolt and reached out for David. He wasn't there and she—who had never been other than revolted by the sight of a man in her bed—felt an anxiety so great at the lack of him that it took her breath away. She was out of bed at once. There was a light from the living room. She ran toward it, threw open the door.

And there he was.

He looked up at her, and for a moment she couldn't speak. "Why aren't you asleep?" she said then.

"Should I be?"

"Men sleep afterward." He was only partially dressed, shirt still open. She had never wanted a second look at any other man—not even a first look if she was honest about it—but she could not bring herself to look away. "Do you think . . ." You see, the shoulders, the body were precisely as she'd imagined them for so many months: this is not easy for a mere mortal to grasp, and she could not bear to have him hidden from her.

"Do I think what?" he said.

"I'd rather like . . ." She sighed, tried to tear her gaze away, failed. "This is very embarrassing."

He got up. "Don't worry. I'm just about to leave."

"No, no. That's not what—" She broke off. "David?"

He waited for her to speak again.

"You smell of cumin and mustard seed, and I . . ." She stopped, took in her breath, then went on in a rush. "Would you come back to bed with me?"

29

THE SKY WAS STILL FULLY DARK—SOMEWHERE AROUND
five o'clock Monday morning, not yet a hint of dawn—as David approached the turnoff to his new house. The four-lane highway of
Grover Cleveland Boulevard glowed orange from the arc lights; the
antiqued streetlamps of Jefferson Place lit up the tree-lined
macadam of the close in interlocked pools. He'd only just left Helen,
and his mind was still on her; that's why he didn't notice sooner
that the lights in his own house were blazing. It wasn't Tony. Tony
never left Mrs. Hunter alone at night. It could hardly be Stephanie.
She'd always gone back to the motel before midnight, usually long
before. David stopped the Chevy some three hundred yards from his
garage.

Nobody else even knew where he lived—except for whoever
was tailing him (if anybody really was). He got out of the car and
skirted the back of the neighboring houses until he reached his
own; he was good at walking silently. Some of it's care in choosing a
place for the foot; most of it's muscular control. There were no
drapes over the glass doors to his patio, and even as he approached
he could see a woman seated at the big round table in the middle of
the room. She wasn't moving, the top of her body sprawled out over
the surface, back and shoulders hidden by the computer screen,
head and arm flung out to one side, face turned away from him. His
first thought was Helen because her hair was dark even though he
knew perfectly well that she was safely asleep in her own bed more
than a mile away—and yet he already knew it was Stephanie. He'd
left her at his house before Lillian's lunch of yesterday, which
meant she was dead. If she'd been alive, she'd be as safely asleep as

Helen; she'd have got a taxi hours before. No blood was visible. Gunshot. Knife. Garrotte. Hands. From this vantage point, he couldn't tell. He knew knife, garrotte, hands. He knew them intimately, how the dead from them looked. Not guns, though: only guards carry guns.

He leaned against the outside wall—cold stucco finish at his back—and breathed slowly in and out: an old trick to force the nerves into submission. You can't let the adrenaline take over. Lay out the ground before you make your move: what's known, what isn't and what has to be done. Since there was no evidence of medics or police, nobody had seen her yet. That left the question of what to do with the body. Get her into the trunk of the Chevy—no problem since the garage was connected to the house itself. After that? There's a lot of open land in Illinois, and he'd seen a spade in a yard along Grover Cleveland Boulevard on his way here.

He took a pick from his pocket and began work on the lock to the patio door. That was when he realized he couldn't remember if the lights had been on or off yesterday morning when he left her to go to Lillian's lunch. The day had been very dark, but there was one of those blank areas in his mind around the time he left; they'd been increasing—the blank spots in his memory—and this one brought a sharp pang of dread with it. He could easily have killed her himself. But what would have provoked him? He never killed without cause. Had she crossed him? found out something he didn't want her to know? No, no. He'd never have left the lights on. He hated that: leaving lights on for no reason. Besides, even at his blankest, he wouldn't have let the body lie there for anybody to see, not for nearly a full day. Nobody else would do that either. So death had to be recent, probably very recent, possibly within the past few minutes. He pushed the final pin of the lock up to the shear line; the plug turned. There was a soft click as the mechanism released. He stepped into the living room and slid the door shut behind him.

As he crossed toward her, she sat up abruptly.

"David!" she cried. "At last! Let me show you." She'd started shuffling through scrambled piles of Internet printouts at once, too preoccupied to notice the shock on his face or the sharp intake of his breath.

"What are you doing here?" he said.

"Couldn't leave. Too busy—no computer at the motel. You always pick your own locks?" He could not bring himself to answer. "You look kind of peaked. Where you been anyhow?" He shook his head. "I'm getting really good at this, David," she went on, too excited by what she had to tell him to notice that he was staring at her blankly, watching each movement she made as though she'd magically come to life in front of his eyes like Lazarus risen from the dead. "Listen, listen. There's 'hard money' and 'soft money.' Isn't that a wonderful distinction? The 'hard money' is the *absolutely* legal stuff. 'Soft money' is only just, well, legal, and vast amounts of it get slipped in sideways, somewhere between the plain legal and the absolutely illegal. See, you can't just hand over whatever you want—it's all got to do with Watergate and Nixon and nowadays no individual can write a check for more than $2,000 to get some guy elected president of the country and a company can't dole out more than $5,000—so there's this loophole—"

"What *are* you talking about?"

"David, I tracked *three* payments from the bankrupt's subsidiaries to Calder. Three! And the campaign's only a couple of days old. The way it works out, maybe individuals can't give direct to a candidate, but they can give anything they want provided they give it to joint fund-raising committees, and these committees—"

"What's that?"

"What's what?"

"Committees?" His brain was just beginning to take hold of what she had to say. "Joint . . . what was it? Fund-raising?"

"Bunch of like-minded groups stuck together—Republicans or Democrats from various states. They're supposed to be playing with stuff like get-out-the-vote drives, bumper stickers, yard signs, maybe TV ads that say 'Vote Republican' or 'Support the Death Penalty' or something. But it's so easy to turn the money in the direction you want it to go, a little hint to somebody in charge is all it takes. So some rich guy writes out a huge check and gives it to one of these committees. The committee peels off $2,000 to send to the candidate as hard dollars and funnels the rest as soft dollars through to *littler* committees all over the place, and *they* can spend the money wherever and however they damn please—which is wherever the rich guy says he wants it to go." She laughed. "It's just another set of twists for that money-laundering trail from Jimmy's safe. The accounting is so complicated—just like you said—that nobody can track it back to its source, and so the sky's the limit. There aren't any restrictions at all. Cute, huh?"

"There's a tie-in to Calder?"

She bit her lip and smiled at him. "I really, really wanted to track something back to Bozo—no such luck, I'm sorry to say—but guess what? *Hugh's* dog paid up. Poor old Athena made her contribution . . . See?" She held out a printed sheet. "Jimmy's Number One Fund file shows up a 'Consultation Fee' of $673,000 that Athena Corporation paid out to a guy named Stuart Henry Ederly. That was just a couple of weeks ago, and right here—see? right in the *St. Louis Post-Dispatch*—it says that a Stuart Henry Ederly wrote out a check for $673,000 to the Victory Joint Fund-raising Committee, which just turns out to be the very one set up to elect Calder. *Exactly* the same amount. It's all down here in the paper in black and white, and I'm talking about *last* Saturday, just . . . what? two days ago? It's got to have been within hours of Calder's announcement—*hours!*"

David took the piece of paper from her. She'd printed out a section from the *Post-Dispatch* coverage of Calder's announcement of his candidacy.

"There's more," she said, picking up another sheet. "I found some subsidiary . . . Damn, where is it?" A sheet of paper escaped her and went flying off the table. He reached out, picked it up, handed it back to her. "One of the directors of CAUC or something, name of Dewey C. Morrison." She was pointing to an entry in Jimmy's Number One Fund file. "See? He got $432,000 as a 'Consultation Fee' and here . . . in the *Chicago Tribune* this time, it says a Dewey C. Morrison gave the committee $432,000. Exactly the same amount *again*."

"What's a campaign like this cost?"

"Dunno, really. I found a story—God knows where—saying that Bush spent something pushing $2 billion. Can't remember the exact amount. But here's my prize. Here's the lollapalooza. Here's the . . . Are you ready? I guess there's not anything stopping anybody giving whatever he wants to his favorite joint fund-raising committee. Because here we have the legislative director of . . . let's

see . . . it's UCA. Or is it . . . No, no, it's UIC. Anyhow, on Saturday—the timing here is *really* cute—this legislative director pitched
$359,000 at the Republican Party like the good citizen he clearly is.
And guess what his name is." David shook his head. "Guess. Go
on."

"Jimmy wouldn't do anything *that* stupid."

"Hugh Freyl!" She crowed with delight. "Now, what do you
think about that? Kind of complicated since he had no interest in
politics and would have come down as a Democrat if anything at
all—to say nothing of the little problem that he's been dead nearly
four weeks and has to be supporting the electoral process even from
the privacy of a still-unmarked grave. But you can't expect the
Calder lot to let a couple of little hiccups like that bother them, can
you?"

David took the sheet she handed him and scanned it. "This certainly wasn't any part of Jimmy's file. I wonder how many more
there are."

"Just could add up to quite a campaign coffer, couldn't it?"

"Um."

"Is it enough?" she said, watching David's every move as he
checked the various papers. "Will it work?"

"I'll go and see old Mrs. Freyl a little later this morning," he
said. He began gathering the printouts into piles and selecting various of the documents that had come from Jimmy's safe.

"Can't you go *now*?"

He looked up at her. "It's not even six o'clock."

"Oh," she said, abruptly deflated. "I'd probably better keep my
distance when the time comes anyhow, hadn't I?"

David nodded. "At least to start with. I'll drive you to the motel
on my way over."

30

THE FOLLOWING AFTERNOON, TUESDAY, AT A FEW MIN-
utes past three o'clock, Becky herself answered her front door to
John Calder. An army of reporters and photographers surged forward from the front yard. The whole of the Freyl property seethed
with them. Cameras on trolleys swiveled into position. So did cameras on shoulders. Flashbulbs blinded the eyes. Huge furry microphones waved in the air over a shouted babble of questions.

"Good morning, John," Becky said to him graciously, ignoring it
all and holding out her hand, which he took. "How very good of
you to come to see me."

"You're the one who does me the honor," John said, holding her
hand in both of his: that famous Calder handshake again.

"It's an exciting time for all of us."

They held the pose a moment longer, and it did make a pretty
picture for next day's front pages: Springfield's first presidential candidate since Abraham Lincoln—still young enough to be dashing (if
the camera caught him from the right angle)—paying homage to the
town's leading citizen who had married into the family that led
straight back to the great man himself. There was frost in the air.
The sky was cloudless. The sun shone. Becky's copper roof glistened.

"Is that enough now?" she said before releasing his hand. "They
can't need *more* pictures, can they?"

He smiled. "I think that'll hold them." The Calder public rela-
tions representative—that odd, epicene individual from his interview with Georgie Pickles—appeared discreetly at his side. "You
remember my PR?"

"Oh, John, I so dislike discussing finances in public."

"One PR isn't usually considered to be the public at large."

"All this"—she waved at the massed reporters—"is quite overwhelming for a private person like me. I do apologize if I seem less than friendly," she said to the PR. "I assure you it is no more than feminine weakness."

Becky's words were pure southern belle, but the steel in her voice belonged on an armor-plated tank. "Of course. Of course," John said. "Forgive me." As she shut the door behind him, he went on, "I'm afraid those guys are trampling on your flower beds. They're not exactly known for their sensitivity."

"Flower beds have little to fear in winter."

John removed his heavy coat. She took it from him, shook it out and handed it to Lillian, who stood in attendance. "Morning, Lillian," he said.

"Morning, Mr. Calder."

"You going to vote for me, old friend?"

Lillian knew her place all too well. She'd learned how to keep it in her cradle, and he'd turned the full beam of his charm on her. "I ain't heard what you got to say yet."

"That's my girl," he said fondly, putting her restraint down to the inexplicable adherence to the law that chains the respectable poor to the bottom of the ladder. To Becky he said, "I'm amazed that you allowed the press in at all. Very pleased, of course—but *very* surprised. They were pretty surprised too. I bet they've been wondering for years what this place looks like up close. It'll make every gossip column in the country."

"Sometimes one must suffer for one's principles." Becky led him across the large entryway to Hugh's study. "In here," she said, opening the door.

"Oh, good. This has always been one of my favorite rooms. You know, the last time I saw Hugh in here—" John stopped short.

There in front of him, beside the window and looking out at the crowd of reporters, was Stephanie.

"Company?" he said to Becky with a frown of puzzlement.

"As you see."

"Well, well, well," he went on with a laugh. "It's Stephanie—let me see—Willis, isn't it? Didn't you used to work for Hugh? Are you working for Becky now? You're hardly the person I expected to see this morning." It was only then that he sensed someone at the door behind him. He turned to find David there. Another unexpected development, which compounded the puzzlement of the first. He was not at all certain what David's position had come to be in the Freyl household, nor what response Becky might be expecting. He mixed caution and condescension. "And you . . . my old client and the man who gate-crashed a funeral. David . . . ? What's the last name? I'm usually good at names, but somehow . . ."

"Marion."

"Of course. Like the prison. How could I forget? Goodness, Becky, you do surround yourself with an interesting mix of people. You have such a kind heart."

Becky's smile was as frosty as the ground outside. None of this was easy for her. She'd trusted John Calder. She'd believed in him. She'd been ready to write a substantial check to the Republican Victory Committee on his behalf; his campaign manager had dreamed up this morning's meeting weeks ago to get the Springfield ball rolling—and thereby the entire country. She'd been happy to do it provided the press was limited to his PR. And then David arrived yesterday to destroy all that: David who seemed to destroy everything in his path. But Becky was nothing if not tough. She knew what she wanted, and the hunt for Hugh's killer erased all other concerns from her mind. So she'd forced herself to read the material David presented, and when she could not help seeing what it meant—when she had not been able to persuade herself that he had misconstrued it—she agreed to his plan of attack. She even enlarged on it; it was she herself who proposed that the press should attend in strength. Then he brought up Stephanie Willis. That was the only point where she balked. The very *idea* of that woman in her house—the upstart who'd so very nearly stolen her son from her—was more than she could bear. The reality was torture.

How could she have let David maneuver her into it?

"These people," she said, keeping her eyes averted from Stephanie, "have some things to discuss with you, John. I think you'd better sit down. It may take a few minutes."

"Becky Freyl, you lured me here," he joked.

"I'm afraid I must plead guilty to the charge."

"Something to do with the campaign?"

"You could call it that."

"Why so mysterious?" She didn't reply at once, so he turned to David and Stephanie and did his duty as a man of the people. He was jovial, urbane. "I'm so glad to have met up with you both again. I'm afraid today is turning into some kind of a cross between a circus and a full-scale riot—I'm already beginning to wonder if I'll survive a campaign that's no more than three days old—but do let's arrange to get together another time." Becky usually wrote her checks for him in her own study; as he talked, he took her arm to lead her there.

She pointedly removed his hand. "Perhaps you did not understand me, John. I wish I could persuade myself that the business these people present is extraneous. If I could, I most assuredly would."

"You're not sick or anything, are you?" John said. She was not bothering to hide her distaste; this made his worry very real.

She had her hand on the doorknob. "I'll be in the living room if you need me, Mr. Marion."

"Hey, wait a minute," John said. But she had already disappeared behind the door and shut it after her. Besides, David blocked his path.

"I suggest you take a seat," David said.

"You're not going to hold me hostage, are you? What a fascinating thought. You know, I have a whole security team out there. What *are* they going to say when I tell them I was kidnapped right in front of their eyes?"

John's smile was wry, superior, indulgent while he groped about in the corners of his mind for a dignified way to get past David. Whatever was going on, he didn't like it. It wasn't presidential. Presidents are not commandeered by convicts, especially when they're in the process of collecting money from rich dowagers. And yet what could he do? The press waited beyond the study windows in the cold. He could hear them yapping and growling out there like the jackals they were, and they would eat him alive if there was some kind of a flare-up today, however modest—especially a flare-up in Becky Freyl's house. Besides, John knew too much about criminals and prisoners, and David's gaze unnerved him just as it had unnerved guards and fellow prisoners at South Hams.

So John gave up and sat, and it turned out to be a good idea. He was more tired than he'd realized. The weekend's celebrations had gone all through Saturday night and on until the early hours of this morning—a little much even for his enthusiasms. Besides, now that he was seated in a large leather chair, the position seemed more, well, presidential. He turned to David and said pleasantly, "This must mean a great deal to you, whatever it is. So who's going to start? You or Ms. Willis?"

"You don't happen to remember the details of David's release from prison, do you?" Stephanie said as though the thought had just struck her.

"His release?"

"The writ of habeas corpus. Surely you remember that. Judge Julius Roxon, the fat man who wheezes. Hugh told me he let David off to pay you back a very substantial political favor."

"Are you seriously . . ." John burst out laughing. Hugh Freyl was one thing, but this woman . . . Maybe Hugh had scared him, but Hugh was Hugh *Freyl*. This person was a nobody. Besides, she'd left town before the hearing, such as it was. "Come on now, boys and girls, you *can't* be serious. Is this really what all the fuss is about? A plea bargain a couple of years back? I know it's difficult for non-lawyers to understand, but lawyers broker deals all the time. It's an integral part of our judicial system. Fortunately for Mr. Marion old police files get lost, as they did in his case. The prosecution didn't have any evidence anymore." He began to pull himself out of the chair. "Now I really must take my leave of you both."

"That's the very thing," Stephanie said. "You see, *I* have the only known copy of the files right here in Springfield. It's that other suitcase, David"—she was responding to the question on his face—"and I can't help thinking that some of the papers might interest some of those people out there." Stephanie peered through the venetian blinds. "Isn't that Georgie Pickles? Hugh loved her column. It made him laugh. He told me just what parts of the file on David would particularly interest her. All that stuff about ineffective assistance of counsel: the forged confession you knew about and the evidence of torture you ignored. And that's just a start. Did you know Georgie is syndicated all the way to the West Coast?"

John shook his head in exasperated contempt. "Oh, dear. Oh, dear. What's this turning into now? Old-fashioned blackmail?"

"Forget the past," said David.

"I can only assume that means you've found your own stick to beat me with this morning. Well, come on. Out with it."

David opened his briefcase and handed over the power of attorney that Stephanie had found. John glanced over it. It was a jolt to the system; he had to admit that. Nothing he couldn't handle, but, damn it, this had been set up to be one of the best days of his life. "I don't know quite what you have in mind here." He paused. "Where'd you get this?"

"Jimmy let me have it."

"Jimmy . . . ?"

"Zemanski."

"Hugh's young partner? Successor, I suppose I should say." John frowned at the sheet of paper, then looked up at David. "So?"

"Hugh appears to have been signing contracts and checks that you should have signed yourself."

John shook his head. "No wonder poor Becky is so upset. You amaze me. You really do. A more sophisticated man would be thoroughly ashamed of himself, Mr. Marion. God knows what fairy tales you put into her head about this wholly innocent document." David said nothing. "It's going to be like that, is it? A nasty incident unless you have an explanation that satisfies you? and hence Becky? But she already knows, you see. She's just forgotten. She isn't all that young anymore." He studied his fingernails a minute, sighed irritably, then went on. "Like all too many people in public life, I have a deep, dark secret. I got into pretty bad shape a while back—that was before I ran for senator—and my wife called on Hugh for help. At about the same time my father made a few very ill-advised financial moves. The poor man lost a fortune—literally—and Hugh took over bank balances, investments, bills—all of it—until I could get on track again. Becky helped too. I owe them both a debt of profound gratitude."

"Yes," said David.

" 'Yes'? That's all you have to say?"

"He means we figured you'd say something like that," Stephanie said.

John cast his eye over his antagonists. "You did, huh? So that's the case for the prosecution, is it? Now let me see if I can get it straight. Ms. Willis here is going to call in the press and show me up as a man who once lost a case that resulted in a miscarriage of justice and did some hard bargaining to right the wrong, while Mr. Marion—the client for whom all this was done—is going to point a finger and say, 'That bad man drinks too much.' " The irony was heavy in his voice, and he was completely unfazed by the discrepancies between the version he was giving David and the one he'd given Georgie only a couple of days before. "On the other hand, George W. Bush was a drunk," he went on, "and it didn't do him any harm. Just for your information, I'm following his example. A press release goes out as soon as I leave this house. It's the official reason for the visit. Didn't Becky tell you? I'm giving thanks for her family's help through some dark days and at the same time clearing the air so people like you will crawl back under the rocks where they belong." He shook his head once more. "Strange of Mr. Zemanski to take possession of the power of attorney, though. I assumed Hugh had shredded it long ago. Is Zemanski dabbling in the blackmail business too? Don't bother to answer. I've had quite enough for one morning, and I have no intention of continuing this farce any longer. Interview terminated."

He got up, dignity fully intact. He took a step toward the door.

That's when David said, "Tell me about Uniplex Advanced Ceramics."

When John was little he'd had a recurrent nightmare about being buried alive. It always came on him abruptly, just like this. He hadn't thought about it since he was twelve years old. Not until this very moment, that is.

"Mr. Calder?" David said.

"I don't see why you insist on boring me with your . . ." John could hear the edge of panic in his voice. "Surely you haven't got me here to talk about the stock market."

"We've traced several contributions to your joint election committee right back to the corporation before it went broke."

"How should I know anything about . . . ? Committees are independent of . . ." John knew he wasn't making much sense. In his childhood dream, a rough coffin lid slammed shut over his chest. It squeezed the air out of his lungs. He'd made an abrupt, undignified duck in the direction of the door before he had a hint of his own intention. And yet somehow he ended up precisely where he had been before he started.

He hadn't even felt David touch him.

"Now, that's really strange," Stephanie said, "because I managed to track a handful of contributions to something called the Number One Fund. Remember that? One of them even carried Hugh Freyl's signature. What amazing power you gave him when you signed that power of attorney. It managed to raise him from the dead."

"Hugh's . . . ? You shock me, Ms. Willis. You . . ." John's voice cracked. "You really shock me. First, veiled threats of blackmail over trivia and now ill-founded questions about campaign . . ." He trailed off, watching uneasily as David went to Hugh's office telephone and dialed. "What could possibly be amiss in legitimate contributions from highly reputable corporate entities?"

"Give me Christina Haggarty's office," David said.

This time John's whole body jolted with the impact. "What are you doing?"

"Tell her it's David Marion."

"You don't mean you know . . . Isn't she . . . ?"

David cupped his hand over the mouthpiece. "You may drink like George W. Bush did," he said, "but nobody gets to be president these days without money like his as well. As you say yourself, you were flat broke only ten years ago. A network of controlled donors isn't a bad way to fill the gap. A bleedout to create cash flow: that's excellent business sense. The snag is that Ms. Haggarty seriously disliked getting burned in the process."

"You've shown her the file?" The question was ripped out of John before he could stop it.

"I wanted to discuss it with you first."

◄◦►

Once David had mastered the basics, I set myself to teach him the more advanced techniques of society.

At South Hams prison, only the violent had peace, only killers were respected and all crimes had equal weight. Expressing concern for a mere acquaintance was a show of weakness that could end in a knife at the throat.

If one prisoner stole a cigarette from another, the sentence was death because a man who gets away with stealing cigarettes will try rape next. To give an inch—anywhere at any time—was to offer oneself up to whoredom or murder. This was the only kind of social intercourse David had known as an adult. Over the years of regular lessons, he had of course learned to behave differently with me, but the relationship remained formal; for all that time it had been conducted in the ugly, noisy confines of a prison conference room with wire-mesh walls, guards patrolling, regulations strictly enforced.

Such goings-on make quite a contrast to the mannered dance of pressure and withdrawal that constitutes a civilized conversation over a dinner table where what looks like attack can just as readily be a show of friendship and what looks like friendship could easily be an act of war. All this must be carried on while juggling delicate silver utensils, crystal glasses, napkins as well as passing salt, pepper, butter, salad bowl: a far more difficult feat than most of us are aware.

The surprise came when I realized that what I had to learn from him was more complex—at least to my way of thinking—than any such delicacy even pretends to be. A prison is a place stripped of the ornate rituals that most of us hide behind and that a dinner party characterizes so well. It strips the human machinery to the motherboard, on which everything else depends and from which there is no court of appeal. This I had sensed. What I had not sensed was that the state of alert that rules a prisoner's life really ought to rule us all. Only because of David's tense vigilance and contempt for the hypocrisy of civilized friendship did I stumble across the saddest rule of human contact, and one that I had always assumed belonged to his world, not to mine: watch your back most carefully when someone you trust steps behind you.

Without him, I would never have started watching Jimmy. There are even times when I find myself furious at David for revealing Jimmy for what he was. I hate being manipulated like that. It is humiliating, and I hate being humiliated even more than I hate being manipulated. How could the son of my old friend have made me a dupe in John Calder's corporate scandal?

President of the United States? John Calder? Over my dead body.

◆

John sank back into the big leather chair in Hugh's study. The skin on his face prickled. He thought he might faint. He opened his mouth, but he had no idea what might come out or what possible bearing it might have on anything.

"I trust you understand," David went on, "that if I complete this call, you're likely to be one very dead senator. Or presidential candidate, rather. What we have told Mrs. Freyl is that we know Hugh had discovered the bleedout. We think he probably knew that the Number One Fund was set up to finance your presidential bid. It was only a matter of time—probably only days—before he exposed you. Jimmy saw it coming. You probably did too. Ms. Haggarty is as yet unaware of these—" He broke off and spoke into the telephone. "It's important. I'll hold."

"Okay. Okay," John shouted. "Just hang up the phone, huh? Hang up! Come on, hang up."

David held the handset away from his ear a little. "Are you sure?"

"Jesus. Sure I'm sure. Christ almighty, hang up, will you? So we helped on the Uniplex bankruptcy a little, so what? It happens all the time. So Galleas got burned. People in their business ought to know how to swallow a loss. Ten million? It's nothing. You can't want records. What would you do with them? What *do* you want from me? Money? Power? I'll give you whatever you want. A position on my staff? What?"

"I want to know who killed Hugh Freyl."

The telephone handset still hovered over the cradle with John's eyes glued to it. "Hugh?" he said.

"Yes."

"This is about Hugh?"

"I want to know who killed him."

"How should I . . . ? You think I . . . *That's* what you think? That *I* killed him? Or had him killed?" John laughed. "You're mad. Me?" He laughed again, tried to suppress it, couldn't. "You can't seriously think I'd kill Hugh over a bankruptcy. Jimmy Zemanski maybe. Who'd miss him? Hey, I can see how convenient it looks, but Hugh *Freyl*? To be perfectly honest with you, I had no idea he knew anything about anything. Jimmy never said a word. Why should he? What difference would it have made to the project?

Hugh would have come around in the end. I'm sure he would have."

The sweat John wiped off his brow was pure relief. He took in a lungful of air, savored it, let it out slowly. "Oh, boy, you had me real worried, know that? I was figuring Galleas had hired you to . . . Jesus, how could you think I'd kill Hugh? Some things are sacred."

"Are they?"

"I'm not claiming to be perfect, but I'm not willing to run down *every*body who stands in my way."

David surveyed him slowly. "Then you'll never be president," he said. It wasn't contempt, just a statement of fact. "You don't want it badly enough."

31

STEPHANIE HAD HELPED ME PLAN DAVID'S TRIUMPHANT return to the outside world, and yet she was not there to share it with me. Only days before his release—nearly a full two years ago now—she disappeared from my life. All she left me was an e-mail saying how much she had enjoyed working with me and how sorry she was to be leaving before I had found a replacement for her; a postscript added that a check on my desk covered her wages for the two weeks' notice she should have given. My frantic response bounced back as undeliverable.

I tore over to her house. It was empty. The belongings that I had gradually transferred over the months from my house to hers stood in a neat pile in the middle of the living room downstairs so that Athena would make sure I located it at once—so that there was no risk of my tripping over it unawares. There did not seem to be anything of Stephanie herself; Athena could find not so much as an abandoned article of clothing or an unwanted newspaper. That bed with its many pillows might never have existed, much less the nights and afternoons we had spent in it. Neighbors seemed to have no idea where she had gone. The post office could supply no forwarding address. Her friends would tell me nothing. It was as though the relationship had taken place only in my imagination.

We had been so much at ease with each other—or so I had thought—that I just assumed we would set up something more permanent as soon as we got around to it. Fool that I was. Idiot. We had not discussed it. She had made no commitment, and she is nearly twenty years younger than I am. There were nuances of speech I had missed. There had to have been. There were hints I had not recognized. It shamed me to think that I could have made my feelings so oppressive. I felt as though I had stalked her rather than loved her. How could I have forced her into a position where she felt she had to leave town altogether to escape me?

◄◦►

The press had endured the biting cold in front of the Freyl house for half an hour, and the wait had been worth every minute. John Calder's relief came across to them as jubilation; photographs of him leaving the dowager's house showed that winning, childlike delight for which he was famous. The announcement of his onetime drinking problem only endeared him to everybody and the brushed-off questions about Becky's contribution led to the conviction that her donation had been in the millions rather than the hundreds of thousands.

As soon as he climbed into his limousine and drew away, a team of policemen jostled the reporters and cameramen off the Freyl property and a small force of groundsmen moved in to clear up after them. Lillian saw David and Stephanie to the front door of the house.

"Could you wait for me in the car?" Stephanie said to David, turning back into the foyer. "I won't be a minute."

Becky was in a small library off the living room. She sat in a chair that had belonged to Hugh's father and to his grandfather before him. It was an ornate, carved piece of furniture, strong in its lines, clearly a man's chair and wholly out of keeping with the Japanese refinement that dominated the house. And yet the chair suited her. It confirmed the authority she wielded; it accentuated what even now—even at her great age—showed itself as a delicate femininity. Despite her rigid control, it was the femininity that ruled. She was close to tears. Not that she would cry. Her son might be dead, her drive to find his killer at a stalemate, her belief in John Calder dashed along with her belief in the system of power that allowed him to flourish. But she would not cry.

She *never* cried, and Stephanie's appearance removed whatever minor threat remained.

"Why are you still here?" Becky said.

"I'm not going home until I find out who did this to Hugh, but I have a—"

"I can't see what possible interest any of your plans are to me."

"—few things to say to you before I go any further."

Becky shook her head. "Not today, Ms. Willis."

"I loved your son."

"We *all* loved my son."

"You told me—"

"*Please,* Ms. Willis."

"—that I embarrassed him, that he couldn't possibly return the feeling I had for him. You're a very smart woman. You knew all the time that you and I were asking the same question: how could somebody as miraculous as Hugh love somebody as ordinary as I am? I kept thinking, 'Am I misreading things? Could I be wrong?' Nobody can be as happy as I was and not have to pay for it. More than anything I was afraid I'd find out that I'd been so wrapped up in myself that I couldn't see what was in front of my eyes—that I'd become a tiresome burden without even realizing it. You knew I loved him too much not to believe that my own worst fears were true."

Becky sighed. "And so they were."

"No, they weren't, Mrs. Freyl. You robbed him. I know you loved him. I do know that. I try to tell myself that you meant for the best. But how could you bring yourself to strip him of everybody but you who meant anything to him? You tried to take Rose away from him. You sent Helen away when he needed her most, and you talked me into deserting him just as he was beginning to come to life again. How could you do those things to your own son? How could you hurt him like that?"

Becky shook her head. "I have nothing to say to you."

"Do you know what he did before he died? The very last thing? his very last act as a living—?" Stephanie broke off because she had the abrupt sense she was watching the first crack appear in an ancient historic monument. "He tried to phone me. He was *happy,* and he tried to phone me." But she could not stop even here. "And what this means is that in the end he *knew* what you had done to him—to us."

Becky held on tight. She pursed her lips. "You were not worthy of him," she said.

32

USUALLY DAVID DROVE WITH ONLY ONE HAND ON THE
wheel. As he and Stephanie started down the drive away from the
Freyl house, he gripped that ring of plastic with both hands. If he
took one off, he'd be able to see it shake. That would scare him
more, and he was scared enough already. All it had taken was a five-
minute thought process while he waited for her.

He'd suddenly remembered a piece of science he'd run across on
the Web somewhere in a search for something else, a big project involving universities all over the world. He hadn't bothered with details for the simple reason that he knew he wouldn't understand
them, but the general outline was easy: the universe looks flat—just
like the Old World was supposed to be. The troubles start because it
might only look that way if we're inside a black hole. On the other
hand, we might *not* be in a black hole; we could be somewhere else
entirely. The joke is that we haven't any way of finding out where.

And the joke in the joke is that if we don't know where we are,
we can't make sense of anything we see.

Stephanie sat huddled and silent beside him, struggling to keep
control of the rush of emotions that the interview with Becky had
provoked in her just as he was struggling to keep control of his own
thoughts. Try it this way: with all the possible explanations ruled
out, a single, terrifying glance turns the impossible into the obvious.
And yet if the signposts are down, who can prove it? Proof or no
proof, who can stop what's got to come? How?

The Chevy crossed the stream through the Freyl property. Turn
left at the big gates, a couple of blocks along Williams Street, then
right onto the highway beyond. One of the camera crews had blown

a tire no more than two hundred yards away and crashed into a hydrant: water everywhere, horns honking, scream of police siren, long lines of stopped cars and angry drivers. David and Stephanie stared ahead, too wrapped up in their own intensities to be more than marginally aware of the commotion.

By the time the traffic jam eased and the Chevy picked up speed, she was calm enough to know she wouldn't burst into tears if she spoke. She sighed and turned to him. "So it was all for nothing?" David didn't even hear her. "David? Hey, wake up."

He glanced at her quickly, then shook his head, more to clear it than by way of response.

"How could all that truth turn out to be only a dead end?" she said.

"All what truth?"

"What do you think?" He shrugged. "Well, Calder's a dead end. I mean . . . isn't he? You do agree about that, don't you?"

"Yes."

She frowned, irritated at him for not seeming to care, irritated at herself for caring so much. "How come you're so calm about it? Doesn't it bother you? I hate it when what's right turns out to be wrong. A perfect theory, and we're right back at the beginning where we started." She took David's exhale of breath as reaffirmation of the alliance between them. "On the other hand, what the hell, I never thought I'd see a presidential candidate scared out of his wits, and that poor guy . . . My God, the relief on the man's face! No lie detector test could have been half as revealing. What do we do now? What have we got left to work with?"

"I'm taking you back to the motel. I want you to pack as fast as you can. I'll check you out."

She turned sideways to face him. "You're doing what?"

"You heard me."

"You're not serious." When he said nothing, she went on, "I'm not leaving until we have some kind of an answer."

"You're leaving as soon as I can get you to the airport."

Stephanie was outraged. "Oh, no, I'm not. You can't dump me just because Calder's bleedout business wasn't responsible for Hugh. I didn't give a damn about any of it until you forced me to. All I cared was that Hugh was dead and that everything meaningful in my life died with him. You forced me to care about who did that to him—and because of him, to *me*. It's too late to back out now. Now I have to know. I *have* to. I'm not going anywhere until I do."

David made another turn onto the next road; he kept his mouth shut and his eyes straight ahead. Left at the traffic lights. Then left again.

"What's the matter with you anyway?" Stephanie said then. "Are you mad at me or something? One minute you act as though we're working together. The next you've made some decision that excludes me entirely. That's not fair." She studied his resolute profile. "Wait a minute. I know. You think there's some kind of threat to me, don't you? That's it, isn't it? Oh, come on, David, that's nuts. Who would threaten me? Why? I haven't lived here in two years. I'm no part of anything that means anything to anybody." He concentrated on the road. Two blocks farther and they crossed the broad four-lane highway of Grover Cleveland Boulevard, no more than a mile from his new house. "Won't you at least do me the courtesy of telling me what this sudden about-face means? Don't you think you owe me some kind of explanation?"

David sighed irritably. "Samuel Clark thinks somebody killed Hugh to force *him* to the wall."

"He said that?" She thought a moment. "I suppose . . . You know, David, there just could be something to the idea. He and Hugh were the very closest of friends, and we didn't find anything to tie Samuel to the Calder mess. On the other hand, that's hardly grounds for thinking . . . But wait a minute, there was his daughter too, wasn't there? Samuel's daughter, I mean. A year or so ago? I read about it in the papers. I almost called Hugh at the time, but . . ." She sighed unhappily, then went on. "Samuel's only child gets killed by an unknown car in the street and then his best and oldest friend is beaten to death by an unknown person for unknown reasons." She paused again. "Kind of hard work, but I can see him forcing it into a pattern. I *know* how much he adored Vivian."

David said nothing.

"But that must mean that you think she could have been murdered too." Stephanie paused. "Well, do you? David? Talk to me, damn you."

"What difference does it make?"

"Quite a lot, I'd say. So some guy kills Samuel's daughter and fixes it up to look like a hit and run. Then this somebody decides to bash Hugh's head in just to . . . Well, however screwy it sounds, it certainly lets me out. I met Samuel several times, and we got along very well but nobody would ever think I was anything more to him than a close friend of Hugh's. Hardly anybody to be eliminated. Come on, David. You can't mean it."

"I won't be stopped in this."

They drove in silence, leaving the rich west side behind them, entering the barren areas of industry, motels, gas stations, malls that make so deep a fringe all around the town. She stared out at the desolate landscape. "It just could be that there's no flight out today, you know," she said.

"You'll be safe at the airport."

"I'll be safer with you."

"Nobody's safe with me."

She swung her whole body around to face him this time. "You think they're after *you*, don't you? That's what it is. Not Samuel. You! You've suddenly decided somebody's trying to take whatever *you* love away from you. Okay, that settles it as far as I'm concerned. You didn't even meet me until after Hugh died. I couldn't possibly be a part of some weird plan or other. So there's no need for all this airport stuff. Besides, David, listen to me, Samuel's nuts. People don't *do* things like that. Even if they did, the only person we can add into the pot is Vivian. She's the only one whose death could possibly be related, and you hardly knew her."

How could he tell Stephanie about Vivian? that he knew she had been coming to his east-side apartment on the night she died? that they'd more than half planned to live together, have children, lead the normal life he'd dreamed of when he was little? that she was pregnant by him already? And even if he could tell Stephanie those things, he could hardly tell her that despite himself, he'd welcomed Vivian's death as a release, that a part of him hated and feared her almost as much as he'd come to hate prison walls because of her—almost as much as he'd come to fear himself in the past half hour.

Because for the very first time it had become clear to him that the person who probably killed them both was David Marion.

◄◦►

Sure, the cops had had him at the top of their list of suspects from the beginning, but that was only to be expected, only one more trap to work his way out of. His own list was an entirely different matter. That's the thing about insanity. You can't see it coming from the inside. The landscape looks calm, controls in place, order enforced, directions clear. That's how it looks, and that's how it feels. Then there's a small flurry of breeze—just a stirring of dust at the feet—and the blast hits before there's a chance to run for cover: hurricane on the Mississippi coast, tornado in Pensacola. Afterward there's nothing but wreckage. Trance states, fugue states, blackouts—those blank areas in David's memory—are all well documented in medical texts: acts committed in a state of extreme emotional arousal. The deaths of the Fowlers, the actual killings: he remembered nothing between the splattering of the oil pan when they knocked it out of his hands and the sight of the bodies in the mess of blood and black engine oil: an oddly gentle embrace, father and son entwined, arms around each other, faces so badly battered it was impossible to tell which was which.

It's why he'd felt he belonged in prison, had no right to appeal, needed bars to restrain him. He had a point too. In prison, things functioned according to law. The laws may have been harsh and erratic, but they started here, inside the man, and they ended at the thirty-foot walls that enclosed a fully functioning society with a pecking order as rigid as a caste system, a society where everything that went on fitted in, even murder. His kills in prison were, given the setting, just and lawful. They were planned, professional, experienced to the full, not at all like the Fowler murders which took place in this world outside and got sucked down somehow into a wild confusion of images, sounds, sensations. Even the outermost edges of this place shimmered with uncertainty. He'd had a hard enough time keeping his balance out here before he went to South Hams; during the prison years, he'd lost whatever savvy he'd had as a boy. There was no proof that he *hadn't* killed Vivian and Hugh. None at all. He didn't even know how long the islands of amnesia lasted. Seconds? Hours? If he'd killed those two people himself,

Stephanie was in danger because she was all he had left of Hugh and he might well do the same to her. If he hadn't killed them, she was in danger because she was close to him—and that just could turn out to be even harder to bear.

He kept his eyes on the road. "Somebody's been following me for the past week," he said.

"Like the other night? That was a joke." But his gaze didn't alter. "No, it wasn't," she said then. "Good God, you mean that too." She shook her head. "David, David. Have you entirely lost your grip on reality? You don't get enough sleep. I mean it. You really don't. That's just plain crazy. You're imagining things."

He glanced at her, and for the first time in her experience of him she caught a full view of that explosive anger just beneath the surface of his skin. "Okay, okay," she said quickly. "So somebody's following you. *Why?* What's the point? If they want to kill you, why don't they just go ahead and do it? Same for me. They could have got me any time in the last two weeks. It would have been easy. Why didn't they?"

"Just do as I tell you."

When they arrived at her motel, she got out and slammed the car door behind her. He got out too, followed her to her room, pushed his way in. "The suitcase, Stephanie," he said, taking it off the luggage rack and throwing it on the bed. "I'll give you fifteen minutes. If you're not packed and out in front of the motel by then, I'll come back and pack for you."

He went to the motel office, checked her out, then went to the car and phoned the Monaghans. He told them to lock the doors, put the chains across and stay inside, not to open up for anybody—not even him. Especially not him, no matter what he said.

"We can't stay locked up here forever," Mr. Monaghan said.

"I'll call when it's okay."

"Why can't we let *you* in? What's going on, David? Are you in trouble?"

"You still have a gun in the house?"

"Is somebody going to hold you hostage or something? Come on, tell me. We can help."

"What about the gun?"

"I got it."

"Make sure it's loaded."

"This doesn't make any damn sense at all. Can't you at least tell me—"

"Just do it."

"I don't see why the hell we can't let *you* in. I really can't see—"

"Promise me you won't let *anybody* in until I call you."

"Okay, okay."

"The gun. *Chains* across the doors, front *and* back. Right?"

"Whatever you say."

David clicked off and stared out at the heavy traffic: people on one side of the highway hurrying to get to some place that the others were hurrying just as fast to get away from: a meaningless, aimless, hopeless dash to escape what cannot be escaped. He punched Tony's number into the cell phone.

"Remember that jewelry store?" he said. Tony had picked up the phone on its first ring.

"How can I forget it?"

"You were right. There's no reason not to do it. They're pressing hard. Two calls in the last couple of days. Why don't you try this one by yourself?"

There was a pause, and David could sense him calculating. "How come they're calling you instead of me?"

"You want to go or don't you?"

"Where the fuck are you anyhow?"

"I got things to do."

"Stephanie, huh? What are you? Irresistible or something? Don't you never get tired of fucking?"

"They want you there tomorrow. There's a flight to Bloomington this afternoon at four."

There was another pause. "I don't know. I guess so. What's the rush?"

"They say they'll call in somebody else."

"That never bothered you before."

"It bothers me now," David said irritably. "Isn't that enough?"

Here's how to stay in control in solitary, in the hole, in the punishment blocks. Never think big. Never think about what it *means*. Hold resentments, guilts, bitternesses, betrayals, dreams of freedom in check even if you have to cut into your own flesh to do it. Concentrate only on the parts that turn something—*anything*—into a puzzle that must be solved, a jigsaw, maybe. Lay out pieces on the blank table of the mind. Puzzles like this always look advanced to start with. There are so many pieces and so many of them could have wandered in from other puzzles that have no connection whatever to the problem.

If David was insane, he had to find some way to prove to himself that he'd done these things. If he was sane, there were three possible alternatives. One: the driver of the Honda, but he could all too easily be no more than some other hobgoblin of David's disordered imagination. Two and three existed simply because David knew—he *knew*—that one way or another he had created this chaos. And yet this also sounded like a mind that had already disappeared down a sinkhole. But he was the one from whom Hugh had learned so hard a lesson about trust and Jimmy: watch your back most carefully when somebody you trust steps behind you. Sometimes when you give a truth away, you lose your own hold on it.

That brought Tony and the Monaghans into the picture. What kind of person sees people like that as possibilities two and three? his only lifelong friend and the closest to family he'd ever be likely to come? But there was no escaping the logic—not that all of them hadn't hovered at the paranoid edges before along with the Honda and the battered Ford that had preceded it.

No matter what the reality, Tony and the Monaghans had to be isolated from each other and from him. Just like Stephanie.

◄o►

As David drove Stephanie away from the motel, a heavy, icy-cold rain began to fall. His face still bore the threat of anger that she assumed she'd put there.

"I'm sorry if I said the wrong thing earlier, David," she said after a few minutes. "I wouldn't hurt you for the world. You must know that. I *know* you'll find whoever did this to Hugh for whatever reason and at whatever cost." His jaw clenched again beneath his cheeks. "I also want you to know that I'm touched by your concern for me." She laughed gently. "I used to resent it when people seemed to be taking care of me, but the older I get the more I realize what a miracle it is. Mostly people don't give a damn what happens to anybody except to themselves. So . . ." She shrugged, smiled. "Thank you." They drove in silence for a few miles. "So you knew Vivian better than I thought?"

The abrupt confusion on his face entirely drowned out the anger. "I loved her," he said.

"Oh, David, I'm so sorry. I didn't know. I never guessed. Oh, dear, you're so secretive. I always thought of you as . . . I'm not sure, invincible in such areas." She touched his cheek with the tips of her fingers then. "I'm so terribly sorry. Vivian was a wonderful person, and I can certainly see why you felt the way you did. And, damn it, she was a lucky woman to have got so close to you as that. I'm sure she realized it too. Do you know, from the very first sight of you across this airfield—" She broke off and scanned his face. "All those months of studying photographs of you, right side, left side, full face . . . You see, even I had trouble not thinking of you in terms that hardly become . . . Hugh was the only man I ever loved, and, my God, I loved him. There wasn't anybody else in my life before. There never will be again. And yet . . ." She shook her head. "I tried to tell him, you know. I talked and talked, but there are times when it's no good just talking. There are things a person has to see for himself."

David felt a rippling across the musculature beneath his skin. That's how a whiff of danger comes across sometimes: dragonfly over the surface of a lake. "What are you saying?"

"It was the big question of his life, or became that anyhow. He'd never have talked much to you about it, of course. He was amazingly gentle for a corporate lawyer. I guess he was amazingly gentle for any man at all. He always tiptoed around the people he liked."

"You're going to have to be clearer than that."

Stephanie turned a puzzled smile on him. "You've thrown my radar completely off track today. Are you really asking that?" David nodded. "It never occurred to me that you wouldn't know what he . . . Look, I'm beginning to think I shouldn't have brought this up. It's not any of my business."

"Say it."

"Oh, Lord, I'm always blurting out what I shouldn't. Maybe he wouldn't have wanted me to say any more." But she scanned

David's face and sighed her resignation. "It's just one of those things blind guys like him face. The answer is right in front of them but no matter how hard you try to describe it . . . If you've never seen the ocean, no amount of talking is going to make you feel the impact of the real thing. He never *saw* you, kid, did he? How *could* he know? He never saw Ellie either. There are—"

"Ellie?" This time the tension in David was abrupt. "Ellie Fowler?"

"I really wanted to lend him my eyes that afternoon. Just for a second. All he'd have needed was one look at her and at that picture—"

"You *saw* her? She's *alive*?"

"Why shouldn't she be?" Stephanie laughed. "I know. I know. When you're only fifteen, somebody who's thirty-three seems as old as God—already dead and buried."

◄o►

They drove into the airport in silence. Rain poured down in icy sheets. When they swung across the entrance, she said, "You can let me out here."

"I'd feel better if I saw you into the building."

"You'll only get wet. Just give me the keys to the trunk. I'll phone you as soon as I get home."

She took the keys from him, reached for the door on the passenger side, then turned back. "Thanks anyway."

It wasn't until she got out and began battling her way through the rain to the trunk that he caught sight of the tattered Ford heading toward her, driver's face hidden by the sloshing windshield wipers and the darkened sky. It was the very same car he'd thought was following him days before—this time there was no doubt in his mind, none whatever—and it yanked his attention back to the danger of the long-distant past of a few minutes ago, before her revelations. How long had the Ford been waiting there for them, engine running? How could he have been so wrapped up in himself that he failed to see it altogether?

A heavy thud, impact of metal against flesh, came at the very minute he yanked open the Chevy's door. Maybe airports are usu-

ally pretty well guarded these days—and least in general—even little airports, but weather like this drives everybody inside. David
was the only witness, and he'd known what was happening even
before it happened. It's the most elementary of physics. An impact
like that—car against woman—hits below the center of gravity. Her
body catapults up in the air, leaving only her shoes behind on the
macadam filling up with rain. The Ford careened away from him,
yawing from side to side of the road, aiming for North Walnut Road
into Springfield. By the time David reached Stephanie, she was a
broken heap on the ground. He took off his heavy coat, laid it over
her, took out his cell phone, dialed 911.

"We need an ambulance. There's a hit-and-run at the entrance
to the passenger entrance—"

"Your name, sir?"

"—at Capital Airport. Serious injury, possible fatality."

He clicked off the phone before the operator had a chance to interrupt him again and ran into the airport.

"Accident," he shouted at a couple of guards who were mid-
laughter with paper cups of coffee in their hands. They followed
him outside and stood there, mouths open, staring down at the
blood that mingled into pools of water—surfaces spattering with
heavy rain drops of sleet—around the disorderly mess that had been
a healthy person only seconds before.

It is because of Stephanie that I began spending my evenings at the office. I feel closer to her here. At first I just sat in the room near mine
where she used to sit. But it was not enough. Of course it wasn't—not
anywhere near enough. I searched for her; almost as soon as she found a
place to live I knew about it. She had gone to the West Coast, where she
had family.

I spent whole evenings—more evenings than I dare admit—drafting
letters to her that I knew I would never send and rehearsing telephone
conversations with her that I knew I would never conduct. What right did
I have to track her down? much less start pestering her? What right did I
have to pry into her life? her new life? She had made her wishes painfully
clear, and I could not bear to hear them spoken out loud.

But at the very least I could spend my evenings in the rooms where she had spent so much time herself.

◄◦►

"I called an ambulance," David said to one of the guards. "You'd better call again and make sure they understood the message."

"I'm sorry, sir, but you can't leave before . . . " the guard began, but David was already near enough to the Chevy to be opening its door. "Hey, come back!" the guard called, starting after him. But a gust of wind whipped the voluminous police coat across the guard's legs, webbing them together. He stumbled and fell to his knees. By the time he'd got to his feet again, David was driving off. In the heavy sleet, not even the license plate was visible—much less the numbers on it.

"You a friend or something?"

"We go back a long way."

"How come?"

"She's my foster mother."

"She's never said anything about relatives." The woman looked him up and down, a stranger in the rain, no umbrella, no hood, water running down his face. "Foster mother, huh?"

"That's right."

"Where you been all this time?" David made a gesture that indicated he knew he hadn't been doing his duty as he should. "Yeah, well," she said, weakening a little, "families do tend to get kind of put off. Know what I mean? Most of them fall away in the first couple of weeks. Sometimes I can't even get them to the door to wave."

"I can imagine."

"You're awful wet."

"Yes."

"Now that's real nice, a young guy like you. It isn't as though you can do much but sit with her, you know."

"I know."

"Well . . ." She hesitated. There's nothing like an educated voice to break down barriers, especially when it has an English tinge to it as David's did; in the Midwest, anything English is as harmless and quaint as *London Bridge is falling down,* so she took the plunge. "You got to promise to leave when I say so."

"I promise."

She opened the door, let him in, took his coat and his scarf, clucking as she shook them out and hung them on a shiny brass hook beside the door. There was textured paper on the walls in the hallway and thick flowered carpet on the floor. Not at all like the house of twenty years ago. Not like the house Stephanie had described either.

"Ellie's still talking some," the nurse said. He followed her, brushing at the rain on his face with the back of his hand. "That's real good 'cause she's pretty far advanced. Multiple sclerosis is hell on wheels. Know anything about it? She's had it for years already. Nobody can figure out how come she's managed to last this long. Kinda like she's hanging on for some special thing. They do that, you know. Hang on for Christmas and birthdays and . . ."

David decided she was a private nurse, an extraordinary expense for an inhabitant of this part of Springfield; she was wearing one of those wildly flowered tops that are supposed to cheer up patients and have come to scream *hospital* while hinting, despite themselves, at not-very-hygienic hospital. A little decal on her shoulder read "RN." She led him past the living room where Hugh and Stephanie had sat. This room too was newly decorated: wallpaper, carpet, pink plush furniture, lamps with frilly lampshades and a picture in a gilt frame: two huge-eyed, doll-like children painted on a swatch of navy blue velvet. The open door to the kitchen showed off shiny appliances and a fresh coat of paint. None of this bore any relationship to the house burned into his memory: dank, dark walls, Ellie tearing at his clothes, he tearing at hers, a half run, half stumble that often failed to make it as far as the bleak master bedroom at the back of the house, that often didn't even try—a wall, the floor, a table, anything solid enough to serve the purpose.

". . . got to keep a sharp eye on her muscle tone, though," the nurse was saying. She checked her watch and turned her head to smile at David. "Imagine Ellie having a foster son that's done so well for himself."

The nurse opened the door to the back bedroom. It too was newly wallpapered and carpeted. The dirty, tousled bed from the long-ago days was nowhere to be seen. A huge, impressive electric bed had replaced it, high on shiny metal legs: gears, cogs, axles beneath it. A bank of buttons operated the thing. Side rails tucked neatly away for use when needed.

"Ellie, you got yourself a real handsome visitor," the nurse said, pulling up a chair for David to sit on.

Stephanie had said that Ellie was still beautiful. Even so, David had expected to find a broken relic. He'd figured the flattery was just one of those indulgences of mind that people comfort themselves with as they get older, seeing beauty or strength or intellectual prowess when it's no longer there, when it no longer *could* be there. He'd heard too much of that kind of thing and seen too much of the reality behind it. A prison, after all, is a community very like a small town, where long-term inhabitants watch the relentless progress of the young turning into the wizened old and the powerful sinking into tremors and dotage.

But the figure on the bed, despite time and disease, seemed largely untouched. Maybe not so strongly aglow. Maybe not so lush. But this was the Ellie of twenty years ago—and every bit as beautiful. In a way, she was even more so; illness seemed to have cast an ethereal fragility over the coarser edges.

"You kept . . . me waiting . . . too long," she said.

"Says he's your foster kid. That right?"

Ellie flicked her eyes at the nurse—a wordless dismissal as clear as a military command.

David shut the door behind her, but he couldn't bring himself to sit down. "So you've been waiting," he said.

"Fucking . . . right."

"I'm easy to find. Why don't you tell me what you have been waiting *for*."

She struggled for breath. "This . . . fucking . . ." She gasped, swallowed.

Multiple sclerosis is one of those incurable wasting diseases, a relentless progress that destroys the nervous system and can reduce its victims to helpless, dribbling hulks of insensate flesh. It's yet another bleedout of the frail human entity (there are so many). But David knew she was not referring to the disease, not in itself anyway.

"You've robbed everybody who ever got near enough to you," he said. "What is it this time?"

"You're out."

"Yes."

". . . second chance." But what he heard in her voice was hate, not hope.

"A second chance for what?"

"For *me*!"

"You going to tell me where the money comes from?" he asked.

Ellie shut her eyes: a silent affirmative.

"So?"

She paused to savor the moment. The response gave her a depth of pleasure she hadn't felt in years. "You," she said.

34

THAT'S WHEN HE KNEW—WHEN HE WAS SURE WHAT ALL
this was about—and there was a fleeting elation. How could he help
it? He was in the clear. The moment Stephanie was hit, he'd known
he wasn't completely crazy. He couldn't possibly have run her down,
so the probability became high that he hadn't killed Vivian either. If
he hadn't killed Vivian, very likely he hadn't killed Hugh. And
Ellie's triumph turned the probabilities to virtual certainties: he
hadn't killed anybody since he got out. Nobody. Not one single person. The relief of it boiled up in him—fizz in a shaken soda bottle.

The Chevy's tires threw sheets of water up into the air as he
tore out of Plymouth Road heading toward the Monaghans. With
one hand controlling the wheel, he keyed in their telephone number. He let it ring ten times. No answer. They had no answering machine. Mrs. Monaghan hated them. He tried again. Again no
answer. They'd probably gone out. He hadn't told them not to go
out. Yes, he had. Please God, don't let them have answered the door
to some plea of Tony's.

The moment John Calder had said he couldn't possibly kill
Hugh, David had thought of Tony. It wasn't the first time either.
The idea had been lurking at the back of his mind ever since the
trip to Washington and Samuel Clark. "Take away what a man loves
and you take away whatever it is that makes him the person he is,"
Samuel had said. "You take away his will to live." And David's first
thought had been Tony. He'd dismissed it at once: a madman's hallucination, the kind of thing that occurs only to a screwball who
might start thinking the Monaghans were plotting against him or
black Hondas were following him. Or that battered Ford with its

broken taillight. "You're getting jumpy," Tony had said of the battered Ford, and he'd gone to the trouble of taking down the name of the rental agency and seeking out the very same car so he could run down Stephanie with it.

As David passed Oak Ridge, going south, the memory of Vivian as he'd seen her first caught him unawares: on the other side of that glass barrier at South Hams prison, a slender, opulent force of life that had been an agony to him because he could only look. Now he yearned for a privilege nowhere near as great as seeing her, just of knowing she was alive somewhere, anywhere.

How could *Tony* have done such a thing to him?

Think puzzle. Only puzzle. An English printer by the name of John Spillsbury invented jigsaws in 1762 to teach geography to children. Practically every border has changed since then but solving techniques remain the same. Sort the pieces into piles according to color, say, or maybe some peculiarity of shape. Some of them will fit together almost at once, just a fluke of the way they've been tossed into the pile.

Ellie Fowler was Tony's beloved Mrs. Hunter.

The thought had seemed as insane as the rest of it the moment it occurred to David—which had been the moment Stephanie said the woman was still around—but now it was obvious. Money for Mrs. Hunter was money for Ellie. The sickness wasn't Alzheimer's but multiple sclerosis. The pleasure she'd got from telling David that he was the source of her luxuries—wallpaper, carpet, occasional nursing care, all bought with Tony's share of the profits—meant only that she had been a part of it for a long time.

David punched the Monaghans number into his cell phone again. Again no answer. A cell phone can develop flaws in the memory card. He punched in the numbers yet again, slowly, carefully. They wouldn't have gone out. Of course they wouldn't. They weren't that stupid. They'd heard the urgency in his voice. Maybe one of them was in the bathroom. Maybe the other couldn't hear the ring over the TV. The TV was always on. He cut through side streets, the speedometer hitting sixty as he tore around tight corners. Only a mile or so to go.

The straight-edged pieces of the jigsaw make the frame; they're the structure that holds it all together: a bleedout, just as Samuel had said. Vivian had been the profound passion of David's life. Hugh was teacher, mentor, liberator. Stephanie had helped him get David out of prison, and Tony figured she'd become Vivian's replacement. David had known that, and the misapprehension had seemed so unlikely that he hadn't bothered to correct it. Take away these people, and the meat loses its savor.

But why? What possible reason was there?

And yet Tony's hand was so clear: Tony the practical joker. He'd killed Vivian almost on David's doorstep; there's nothing so funny as pleasure snatched away right at the point of consummation, the spoonful of ice cream slapped out of the hand just as it goes into the mouth. He'd bludgeoned Hugh to death much as David had bludgeoned Ellie's husband and her son: a thumbing of the nose that meant the mysterious weapon the police failed to identify could only have been the lug wrench that David had feared it was all along, fearing that he himself had killed Hugh with it. The battered Ford to run down Stephanie was funniest of all: David's paranoia just rising up out of the road in front of the airport building and snatching her away from him.

Only the Monaghans were left.

They'd always been reclusive; theirs was the only house on Cooper Street with any hedge at all, much less the six-foot privet barrier that Mr. Monaghan had trimmed so carefully for so many years. The icy rain had turned to full-blown sleet by the time David arrived. He forced himself to think each move, to park around the corner, open the gate with gloved hands—hardly an oddity in weather like this—and yet he ran down the steps despite his own pleas for calm. He rang the bell, terrified by the empty sound that echoed through the house and even more terrified by the silence that followed it. He rang again. Again there was only silence. He got out the key the Monaghans had given him on his first visit to them as a free man, and fumbled it into the front door. But there was no need for it; a gentle push, and the door opened. They *hadn't* put the chain on. He cursed himself feverishly for not insisting harder. But Tony could have talked his way through it even if they had. He'd have convinced them that David had sent him, that everything was all right now.

Blood has a semisweet, living smell, and yet the blood of a stranger—or of an enemy—is only the blood of an animal. The blood of someone close is a different composition altogether; seeing it makes the brain spin. A pool of it had collected on the wooden floor of the small foyer. Some part of David's mind had known this was what would greet him when the Monaghans didn't answer that first cell phone call. Even so, there was an electrifying moment when he thought he might faint for the first time in his life. He held still. He breathed slow. One or the other of them must have tried to escape; an old man or an old woman trying to get out of the way of the onslaught—and failing miserably. A wide smear that marked the failure ran across the mirror facing the front door. David took off his shoes and picked his way toward the living room, careful not to step in the coagulating patches, pools, drops, smears, careful to leave no trace of himself. What he had to do was clear to him, and anything that compromised the crime scene with a second intruder was no part of it.

The living room that had once been a calm, ordered place—photographs of the Monaghan children and grandchildren (David too) on the mantelpiece, pictures of Springfield scenes and portraits of Springfield notables, comfortable easy chairs grouped around the fireplace with antimacassars tatted by Mrs. Monaghan's grandmother—was now a garbage-heap confusion of broken glass, upset and broken furniture with blood everywhere. An arterial swath arced across the fireplace wall. David edged his way into the dining room. Devastation here too. In the kitchen, the big red table—the very same table where he'd eaten his first dinner with the Monaghans as a small boy—had huge gashes in it. Tony had turned it into a butcher's block.

But no bodies.

A trail of blood ran to the kitchen door that led into the backyard where David had played ball with Mr. Monaghan after that first dinner and after so many others that followed it. Sometime while David was in prison, Mr. Monaghan had installed a fishpond in the middle of the lawn that had once served as ballpark. He'd dug the pit himself, poured the cement, plumbed in an elaborate drainage system so that a change of water was no more than an hour's job. In summer, lily pads floated on the surface; dragonflies hovered. The lawn that Mr. Monaghan had trimmed so neatly at the end of last summer went to the edge of the pool on the front and the sides.

David had hated that pond the moment he laid eyes on it. Even in summer its size and proportions brought to mind the oil pit out at the Fowler garage. In winter, drained and raw—sleet gathered like snow in the branches of the short hedge at the far side—it was a carbon copy. He must have said so to Tony once, some now-forgotten moment of weakness. He *must* have. Because in the empty concrete pit itself lay the two bodies, one on top of the other in the gentle embrace that had haunted David's nightmares, that mimicked the way the Fowlers lay together after he'd killed them.

David had seen a lot of death, and a lot of it had been messy. The professional's eyes registered the impact wounds that had reamed open flesh, broken bones, crushed skulls. The professional's eyes also took in the two little boxes carefully wrapped in plastic to protect them from the weather—two Rolex boxes—and the dead wrists that did not wear the watches he'd given them only days before with such an agony of embarrassment. But it was the beige and tan silk shawl that tore at the man. There was so much blood—and so much sleet-diluted blood—that only a close friend or a relative could have guessed that Tony had wrapped Mrs. Monaghan in her favorite shawl, the one David had given her. Maybe he'd never mastered giving presents just for the sake of it, but Hugh and the Monaghans together had taught him the elements of the ritual gift exchange at Christmas. This scarf—the first Christmas gift David had bought as a free man—was the first real silk she'd ever owned, and he'd glowed with the pleasure he'd seen on her face when she opened the package.

When the police had arrived at the Fowler garage all those years ago they'd found fifteen-year-old David on his knees, his head bowed as though awaiting execution by the sword.

"What's all this?" the cop had said.

"They're dead," David had said.

"Jesus, I can see that, kid."

Imagine so fragile a thing as a shawl felling a grown man to his knees just as a sledgehammer of guilt had felled the boy so long ago.

◄○►

A narrow alleyway ran along the rear of the Monaghans' property, guarded by a wooden fence. David had found a secret route through when he was little, and it had amused him, returning here after so many years in prison, to find his secret exit unaltered. Lift the crossbar and the palings behind just eased off to one side, a perfect way for a kid to slip out at night and do a little pilfering.

He was certain that Tony had been as hygienic this time as he had been with Hugh. That's why it had been important not to upset the pattern of bloody footprints in the house: it would be David's job to supply something a little more substantial for the police to work with. A few strands of Tony's hair would serve, perhaps a small clump as though one of the Monaghans had managed to pull it out in the course of the attack, perhaps scrapings of skin to go beneath dead fingernails. After all, Tony's practical joke with the beehives had ended up getting his DNA into the police files.

David kept to the path in the yard. The unrelenting sleet would wipe out any other traces of his visit. When he returned, he'd be better prepared.

35

THE ULTIMATE GOAL AND THE GREATEST PLEASURE OF
the practical joker is catching the full force of the hapless victim's
reaction. That's why Cockran's was a likely place for Tony to go—
more than likely. Confront David where they'd spent so many hours
as friends, wait for him over a bourbon as though what had happened was all in a day's work, watch David the madman reeling
with grief, fury, the devastation of a life. How could Tony resist it?

David slammed on the brakes in front of the bar. The room was
largely empty. Jason, the bartender, stood behind the bar polishing
glasses.

"Tony here?" David said to him.

Jason turned in that slow, dreamlike way of his. "Nope."

"He been here today?"

"Nope."

"You wouldn't lie to me, would you, Jason?"

"Kind a steamed up, ain't you? Something the matter?"

"Just tell me if he was here."

"What do you want to be talking to him all the time for anyhow? He's a piece of nothing. Zilch. Zero. I been meaning to say
that to you ever since I first—"

"Just give me the answer."

"No, he hasn't been here. But if you ask me—"

"I didn't."

"—he wouldn't be nowhere without you. He's nothing but a
two-bit lowlife, and if this was my joint I'd a kicked . . ."

David was on the street outside before Jason could finish, and
that's when he realized that the next move would have to be Tony's,

not his. There was nobody left that David cared about, nobody left to kill but David himself. He drove slowly back toward his house just off Grover Cleveland Boulevard.

◄◌►

It had taken David years to learn to claw his mind back *before* it spiraled out of sight, to throw up walls around it, force it into submission. That last seven months of his prison sentence in the hole without a single ray of light was by far the longest and hardest of too many stretches in solitary. All that time, he'd worked on the puzzles. When he'd put one together, every piece in place, he took it apart. Then he rebuilt it. After the first few weeks, pressure on the eyes caused bursts of light inside his head, red and blue Catherine wheels like some New Year's Eve celebration. He'd dismantled the Catherine wheels, worked out their trajectories, the amount of explosive needed, the angles—and then rebuilt them.

A fowler is a hunter who catches only birds for sport while a hunter traps all wild animals. Word games were hardly Tony's forte—or Ellie Fowler's, for that matter—and the name Mrs. Hunter must have begun as a lover's joke between them. They knew David was being educated behind bars, and they must have spent whole days seeking out this leaden play on words for him. Tony had mentioned it right back in the early days of David's sentence. Which meant some aspects of the plan had to have been in the works for a very long time. How close they skirted to the wind. They must have figured he could tumble to the truth at almost any moment—and what a kick they must have got out of that. It wasn't just the name either. David had killed Ellie's husband and son, and Tony's letters had mentioned that Mrs. Hunter's husband and the child were dead in sad circumstances. There must have been other hints too, details that David simply passed over in the way of all convicts; there's not a one of them who won't excuse almost anything to keep the goodwill of a contact on the outside.

He telephoned the hospital as soon as he got back to his house. News of Stephanie was not reassuring, but at least there *was* news. He paced the floor, back and forth, back and forth, telephoning every half hour as afternoon worked its way into evening; there was no change. In exasperation, the nurses told him to wait until morning; he slammed the receiver down. With the last rays of daylight he forced himself to begin clearing the round table of the files they'd put together while they'd worked out the details of John Calder's financial bleedout. He packed a box partway, stared at it emptily, lifted a couple of pages out of it, threw them back, slumped in a chair, head in his hands, then got up and started again. He packed a second box and stored them both on the top shelf of the mirrored closet in the hallway. If there'd been a little more of the afternoon left, he might have been able to make himself open the crates and begin to hang the Escher prints, but there wasn't. By seven o'clock it was already too dark, and he was sitting at the round table, staring out into the patio, watching the last of the daylight fade, mind scrambling to stick together more of the puzzle before whatever happened that had to happen.

Tony and Ellie's minor practical jokes at his expense must have begun as a matador's banderillas stuck into the bull's flesh through the bars. When the bull got out, the possibilities picked up wondrously. David's apartment was his and Tony's office, and Vivian spent many hours there, sometimes whole nights. Evidence of her slowly gathered in the medicine cabinet, on the bedside table, among David's reading material, even what he ate and drank. There'd been a small bunch of straggled flowers that she'd picked on the way to see him one afternoon. Tony hadn't liked that. At the time, David paid no attention, but she'd been the one who'd bought the Escher designs that decorated the walls. "They're so like you," she'd said. "They try to control what can't be controlled." Tony had known they were hers the moment he laid eyes on them, and he'd never bothered to hide his disgust with them. He made no bones about hating the idea of the move to the west side either, and he'd been all too clearly irritated when the influential Hugh Freyl didn't drop by the wayside as predicted.

Sometime around midnight David heard cautious footsteps on the patio outside where in another few months there would be daffodils blooming. He got up slowly. The night was as black as the hole at South Hams prison—moonless, starless—and David was as blind as Hugh had been. He had to imagine Tony hunching outside the glass door and setting to work on the lock. David listened—and

was impressed despite himself. Tony had always managed to appear
so clumsy at locks; he'd been a crude user of tools—or so he'd
seemed to be—an impatient batterer who saw mechanical things as
stubborn mules to be whipped into compliance. So he'd fooled
David in this too. Clearly he'd been learning even while he dispar-
aged it because what was going on here was expertise. Nobody
would claim that the level was all that high—even good door locks
like this one hardly called for an artist—but he wasn't forcing; he
was feeling for the pins as they sprang back into place. The job was
quick, efficient.

The patio door slid open.

Just as you can tell the quality of a lock picker from the sounds
of the work, you can tell professional training from the first move a
person makes: fighter, dancer, skater, murderer. Tony was not professionally trained in any such field, not even murder. Maybe he
overcame an indifference to technique with an unexpectedly imaginative element of surprise, but he had only brute force to back it up
with. The moment David's first blow landed—a chop to the back of
the neck—he knew the man wasn't Tony. The force threw this person to the floor and yet the reaction—instinctive buckle and roll
away from the onslaught—was something Tony would never have
bothered to master.

David backed off, head buzzing with the intensity of it. He
flipped on the light.

The man on the floor was massaging the back of his neck.
David recognized him at once: the driver of the Honda. "Jesus," the
driver said, "you could have killed me."

"Get out," David said.

The driver struggled partway to his feet, then fell back. "Give
me a minute."

David jerked him to his feet. "Your minute is up."

The driver leaned heavily against the wall. "I figured you might
be hurt in here." There was the hint of a self-righteous whine in his
voice. "Or worse than that. And then there'd be hell to pay."

"What's that supposed to mean?"

The driver made a self-deprecatory gesture. "Can I sit down? I
don't think I can stand up all that much . . ." He eased himself into
a chair, dropped his head into his hands and tried to force his lungs

to work properly again. "Deputy marshals don't get paid any better than cops. Did you know that?"

"Samuel Clark," David said, the source of all this careful following clear to him at once; the U.S. Marshals Service protects federal judges. "What do you think you're doing? Keeping me safe?"

The driver nodded, then shrugged. "I know you spotted us. I told him. We *all* told him. He said he didn't care, he said our job was to be there just in case—"

"How many of you are there?"

"Four."

"*Four?*"

"At two hundred bucks an hour. *Each.* Can you imagine money like that? I can't turn that down. None of us can. Nobody ever offered me that much for anything. Nobody ever will again. I'm awful sorry about the woman at the airport and that old couple, though. I can see that really upset you." He massaged his neck again, twisted it back and forth under his hand. "I don't know how the hell you kept hold of your lunch, seeing them two done up like that. If it hadn't a been for a couple of years on homicide, I just might a upset the whole—"

"You leave any traces?"

"Hell no."

David flipped off the light and sat down at the table opposite the driver. "What were you *doing* there?"

"Look, if I tell you it's gonna sound kind of weird—"

"Just say it."

"I don't really know as I ought—"

"*Say* it."

The driver sighed. "The justice figures you can take care of yourself okay, but if anybody picks you up or anything, you *got* to have witnesses. I mean, it's a real good idea, and Marshal witnesses are the best kind of witnesses. Juries always believe them. They see a five-pointed star, think of Wyatt Earp and go weak at the knees. See what I mean?"

"Go on."

"We got play-by-play notes of you every hour. I know when you eat, when you piss, when you sleep, when you run. I know every move you make. It's all down in the book. Ain't nobody can deny that kind of testimony. What else do you expect the justice to do? Hire a couple of Supreme Court cops? Nobody believes cops. Why should they? They could swear themselves blind on a heap of Bibles, but they're a bunch of lying assholes, and everybody knows it. Private cops are even worse. Look, Mr. Marion, I don't know what this is all about, but somebody's sure as hell mad at you."

"How long have you been after me?"

"Since you left Washington."

David studied the driver. "Suppose I *had* killed them."

"You didn't."

"I might have."

"Aw, come on, there ain't no point—"

"*Suppose* I'd killed them."

"What the fuck, we'd a seen you being somewhere else. We'd a written it all down in the little book. Mr. Marion was on the other side of town eating a sandwich and reading the newspaper. You got to know that."

"Those your instructions?"

"Along with a little housekeeping."

"Swear I wasn't there and clean up any mess I make. That it?"

"Something like that."

"For two hundred an hour?"

"For two hundred an hour, I'd swear myself black and blue that you'd died and gone to heaven and come back down just like Jesus Christ. I only hope I get a chance to do it again sometime. I got me a mortgage and a couple of kids. I got loan sharks all over me. Don't screw me up with the justice, huh?"

David got up from the chair he sat in. "You might have to do a little work for your money."

"Yeah?"

"I want you out of my way until I call for you. Understand me? I catch you near me again when I don't want you, and you won't walk away. What's your cell phone number?"

36

THIS IS TRUE IRONY, THIS . . . RIDICULOUS DEATH COM-
ing at just this time.

You see, as I left this evening, I happened to mention Stephanie to
my mother—something about her ability to see through the unimportant
things to the core of the matter—and my mother said, apropos of nothing, "She had no breeding." I have heard my mother say that about a
number of people, but there was something in her voice this time, some
unexpected, unfamiliar tone. A hint of triumph? Why use the past tense?
Why emphasize the "she"?

And all at once I knew what had happened. David's harsh lesson was
again the key, just as it was with Jimmy Zemanski: only fools trust the
people closest to them. After all, it was not the first time. My mother had
tried to drive Rose away. I had caught that one before the damage was
done, but with Stephanie I had been too slow. Or just as likely, my mother
had perfected her technique. One telephone call was all it would take.
One telephone call and Stephanie would understand what had happened
too. The very fact that she had responded so forcibly gave me hope. More
than hope. I was certain.

As Hiram drove me here tonight, I felt happy for the first time since
she left me.

37

AFTER THE DRIVER OF THE HONDA LEFT, DAVID SAT IN
the dark at his house, and the minutes trickled by as slowly as minutes do in solitary when a minute is a day long and a day is a lifetime. At about three o'clock in the morning, his cell phone rang. He
pulled it out of his pocket and checked the caller:

Hugh Freyl.

Even though he had been expecting just this ever since he left
Ellie, he could not help the shock he felt at actually seeing it.

"Yes," he said.

"He's here." The voice was Helen's.

"Your house? Your grandmother's?"

"Mine."

"Are you all right?"

"He killed my father."

"I know. Are you hurt?"

"He's waiting for you."

"Tell him I'll be there in twenty minutes." He clicked off the
phone.

Hope is stupid. David suddenly realized that up until this very
moment, he'd been hoping that somehow or other Tony hadn't
killed those people, that some other person had. *Any* other person.

He called the driver of the Honda.

"He's got the Freyl girl?" the driver said.

"That's right."

"He's probably going to kill her too."

"It's what she wants."

"What's that supposed to mean? Where are they?"

"I find you following me, I'll kill you before he gets a chance at either of us, understand?"

"You're condemning her if you don't beat the shit out of him first?"

"I'm giving her what she wants if I fail. Either way she loses."

"Jesus, you're a cold bastard."

"I'll call you in a couple of hours. If you don't hear from me by morning, it's not going to make much difference what you do."

◄o►

Helen opened the door herself as soon as she heard David's footsteps on the stairs outside.

"Thank God. At last, you're here," she said, throwing her arms around him. Her breath came in ragged gasps. "I don't know what he wants."

David held her a moment, then released her slowly to face Tony.

The past may be a waste of time, as David had said so many times, but Helen was right: there's no escape from it, not for anybody. There's no escape from the betrayal when it comes either, and it always will come for the simple reason that everything—however rock solid it seems—is just one more illusion like all the rest. There's not even an escape from the loneliness that reaches back to reclaim all the years before the betrayal took place.

Tony's face showed that childlike delight so familiar from the practical jokes he'd pulled on Jason. "Fooled you, didn't I?" he said.

"How long?"

"Oh, God, I been planning this ever since . . . Let's see, ever since you got out. Nope. I tell a lie. I been planning it ever since Ellie told me you were getting educated inside. Nope. Even that's a lie. At least it ain't just exactly right. Some ways, I been planning this since the very first day I met you when we was little kids together."

"Not that. You and Ellie."

"You wouldn't understand nothing about it."

"How long?"

"We go right on back. All the way." It was one of those periods when David and Tony crossed paths again, both of them just turned fifteen, David barely out from under Ellie's spell and looking for a liquor store to rob or a car to jack. He and Tony made plans, and she saw them together. She saw how close they were; she was very intuitive about such things.

"Who's idea was it?" David said.

"You gone soft, David. It shouldn't a taken you all this time to catch on."

"Just tell me whose idea—"

"She's the one come on to me. I never seen nothing like that before—or since."

"Not *that*."

Tony gave a sharp snort of contempt. "You think *she* put me onto all them people of yours? Aw, come on. Sometimes I think you don't understand *nothing* no more. You used to be real smart about people—used to see right through them. Scared the shit out of me. But her? You didn't know her at all. I ain't saying she didn't like the idea. A course she liked it. She *loved* it. You could even say it kept her alive, know what I mean? Every time we talked about it, some of the old sparkle came back and we'd fuck like we did when I was a kid." Tony stopped, then went on irritably, "Can't you blink or nothing? I hate it when you look at me like that. You don't seem hardly human." But David's gaze didn't waver, and Tony turned to walk around the room, dragging his fingertips along the wall as he went.

"Jesus, this sure is some place you got here, Helen. Just look at them pictures."

Tony scanned the Goyas that papered one wall of the room from floor to ceiling: the hanging, dismembering, disemboweling that the Spanish artist had seen on battlefields and recorded along with his own night horrors—and he was a man who'd had bad dreams.

"I think that one's me," Tony said, pointing to one of the nightmares where an indistinct, hooded figure in cloak and cowl torments a creature made up of arms, legs, wings: some amalgam of bat, cat, human, owl.

Helen followed his gaze. She stared at the hooded figure, then moved her eyes across the whole bleak panorama, frowning in puzzlement as though she were seeing what was there for the first time.

"I don't know why I put them up," she said in a half whisper, more to herself than to him. Revelations come in the strangest guises, and there was awe in her voice. "I never have known." She glanced quickly at David, then down at her hands, which were folded schoolgirl-like in her lap, then back at him. "I hate all of them. I always have. They made me feel safe. I don't know why."

"Hey, kid, put your mind at rest," Tony said. "I'm going to give you everything you ever thought Daddy ought to a done to you." Helen looked up at him, uncomprehending. He laughed. "I met an awful lot of whores that think they don't deserve nothing but getting hurt. No reason why a rich girl's got to be any different."

"I hate pain."

"Come on, I bet you're going to learn to love it."

"Leave her alone," David said.

Tony gave him a broad grin. "Ain't going to be *no*body left to put flowers on your grave."

David still wore his heavy winter coat. He sat down opposite Helen. "You're going to be all right," he said to her. "Just keep out of the way, mine as well as his." Then he turned to Tony, who was watching the two of them, the grin still fixed on his face. "Stephanie Willis isn't dead."

"Nah. You're having me on."

"You were careless."

"I don't believe you. You checked the hospital recently?" David nodded.

"Her too?" Helen said to Tony in terrified wonder. "Why? What could she have done?"

Tony shrugged. "See, that's the funniest part of the whole deal. Here I am looking and looking and looking. Can I find that woman? No, sir, I can't. She's the one helped get David out, and we want her. We *really* want her. Me and Ellie was thinking we wasn't never going to find her, then David just ups and brings her to me. Just like that. I was shitting myself—couldn't hardly believe my luck. You sure she ain't dead, David? That's a shame. That surely is a shame. But what the hell, if at first you don't succeed . . . and all that shit."

"She's the best thing that ever happened to my father," Helen said then.

"Yeah?"

"She was so . . . normal."

"David here was fucking her just like your daddy was. That make you feel any better about it?"

Tony continued his walk around the room. He paused in front of the windows; the night lights threw shadows into the trees and undergrowth outside. They shifted and shivered in the wind, and he sounded almost dreamy when he spoke again.

"Ellie thought up some real good things. You know about the lug wrench? like you used on her old man? That was her idea—so was wearing one of them sterile body suits like they got in hospitals for infectious guys: she sure knows hospitals good. See, there's something about Ellie . . . I ain't never wanted to kill her. I can't rightly figure that one out. I washed her. I dressed her. I fed her. I wiped her ass. I bought her pink curtains and a bed that cranked up and down. And I didn't want to kill her.

"That's the thing, see?" There was an abrupt look of pain on Tony's face. "Ellie is . . . She's dead." His voice caught in his throat; it cracked on the words. "Don't you got feelings or nothing? You only left her a couple of hours ago, and I just told you she's dead."

David said nothing.

Tony glanced at him, then reached over to stroke Helen's hair. She shrank away from him. "I sure did get a kick out of buying her all that crap with the money you and me got. About the only kick there was in that security business of yours. What you want to do a legit business for anyhow? That was the hardest part of the whole plan. That wasn't no fun. Why did it have to be some stupid legit operation? We could a made a fortune. Then you turn out to be better at it than me. I hate that almost worse than anything. 'Cept when you do this quiet thing on me. You got *nothing* to say to me? You're the one kept her alive, you motherfucker. Twenty years, she thinks of nothing and nobody but you. Twenty fucking years, then ten minutes after she sees the last of you, she chokes to death on her own spit. I wasn't even *there*. She'd a dumped me any day if she could get at you, and she couldn't even hold up dying till I got back. How am I supposed to live with that? You tell me, huh? We're talking justice here. What kind of people can live with that kind of *in*justice? It wears you down. You been beating me since we was kids. How come you got to win every time? Even with Ellie? Even after they locked you up and threw away the key? It eats at me bad. I'm telling you. Then one day this old blind guy and that Stephanie of yours show up at the door saying you're going to walk, and me and Ellie, we *both* start living again. Know what I mean? We was really *living*."

Uranium is an unstable atom; it's the source of a fission reaction in a bomb, and because of it not even old weapons are safe. You can't destroy them when you don't want them anymore. You can't recycle them either. You can only bury them and hope for the best. But then one day you see blue fire above the surface of the ground—and you know you're losing control despite yourself. It was much the same with David. The face, eyes, planes of the cheeks, the neck that both Tony and Helen had traced in imagination—the radioactive intensity that had never dimmed—glowed so strongly in this room that Tony felt it on his own skin. Helen felt it too, just as she'd felt the heat of him when she was a child and he'd given her the sense of a way out even though she knew there was none—even though he was wholly trapped himself.

"I don't mean to be saying I wasn't enjoying myself," Tony went on as though she wasn't there at all, as though it was only the two of them, only David and Tony as it used to be, as it had been for all those childhood years when David won every single battle. "There I was, beating the crap out of Freyl, him coughing up blood like he'd swallowed a whole tomato or something and was trying hard to keep it down, and me laughing myself sick. But I couldn't hardly shut him up. He kept on talking about you. I kept trying to shove what he was saying back down his throat, but he wouldn't stop. So I just kept pretending it was you, not him. I watched the blood pour out and I just kept on pretending. I ain't felt that good, not since, Jesus, maybe not since we was seven years old together."

Tony laughed happily. "The old man and old woman was fun too. He squealed like a pig. I never knew people did that in real life. And she kept slipping out of my hands." He laughed again. "Whoop: there she goes." He made a grabbing gesture. "Whoop: she's off again. That was something special. Right now is best of all, though. Right now, it's Christmas all over again. I told you they'd filled you with cat piss where your guts should a been. But you wouldn't listen. You gone *really* soft. Know what I mean?"

"Couldn't resist Hugh's cell phone, though, could you? Or the Monaghan watch? What's that all about? Trophies?"

"You didn't bring *me* back nothing from New York," Tony said, holding out his wrist and admiring the Rolex that David had given to Mr. Monaghan. "Why is that anyhow? How come you did that? That wasn't very nice. You hurt my feelings."

David shut his eyes. He pressed them with his fingers. "What did you have to hurt Vivian for?" he said, and he didn't bother to hide the pain in his voice.

"That was ages ago," Tony said, a little puzzled by the question. "Trial run, kind of. Just to see if I could do it. Know what I mean? Just to see how it felt. She called the office and you was out. I took the call—bubbling all over herself about getting knocked up. I knew before you did. That was cute, I thought. A nice touch."

"And Helen?"

"She gets a ringside seat. That's what she wants even if she's kind of forgot. Look at her eyes, all lit up like the lights on the tree." All David could see in her eyes was terror. "Best thing that ever happened to her. Only one of us is going to leave this house alive, and it ain't gonna be you."

"Then what?"

"That's between her and me."

David stood up and took off his heavy coat. He folded it carefully—meticulously—and set it down on the chair he'd been sitting in himself. "You're stupid, Tony," he said.

"You killed a couple of guys when you were fifteen. Me? I been practicing a lot." David only shook his head. "Hey, David, what do you think I'm doing here? I even brought my own lug wrench."

38

HOW CAN THE IRONIES KEEP ON MOUNTING? HAS GOD NO shame? no respect for a man's principles in the moment of his death?

I was as proud as a father—as proud as God Himself—to watch David master the techniques of a civilized society, to see the onetime criminal fade from view behind a man of culture, to change him with my own hands into a man of my world who had deserted the one that had been his. Is it punishment for the sin of pride that David the murderer is the only person who could help me now? That what I destroyed is what I need?

So is it he who betrays me in this final—

39

BEHIND THE REACHES OF THE FREYL MANSION IN ITS private park stood a large greenhouse that glowed lanternlike on dark winter evenings. Its curved glass panels arced into the sky with all the promise of an enchanted castle in a fairy tale. Inside, the temperature was June—hot, humid, in the eighties—and the light was sunshine rich and yellow: bougainvillea, orchids, gardenias bloomed. But this was not a place for pleasure alone (if scent as heavy as gardenias give off can be called a pleasure). A whole section of the floor space was devoted to vegetables, herbs, fruits: carrots, lettuce, beans, chervil, chives, strawberries. The Freyls had always liked their comforts.

Becky was tending the tomatoes. She cultivated them English-style because that's how Hugh had learned about them in school, a single stalk per plant, four trusses per stalk, the plants themselves graduated to produce all winter long. She wore surgical gloves and continued her pricking out as she talked.

"Tomatoes are particularly difficult," she said to David who stood in the middle of this space, watching her back without expression. "This disagreeable heat is essential if the fruit is to have any taste. Surprising, don't you think? I would have thought light and careful grooming were enough. So," she went on without a change of tone or a pause in her work, "what you are telling me is that you are in fact responsible for Hugh's death."

"Yes," said David.

"Just as I suspected."

"Yes."

"I was right."

"And I was wrong."

"You even showed that . . . that person how to get into Hugh's office—how to manipulate his way through all Hugh's security."

"Yes."

"Why would you do a thing like that?"

"He needed the practice."

"For that ridiculous security firm of yours? How could Hugh have set up a convict in so foolishly tempting a business?"

"He wasn't good at locks."

"You mean Hugh?"

"Both of them."

Becky carefully gathered her small clippings of tomato vine into a container beside her and turned to face him. She opened her mouth to speak, then shut it at once. Emotion is so contrary. It lacks sensitivity to the proper order of things. She stiffened herself against it. She gritted her teeth. All in vain. For the first time in more than half a century, tears rolled down those cheeks.

"What is an old woman to do when her only son is dead?"

"You have a granddaughter."

Becky turned abruptly back to her tomatoes and went on gathering up clippings, although there were none left to gather on the greenhouse floor. David waited. Several minutes passed while she wept in total silence, body shaking from the impact, mind struggling in vain to find something to take hold of, anything to help her hoist herself out of this quicksand of emotion.

"You also have a presidential candidate," David said then.

"I do not approve of people who cheat." Such a prickle of annoyance was her only hope; she knew it, and she knew David knew it. A thoroughly irritating person. How dare he be kind to her? "The country will not be fooled so easily."

"Calder didn't have much trouble fooling you."

This further barb stiffened her spine enough to stop the tears, but she couldn't turn around, not yet, not until she could be certain there'd be no more weakness on show. "Why didn't that . . . that man wear the hospital uniform last night? Wasn't he worried about leaving traces? Or whatever people like him worry about?"

"I imagine his story would have been that he tried to stop me killing Helen—but failed."

"What did you do with him?"

"I had a little help." The driver of the Honda had been as good as his word.

"I trust he is not going to show up in Peoria next week killing blind men for no reason."

"It's probably better if I don't give you full details."

"No." She hesitated a moment. "I understand it's far harder to kill people than most of us think."

"Not for me."

"What will they do?"

"Who?"

"The police."

"Try to track him down and fail. The case will be closed." The driver had ensured that the Rolex's wristband held enough of Tony's epithelial skin cells for DNA analysis.

"And you were in Helen's bed at the crucial time." It wasn't a question, and he didn't answer. She tapped the flowers on the tomato trusses, working her way down each of them to scatter the pollen as bees do in the rough world outside.

David watched her a minute, then eased himself into one of the teak chairs.

"Has anybody tended to those bruises?" she said without turning around.

"It isn't necessary."

"You move like an old man."

"I'll get over it."

"I trust that there is nothing to tie Helen or me to this person's . . . disappearance."

"No."

"Mr. Marion—David—I owe you my granddaughter's life. Do not think I have forgotten that. Do not think I am ungrateful. That was not part of our original bargain, and I intend to pay you handsomely for it."

When he said nothing, she turned again and looked him over. There was true incomprehension in her voice as she said, "One piece of filth killing my son out of jealousy for another and threatening to kill my granddaughter as well . . . It is a matter of wonder to me that there could be people jealous of such a man as you. I cannot see a single thing in you that anybody could possibly covet."

A frosty smile flitted across her face despite her grief. "But then of course," she added, "I do not have a jealous nature."

40

INTENSIVE CARE UNITS ALL HAVE THE SAME FEEL TO THEM. Plastic sheathing inhales and exhales like a weary asthmatic. There are beeps and bleeps. Misshapen waves glide across screens: heart, kidneys, lungs. Wires drape; an inordinate number of them disappear into dormant figures on beds. So do tubes, air tubes, blood tubes, oxygen tubes, gastric tubes. The clocks overseeing all this are calibrated by satellite, accurate to a millionth of a second in a century. A visitor can't help feeling that the real purpose here is only to pinpoint the magic moment that separates life from death—to catch it on the wing.

Stephanie lay in the middle of a row of identical cubicles separated by glass, but she was not the Stephanie that David knew. She was just one more frail ecosystem dependent on a hospital generator and a bank of on-off buttons behind the nurses' station. He pulled up a chair and sat beside the bed; nobody discourages visitors when patients are in her condition.

At midnight the nursing shift changed, a modest bustle that died down as quickly as it arose. Just after dawn, the shift changed again. It must have been an hour later that Stephanie opened her eyes and smiled. It was not a strong smile, but it was a happy one.

He leaned forward.

She smiled again. "David."

"Are you in pain?" There was anxiety in his voice, and she smiled once more, very languidly this time.

"I dreamed about you last night, kid," she said.

Acknowledgments

The period during which the South Hams District Council prosecuted me was a very difficult one, and I want to thank the many people who helped me through it—and with the book that grew out of it. Jules Preston was the person who suggested I try a thriller to take my mind off the council itself and the shoe factory they had inveigled into position beneath the same roof with me; I owe him a huge debt of gratitude for that suggestion as well as for egging me on through nearly a year of Saturday morning discussions of early drafts and for supplying many ideas crucial to the project. I owe just as much to John Saddler, who told me where those rough attempts had gone wrong—and how to right them. I owe as much again to my cousin Eleanor Barrett, retired deputy district attorney for Los Angeles County, for her endlessly patient e-mails, her meticulous care with the final draft and—when I couldn't get it right—the prosecutor's speech toward the end of the story. Any legal expertise I may appear to have I owe to her (all errors are my own). And I owe as much yet again to Flora Dennis and my son, Alexander Masters, to whom this book is dedicated, not only for their support but also for their extraordinary editorial skills that helped me first to fill out what amounted to only a sketched-in plot, then trim it down to size—and speed. For information on scams, elections, blindness, lock picking, prisons, practical jokes and a myriad other subjects, I owe my allegiance to Google. Then there are debts I owe to Rosemarie Buckman, Al Hart, Sylvia Sutherland and Lynda Kinzey, all of whom contributed wonderfully to my spirits as well as to the text. Nor can I omit my deep gratitude for the work done by my marvelous editors, Suzanne Baboneau and Doris Cooper, by my doctor Tim Manser, who oversaw the medical aspects (and the spelling of midwestern place names) and by Martyn Torevelle, who reassured me on the subject of finances.

Perhaps most important of all, I owe my thanks to Dette Lange, the first Totnesian to have the courage to support me openly in my battles.